A Witch Steps into My Office

i

A Witch Steps into My Office

By

Douglas Lumsden

To my parents, Bill and Carolyn, for a lifetime of support and encouragement

Books in this Series

Alexander Southerland, P.I.

Book One: *A Troll Walks into a Bar*

Book Two: *A Witch Steps into My Office*

Book Three: *A Hag Rises from the Abyss*

Table of Contents

Pronunciation Guide

Many of the names in this book come from the Nahuatl language, which was spoken by the Aztecs and is still a living language in many parts of Mexico today. Many words in Nahuatl (including the word "Nahuatl" itself) end with a sound that is commonly transliterated as "tl." This "tl" sound is unique to the Nahuatl language, and its pronunciation amongst Nahuatl speakers is inconsistent. Many speakers simply drop the "l" altogether, so that "Nahuatl" is pronounced NAH-wăt. Technically, however, "tl" should be pronounced as a soft "t" that doesn't quite come to a clean stop, or something like a "t" sliding into the beginning of a "j," so that "Nahuatl" is pronounced NAH-wătj.

Brujería: broo-hār-Ē-uh
Cuetlachtli: kĕ-TLAHCH- tlē
Citlali: sĭ-TLAHL-lē
Coyot: KŌ-yōt
Huaxian: WAH-tzyĕn
Huitzilopochtli: hwēt-zĭl-ō-PŌCH-tlē
Itzel: ĬT-zl
Mexica: mĕ-SHĒK-uh
Mictlan: MĬKT-lawn
Nahuatl: NAH-wătj
Omecihuatl: ō-mĕ-SĒ-watj
Ometecuhtli: ō-mĕ-tĕ-COO-tlē
Ometeotl: ō-mĕ-TĔ-ōtj
Quetzalcoatl: kĕtz-ĂL-kwătj
Qusco: KOOS-kō
Tenochtitlan: tĕ-nŏch-tē-TLAWN
Teotihuacan: tē-ō-tē-waw-KAWN
Tizoc: TĒ-zōk
Tloto: TLŌ-tō
Xolotl: SHŌ-lōtj

Yerba City was into its third morning of a rare heat wave when a witch stepped into my office.

"Mr. Southerland?" the witch asked from the open doorway.

I rose from my faux leather office chair. "Yes, ma'am. Please come in."

As the witch closed the door behind her and crossed the room to my desk, I took note of the colorful snake tattoos whose tails coiled around each of her moccasined feet and on up her gams before they disappeared under her chic apricot sun dress. She sat down in one of the chairs I provided for clients and crossed her legs, causing the hem of her dress to rise above her knees and expose another inch and a half of the two coiled serpents. I spent a few moments admiring the exquisite detail of the skin art. The snakes seemed to be shaded in darkness, with the scaled red, yellow, and black rings reflecting a pale glow, as if the creatures had been caught on camera crawling up the witch's body on a moon-lit night. It was remarkable work. I couldn't stop myself from wondering where the snakes' heads might be resting.

The witch waited for me to sit down and said, without preamble, "A man is going to die this afternoon at precisely 1:30 p.m. I will be the cause of his death. Do you mind if I smoke?"

"Go ahead." I indicated a clean ashtray on my desk. "Are you saying that you are going to kill him?"

The witch pulled a homemade cigarette and a lighter from her purse and shrugged. "I already have. He just hasn't died yet."

I waited while the witch lit her cigarette with the silver lighter. Silver, as in made of pure silver, not simply silver in color. I know the difference. She put the lighter away in her purse, drew in some smoke, and breathed blue-gray haze into the air above my desk. The haze drifted up toward a ceiling fan that, despite spinning at its highest setting, did precious little to disturb the warm dank air that hung in my office like a wet shroud.

The witch watched me and waited. I was struck by her lack of urgency.

I glanced at the clock on my desk. "It's 9:30."

The witch took another drag off her cig. I caught a whiff of something sweet blended in with the tobacco.

"Shouldn't we try to stop this man from dying?"

The witch shrugged. "There's nothing we can do, Mr. Southerland. If his death could be stopped, I would have already stopped it."

"And, to be clear, you are the cause of his impending death?"

She sighed, but didn't frown. "Yes. It's very unfortunate." She tapped her cigarette on the side of my ashtray, and a quarter-inch of spent ash dropped from the tip into the tray.

"Any reason I shouldn't be calling the cops about now?"

She stopped in the midst of raising her cigarette to her lips, and her eyebrows arched. "Whatever for?" she asked, mystified by my suggestion.

"I don't know. To have you arrested for murder?'

The witch's lips parted in a smile that reached the corners of her dark eyes. Her arched eyebrows relaxed. "Oh please, Mr. Southerland. Do you know who I am?"

I took a good look at the woman seated across the desk from me. She was a polished-up dame of indeterminate age. The silver streaks in her dark auburn hair, tied in a thick bun, said middle age, maybe mid-forties. But her smooth caramel face, free of all but the faintest of creases, suggested that the silver in her hair might be premature. Early thirties, then, one might conclude. Her nose was flat, her lips thin, her cheekbones high, and the irises of her eyes almost black, so that the pupils were difficult to distinguish. Not a face you would see gracing the cover of a glamor magazine, but an attractive face nonetheless. In a similar way, her body was more elegant than beautiful. She was neither thin nor stout, and I guessed that she was no more than five feet tall in bare feet. Besides the twin serpents winding their endless way up her legs to who knows where, colorful tattoos of flowers, spiders, and birds covered every visible inch of skin that was exposed by the sleeveless sun dress, including her arms and the backs of her

2

hands. Only her face and the palms of her hands were free of ink. More than her appearance, though, it was the way she moved that caught my attention. She had swept into my office with an ephemeral grace, as if she were a mere projection of light, or a hologram. Or, perhaps, a bodiless spirit. I had a sudden urge to reach out and touch her shoulder just to ensure that it was substantial, but I resisted, proving once again that, reports to the contrary notwithstanding, I was still a gentleman.

I knew who she was all right. I had recognized her the moment that she stepped through the door. Everyone in Yerba City knew the infamous Citlali Cuapa. Dubbed the "Barbary Coast Bruja" by a long-dead newspaper columnist some fifty or sixty years ago, Madame Cuapa was the most powerful witch in western Tolanica, and she was much older—and infinitely more dangerous—than she appeared.

"Madame Cuapa, maybe we should start from the beginning."

"Of course." The witch placed her cigarette in a slot on my ashtray and let it smolder unattended. "Exactly one week ago, I placed a curse on a man named Donald Shipper. He's the general manager of Emerald Bay Mortgage, one of the many subsidiaries of Greater Olmec International. I, as you no doubt know, am the CEO of Greater Olmec, a holding company that was started by my father more than a hundred years ago. The curse is a powerful one. It will culminate in Shipper's death this afternoon at, as I said, precisely 1:30."

"I see," I nodded, more to show that I was listening than because I actually understood what she was telling me. "And why did you put the whammy on Mr. Shipper?"

The witch sighed, and this time her sigh was accompanied by a frown. "Now there's the problem. I don't know. I didn't wake up that morning knowing that I was going to do it, and afterwards I didn't know why I had done it. I hadn't been thinking about Shipper at all that morning. He's not a man who is often on my mind. I simply got out of bed, walked into my lab, put the necessary ingredients together, conducted the ritual—it's an unusually powerful one—and set the proper elements into motion. I was aware of what I was doing, but I had no idea why I was doing it,

3

nor did I question what I was doing *while* I was doing it. It's a ritual that I haven't performed in decades, and one that I never thought I'd ever perform again. And yet it seemed as right and natural as drinking my morning coffee. It was only when I had finished the ritual that I thought to ask what had just happened. Very odd. And very, *very* unsettling."

"Uh-huh. And what did you do next?" I asked.

"I tried to reverse the spell, of course," answered the witch. "But my mind wouldn't respond to my desire. It was then that I realized I was under a compulsion."

"What do you mean?"

"I mean that I was forced in an unnatural way to curse Mr. Shipper, and I am unable to gather up the will to undo the curse." She reached for her cigarette, and for the first time I detected a trace of agitation in her demeanor, just the slightest break in her self-assurance. It passed in an instant. Her hand was steady as she smoked her cigarette, and her strange dark eyes were cool as she regarded me across my desk.

Meeting those eyes was a disorienting experience. At a shade over six-one and a solid two-ten, I was a giant compared to the woman seated across from me. Even in my shirt and tie, I was not what anyone would consider to be a picture of refinement and sophistication. My mug has been referred to by polite people as more rugged-looking than handsome, something I've learned to live with seeing as how I have little practical choice in the matter. As a private investigator, I've found that passing myself off as a tough guy can be good for business. It tends to make my clients feel like they've found the right man for the job, especially when the job borders on, or crosses over into, the shadier side of life. My life has not been pretty. I've seen action in the thick of the Dragon Lord's border war against the Qusco insurgents, where I killed enemy combatants and watched them kill my fellow grunts. I gained the respect of the baddest streetfighter in the City by taking him on in front of his gang in brutal hand-to-hand combat, rising out of a pool of my own blood to batter him into submission. I once went toe-to-toe in this very office with a murderous troll twice my size, and, although I was forced to take the run-out (he *was* a troll, after all), I gave as good as I got and left him bleeding before I scrammed out of there. By most accounts, I'm a dangerous individual. But Madame Citlali Cuapa, all five-feet nothing of her, showed no signs of tension or discomfort whatsoever as she sized me up with her coal black peepers. She sat in her flimsy sun dress, legs crossed, demure as a schoolgirl, and showed as much fear of me as a sated cat in the company of a canary. And yet, I knew that underneath her appearance of unshakeable serenity, this powerful lady was troubled. Something had happened to her—something unfathomable—and, for perhaps the first time in her storied life, she was faced with a problem that appeared to be beyond her incredible resources. So she had come to me, an ordinary private dick, for help. As unruffled as she appeared, I knew that she must be desperate.

"Madame Cuapa," I began. She waited. "I've read about you. They say that you are the preeminent practitioner of native Nahuatl magic in Yerba City."

Madame Cuapa's face remained impassive. "I would say in the entire west of Tolanica, at least. In fact, when it comes to the practice of brujería I have few rivals anywhere." She smiled. "The Barbary Coast Bruja, right? It's a well-earned title, believe me."

"And yet you say that you were forced, against your will, to conduct a ritual that is going to result in the death of this Mr. Shipper."

"That's right."

"And you are powerless to stop it."

"Also correct."

"How is this possible?" I asked.

Madame Cuapa took a quick puff from her cigarette and placed it in the ashtray. "I've come up with three possibilities. First, someone with an enormous amount of strength, perhaps more than my own, has overpowered my defenses. Second, someone unknown to me has uncovered a spell of compulsion against which I have no defense." She paused. I waited.

"Third," she continued at last. "Third, it's possible that I'm doing this to myself. It's possible...." She enunciated her words with care. "It's possible that I've lost control of my own mind." The witch's impassive expression hardened. "I *truly* hope that this is not the case. If it is, the consequences could be extremely dire."

5

"How dire?" I asked.

The witch took a final puff on her cigarette and crushed it out in the ashtray. "Are you familiar with the term, 'extinction event,' Mr. Southerland?"

I rolled this concept around for several long moments. She let me. The leaden air in the room was causing beads of sweat to trickle down my forehead and into my eyes. I took a handkerchief from the breast pocket of my suit and wiped my brow. I folded it and returned it, quite damp now, to my pocket. Madame Cuapa, in contrast, appeared to be as cool as a daisy in spring. No evidence of perspiration. Not even a glow. She was waiting for me to break the silence, so I did. "You're that powerful?"

The witch smiled with some amusement. "A television news host once tried to frighten his audience by declaring that I could destroy an entire battalion of soldiers with the wave of my hand. Sadly, that isn't true. But with my abilities and the resources at my disposal, I could, if I wanted to, set events into motion that would eventually wipe out whole populations and make the planet all but uninhabitable. It wouldn't be that hard, actually. Our governments control technology that could do the same thing." She shrugged. "Do you realize how precarious life is for thinking creatures? It's a fact that we live only at the sufferance of ruling authorities, both earthly and unearthly. There are many who encourage rebellion against the rule of the seven Dragon Lords, but it is only due to their firm guidance that many deadly forces—natural and unnatural—are safely contained, at least for now. There are enough storehouses of massively destructive weapons—nuclear bombs, chemical and bioweapons, cursed artifacts, and so forth— to bring about the permanent extinction of all life on this planet many times over. The Dragon Lords and their subordinate rulers stockpile these weapons and wave them at each other from time to time in order to show that crossing certain lines would cause mutually assured destruction, and this threat has so far produced a surprising geopolitical stability. But a ritual here, a few billion spent there, and it would be an easy matter for me to upset the applecart and, to mix my metaphors, send blood spilling everywhere. And then there is the matter of environmental conditions, which are about as balanced as a tightrope walker on a spider's thread in a windstorm. Do you realize that if the average temperature of the planet rose or fell by just a handful of degrees over an extended period of time all sentient life would be destroyed? Tipping that balance would be child's play for me. For that matter, even for hundreds, maybe thousands, of gifted fools who are less skilled than me. When you think about it, it's a miracle that we've lasted as long as we have."

The witch laid this all out for me in a calm, reasonable voice. These weren't the deluded ravings of a fanatic or some conspiracy nut with an internet blog. I knew that everything she was telling me was true, and that she knew that I knew the score. I guess at heart we all do. And yet, somehow we muddle along, ignoring and even denying the dangers, making the best of things while we still can. Rather than let myself get swept away by the big picture, I tried to keep myself focused on things that I could do something about.

"What you're telling me is that you'd like me to get to the bottom of your current dilemma before it gets out of hand. Specifically, you need me to find out who or what is causing you to perform dangerous rituals that you never intended to perform."

Madame Cuapa nodded. "Exactly, Mr. Southerland. I'll give you access to whatever information and whatever resources you need to do the job, and, of course, I'll pay you well. I'd like you to, as you say, get to the bottom of this as soon as possible. As you can probably imagine, I'm not comfortable with the idea of not being fully in control of my mind and actions."

Nicely understated. Not for the first time, I marveled at Madame Cuapa's show of calm. I could only imagine the inner turmoil that she was holding at bay behind those cool dark eyes.

"I understand." I wiped sweat off the corner of my lip and nodded at her. "But I still think we need to start by doing something about this Mr. Shipper. He's not dead yet, and we still have..." I glanced at the digital clock on my desk, "nearly four hours to keep it that way."

The witch shook her head. "No, Mr. Southerland. Shipper isn't the issue. His death is inevitable. The issue is finding the cause of the compulsion that has overwhelmed my will. You need to concentrate your time and attention on that."

I shifted in my chair and rubbed the stubble on my chin with the palm of my hand. "I'm sorry, Madame Cuapa. But I can't stand around and allow someone to die if there is any way at all that I can prevent it from happening."

"There isn't."

I continued, "Nor can I let his death go unpunished."

"You will."

I had nothing to say to that. This lady might be a big deal in her own world, but she had come to me, and, when it came to doing my job, I made the rules. I felt steam beginning to build in my head. It must have shown in my eyes, because Madame Cuapa uncrossed her tattooed gams and leaned forward an inch. "Mr. Southerland." Her voice was quiet, but her tone was hard. "I realize that you are feeling a little frustrated by all this. I'm aware of your capabilities, your career, and much else about you. I probably know things about you that even you are unaware of. About what kind of man you are, who you are inside. I'm a very perceptive person, not to mention a very well-informed one. I know that you are a man who believes strongly in justice, a rare thing in this unjust world. I know that until several months ago, you were a mediocre elementalist with an affinity for the spirits of air. I know that your mastery over air elementals increased suddenly at about the same time that you had a rare and secret meeting with an elf, a creature that most people believe to be extinct. Until this encounter, you were beneath my notice, but I've had an eye on you ever since. It's no accident that I came to *you* this morning rather than to someone else. But I hope that I haven't misjudged you. Believe me when I tell you that Mr. Shipper is an odious little man, loved by no one, not even by his wife and children. He's been a useful tool, but he's nobody special. The world will hardly notice his passing, and it might actually benefit in some ways by it. Yet if I thought for one second that you could prevent this fool's death, I'd encourage you to do so. But you can't. It isn't possible. Forget about Shipper. Move on."

In that moment, I formed a plan. My office was situated in an innocuous two-story free-standing rental located just outside of the more fashionable parts of downtown Yerba City. A staircase behind my desk crossed diagonally up my back wall and led to my living quarters on the second floor. A door on the side wall to the right of my desk and beneath the top of the staircase opened into a hallway that led out to an alley in the back of my building. From this hallway, I had access to a laundry room, which, after I bought a few free weights and hooked a heavy bag to the ceiling a few months earlier, had begun to double as a home workout center. My plan was to take a set of handcuffs out of my desk drawer, physically overpower and cuff the tiny dame sitting on the other side of my desk, brace her to a thick pipe in the laundry room, and then quickly find Mr. Shipper and prevent him from dying. After that, I would call the coppers, bring them back to my office, and give them the person who had tried to murder Shipper, albeit unwillingly, if Madame Cuapa's story was to be believed. After that, justice would be a matter for others to sort out, but my conscience would be clear.

I've had worse plans, but probably none that fell apart so fast. I never even got my desk drawer open. As I reached for it, I found myself falling headlong into a black pit. All semblance of light vanished in an instant. I felt myself plunging into nothingness, accelerating at an alarming rate. Within seconds I was falling too fast to survive the end of it. As I dropped faster and faster, I reached out in desperation for something to grab onto, knowing that even if I succeeded my arms would be ripped from their sockets. Finally, I curled into a ball and braced myself for an impact that I would never feel. My mind began to go black.

And then I was seated once again in my desk chair as if nothing had happened. The witch, legs crossed once again, sat composed with a hint of an amused smile on her plain, supernaturally youthful face.

"Satisfied, Mr. Southerland?" she asked me.

"I get it. I can't touch you."

"Well, not without my permission," she drawled, and I could swear that she was flirting with me. Just a little. I told myself that she was just enjoying her little show of dominance. That seemed more likely.

"Okay. But I still have to try to prevent Mr. Shipper's death. At least tell me where I can find him."

"Such a stubborn man. Oh very well." The witch sighed with a dramatic show of resignation. "But be quick about it. I need you to focus on solving my problem. He'll be at his office. It's not far from here, although the traffic is going to be miserable, and as for parking, well...." She waved her hand and snorted her dismissal. She gave me the address for Emerald Bay Mortgage, which was located in the upper floors of an office building on Market Street. "His weekly managers' meeting is scheduled for one o'clock this afternoon. The purpose of the meeting is to show the department managers who work for him that he has the authority to call such a meeting and to require them to attend. They'll file in by 1:10 or so, pour themselves drinks, light up cigarettes, and wait for Shipper to make his grand entrance at about 1:15. He'll make some small talk, and then at about 1:20, he'll bring the meeting to order. He'll yammer on about inconsequential matters that he's suddenly decided are important. And then, at 1:30 p.m., he'll die. You can look up his phone number online if you want to make an appointment. I doubt that you'll get to him that easily, but go ahead and do your best. You're a private eye: maybe you can come up with a clever disguise or some scam that will do the trick."

She was giving me the rib now, but I was thinking about the dozens of ways that I might be able to gain quick access to a self-important executive who was apparently an asshole and who had no logical reason to see me on short notice.

"I'm curious, though," Madame Cuapa continued. "If you manage to see him, what will you do? The ritual has been performed, and the curse has been unleashed. Nothing can stop Shipper from dying at the appointed time. Believe me, if I can't stop it, neither can you."

I thought about this. "You said earlier that you tried to reverse the whammy, but couldn't summon the will to do so. Could somebody else reverse it?"

Madame Cuapa shook her head. "Sorry, but no. Naturally, I had the same idea. But the ritual involved using some of my own blood and a pact with a certain unearthly power. A particularly nasty one. The reversal would also require my blood, which the compulsion would not allow me to give up even if I wanted to, which I don't, and the pact can only be broken by an agreement by

10

the original participants. The compulsion will not allow me to cooperate. Good question, though. You're sharp, I'll give you that."

I thought some more. "This unearthly power.... Could anyone else persuade him to act independently of you? Get him to retract his claws, or whatever is involved here? Maybe give him something that would make it worth his while?"

"Another good question! I think I like you!" Madame Cuapa, smiled. "Sadly, it's more complicated than that. The...spirit, let's call him...has already set in motion the forces that will result in Shipper's death. It's hard to explain, but time doesn't work the same for these unearthly powers as it does for us. The spirit's work is done, and he doesn't have to actually do anything further at this point."

"But could he prevent the death in some way?" I persisted.

"In theory, yes," Madame Cuapa agreed. "But the spirit would almost certainly require another death in Shipper's place. That's how these things generally work. And if someone has to die, well, better a lowlife like Shipper than pretty much anyone else."

"Would this spirit accept another form of compensation, other than someone's death?"

"Only something even more undesirable, I suspect." Madame Cuapa wrinkled her nose, as if she'd just sucked a lemon.

"Such as?"

"Such as my unending servitude. And I'm not willing to become his eternal slave."

I did some silent brainstorming, but the witch quickly interrupted my thoughts, as if she had been listening in. "Yes, you could try to seek the aid of another practitioner, get him or her to intercede with the spirit, or with another, more powerful spirit, and try to prevent the curse from taking effect. It won't work. Do you suppose that you were the first person I contacted for help? I've already consulted with my most trusted peers, and I'm sure that word of my troubles has spread to the rest of the witching world. There's nothing any of them can do, or would do if they were willing. No one with the power to help you will agree to do so. You can't imagine the risks in interfering with matters like this."

"And yet, you want me to get the dope on who or what is behind it all. Doesn't that carry some risk?"

11

"I'd be lying if I said otherwise," Madame Cuapa admitted. "But you seem like a capable fellow, and I'll help as much as I can." She hesitated. "Did I mention that I'll pay you well? Some of that will be what you might call 'hazard pay.'"

I took another look at my clock and pulled my phone from my breast pocket.

"All right," Madame Cuapa sighed. "You've got a conscience and you feel obligated to try to save Shipper's life. I suppose I have to let you." She stood. "Walk me out first. After you've failed to prevent Shipper's death, call me. I have an assistant outside who will give you my card and a retainer. You'll be wanting more information from me, and I'll give you whatever I can." She waited for me.

I put my phone back in my pocket and stood. I came around my desk, and the witch placed her hand on my arm as I walked her to my door. It was an oddly intimate gesture. I reminded myself that this wasn't some ordinary bit of fluff and couldn't help wondering whether she was syphoning away some of my life's energy, or something like that. I think that I might have trembled slightly at her touch, because she looked up at me from more than a foot below and gave me a wry smile. "Don't worry, big guy. I won't bite you. Not yet, at least."

We went outside. A beige luxury SUV that cost more dough than I earned in a typical year was waiting for Madame Cuapa in front of my building. I wondered how she had managed to secure such a prime parking spot on a weekday morning, but quickly dismissed the thought. I probably didn't want to know. Standing on the sidewalk in front of the SUV was a young jasper with a smirking grin and a thick mane of jet-black hair that fell below his shoulders. His eyes were hidden by a pair of cheaters with black rims and black lenses. A gold short-sleeved silk shirt, unbuttoned nearly to his waist, exposed a pair of tattooed biceps the size of bowling balls and a thick hairless chest that was nearly as broad as a troll's. One thumb was hooked in the pocket of a pair of skin-tight dark brown leather trousers that no sane person would wear on a day that was as hot as this one was shaping up to be unless he was trying to impress somebody special or the world at large. Gripped in his other hand was an iron chain. The chain was attached to an iron collar. The collar was around the neck of a creature that I had heard of, but never before seen. The beast stood on four massive legs, the top of its head even with the man's chest. Each of its paws was the size of my head. Yellow eyes glared at me from a fierce lion's face, surrounded by a spiky mane. Leathery black wings were folded against the big cat's powerful body, which was reddish brown with black tiger's stripes. The long segmented tail of the beast arched upwards over its back and was capped by a horned shell that narrowed to a pointed scorpion's barb. I stopped in my tracks and turned to the witch at my arm.

"Is that a manticore?" I asked.

"Magnificent, isn't he?" Madame Cuapa looked up at me. "Do what you must to help Mr. Shipper, but then find out why I am compelled to commit acts against my will." Her dark eyes flared. "It does not benefit the world for my mind to be outside of my conscious control."

I turned to gaze into the manticore's feral eyes and nodded.

Chapter Two

Madame Cuapa left me at my door and walked to her SUV. The beast-handler handed her the leash and approached me, pulling an envelope out of his shirt pocket. He was taller than me by nearly half a foot and moved like a jungle cat. He had a boyish face, and I guessed that he wouldn't see his twenty-fifth birthday for another couple of years. When he reached me, he smiled his smug smile and held out the envelope.

I looked past him to the manticore, who appeared to be sizing me up with murderous intent. "Nice animal."

"Oh, him?" He glanced back over his shoulder at the manticore and then back at me, beaming from behind his shades, happy to be alive. "He's a pussycat, sir. In the right hands. In the wrong hands, he can be a fuckin' monster."

"And Madame Cuapa?"

The jasper's smile faded a bit. "Sir?"

"Pussycat or monster?" I asked. "In the right hands."

He considered this for a second, going through his options. Then he manufactured a broad grin that exposed a mouthful of thick white teeth that didn't look capped, "I'd stay on her good side if I were you, sir. Otherwise she might turn you into a frog."

"I take it that there's a check in that envelope?" I asked.

He shrugged, "I wasn't asked to look inside, sir."

"I'm asking. Open it."

The jasper hesitated for a second, shrugged again, and ripped open the envelope. He reached inside, drew out a business card and a check, and held them up like a magician that had just performed a clever trick. Ta-da!

"I'll take the card. But tell Madame Cuapa that I'm not working for her until I see Shipper. I'll call her this afternoon."

"Are you sure, sir?" the young man asked. "Remember what I said about staying on her good side."

"I'll take my chances."

The jasper nodded once at me and held out the business card with two thick fingers, a smirk on his face. "Sir? If you start growing an appetite for flies, you'll know why."

I took the card without commenting.

"Have a nice day, sir." I didn't feel a lot of sincerity in the young man's tone. With a stride that might be described as "jaunty," he returned to the SUV. Cheerful guy. Smiled a lot. Wouldn't have looked out of place on a stage fronting a heavy-metal rock band. As far as he was concerned, life was swell. I watched him hand the check to Madame Cuapa, who took it as if she had been expecting it. The jasper opened the back door and guided the manticore inside. The creature turned in his seat until he was staring back at me out the closed window. I thought he looked a little disappointed. He licked his lips with a massive tongue, revealing an impressive set of ivory carnivore teeth. Then the jasper opened the front passenger door for Madame Cuapa and guided her in with a hand on her elbow. After she was inside, she turned in my direction, gave me an encouraging wave, and leaned back in her seat. The jasper hustled around the front of the SUV and took his seat behind the wheel. As they all drove away, I held up my hands and checked them over, front and back, looking for webbing. Satisfied that I had not yet been transformed into an amphibian, I returned to my office.

***

Once at my desk, I used my computer to find the website for Emerald Bay Mortgage. After clicking on a couple of links I found myself staring at a photograph of Donald Shipper seated behind an impressive looking desk. He was a middle-aged goose with thinning light brown hair, a pale clean-shaven mug, and a reluctant smile that said "I'm too important for this shit." I found a company email address and a phone number and jotted them down on a notepad.

Concluding that an email would be a waste of time, I punched the phone number into my cel. After one ring, a throaty female voice responded. "Emerald Bay Mortgage. Mr. Shipper's office. How can I help you?"

"I'd like to speak to Mr. Shipper, please. It's an emergency."

"Mr. Shipper is away from his desk. What is the nature of your emergency?"

I had considered a number of tactics, but decided that the direct approach would be simplest. "Mr. Shipper is in danger." I tried to keep my voice level and clinical, like a doctor delivering an unfortunate diagnosis. "I've discovered that he has received a deadly curse, and that if nothing is done to reverse it he will die this afternoon."

"I see. And may I ask who is calling?"

"My name is Alexander Southerland. I'm a private detective."

The voice didn't respond right away, and I heard clicking on a keyboard. After half a minute, the voice returned. "Can you please leave me your number, Mr. Southerland? I may have to have someone get back to you."

I gave her my cellphone number and asked, "Are you sure I can't speak to Mr. Shipper? This is an urgent matter."

"I'm sorry, Mr. Southerland." I didn't think that the voice sounded apologetic at all. "Mr. Shipper is currently unavailable. Are there any more details that you would like to leave with me?"

Whoever I was talking to was showing no signs of alarm, and, although the woman oozed professionalism, I thought I detected a note of condescension in her voice. "What is your name, please?" I asked.

After a short hesitation, the voice responded, "I'm Mrs. Turlock. I'm Mr. Shipper's executive assistant."

Executive assistant. Right. No one is a secretary anymore. "Mrs. Turlock, someone needs to find Mr. Shipper right away. He's been cursed by a powerful witch, and unless this curse is lifted, Mr. Shipper will die at exactly 1:30 this afternoon. To be honest, I don't know what anyone can do about it, but Mr. Shipper should at least be told. Maybe he'll have some recourse that I don't know about. I mean, I don't even know the man, but, who knows, maybe he has his own witch on staff."

"Yes, well...." I had the feeling that Mrs. Turlock was ready to get on with her day. I couldn't blame her.

"Mrs. Turlock, I know what I sound like, but I assure you that this is on the square. By now you've looked my name up online and verified that I'm a licensed private investigator. I've been in business for almost eight years and my reputation is stellar." That last part might have been a stretch, but under the circumstances I didn't feel like elaborating. "We've got a definite time problem here. Mr. Shipper needs to be notified of the situation right away. It's a matter of life and death!"

Mrs. Turlock was silent for a few moments. Then she spoke the words that I hoped I wouldn't hear: "I'm going to put you on hold, Mr. Southerland."

"Wait! Are you getting Mr. Shipper for me?"

"Someone will be on the line with you shortly."

I broke the connection. The executive assistant wasn't buying it. She had intended to forward my call to some lesser boss, or maybe to the police. Either way, I knew that I was wasting my time on the phone. I needed to get to Emerald Bay Mortgage and find Shipper myself. I didn't know what good I could do, but I felt that if I could alert Shipper to the danger he was in then maybe he would have some idea what to do about it. I at least had to tell him what was coming. It seemed like the right thing to do.

***

I hurried out of my office and made my way down the block to get my car. Eight months earlier, I had come into possession of a ridiculously large automobile that I referred to as the beastmobile. It had belonged to the proprietor of an escort agency, and it looked like something that a high-end pimp would drive, especially before I had a detailer remove the oversized decal of the winged bare-breasted nymph rising out of purple flames from the hood. I'd also had him remove the purple racing stripes that had streaked down the length of the car, and I'd had him repaint the jet black exterior an innocuous brown color that he had referred to as "deep taupe," whatever that was. I'd kept the plush red leather interior, though. I told myself that it was too much trouble to change it.

The car was parked a block from my building at a small auto repair shop owned by an honest mechanic named Giovanni. I paid Gio a monthly fee to keep the car safe. His fourteen-year-old son, a good kid named Antonio, loved the car and spent his free time tending it, making sure that the engine was clean and in good shape. I'm sure that he would have loved the car even more if I had kept the nymph decal and the racing stripes, but the beastmobile was ostentatious enough without them. A small family could have lived comfortably in its spacious interior, and they could have run a mobile lunch-wagon business out of its massive trunk.

Antonio wasn't around when I reached the repair shop. It was a Monday morning in late April, and I used my powers of deduction to conclude that the kid was at school. That's the kind of skill that makes me a successful P.I. The office was empty, but in the garage I spotted a portable fan on the floor pointed at a two-door coupe that was propped up on jacks. I walked to the other side of the coupe and saw a pair of stocky legs sticking out from underneath.

"That you under there, Gio? It's Alex."

"Hey, Alex. You getting your car?" Gio asked from under the coupe.

"Yeah. Got an errand."

"No problem. Stay cool, man. It's already hotter than a motherfucker. I hear it's gonna top a hundred today!" I heard a grunt as Gio loosened a nut, or whatever it was that he was doing under there.

"How's Antonio?" I asked.

"Little prick's a pain in the ass!" Gio growled. "If you're smart, you'll never have kids."

"I'll keep that in mind."

***

A few minutes later I turned the beastmobile onto Market Street and began the tedious process of searching for a parking place. I figured that if nothing was available on the street, then I would make for the nearest parking garage, which was nearly four blocks from the building housing Emerald Bay Mortgage. The air

19

coming from my dashboard vent was as cool as a mountain breeze, but it was already in the nineties outside. I didn't want to leave the comfort of my car, but I had to try to stop a man from dying, and I still had no idea how I was going to do it, or if it was even possible. The chances of even getting to see the man were slim. Most likely, I was going to get the bum's rush, or I'd wind up getting elbowed by the cops. In either case, it wouldn't be the first time. I wouldn't be able to square it with myself if I didn't give it my best shot, though.

I was halfway to the parking garage when I saw a car pulling out of a parking spot on the street. I let him go, and with great care and much patience, ignoring the angry honks from cars stacking up behind me in my lane, I parallel-parked the beastmobile, leaving no more than a dozen inches between it and the vehicles parked in front and behind without once bumping bumpers. I was only two blocks away from Emerald Bay Mortgage. This was going to be my lucky day.

Stepping out of my climate-controlled beastmobile into the scorching hot Yerba City morning was like waking up from the midst of a pleasant dream and getting kicked in the balls. My lungs refused to breathe the heated air, my eyes closed against the glare of the sun reflecting off the glass fronts of the office buildings on Market Street, and sweat immediately began to pour down my face. My brain threatened to shut down in protest against the abuse I was subjecting it to. Feeling lightheaded, I stopped in my tracks outside my car and took some slow deep breaths until my mind started to clear. That works when you get kicked in the balls, too, if the impact isn't too severe.

After collecting myself, I slid my credit card through the parking meter and began to walk down the crowded sidewalk to Emerald Bay Mortgage. The heated air was absolutely still, a rarity in a city known for its winds. It was only late-morning, but the people I passed appeared glassy-eyed and confused. I wasn't born in Yerba City, but I'd lived there for eight years, and I'd come to feel like I belonged. The good citizens of Yerba City are accustomed to June temperatures in the high sixties. We can tolerate temps in the seventies, or even in the eighties if we must, although we will complain about it with a justified sense of moral outrage. Ninety-degree heat is a direct insult to our sense of entitlement. A hundred degrees is beyond the bounds of endurance for sentient beings. We never even consider the possibility, because it's unthinkable. The temperature in Yerba City had only exceeded a hundred degrees six times in the last century, but weather reporters had projected today's temperature to reach one-oh-three, give or take. I took out my cel and entered my passcode. The time and temperature were displayed on my home screen. Not even eleven o'clock, and it was already ninety-seven degrees. I loosened my tie, rolled up my shirtsleeves, and started hoofing it.

I'd only taken a few steps when a black cloud of more than a dozen crows descended out of nowhere and began swirling in front of me, cawing and screeching, individual birds darting almost within my reach and then shooting up over my head, only to dive back into the maelstrom. The other pedestrians scattered, waving their arms over their heads and shouting in surprise, but the birds were leaving them alone and coming at me. What the hell? I stomped my way forward, waving my own arms to try to scare the birds off and determined to bull my way through the swarm, and some of the crows began to throw themselves at my head with impacts that felt like heavy jabs from a prizefighter. I threw some punches of my own, but the birds dodged them with ease. Then one of the birds shot toward me and slashed at my face with a claw. A burning sensation in my jaw told me where the claw had struck. I slapped at the bird, and managed to bat it away. I wiped at my jaw, and my hand came away with blood.

I had never seen anything like this and didn't know what to make of it. But I knew what I could do about it.

I stopped walking, closed my eyes, and crossed my arms in front of my face. The birds continued to slam into my body. I ignored the body blows, relaxed my mind, and formed mental images for the appropriate sigils. Putting them together, I sent out a call. The crows continued to dive and screech, but, at least for the moment, I succeeded in keeping them away from my face. I waited, peeking past my arms at the swarm.

Less than half a minute later, a funnel of whirling wind, a twelve-foot tornado of gray haze, automobile exhaust, and the grit of the city, descended from high overhead, picking up dead leaves and waste paper as it headed in my direction. As the whirlwind drew near, I pointed at the crows and shouted, "Scatter them!" The whirlwind picked up speed and plunged into the swarming crows. The birds were tossed about, some smacking into the building, others out over the street. One caught me square on the noggin and sliced my forehead with his claw as he struggled to find a grip. Soon, the birds were gone. The wind funnel stopped whirling, and, as the dust and debris settled, it transformed itself into a nearly invisible pulsating blob of air.

"Hello, Badass."

A low-pitched howling moan came from the rippling air, "Greetings, Alex. This one is pleased to serve."

Chapter Three

Badass was one of my two favorite elementals. When I was in school, my teachers taught me that elementals are barely sentient natural spirits of air, earth, fire, and water. I learned that elementals are as old as the earth itself, and over an immense period of time, some have learned a few words and can be taught to follow simple instructions. According to my teachers, a lucky few people are born with the talent to use special sigils, or symbols, to summon and command elementals. We were taught that elementals are not pets, but tools. For the sake of convenience, a summoner can assign a name to an elemental that has learned a set of instructions and then re-summon it, as needed. But personifying an elemental—giving it the qualities of a person and treating it as a friend—was discouraged by our teachers as childish. Elementals, we were told, do not have personalities. My teachers drummed the lesson home time and again: after accounting for differing sizes and degrees of power, one elemental is pretty much the same as any other.

It was all bunk. Madame Cuapa knew about my encounter with the elf in the previous fall. She correctly concluded that the elf had done something to me, and that it had affected my ability to command elementals. What she didn't know was that the elf had somehow, as he put it, "enhanced my awareness." I don't know exactly what that means, or what he did to me, but afterwards I could see in the dark and hear things from blocks away. There were other benefits, too. The command centers in my brain became more aware of how my body functioned, and, as a result, I never got sick for any length of time, and the wounds and injuries that I seemed to pick up with alarming frequency healed in a hurry. Another bonus was that I better understood the spirits of the air. I could still only summon air elementals—earth, fire, and water have always been outside of my control—but I no longer had to write the sigils down, as other summoners do. All I had to do now was envision the summoning sigils in my mind and send out a call. More important, I came to know elementals in a way that exceeded everything I'd been taught. Turns out that elementals *do* have distinguishing quirks. They aren't different from each other the way snowflakes are different from other snowflakes, they are as different from each other as people are from other people. And they *do* have personalities, if you are willing to discover and acknowledge them.

Badass bowed slightly as I dismissed it, and I watched it shoot into the air like a rocket, leaving a cooling wind in its wake. It didn't last, but for a few brief moments, I felt refreshed enough to bear up against the hot sun. Badass lived in the winds high above Yerba City, and it once revealed to me that I was never out of its sight. The spirit was the largest that I'd ever been able to summon and command, and I called it to my aid whenever I needed extra muscle. Badass seemed to enjoy its role as my guardian, and I had the distinct impression, based on some hints from the spirit itself, that it did so as a favor to the elf. Whatever the case, I felt good knowing that I could always count on the big whirlwind.

I was in a hurry to get to Emerald Bay Mortgage, but I took the time to duck into a café on the way and use its restroom. After the bird attack, I needed to clean up and make myself pretty again. I examined myself in the restroom mirror and discovered that the cuts on my jaw and forehead, though messy, were superficial. That was probably my healing powers at work. The wounds were already closing, and, after I washed off the blood, I was left with nothing more serious than a couple of long red scratches that I knew would disappear in a couple of days.

My shirt was another matter. It had been slashed in several places. There wasn't much I could do about that, short of buying myself a new shirt, and I didn't have the time. I'd just have to live with it. Maybe no one would notice. Yeah.

I hit the streets again, searching the skies for crows. I had no doubt that the birds had targeted me personally, but why? To keep me from reaching Shipper? Although I suffered some minor damage, I knew that it could have been much worse. It hadn't been so much an attack as a warning of some kind. But against what? I was lousy with questions and short on answers. Well, nuts to that. I'd have to get the lowdown on the crows later. Right now I had a death to prevent, if it was in the cards. The odds were against me, but I told myself that I might still find a way. The eternal optimist, that's me. I swaggered down the sidewalk with a smile on my face and a song in my heart.

***

When I crossed through the doors of the commercial high-rise that housed Emerald Bay Mortgage, I was relieved to discover that the building was air conditioned, something uncommon in a Yerba City structure. Air conditioning isn't cheap, and it's rarely necessary in this town. I noticed a few ragged-looking street people—three humans and a dwarf—sitting on the floor just inside the doorway. Normally they would have been outside flimflamming the tourists, or squatting on the sidewalk with cardboard signs bumming for scratch. Now they were just riding out the heat and hoping that no one would give them the heave-ho.

I rode the elevator forty-two floors to the reception level of the Emerald Bay Mortgage Company. The elevator doors opened into a lobby, and I was greeted by an attractive blonde seated behind a counter. She looked up from behind a computer screen and asked if she could help me. I had my doubts about that, but I asked to see Mr. Shipper.

The receptionist checked her screen briefly and frowned. "Do you have an appointment?" she asked.

"No, but it's an urgent matter"

I caught her giving me the once over and frowning at my scratches and ripped shirt. "Let me see what I can do," and picked up a slim phone receiver. She connected to someone, and it soon became apparent that she was speaking with Mrs. Turlock. After a brief exchange, the receptionist began staring at me as if I might pull out a roscoe and start shooting up the lobby at any moment. She tilted the receiver away from her mouth and asked me, "Are you Mr. Southerland?"

I told her that I was, and the receptionist resumed her phone conversation. After a moment, she hung up the receiver and turned to me. "Please take a seat, Mr. Southerland. Mr. Shipper's executive assistant will be out to see you shortly."

I took a seat far enough away from the receptionist that she wouldn't feel threatened by my good looks and waited. It didn't take long. In less than a minute, the door to a stairwell opened, and a woman who appeared to be a recently retired runway model stepped into the room. She was attractive, brunette, pushing forty, and the picture of poise and composure in her knee-length dress and her half-inch stiletto heels. She smiled when she saw me, but it was a dutiful smile, lacking warmth. "Mr. Southerland? Could you please come with me?"

I rose and approached her. "Mrs. Turlock?" I asked.

"That's right. Do you mind taking the stairs? It's only two flights to the executive floor."

"Fine with me. I hope the stairwell is air-conditioned."

"It's not, but you look like someone who can manage."

Mrs. Turlock didn't speak as we climbed the two flights of metal stairs. If she disapproved of my appearance, she was polite enough not to make any indication. I had to admire her professionalism. She opened the door to the executive floor and invited me to step through. I walked past her and was met by a troll in a tailored suit, his arms, each bigger around than my legs, hanging at his sides. His close-set pointed ears rose nearly to the top of his domelike hairless skull. I had to look up to meet his glowing red eyes, which pierced laser-like into my own from almost two feet above my head, but the expression on his grey leathery face was impassive.

"Mr. Silverblade is our head of legal services," Mrs. Turlock informed me. "He'll be accompanying us."

"Suits me." The troll didn't offer to shake my hand, but neither did he make a move to frisk me. I wasn't packing a rod, but I doubt that he would have been scared by one. I followed Mrs. Turlock down a wide wood-paneled corridor through the center of the executive floor, and Mr. Silverblade paced me from close behind. We passed by a number of doors on either side of the hallway, each one labeled with embossed signs indicating the office's occupant. Most of these doors were closed. One was open, and two men in suits were holding a conversation in the doorway. They stared at Mrs. Turlock's legs as she passed by and glanced down their noses at me as if I were beneath their notice. They

26

avoided looking at Silverblade. The last door on the left opened into an empty glass-walled conference room. The last door on the right was open, and the label on the door revealed that this was the office of "Claudius Silverblade, Director of Legal Services." At the end of the hallway was a door that was facing us as we approached. The sign on the door read, "Donald Shipper, General Manager," and beneath that in smaller letters, "Patricia Turlock, Executive Assistant." Mrs. Turlock opened the door, and I followed her into a small windowless office dominated by a desk to the left of the doorway. The desktop was neatly organized, but every inch of it was covered with stacks of folders and papers, along with a landline telephone and a computer with a 21-inch screen and an oversized ergonomic keyboard. File cabinets lined most of the back wall of the office. On the right side of the room, opposite Mrs. Turlock's desk, was a door that no doubt led into the general manager's office. I guessed that it was much bigger than Mrs. Turlock's working space. I had a feeling that the size of the offices in this part of the building was inversely proportional to the actual amount of work that was done in them.

"Wait here, Mr. Southerland," Mrs. Turlock instructed me, and she walked through the door on the right.

I looked up at Silverblade, who was standing beside me with his huge knobby hands and eight taloned fingers clasped on his abdomen. "So, Claudius, you're a lawyer?" I asked, being sociable. The troll made a quiet grunting sound in response. So much for conversation.

Presently, Mrs. Turlock emerged through the door. "You can go in now, Mr. Southerland. Mr. Silverblade will accompany you."

"In case I get lost?" I asked.

"There's always that possibility," Mrs. Turlock replied.

I stepped through the open door and emerged into an entryway that was nearly the size of Mrs. Turlock's office. Near the door was a coatrack holding a lightweight navy blue blazer on a wooden hanger. The bottom of the coatrack opened into a black mesh umbrella stand, which was holding three folded black umbrellas. Next to the coatrack was a chest of two drawers, no doubt filled with spare shirts, ties, pocket handkerchiefs, cufflinks, and, who knows, maybe boxer shorts. On top of the chest were three hat stands upon which three homburgs were mounted: one black, one brown, and one plaid. Evidently, Mr. Shipper was a man who liked to be prepared for any fashion emergency. A set of three full-length mirrors, hinged together and angled like the ones in clothing stores, stood right next to the door so that Mr. Shipper could check out his appearance on his way out of his office to meet the rank and file. The entryway opened to the left into the general manager's office.

The main part of Donald Shipper's office wasn't large enough for a regulation basketball court, but it was close. It stretched from one side of the building to the other, and the glass walls on three sides of the room displayed a sprawling panoramic view of the Yerba City cityscape. Shipper's polished walnut desk, near the back right corner of the spacious office, was the size of a grand piano, and the desktop was empty apart from a phone, a computer, and a single framed photo of a pretty blond-haired woman and two teenagers, one boy and one girl: Shipper's wife and children, I assumed, although the woman didn't look that much older than the children. Much of the room was filled with living room chairs and sofas that formed a half circle in front of an enormous flat television screen standing like a shrine on an entertainment consul in the center of the office. What appeared to be a fully stocked mobile bar stood off to one side. A news station was broadcasting from the television screen, but the audio had been muted.

Shipper was seated in a plush leather office chair with a four-foot back, and he waited for Mrs. Turlock to announce me and exit the office before rising. The general manager of Emerald Bay Mortgage looked just like his picture on the company website, except that he wasn't bothering to smile since no one was asking him to.

"Take a seat, Mr. Southerland," Shipper said in clipped tones, indicating an easy chair near his desk. I guess I didn't rate the living room set near the television. He didn't offer me a drink, either. But at least I got to sit. Silverblade was left standing just behind my right shoulder, out of sight, but not out of mind.

Shipper sat after I did. I couldn't help but notice that I had sunk so low into the padded easy chair that, although I was at least four inches taller than Shipper, he was looking down his nose at me from his own perch. He crossed his arms over his desktop and leaned toward me. "Now, what is this urgent matter that you wish to warn me about?" Shipper's voice was deep and resonant, like a newsman's voice. I bet he didn't sound pompous at all in meetings.

"Thanks for seeing me, Mr. Shipper," I began, making an effort to lean forward in the soft chair to cover the rip in my shirt and trying to sound as sincere as I could. "I'm a private detective. I had a meeting this morning with a well-known practitioner of witchcraft. In the course of our conversation, she informed me that you have been targeted with a powerful curse. She told me that the curse will take your life this afternoon at exactly 1:30. I immediately called your office and spoke with Mrs. Turlock. She seems like a capable-enough assistant, but I don't think she was altogether convinced that I was on the level. I can't say as I blame her, but, wanting to make sure that you received my message and understood its gravity, I made the decision to seek you out in person. I'm hoping, for your sake, that you might be able to take some action to prevent the curse from taking effect." Message delivered, I leaned back into the chair, which threatened to swallow me whole.

Shipper nodded, his face betraying nothing of his thoughts. "And who was this 'well-known practitioner' that you met with?" he asked, emphasizing my description of the bruja in a way that grated on me a little.

I hesitated. I hadn't accepted Madame Cuapa's check, so, technically, I wasn't working for her yet, but she was very likely going to become my client before the day was done. As my client, she had a right to confidentiality. "I'm sorry," I told Shipper. "But for professional reasons, I would rather not say. I'm sure you understand."

Shipper sighed. "Why am I not surprised. But if my life is really in danger, wouldn't that supersede your desire to protect your client's identity?"

I could see that I wasn't getting anywhere with him. He was predisposed to dismiss me as an inconvenient interruption to what was apparently slated to be an interesting day of financial transactions, martini lunches, and board meetings, or whatever it is that general managers of mortgage companies do.

"I can see your point. But before I reveal my client's identity, let me ask you a question. Are you taking this warning seriously? I know what I must sound like."

Shipper raised his eyebrows and looked at me down his nose. "Oh, do you? Because, quite frankly, Mr. Southerland, you sound like a lunatic. And you look like a hobo! I suspect that if you even *have* a client, he's not a 'practitioner' at all, but rather a disgruntled customer who has hired you to make a ridiculous attempt to rattle my cage. Honestly! A witch's curse? I'll admit that's a new one, but I get all manner of threats from deadbeats who have lost their homes because they were no longer able to make their payments. This one is more creative than most, but still...." Shipper shook his head and sniffed. "A private eye! I didn't think you guys even existed outside of the movies. And a witch's curse, honestly!" He glared down at me, a prince on his leather throne rebuking a peasant. "Mr. Southerland, go tell your client that I enjoyed his little prank, but that I have no time for such nonsense. If he can afford to hire you, then he can afford to pay his bills."

Shipper sat back and dismissed me with a small hand motion. That was Silverblade's cue, and the troll laid a giant paw on my shoulder. I looked up at him, and he motioned me toward the entryway with his chin.

"You're making a mistake, Mr. Shipper."

"I make many," Shipper proclaimed in a grand voice, pleased with himself.

Silverblade's fingers tightened on my shoulder, and I could feel myself getting a little steamed.

"Well, Mr. Shipper, I tried," I rose from my chair. Silverblade's fingers held their grip. "But if I were you I'd find an expert in these matters to check you out. I imagine that these sorts of things are detectable by other practitioners, and you've only got a couple of hours. Whether you live or die is none of my concern, except that I thought you deserved a head's up. Whatever you choose to do at this point is on you."

Shipper made a show of ignoring me. He opened a drawer in his desk and pulled out a printed sheet, which he pretended to read. He even furrowed his brow while he studied it, showing me that he was a harried executive with no time to waste indulging riffraff like me. Silverblade guided me toward the entryway and I made no move to resist.

Mrs. Turlock was seated at her desk when I entered her office and shook myself loose from the troll. "Your boss is an idiot," I told her.

She gave me a thin smile, but said nothing.

I gave it my best shot. "Look. Find a brujo or bruja. There are many in the city, and I'm sure a few have offices or shops nearby. Bring the witch to your boss to try to detect and reverse the curse. What can it hurt? But you need to act fast if you want to save his life."

Mrs. Turlock pursed her lips. "I don't think that Mr. Shipper would appreciate that, Mr. Southerland. You've had your joke, but it's gone on long enough. Mr. Silverblade will show you to the elevator. Good day." She buried herself in some paperwork.

Silverblade laid a hand on my elbow. "Shall we?"

He led me to the executive elevator, which could only be opened with a key card. We had the elevator car to ourselves. On the way to the ground floor, I turned to the troll. "Despite what Mrs. Turlock thinks, this is no gag. Your boss is dead man walking."

Silverblade looked down at me with a bland expression. "If you say so."

"And you're okay with that?"

"I can roll with it either way."

I glanced at Silverblade, but he didn't meet my eyes and his expression remained bland. Interesting.

The troll gave me a quick glance. "If it's any comfort to you, Mr. Shipper is protected from magical attacks by a number of charms. He's a man who receives threats. He's not unprepared."

I nodded. "Good to know, though I doubt they will help. Not against this particular witch."

We reached the end of our descent then, and the elevator door slid open. We emerged on the opposite of the main elevators

31

and crossed the lobby floor to the front door. Silverblade was going to make sure that I left the building. I had no intention of resisting him. He was a troll and a lawyer. I've dealt with both many times, and the experience has rarely been pleasant.

I soon found myself outside on Market Street with a bruised ego, sweltering in the heat and feeling like a sap. Shipper was a self-important, arrogant ass, and the smart thing to do would have been to walk away. I had no reason to care about him. It was time to fold my cards and go collect that check from Madame Cuapa. I'd done all I could.

***

But that wasn't true, was it. Maybe no one at Emerald Bay Mortgage was going to contact a practitioner, but that didn't mean I couldn't try to do it myself. Sure, Madame Cuapa had told me that no one could reverse the curse, and that no one with any real skill was even going to be interested in talking to me about it, but I had no reason to simply take her at her word. I still had an hour and a half or so to act before my 1:30 deadline, and I couldn't bring myself to let a man die without doing everything I could to prevent it, not even when the man himself had waved away my efforts to warn him. Or maybe I was just annoyed because no one was taking me seriously. I like to be taken seriously. I'm a serious person. Serious as a heart attack.

I logged into the net from my phone, and a quick search revealed far fewer practitioners of witchcraft in the immediate neighborhood than I would have hoped, at least ones who advertised their services to the general public. In fact, my only real choice had an office about four blocks away. He went by Dr. Coyot, and his website proclaimed him to be an accomplished master of the brujería arts. I hoped that he wasn't a charlatan. I'd have to take my chances. It's not like I had any time for a formal vetting process.

I walked as fast as the intense heat would allow and reached Coyot's office in less than twenty minutes. The brujo's shop was located above a clean-looking restaurant that served Quscan food, and I climbed the flight of stairs to a glass door with Dr. Tizoc

Coyot's name across the front, happy to see that the establishment was an actual office and not some lurid strip-mall shop selling fake charms, cheap straw dolls, and other souvenirs of The City to gullible tourists. I walked into an empty waiting room and over to a receptionist seated at a counter behind a sliding glass window.

The receptionist was a dwarf whose narrow nose, thin lips, and silky beard indicated that she was a female, and probably an attractive one to other dwarfs. She slid the window open and asked in a thick gravelly voice, "May I help you?"

"I hope so. Is Dr. Coyot in? I don't have an appointment, but this is an emergency."

The receptionist's eyes told me that she had heard that story too many times to count. "Let me check."

She disappeared through a door behind her counter and reemerged through a door that opened into the waiting room. "The doctor can see you now," she announced. "This way please."

I was led down a short hallway to a room containing a wooden table and two wooden chairs. The walls were lined with clay pots and glass bottles of various shapes and colors filled with powders, leaves, and roots. "Wait here please. The doctor will be with you shortly." The receptionist shut the door as she left.

I took one of the chairs and decided to give Coyot five minutes before I packed it in. I hate waiting for any doctor, and witch doctors are no exception. What makes them think that their time is more valuable than mine? I admitted that if we compared the dough earned per hours worked, a doctor's time might actually prove to be worth a great deal more than mine, even if the doctor was a quack working above a restaurant, but the idea didn't make cooling my heels with nothing to do any more bearable. At least no one was trying to put me in one of those stupid robes that exposed my backside for no good reason.

As it was, Coyot entered the room in less than three minutes, making him a right joe in my book. An old short-haired dog, big as a wolf, black and white with a significant amount of gray on his muzzle and over his eyes, limped into the room on the doctor's heels, and, without even a glance in my direction, promptly curled up on a pile of old blankets and pillows in a corner of the room and prepared himself for a nap. The doctor was a tall,

33

soft-looking middle-aged man with spindly arms, a thin chest, and a paunchy midsection. He had an amazing head of thick gray hair tied back in a ponytail and large droopy brown eyes under bushy gray eyebrows. The bags under his eyes bulged like coin purses. He had a broad smile and seemed happy as a clam to see me. Remembering the empty waiting room, I wondered just how many patients he saw on a typical day.

"Hello, sir!" Dr. Coyot held out his hand, and I shook it. "Hope you're not allergic to dogs. Ol' Chichi thinks he's my consultant, but he won't get in our way. Now, what can I do for you today?"

I once again found myself explaining my situation, trying to be as efficient with my words as possible and emphasizing the need for haste. Coyot's eyes widened as he listened to my story without interruption. When I finished, he nodded. "This bruja, she would not by any chance be Madame Citlali Cuapa, would she?"

I didn't answer, but he let out a slow breath and shook his head. "I've had some word of this already. I agree that this is serious business, and I doubt that I will be of any use. But I suppose we should at least try." He nodded to himself, took a deep breath, and looked at me with an amused expression. "I'm free until later this afternoon, and I will, of course, be billing you for my time."

Of course. I'd add it to my expense report. I hoped Madame Cuapa wouldn't object to paying me for my efforts to stop her from killing Shipper. She *did* give me permission to try. Of course, I reminded myself, I wasn't technically working for her yet, but I was confident that I could find a way to pass the cost on to her.

"Does Madame Cuapa know that you have come to me?" Coyot asked. "I can't imagine that she recommended me to you. I'm not in her league. Not even close."

"I admit that I'm desperate."

Coyot's smile looked a little sad, but his eyes betrayed amusement. "I understand. And, as I said, I doubt that I'll be able to help you. But, as your last resort, I suppose I should take a look. And maybe I'll learn something by observing the Barbary Coast Bruja's work in action. She's a real artist, you know!"

Chapter Four

Coyot was soaked with sweat by the time we reached the entrance to the building housing Emerald Bay Mortgage, and I think that he was regretting his choice to accompany me. He had taken time to gather a few materials, which he carried in a crocheted pack that he'd strapped to his back. His gray ponytail trailed down his back from a shapeless woolen cap that drooped to one side and he carried a thick walking stick that was nearly as tall as he was. If he was trying to pass himself off as an eccentric wandering wizard, he was succeeding. But we attracted no attention as we walked the four blocks to Emerald Bay Mortgage. This was Yerba City, after all.

At least he'd left his dog back at his office. "Ol' Chichi was a real redhot back in the day, but he isn't much for long walks anymore," Coyot explained.

Once outside the building, I turned to Coyot. "I should warn you. I don't think that anyone up there is going to be happy to see us. It may get a little unpleasant."

The brujo's droopy face lit up with the same sad amusement that I'd seen in his office. "I may be able to help with that."

"Ummm...." I began.

He shrugged. "Don't worry about it."

Right.

I checked my phone. It was already twenty after one. Time was running out. We entered the building and called the elevator. Once inside, I punched the button for the forty-second floor, which was as high as the elevator would go. We emerged into the reception area, and I immediately headed for the door that opened into the stairway leading to the executive floor. Coyot followed close behind.

"Sir? Sir?" I heard the blond-haired receptionist calling and concluded that she was trying to get my attention. I ignored her and continued to the door.

"Sir? You can't go in there. Sir?"

I tried the door, and of course it was locked. I reached into my pocket and pulled out a set of lock picks that I liked to keep handy for times like this. "This may take a couple of minutes," I told the brujo.

Coyot placed a hand on my shoulder. I swung my head toward him. He smiled. "That won't be necessary. I've got this." I hesitated, and he put some pressure on my shoulder. "You might want to stand clear."

Curious, I stepped aside. The brujo took a step back and touched the end of his walking stick to the doorknob. He muttered something to himself that I didn't catch, and a second later the doorknob blew through the door with a noise like an exploding grenade. The receptionist screamed. At least, I think it was her. I leaped backwards and shouted something that was probably coherent, sophisticated, and cool.

A puff of smoke wafted out of the six-inch hole in the door where the doorknob used to be, and the door slowly swung open, creaking a little as it did. Coyot looked at me with a sly grin. "After you."

I stared at him, possibly openmouthed. He shrugged. "The staff is enchanted."

"You don't say."

I hustled through the door and spotted the remains of the doorknob on the stair steps. I jogged up the stairs with the brujo close behind me. This was going to be more interesting than I had thought.

We reached the door to the executive floor, and I pushed it open without incident. At the end of the hallway, Silverblade and Mrs. Turlock stood outside the door to the conference room. Their confused expressions turned angry when they spotted me.

"Mr. Southerland!" shouted Mrs. Turlock, and she advanced toward me as if she intended to toss me down the stairs I had just climbed. I doubted that she would be able to, but, with Silverblade following close behind, I knew that she wouldn't have to.

I held up a hand. "Hold on there, Mrs. Turlock, I come in peace. This man is a brujo. Just give him a minute to see if he can protect Mr. Shipper from the curse."

I was going to add, "I assure you that we mean no harm," but by then Mrs. Turlock had reached me, and she surprised me by slapping me across the face—hard!

I threw up my hands in surrender. "Please, Mrs. Turlock." I made sure to keep one eye on Silverblade. She slapped me again, even harder. I stood and took it.

By now, Shipper and several other men had filed out of the conference room and were looking on with curiosity. "Mr. Shipper!" I shouted. "This man is a brujo. Give him a chance to protect you. Please!"

Shipper's curiosity turned into indignation. He drew himself up to his full height, such as it was, and shouted, "Alkwat's flaming balls! Claudius! Get rid of these idiots! If they've done any damage to this building, sue them!"

Silverblade placed a gentle hand on Mrs. Turlock's shoulder. "I'll take it from here, Patricia. Thank you for your assistance."

I stood up to the troll. "Listen to reason, Silverblade. Your boss may not want to admit it, but he's in danger. This man might be able to help him. Don't you think it's worth trying? Just in case I'm right?"

The troll was the calmest person in the room. "I think that you should both go quietly before I have to take sterner measures."

I sighed and let my shoulders slump. "Okay. You win. I'll go."

I turned toward the door, and with my back to Silverblade I caught Coyot's eyes and made a quick motion with my own to my left. He gave me an almost imperceptible nod in return. Then suddenly, I spun to my left and threw myself into Silverblade, attempting to pin his left arm to his side. It was like running into a tree trunk. Coyot took advantage of the situation, held out his staff to fend off Mrs. Turlock, and attempted to run past the three of us down the hallway.

But Silverblade was having none of it. He easily flung me aside into Coyot before the brujo could get past him. The two of us fell to the floor in a heap, me on top of the brujo, whose breath escaped him with a *whoomph*. I tried to regain my feet, but before I could the troll reached down and picked me up into the air by my collar. He held me seven feet up in the air and glared at me with his burning red eyes. Then he threw me facedown to the floor.

It could have been worse. I didn't lose consciousness, and after a quick inventory I concluded that I had broken no bones. I rolled to one side to see Coyot point at the troll with his staff and begin to mutter. Silverblade was too quick, however. With more speed than I would have thought possible, he reached down and plucked the staff out of the brujo's hand. The troll examined the staff for a second, and then, with contempt, tossed it behind him down the hallway.

Silverblade paused to stare down at the two of us, but his expression was benign. "Shall we try again?" he asked.

I held up a hand, palm outwards. With my other hand, I reached slowly into my pocket and took out my phone. I punched in my access code and looked at the time. The digital readout said 1:29.

I looked up at Silverblade, looming over me. "That's all right. I think we're about out of time." I turned my head and spotted Shipper, still standing down the hallway, surrounded by his department managers. One by one, first Coyot, then Mrs. Turlock, and finally Silverblade also turned toward Shipper.

Shipper stared back at us with disgust. None of us moved for several seconds. Finally, Shipper shook his head, threw a dismissive arm into the air, and said, "Oh for—"

And then he disappeared, replaced by a cloud of flying red goo that covered his department managers from head to toe and flew down the hallway to cover Silverblade, Mrs. Turlock, Coyot, and me.

***

An owl-eyed bucktoothed gnome with a jet-black hairpiece wedged between his huge rounded ears stormed into the police interrogation room. "Alkwat's pecker, Southerland—what have you done this time!"

"Nothing. I tried to save a man's life."

"Is that his blood all over you or yours?" asked the gnome.

"His."

"So you screwed up! Nice work!"

"Fuck you, Lubank! Just get me out of here. I need a shower."

Lubank turned to the homicide detective seated at the other side of the table from me. He smiled, and his voice became pleasant. "Mrs. Kalama. A pleasure, as always. You beat a confession out of my client yet?"

The detective didn't rise from her chair. She turned toward Lubank, and, though she wasn't a tall dame, her eyes were level with the gnome's. "Hello, Mr. Lubank. Hot enough for you?"

"It's a bitch out there, that's for sure. My lowlife clients don't pay me enough to sweat like this!"

"Hey!" I said.

"You charging him?" Lubank asked the detective.

She sighed, "No, not at this time. But we'd like to ask him a few more questions before we turn him loose."

"Nuts to that!" Lubank was already moving toward the door. "Unless you're charging him, he walks. The man needs a shower and some clean clothes. You still wanna talk to him after that, you arrange to meet him in my office. Let's go, Southerland!"

I stood and followed Lubank out of the room. As I walked into the hallway, I heard Detective Kalama tell me, "Keep yourself available, Mr. Southerland. We'll be in touch."

***

Outside the police station, Lubank took out a pack of cigarettes and offered me one. "You know I don't smoke," I told him.

"Never know when you might start." He lit a pill for himself and flipped the spent match into the gutter. "You think they'd get some damned air conditioning in those interrogation rooms. It was like a fuckin' furnace in there! How long did they hold you? We should sue them for excessive torture!"

"I was only there an hour or so. And mostly by myself. At least they brought in a fan."

"Well *that* was big of them. I guess you must rate some sort of frequent-visitor bonus. As often as the cops drag you to their downtown clubhouse it's a wonder you don't have your own office."

"They were pretty decent this time." I shrugged. "No one laid a glove on me. I wasn't even cuffed. And the detective seemed polite enough."

"Well you look like shit." He hung his cigarette on the corner of his mouth and looked up at me to make sure that he had my attention. "Word of advice, Southerland—watch out for Kalama! She may be a good-looking dish, but she's your worst nightmare—a smart cop! She's not like most of those mugs. She doesn't just take the easy way out and call it a day. She's a fuckin' bulldog! If you're hiding something, she'll keep digging until she finds it."

"I'm not hiding anything. I didn't do anything illegal."

"That right?" Lubank sounded skeptical. "Word is you invaded a mortgage company, blew open a door with a bomb, and were on the scene when some big shot—and I'm quoting one of the homicide dicks here—'got blown to bits with enough firepower to paint a whole hallway red with his guts.' Is that pretty much it?"

"Pretty close."

"Alkwat's balls! You sure don't make life easy for an honest lawyer."

"Good thing I've got *you*, then."

"Fuckin' right! Honest lawyers are suckers." Lubank pointed up the street. "My car's just around that corner. Where's yours?"

"Six or eight blocks further up."

"That's not so bad. You can walk."

The blazing afternoon sun was giving me a worse beatdown than a cop's billy club. It was officially the hottest day I'd ever spent in Yerba City. "You can't drop me off?"

"And get blood all over my clean car seats? Look at you— you look like a used tampon! Go home, spruce yourself up, and then come see me. The police still want to talk to you. Better they do it with your mouthpiece present, in case they wanna play dirty." He looked up at me. "Besides, I wanna hear about this. You busted into a mortgage company? Th'fuck, man! Sounds like you're gonna need me to keep you outta stir. Again."

40

"Nuts to you, pal. You just want to squeeze some dough out of me, as usual."

"So sue me for wanting to earn a living. Gracie's been bugging me to buy her a new car. She says the one's she's got is a heap! I told her that if I get her a new model, she can use it to drive me to the poorhouse!"

"Her car's, what, twelve years old?"

"You see? I knew you'd be on her side. Well, I've got news for you, you turncoat—I'm doubling my fee! The cost for her new buggy is coming out of your pocket!"

"You still owe me for the last job I did for you," I pointed out.

"What job was that?" asked Lubank.

"That background check I did on the new councilman."

"You're charging me for that?" Lubank shouted. "You didn't even dig up any dirt that I could use on that operator! You shoulda done that one for free, you chiseler!"

I couldn't help but laugh. Rob Lubank calling anyone else a chiseler was like a whore accusing someone else of only being in it for the dough.

We'd reached his parked car by then, and Lubank stopped. "Okay, peeper. Gotta go. Come by when you're presentable."

"You can't drive me a couple of blocks? It's a hundred degrees out here! And the blood's dry as a bone."

"Sorry," Lubank told me in a manner that implied he was anything but. "To make it up to you, I won't bill you for the walk from the police station." He took a last long drag on his cigarette, and flicked the butt to the sidewalk. He walked to the driver's side of his car, turned, and waved at me. "See you later, pal. I'll tell Gracie that you're picking up some take-out. Some Huaxian would hit the spot." He opened the car door and got in.

I watched Lubank yank his late-model luxury sedan out of his parking space and squeeze into an impossibly small opening between an SUV and a pickup truck without scraping either one. Lubank's driving skills were remarkable, but terrifying. Maybe it was better that I was on foot after all. Wiping sweat out of my eyes, I started hoofing it to the beastmobile.

***

It was after four by the time I pulled into the lot at Gio's shop. I parked and found the mechanic in his office wearing stained overalls, smoking a cheap cigar, and punching data into his computer with one thick finger. He was a burly man with a bald head, a grease-covered face, no neck, and a wrestler's body that had seen better days. He looked up when he heard me come through the open door.

"Alkwat's iron balls!" Gio exclaimed when he saw me. "What the fuck happened to you?"

"It's not my blood," I told him.

"Yeah? Well, you look like someone put you through a cement mixer!"

"You should see the other guy."

"You need a beer?" Gio asked. He grabbed a dirty red rag off his desktop and smeared the grease on his face.

I hesitated. I had things to do, but the heat and the events of the day had caught up to me. I needed a breather before heading out for the next round. "Just one. I've got to get home and clean up. Then I've got to go out again. Day's not done."

Gio lumbered over to a small refrigerator and took out two bottles of brew. He opened them both with a cap remover built into the refrigerator door and handed one of them to me. I tilted the bottle to my lips and guzzled three quarters of the contents in one go. The cold liquid streaming down my throat felt like the best thing that had happened to me all day. I put the icy bottle against my temple and let out a loud unrestrained belch.

Gio laughed. "I guess you needed that!"

I wiped my mouth with the back of my hand. "Hot day."

"That's for sure! You fuckin' kiddin' me? This ain't the Yerba City we know and love. Bring back the damned fog!" He took a gulp of beer and wiped his mouth with his free hand. He motioned toward my bloodstained clothes with the bottle. "So what's up? You in some kind of jam?"

"Long story. Okay if I put it off for another day?"

"Sure, no sweat. I can't stay here long anyway. Connie got a call from Antonio's math teacher today. Turns out that the kid hasn't been doing his algebra homework. So Connie gets me on the horn and gives me an earful. I tell her, so what? What's he need algebra for anyway? The kid's not going to be a fuckin' brain surgeon—he likes workin' on cars, like his ol' man! She was *not* amused. She said something about how the boy should at least have the tools to make a fuckin' choice about his life." Gio took another gulp of his beer. "She's prob'ly right—she usually is! So anyway, I promised to get home early and wise the boy up."

I finished off my beer. "He's fourteen, right? Bad age."

Gio shook his head. "They're all bad ages, brother. But, yeah, fourteen. Still a kid and thinks he's a man."

"Too much of a man to listen to his parents, right?"

Gio barked out a short laugh. "Let me tell you something. Ain't no one dumber than the parent of a teenager. There's not a thing you can tell them that they don't already think they know. You remember your parents trying to teach you anything about life when you were that age?"

I shook my head. "My parents weren't much for giving advice. The only worthwhile thing my father ever told me was that there's no point in buying expensive booze because after the first four drinks it all tastes the same. And the only good thing my mother ever taught me was that I should avoid my father after he'd had that fourth drink."

"Hmmph," Gio grunted. "They sound pretty smart to me."

"Maybe I just wasn't a good listener."

"Show me a teenager who is! Not Antonio, that's for sure. No matter what I tell him, he'll wind up having to learn the hard way, same as the rest of us. Another beer?"

I waved the offer off. "Another time. Gotta see a man about a dog."

"Okay, man." Gio gave the dried blood on my clothes another meaningful examination. "Try to stay outta trouble."

"I always try."

I walked back to my place then. No cops were waiting around to put the arm on me. I showered, put on clean clothes, and put a frozen pizza in the microwave. I hadn't eaten since breakfast, and, although the pizza tasted like rubber and was about as nutritious, it at least filled the gaping pit in my stomach. I washed

43

it down with a shot of whisky and a beer chaser and felt like I could get on with my life.

I found Madame Cuapa's business card on my desk. It listed two numbers for the Madame, a work number and a home number. I punched the home number into my phone. The call was answered by a male voice, most likely that oversized young man with the manticore that I'd met that morning.

"Madame Cuapa's residence," the voice declared.

"This is Alex Southerland. I'd like to speak to Madame Cuapa, please."

"One moment, sir. She's been expecting your call."

A minute or so later, Madame Cuapa came on the line. "Mr. Southerland. Will you be needing that check after all?"

"Looks that way. I guess you know that Shipper is dead."

"Of course! I've also noticed that his death failed to make the news."

Which made me wonder how she had known about it. No doubt her sources were extensive. I reminded myself that it would be a mistake to underestimate the Barbary Coast Bruja.

"I guess the police are keeping a lid on it. They're more than a little disturbed by the whole thing."

"I'll bet. Were you there to see it?"

"I had a front-row seat. You didn't mention that his death was going to be so thorough."

"Didn't I? I hope you weren't too upset by it, dear. I *did* encourage you to stay away."

"That was a powerful curse. The only part of the body left intact was the feet. They had to scrape the rest of him off the walls. I can see why you might not want someone using you to fire off another of those rounds on anyone else."

"To be sure, Mr. Southerland." An admonishing tone had entered Madame Cuapa's voice. "I hope you can see now why I wanted you seeking out the source of my compulsion rather than wasting a day trying to prevent Shipper's inevitable demise. I want you to come to my home immediately and start making yourself useful."

"Can it wait until morning? I was going to see my lawyer tonight."

44

"Your lawyer can wait. I don't like doing business over the phone. I want to talk to you tonight, face-to-face. I'm about to give you my address. Do you have something to write with?"

I wrote down her address and we ended the call. I wasn't familiar with her street, so I consulted an online map and found that Madame Cuapa lived on the extreme western part of the city in a lightly inhabited residential district nearly an hour's drive from my place. I called Lubank and asked him if any cops were waiting for me there. He told me that the coast was clear, and I told him that I would come by his office in the morning.

"Got a hot date tonight, Slick?" he asked me.

"Yeah," I answered. "I've got to go see a witch. I'll give you all the gory details tomorrow."

"Make sure you use protection," advised Lubank.

I groaned. "Yeah, right. I think I'm beyond protecting."

As I was about to go out the door, I decided that a little protection might not be a bad idea at that. I grabbed a tight-fitting shoulder holster from my closet and strapped it on. Then I took a concealable nine-millimeter out of my desk drawer and holstered the gat. I found a clean blazer, adjusted it over the shoulder holster until it was comfortable, and headed back to Gio's shop to get my car.

It was about 5:30 when I reached the lot, and the temperature had cooled into the high eighties. Gio was long gone, probably making his wife happy by saying the right things to their boy. It occurred to me that, although we had become something like friends over the past several months, I didn't actually know where Gio lived. I'd have to meet him for a drink some time. Maybe get to know his wife and kid and see what the domestic life was all about. I guessed that it didn't involve dealing with witches and curses. It struck me how different our lives were. Thinking about Madame Cuapa reminded me of what she had told me that morning about the fragility of existence. Unbidden, the image of Shipper exploding into a ball of red gore flashed through my mind. I thought about how one tiny woman could shed a few drops of her blood into some herbs, light some candles, mutter a few phrases, and cause that amount of pure carnage. What kind of horror was she? And here I was, willingly driving myself straight into the creature's lair. Would I rather be at home with my wife after a long day's work trying to talk sense to my rebellious teenaged boy? I shuddered at the thought and made my way to the witch's house.

Chapter Five

I pulled in front of Madame Cuapa's house just before 6:30. She lived in a nice neighborhood. Most Yerba City houses are crammed next to each other with little or no space between the structures in order to provide roofs over the heads of as many people as possible in the limited space available on the Yerba City Peninsula. Madame Cuapa's home, however, was located in a quiet subdivision with plenty of space between the houses, many of which were large enough to qualify as mansions. Madame Cuapa's cozy two-story bungalow was older and more modest than the neighboring houses. A white picket fence marked off the boundaries of the property, which was large enough to allow a small grove of oak trees to grow in her yard. A driveway led to an old carriage house that now served as a two-car garage. Attached to the pale-green house was a railed porch with an overhead portico supported by wide white pillars. A cement walkway led from the street and up three steps to the front of the entryway. It seemed like a pleasant place, well maintained and welcoming. Nothing about the house indicated that the most powerful witch in western Tolanica cooked up lethal curses within its walls.

I walked up the steps to the entryway and rapped on the front door. It was answered immediately by the smug jasper that I'd met earlier that day. He'd changed into a dark brown leather suit with no tie and a pastel-blue shirt that was open at the collar.

"Come in, sir." He looked pleased with himself, like he knew that he was the strongest and best-looking man on the dance floor.

"Thanks. I didn't catch your name earlier today."

He held out his hand. "Call me Cody." I noticed that the palm of his hand was lined with a number of long, thin scars. The hazards of handling a manticore, I guessed.

I shook his hand. "So, Cody, you're a beast-handler, chauffeur, bodyguard probably, and butler? Any other duties I should know about?"

He chewed on my question for a couple of seconds. "I prefer 'animal trainer' to 'beast-handler. As for the rest, let's just say that I am Madame Cuapa's personal assistant."

"Fair enough." I looked around the front room, which contained a comfortable-looking sofa and two equally comfortable-looking easy chairs ringed around a wooden handmade coffee table. Paintings of plants and animals hung on the wood-paneled walls and old photographs sat on wooden side tables. The room seemed homey and ordinary, if a bit rustic.

"Where's your pussycat?" I asked

"Mr. Whiskers? He's in the pen out back, sleeping off his dinner."

"His name is Mr. Whiskers?"

Cody's smile broadened again. "He didn't want to leave you this morning. I think he likes you, sir."

"And where is your mistress?" I asked.

The smile faded. "My what? You trying to be funny?" he asked.

"Huh? No, I'm just wondering where your...where the bruja is. She *did* ask me to stop by tonight."

"The *Madame* is expecting you, sir." Cody was all business now. He seemed sore. I guess he didn't care for me referring to the lady of the house as his "mistress" and all that might imply. "She's waiting for you upstairs. I'll lead you there."

I followed Madame Cuapa's personal assistant up a flight of stairs to the second floor. I was curious about Cody's relationship with Madame Cuapa, for professional reasons, of course. He struck me as an arrogant young fuck, but he'd be an impressive tomcat for Madame Cuapa if she was interested in that sort of thing. I didn't really know anything about the kid, but something about his flamboyant leather outfits and the self-satisfied smirk he sported made me want to slap him into next Tuesday. Granted, I'm a rude person. Getting under people's skin is part of my job. It can make people careless with their secrets. If Cody's "personal assistant" responsibilities included intimacy with the lady of the house, then that was a bit of data that might be good to know.

But I also had to admit that my reaction to the kid was a little over the top, and that my judgment of him might be

48

premature. Maybe even unfair. I couldn't put my finger on what it really was about him that raised my hackles. Maybe it was his youthful swagger. Maybe it was the way he referred to me as "sir." We were both in our twenties, but he hadn't been there for long and I wouldn't be for much longer. Moreover, I knew that I'd never been young the way that he seemed to be. I rubbed my hand over my head of short black hair. A few days ago, I'd noticed for the first time that more than a few of those hairs were white. I had shrugged it off, but I couldn't help concluding that a salt-and-pepper look was a natural fit with the new wrinkles and pale scars that had begun to appear on my face over the past several months. I'd never considered myself vain, and I wasn't prone to agonizing over some mythical lost youth, but, still, the last thing I needed at that moment was a reminder that my thirtieth birthday was only a handful of weeks away. I stared daggers into the young assistant's back as I trailed him up the stairs. I was being petulant, of course, but I *knew* that I was being petulant, so that made it okay. Besides, I wasn't thirty just yet. I still had some time to be an immature asshole if I wanted.

The second floor of the bungalow was half the size of the ground floor. It consisted of a hallway and three rooms. The one at the end of the hall was probably a bathroom. Cody led me to Madame Cuapa's lab, and I guessed that the closed door on the other side of the hall from the lab led into the bruja's bedroom. Madame Cuapa, dressed in a long casual dress that concealed most of her tattoos, was seated at a worktable in the lab, and she rose when I entered.

"Mr. Southerland. Good. I'm glad you're here at last. Cody, would you bring us some tea?"

Cody excused himself with a "Yes ma'am" and disappeared through the doorway.

I gave the bruja's lab a quick once over. Overhead track lights lit the room with a warm light. Layers of wooden shelves lined every wall, and every shelf was filled with an assortment of sealed bottles, corked clay pots, potted and hanging plants, glass cases containing dead animals, and wire cages containing live animals. A long wooden worktable with a wooden bench ran down the center of the room, and the table was covered with the same

49

sort of materials that filled the shelves. In addition, the table contained mixing bowls, various utensils, papers, writing materials, and a state-of-the-art desktop computer.

"Are you ready to get to work?" Madame Cuapa asked me.

"I'm ready," I assured her. "I hope you appreciate that I had to do what I could."

"Yes, yes, I suppose." Madame Cuapa's dark eyes seemed to flicker with an inner light. "But you've wasted most of the day. I need you to be more focused on your real job from here on in. I hope that your calendar is clear. You won't be taking on any other clients until my problem is resolved. I'll make it worth your while financially, of course." She reached to her worktable and picked up the check I had seen that morning. "This is your retainer. I trust that it will be sufficient to ensure your full attention?"

I looked at the amount. It wasn't enough to allow me to retire in luxury, but it would keep me comfortable for several weeks, if not months. Maybe a year, if I changed to a cheaper brand of whiskey.

I put the check in my pocket.

Madame Cuapa, gestured toward the worktable. "Please sit, Mr. Southerland. I'm afraid that you'll have to settle for this old bench. I don't have any chairs in here."

"I can manage." I sat on the bench with my back to the worktable. Madame Cuapa perched herself on the bench a few feet away from me.

"Actually, today may not have been a waste of time at all. I learned a few things that might prove useful."

Madame Cuapa's eyebrows raised. "Oh?"

"I met two employees at Emerald Bay Mortgage today: Patricia Turlock, Shipper's secretary—pardon me, executive assistant—and Claudius Silverblade, the director of legal services."

Madame Cuapa frowned at the names. "Yes, I know them. What about them?"

"Neither showed much interest in protecting their boss when I told them that he had been targeted with a curse. I didn't mention your name, of course, but I did tell them that the curse was deadly. Neither took my warning seriously. Maybe that was my fault. Maybe I wasn't convincing enough. And I *was* allowed to

50

see Shipper, briefly. Shipper didn't take me seriously, either, and I have a hunch that Mrs. Turlock set him up to dismiss me out of hand."

"What do you mean?"

"If someone told me that my life was in grave and immediate danger," I explained, "I'd at least ask a few questions. Shipper had me sized up as some kind of kook the minute I walked into his office. He gave me about thirty seconds to make my case. Then he called me a lunatic and had Silverblade escort me out of his office. Forcibly."

Madame Cuapa shook her head. "Shipper was a pompous ass." Then she looked up at me and asked, "Do you think that Mrs. Turlock and Mr. Silverblade have something to do with...my problem?"

"I don't know yet. Let's just say that neither of them showed a lot of concern for Shipper's well-being. That might not mean much by itself, but it puts them on my suspects list."

Madame Cuapa nodded, but she didn't seem convinced. "Anything else?" she asked.

I hadn't been sure that I wanted to mention Coyot, but I didn't want Madame Cuapa to find out that I'd been holding anything back from her. So I said, "I brought along a brujo to help me out. It was kind of a spur-of-the-moment decision."

Madame Cuapa gave me a sly smile. "Ah, yes. Dr. Coyot. I heard from him. Not directly, but through channels. He's smart enough not to get himself involved in my affairs without letting me know about it. He knows that I would find out anyway."

"Not a problem, I hope?"

Madame Cuapa waved a hand in dismissal, "No, no problem. Coyot's a nice enough man. Don't worry about him. He's harmless."

I thought about what Coyot had done to the stairwell door. I thought about what it meant that Madame Cuapa considered the brujo to be harmless. I might tower over the diminutive lady next to me, but I had no illusions about which of us was the most dangerous person in the room.

"Still, he might be useful to me. I don't know much about the Nahuatl arts."

Madame Cuapa laughed. "My goodness, dear! What do you suppose he could teach you that I can't?"

"Probably nothing," I admitted. "But you're on the inside, and he's on the outside. It might help to have a different perspective."

The witch seemed amused. "Well, you're the detective. I'm not going to tell you how to do your business. As long as I get results. And as long as I don't think you're wasting your time. And mine." She was no longer amused by the time she finished talking.

I decided that I'd better change the subject. "What can you tell me about Shipper?" I asked. "Other than the fact that he was a pompous ass, do you know of any reason why someone would want to kill him?"

Madame Cuapa thought about it. "Not really. I mean, sure, a lot of people disliked him. He was an unlikeable man. But enough to kill him?" She shrugged.

"People will kill for a great many reasons. Not all of them make sense to other people."

Madame Cuapa frowned. "You're going to have a lot of suspects, I'm afraid. The hard part is going to be narrowing them down."

"You're his employer, aren't you?" I asked.

"Technically, yes. I suppose. Do you want a cigarette?" Madame Cuapa opened a box on her workbench, revealing a dozen or so hand-rolled tobacco sticks.

I held up a hand, palm out. "No thanks. I don't smoke."

"Well, I do." Madame Cuapa put a cigarette in her mouth and lit it with her silver lighter. She blew out some smoke, and I detected the same hint of something sweet mixed with the tobacco that I had noticed that morning. A drop of hashish oil, maybe. Madame Cuapa took the cigarette from her lips and held it off to one side. "My firm owns Emerald Bay Mortgage, and Mr. Shipper was its highest ranking officer. So I guess you could say that he worked for me."

"Was he good at his job?" I asked.

"You might not think so, but, yes, he was. He wasn't a man that I would socialize with, but I had no problem with him as a businessman. Under his direction, Emerald Bay Mortgage was a successful enterprise that regularly turned a nice profit. I've seen the books, so I know."

"You've seen the books? How recently?"

"Just a couple of weeks ago, as it happens. I ordered an outside audit of his company."

In other words, just before she cast a spell that wound up transforming Shipper into a red mist. "Why did you order an audit?" I asked.

"He was skimming. I wanted to find out how much." Madame Cuapa raised her cigarette to her lips and breathed in some smoke.

"He was skimming?" I was confused. The haze from Madame Cuapa's cigarette was firing up jackhammers on the inside of my forehead. I closed my eyes and rubbed my temple. "I thought you said that you had no problem with him."

"Oh, Mr. Southerland." Madame Cuapa gave me a condescending smile. "Don't be naïve. Everyone takes a little something off the top for themselves. Can't let the taxman know everything, right? I had the company audited, just to be sure it wasn't getting out of hand, and it turns out that Shipper wasn't taking all that much. Certainly not enough for me to trouble myself over it. Emerald Bay Mortgage makes me a great deal of money. Shipper was a good, solid manager. I wish he were still alive! Replacing him is going to be a bitch." Madame Cuapa placed her cigarette in an ashtray on the worktable, where it smoldered amongst a number of its burnt out predecessors. The throbbing in my temples was getting worse, and the thickening haze was rubbing up against my eyes like sandpaper. Madame Cuapa continued, "I wouldn't trust a businessman who didn't take a little off the top. Especially a banker! I'd wonder whether he was interested enough in money. If you don't like money enough to dip your beak in it when you get the chance, then you're not going to do what it takes to make enough of it to matter."

I thought about that. "Well, I hope you don't mind if I give you an honest account of *my* expenses when we're done with this."

She smiled up at me, and not in a condescending way. She brushed her auburn hair away from her face and picked up her cigarette. She took a brief puff and blew a stream of smoke out her nose. "If you *do* skim, dear, try not to take enough for me to notice."

Cody returned then with a pot of tea and two porcelain teacups with saucers on a silver tray. He cleared a spot on the worktable, placed the tray on the table, bowed his head toward Madame Cuapa, and left the room.

I nodded my head toward the door. "The jasper seems like a useful lad."

"Jasper? What's a jasper?"

"A jasper's a good-looking gee."

"Gee?"

"Sorry. A guy. I used to kick around with a rough bunch. On Saturday nights the local gin mill would let us use our fake IDs to get in and knock back shots of cheap hooch. Jaspers were the good-looking gees—guys—mostly from outside the neighborhood, who would come strutting into the joint in their glad rags, all fancy-free like nothing could touch them. The dizzy dishes would go all moony for them and give us pugs the breeze. I guess we might have been a bit envious."

Madame Cuapa smiled. "I might have understood about half of that, but I think I get the gist." She flicked some ash from her cigarette into an ashtray on her worktable. "Do you know that Cody has a psychic bond with that manticore? He and the manticore were born at exactly the same moment in a village near Tenochtitlan. The two of them have been together since they were babies. The boy named him Mr. Whiskers. How cute is that?" Madame Cuapa smiled like a grandmother showing off photos of her new grandchild. "Word reached me about the young boy and his unusual pet. I was intrigued by their connection and traveled south to pay the boy's family a visit. They were living in squalor, and I became a sort of sponsor to the boy. I made sure that the family was cared for, and that Cody received a proper education. When he was old enough, I brought him up north so that he could enter my service and I could complete his education."

"The manticore came with him?" I asked.

"Of course! That was the whole point. The manticore became my familiar."

"And what does that make Cody? Is he your familiar, too?"

54

Madame Cuapa blew some smoke off to one side, directing it away from me. "That's the intriguing part. The rites that bond Mr. Whiskers to me as my familiar don't quite extend to Cody, but the bond between the boy and the manticore is still in place."

"So Mr. Whiskers is bonded to both Cody *and* you?"

"Precisely."

"Isn't that a little tricky?" I asked.

"What do you mean?"

"Seems like Cody might resent you inserting yourself into the special relationship that he has with his pet."

Madame Cuapa waved her hand in dismissal. "Nonsense. We couldn't be closer. Cody is very devoted to me."

I didn't say anything to that. Madame Cuapa glanced up at me with a knowing look in her eyes. "You're wondering if I sleep with him. I don't, though he's certainly a pretty enough 'jasper.' But he's very young, and, to be quite honest about it, I think he'd much rather sleep with you."

"Oh." I paused, surprised. "I hope he won't take it too hard when I turn him down."

"He'll be disappointed, I'm sure." Madame Cuapa made a show of looking me up and down as she took a lengthy puff of her cigarette. "You're just his type."

I felt like it was time to get back to business. "So you had no beef with Shipper as a businessman. What about personally?"

"Personally?" she repeated. "Well, like I said, we didn't socialize. I didn't have anything against him, though." She took a last draw from her cigarette and then reached over and crushed the stub into the ashtray. She poured tea from the teapot into the two cups and handed one of them to me. "Have some tea, Mr. Southerland. It's my own blend. But don't worry!" She picked up the other cup and smiled as she breathed in the steam. "It's spicy, but it won't turn you into a toad." She placed the two saucers on the table.

I held the cup in my hand and sniffed at it. I must have looked doubtful, because the bruja's face broke into an amused grin. "Really! Here, I'll go first." She put her cup up to her lips and took a vigorous sip

"You're probably just immune," I muttered under my breath, and took a sip of my own. The tea was earthy and a little bitter, but it left a pleasant peppery aftertaste. "Not bad!" I said out loud, and I meant it. I took another long sip.

"It's even better with a slug of rum." Madame Cuapa rose from the table and crossed over to one of the wall shelves. She pulled an unlabeled bottle off one of the shelves and carried it back with her, pulling a cork stopper out of the top. "Shall we?" she asked, holding the bottle up to my cup. The heady smell of strong alcohol filled my senses.

"Why not?" I held out my cup and the Madame filled it to the brim. I took a quick sip so that it wouldn't spill.

Madame Cuapa put some of the rum into her own cup, sat on the bench, and took a sip of her own. "How is it?" she asked me.

"Hits the spot!" I took another sip of the spiked tea. The fumes from the rum rushed up my nostrils and cleansed the smoke from my sinuses. My headache began to subside. I took a long sip and held it in my mouth for a few moments, savoring the taste. By the time I swallowed, my headache was gone. Good stuff!

I set my cup down on its saucer. "Let's get back to Shipper. I imagine he was pretty well off. Do you know who gets his fortune now that he's gone?"

Madame Cuapa swallowed a sip from her cup and shrugged. "Mrs. Shipper, I would imagine. And his kids, I suppose. I haven't seen his will." She took another sip of tea and asked, "Do you think that she might have been in a hurry for her inheritance?"

"When it comes to motives for murder, love and money top the list."

Madame Cuapa frowned. "I would think that a desire for power would be at the top of that list."

"You're right. But for most of us average joes, power comes from money."

She sniffed. "I suppose. In my case, it's just the opposite."

"You live in a different world than the rest of us."

The bruja smiled. "We're all from the same world. Some of us just see more of it than others."

The rum and tea had done a remarkable job of driving the ache out of my head. The light in the room seemed brighter, as if the cigarette haze that had been hanging in the room had disappeared. I picked up my cup and finished it off with two long swallows. "This is good."

"Would you like another?" asked Madame Cuapa. Without waiting for my answer, she poured me a second cup from the teapot and topped it off with the rum.

After taking a sip from the fresh cup, I asked, "Have you met Mrs. Shipper?"

Madame Cuapa grimaced. "Oh yes. She's about what you would expect. She comes from decent upper middle-class money, but she never has enough. And her children are a handful, from what I hear. But if you are thinking that she had her husband killed for his dough, I don't know. Unless he was threatening to divorce her. But I haven't heard anything like that." She looked at me. "That's your department, though, right?"

"It's something I'll have to check out. It's a place to start, at least." I gulped down more of the jacked-up tea and was surprised to discover that I had finished the cup. A wave of dizziness, different in tone and texture from the previous aching, passed through my brain, coming and going like an unexpected slap in the face.

"Shall we polish this off?" asked Madame Cuapa, refilling our cups without waiting for a response.

What was I talking about? Shipper's family, that's right. I started to frame another question, but I stopped at the sight of a huge spider, as big as my hand, crawling up from Madame Cuapa's back to her shoulder. It perched there for a second, and then crawled to her neck before disappearing under the collar of her dress.

"Are you okay?" asked Madame Cuapa. A dark green vine trailed down from her mouth, and began to wrap itself around her neck.

I looked at my cup and noticed that it was only half full. Was that because we had emptied the pot, or had I taken another drink? I couldn't remember.

"Mr. Southerland?" Madame Cuapa's voice echoed up from the bottom of a well, but she was no longer in sight. In her place on the bench I now saw a writhing mass of snakes, twisting and creeping, tongues darting in and out as they tasted the thickening yellow haze that was descending into the room.

I wanted to stand, but my legs weren't getting the message. I felt the cup slip from my fingers, and I watched it splinter into shards on the floor. Funny that it was empty. How had that happened? I sucked in my breath and gritted my teeth. I was going to stand! I was an unstoppable juggernaut, battle-tested and hard as nails. No one was going to stop me!

A low soothing voice told me to relax and let myself ease into a restful sleep. "Can it!" I shouted. At least I think I shouted. It might have been a whisper. Or just a thought. A comforting warmth spread from a glow in my midsection, and my arms tingled as they drooped. "Knock it off!" I croaked. Threads of cotton candy filled my skull. I shook my head and gathered up all my strength. "On your feet!" I yelled, or tried to yell. The soothing voice, which sounded very much like my own, told me that I was being a sap. It told me to stop struggling, to give in and let myself rest. "No!" I shouted out loud. Wobbling like a baby deer, I rose to my feet.

The colors in the room blazed like a sudden wildfire. Light seemed to mix together, and then to pulse and flicker. I could hear Madame Cuapa's voice, but it seemed far away and I couldn't understand what she was saying. Images began to emerge from the colors with unusual clarity. Shipper's body exploded into mist and the walls and the bodies in the room turned red with his blood. A landmine went off, and Private Leota's legs disappeared as the rest of him went flying off the dirt road and into the jungle. My father's fist flew toward me and I knew that I couldn't do anything to stop it from smashing into my face. A snarling black dog with no eyes and lightning bolts in its claws bared its teeth at me, spittle pouring from its snout. Its jaws sprang open as it leaped for my throat. Detective Stonehammer picked up an icepick and held its point an inch away from my eyeball, holding it steady for a second before slowly moving it forward. Someone was shouting, but I couldn't make out the words. A pit with no bottom and no walls opened in front of me. A gat was in my hand, my finger on the trigger. I heard another explosion from somewhere near my face. A hundred tentacles came out of the pit and pulled me off my feet. A sound like the screeching of a thousand demons filled my head and the lights went out.

***

A lead weight filled my head. Spikes stabbed into the backs of my eyes and out my temples and forehead. I heard someone groaning and realized that it was me. My eyes were closed, but I sensed that I was lying on my back on something soft. A couch, maybe, or a bed. I felt a pillow under my head and a heavy quilt over my body. Wherever I was, I didn't want to be there. I rolled to my side and opened my eyes. Searing white-hot light poured through my eyeballs, and I lifted up a hand to shade them. I heard a deep growl, like a thick carpet being ripped in two. After a while, the light faded and resolved itself into blurred images. I was on a bed in a bedroom. I had been at Madame Cuapa's house. Was I still there? The images came into focus, and I saw Cody seated in a chair, watching me. The manticore lay at his feet. The animal's head was resting on the floor, but he was watching me, too. I opened my mouth to speak, but nothing came out. I swallowed something dry and tried again. "What happened?" My voice rasped like sand blowing over tin foil.

It occurred to me then that Cody wasn't just watching me. The big man was glaring down at me, his eyes red and angry.

"Where am I?" I asked. "What happened? Where's Madame Cuapa?"

Cody didn't move. "You shot her." His voice was low and filled with danger. "You son of a bitch!"

Chapter Six

From the room's meager furnishings and paucity of decoration, I concluded that it was neither Madame Cuapa's bedroom nor Cody's, but more likely a guestroom. I forced myself into a sitting position. My head felt like it might split open at any moment, and my brain was trying to push my eyes out of their sockets. The blood rushing through my ears sounded like a freight train, and I thought that I might have misheard what Cody had just told me.

"I shot her?" My voice struggled through my clogged throat, sounding like a croak.

Cody's body tensed. He looked ready to spring out of his chair. The manticore raised his head off the floor and let out a low rumbling growl that made the hairs on my neck stand at attention.

"How.... How bad?" I asked.

Cody made a visible effort to uncoil. The manticore stopped growling, but continued to stare in my direction. "She's fine now," said Cody. "No thanks to you. The Madame isn't an easy person to kill, even when she gets a bullet to the heart."

Shit. "Can I see her?" I asked.

Cody stood, and the manticore rose, as well. "I don't like it, but the Madame told me to notify her the minute you were awake. She wants to see you right away." He looked like he wanted to say something more, but after a couple of aborted attempts, he turned on his heel and started walking toward the door.

I stopped him. "Wait! How long have I been out?"

Cody looked back at me over his shoulder. "It's morning. You've been here all night."

"Did you call a doctor for Madame Cuapa?"

Cody's smug smile made its appearance. "I'm the only doctor she needs. I tended to her last night, and she's mostly recovered. You, on the other hand, are lucky to be alive." Then he turned and walked through the door, Mr. Whiskers in tow.

My eyes began to droop, and I had to struggle to keep myself from drifting off to dreamland again. I didn't want to be curled under the covers like a sick child when Madame Cuapa came in to see me. I propped myself up on my elbow, and, after overcoming a brief wave of nausea, I pushed my pillow back against the headboard and sat back against it. I kicked off the covers and discovered that I was still in my clothes, including my shoes. The only thing missing was my shoulder holster. I looked around the room and spotted the holster, with gun inside, draped over a chair. The thought of getting out of bed to retrieve the heater caused another wave of nausea, and I decided that I didn't need it after all. If Madame Cuapa or Cody had wanted me dead, they could have killed me while I was sleeping.

It didn't take long for Cody to reappear, followed by Madame Cuapa. Mr. Whiskers bounded in after them. The bruja sat in the chair that Cody had occupied earlier. Cody stood at her shoulder.

The manticore, with no leash or collar in sight, took a step toward me and sniffed. In slow motion, the tip of his tail began to rise skyward and his wings began to unfurl. "Mr. Whiskers," said Madame Cuapa in a pleasant voice. The manticore stopped in its tracks. His tail curled and his wings returned to his sides. "Go sit in the corner," Madame Cuapa commanded. Mr. Whiskers turned and rubbed his body up against the bruja's leg, emitting a purr that sounded like an electric generator. He raised his head, and Cody reached out and scratched him between his ears. Then the manticore made his way to a corner of the room and began licking his paw with a tongue that looked like a thirty-ounce slab of raw tenderloin.

"How do you feel, Mr. Southerland?" asked Madame Cuapa.

"Like I just woke up in a gutter after a nine-day bender." I cleared my throat. "Cody says I shot you."

Madame Cuapa's lips curled into a weak smile, "Oh, that. Don't worry about it." She looked over her shoulder at Cody. "Can you can get me some water, Cody? And a glass of wine. White. Bring one for our guest, too. He looks like he could use a little hair of the dog."

My stomach clenched against another sudden bout of nausea. "Nothing for me. Thanks anyway."

62

Madame Cuapa let out a brief chuckle. "You don't trust me. Well, I can't blame you." She waved Cody away, and he left the room. Mr. Whiskers remained behind, though, curled up in the corner and staring at me with interest as he groomed.

I heard Madame Cuapa sigh. "Mr. Southerland, I deeply apologize for what happened to you last night."

"To me? You're the one who took a bullet."

"That's of no consequence. I wouldn't be much of a witch if I could be brought down by a mere pellet of metal. But I'm afraid that our problem has escalated."

"*Our* problem?"

"Our problem." Madame Cuapa closed her eyes for a long moment, composing herself before reopening them. "The compulsion has struck again. And this time you were the target. We need to talk."

I agreed, but I kept my lip buttoned for the moment. Madame Cuapa nodded, as if I had spoken, and resumed speaking, "After I returned home from your office yesterday, I picked out some herbs and put them in the rum. When the doctored rum is combined with the tea, the mixture is fatal. I never intended to poison the rum, and I didn't know why I was doing it. And then later, I poured the rum into our tea with full knowledge of the danger that it posed for you, but, how can I put this.... Not caring? No, no, that's not right. It was more like I was powerless to care, or to generate the desire to stop myself. I didn't even realize that I was doing anything that I shouldn't be doing. It didn't seem wrong. It was only when the mixture began to take effect that I snapped out of it and returned to my senses." She grimaced. "Unfortunately, when I tried to come to your aid, you grew alarmed. In your state of mind, you must have found me threatening. So you pulled your pistol out of your holster and shot me in the chest. I must say, that was quite a surprise!"

At that moment, Cody entered the room with two glasses on a tray. He cleared a spot on a nightstand next to the bed and placed the tray within Madame Cuapa's reach. Madame Cuapa picked up the glass of water and drank it down until it was gone. Then she took the glass of wine and took a small sip.

My head pounded as I thought about Madame Cuapa's story. "Fatal?"

"Yes, Mr. Southerland. You should have died. The fact that you didn't is...interesting."

"Any theories?" I asked.

Madame Cuapa stared at me for a long moment, studying me, before saying, "You must have some kind of protection that I'm unaware of. For the moment, at least."

I knew that I had survived because of what the elf had done to me months before, but I didn't want to give that kind of dope away for free, especially to someone who had just admitted that she had tried to put out my lights for keeps. "You put the doctored rum in your tea, too, didn't you? How come you didn't trip out like I did?"

Madame Cuapa shrugged. "Mr. Southerland, you can appreciate my unwillingness to reveal the tricks of my trade."

I nodded. It was clear that neither of us was willing to share all of our secrets. "Still...." I paused "You *did* try to kill me."

That was enough for Cody. He gripped the top of Madame Cuapa's chair and shouted, "You tried to kill her!"

Madame Cuapa turned and placed her tiny hand over Cody's massive one. "Please, Cody. Mr. Southerland isn't to blame. He was not in possession of his senses. He wasn't any more responsible for trying to shoot me as I was for trying to poison him. We both survived. Consider us even."

"But you were hurt!" Cody was agitated. "Omecihuatl may have eaten the bullet, but that shot still packed a big punch."

"Cody!" Madame Cuapa tightened her grip on his hand. The kid reacted like he'd been slapped in the face. "We don't talk about such things in front of others." She held his apologetic eyes with her own stern ones.

"I'm sorry, Madame Cuapa." I detected a slight tremor in the big man's voice.

The bruja held the kid's eyes for a second longer, and then released his hand and turned to me. When she spoke, her voice was smooth and businesslike. "Forgive my personal assistant, Mr. Southerland. He concerns himself with my well-being, and he was shaken by what happened last night. As he said, I did suffer some harm, but nothing significant. A hammer blow to the sternum, which produced some bruising. Hard to look at, but it will heal. I've taught Cody how to treat such things, and he did well. I daresay that I'm in less pain this morning than you are."

Omecihuatl. I had never heard that name before and made a mental note to research it as soon as I had the chance. As for being in pain, my powers of healing were kicking in. The nausea had disappeared, and I had only the hint of a headache. I was hungry and thirsty, though, and I had one other burning desire.

"Before we go on...." I hesitated. "I could really use a restroom."

"Of course!" Madame Cuapa smiled. "Cody, would you show our guest how to find the facilities? And remember to mind your manners."

I rose from the bed without much difficulty, and Cody, acting the good servant, showed me to the bathroom with a clipped, "This way, sir." I closed the door and got myself ready for the day.

While I was washing up in the sink, I examined myself in the mirror. All things considered, I didn't look all that bad, or at least no worse than usual. My eyes were clearer than Cody's, who appeared to have stayed up all night. It seemed that I needed to add "attendant physician" to his list of duties. I was beginning to realize that I had underestimated the jasper.

When I was finished, Cody led me into the living room, where Madame Cuapa was seated on a sofa waiting for us. Mr. Whiskers was not in sight, but probably not far off.

Madame Cuapa waved me to a chair. "You probably have a lot of questions, Mr. Southerland, but my day beckons. I need to attend to my business. It's a wonder anything ever gets done without me, and now there's the matter of overseeing the search for a new general manager at Emerald Bay."

And I needed to eat something that wasn't going to try to punch my ticket.

"One thing before you go, though." Madame Cuapa looked uncomfortable. "I was compelled to curse Donald Shipper. Last night, I was compelled to poison you."

"And you can't guarantee that you won't try to kill again," I finished.

Madame Cuapa's eyes met mine. For the first time since she'd stepped through my office door, she seemed vulnerable. "Not willingly. But you can't trust me." She paused and lowered her eyes for a moment before looking back up. "I can't trust myself. Who knows what I'll do next time I step into my lab. I'm making some arrangements around here to provide additional protections, but I've never been in a position like this before, Mr. Southerland. I need you to help me, but someone may be working through me to try to stop you. You need to make sure that you understand the risks."

I nodded. "I get it, especially after last night. And that reminds me of something. Yesterday, when I was on my way to help Shipper, something strange happened. A flock of crows attacked me. You know anything about that?"

Madame Cuapa's eyes widened. "A murder?"

"Excuse me?"

"A flock of crows is called a 'murder' of crows."

"No kidding? Well, I don't think that these crows were trying to murder me. They could have done a lot more damage to me if they had wanted to. It was more like they were trying to stop me from warning Shipper."

"Crows, hmmm." Madame Cuapa's expression grew thoughtful. "It was none of my doing, I assure you. Perhaps it was just a coincidence, but, if so, it's an odd one. I'll look into it."

I couldn't think of any good reasons to stay, so I rose from the chair and we said our goodbyes. Madame Cuapa had Cody retrieve my holster and gun, and he walked me out the door.

When we reached my car, I turned to Cody. "No hard feelings, okay? I know that you're a little sore at me because I plugged Madame Cuapa, but I was out of my head. I don't even remember drawing my heater, much less pulling the trigger."

Cody looked away for a second, and then turned back to me. He looked down, and then stuck out a hand. "She fuckin' needs you, man." He met my eyes. "Do a good job."

We shook. "Watch out for her," I told him. "Someone is compelling her to do things she doesn't want to do, and she can't keep it from happening by herself."

Cody nodded. "Her coven will help her. She's going to bring a couple of them here to keep an eye on her."

"Coven?"

"She's a witch. She has a coven."

Of course she did. Just what this case needed—more witches!

***

I dropped the beastmobile off at Gio's and walked the block to my office. When I reached my front door, I heard a car door open and close from further up the block. I turned and saw Detective Kalama crossing the street and heading my way.

I waited for her to get close. "Jaywalking is against the law, you know."

"Call a cop." She nodded at my door with her chin. "Do you have time for a few questions?"

I unlocked the door. "Come on in."

When we were inside my office, I switched on the lights, started up my ceiling fan, and set up the coffeemaker. After we had taken seats on opposite sides of my desk, I asked, "Am I going to need my lawyer?"

Kalama shrugged. "That's your option." That's a cop's way of saying that, yes, if you're smart you'll call your mouthpiece before you take your next breath, and then you'll clam up tight until he gives you the go-ahead to open it.

I'm not that smart, though. "Hit me with your best shot. I'll give Lubank a call if it gets sticky."

"I just need to tie up a few loose ends," began the detective, which is what a tiger says just before it tears out your throat. I resolved to keep my head down and my guard up.

Kalama made a point of taking out a notepad and flipping through the pages, reading a few of the entries without speaking. Then she raised her eyes to look at me. "You called Emerald Bay

Mortgage yesterday morning just before ten. Can you explain the purpose of your call?"

We had gone over this at the station the day before, but there was nothing to be gained by grousing about it. "I received information that their general manager's life was in danger. I called to warn him."

"And how did you come by this information?"

"From my client."

Kalama made a notation in her notepad. Probably a reminder to buy a quart of milk on her way home. "And this client's name is?"

"Confidential. But I'm betting that you already know the name."

The detective raised her eyebrows. "Oh? And what makes you say that?"

Five would get you ten that they plucked Madame Cuapa's name from Coyot, but I shrugged and said nothing.

Kalama added something else to her notes. A cube of butter, maybe. Or a dozen eggs. Then she put the notepad away, sat back in her chair, and studied me for a few seconds. I studied her right back. She had a pleasant face. Pretty, but not soft. Angular features, dark hair, serious, no-nonsense eyes. She wore no makeup, and apart from a modest diamond wedding ring on her left ring finger, she wore no jewelry. I figured her to be five or so years older than me. She was medium height, and fit, like an athlete. Not a weekend athlete, but like someone who used to compete and still trains. She was professionally dressed in a business shirt and slacks, but I could see muscle development in her neck and shoulders. A swimmer, I guessed. Ten years past her glory days, but still active.

When we were done sizing each other up, the detective resumed her questioning. "How did you get mixed up with the Barbary Coast Bruja? Isn't she a little out of your league?"

"The Barbary Coast Bruja? I've heard of her. They say she's a witch."

"A bruja is a type of witch," the detective informed me.

"You don't say! What type of witch?"

"A real nasty kind."

"Hnnh!" I grunted. "If I ever meet this Barbary Coast Bruja, I guess I'll have to watch my step."

Kalama put her hands on her knees and leaned forward. "Wise up, Southerland. Madame Cuapa did the murder, and there's nothing that says a private investigator is obligated to protect a killer. She's using you. You may think you're in charge, but to her you're small change. When she's done grinding you up, you'll be nothing but plant food. Help me bring her in before you get in so deep that you can't swim back up."

"I never said that Madame Cuapa was my client, and I'm not saying she isn't. But if she is, then it's my job to protect her interests. Nobody hires P.I.s who sell out their clients. Besides," I cut her off before she could object, "this isn't a cut-and-dried case. My client isn't the one responsible for Shipper's death."

The detective held my eyes for a moment before saying, "Cuapa pulled the trigger. That makes her guilty."

"You've got it wrong. Madame Cuapa didn't pull the trigger. She was the gun. Someone else pulled the trigger."

Kalama's eyebrows shot up again, as if I had told her something that surprised her. It almost looked real. She was good. But I was tired of playing the game.

"Let's cut the crap, detective. You got the straight dope from Coyot, so you know everything that I told him. Are you ready for some coffee?"

Without waiting for an answer, I stood up and stepped over to the coffeemaker. I poured the steaming brew from the pot into a couple of clean mugs and asked, "Cream?"

"Please. Enough to take the heat off. And sugar, too."

"One lump or two?"

"Four if you can spare them. I like it sweet."

I put four sugar cubes in her coffee and topped it off with a half-inch of cream. I left mine black, because I like my coffee to taste like coffee, even on a hot day. I set her cup down on the desk and carried mine with me to the other side.

After I sat down, I turned to the detective to make sure she was listening. "You were right when you said that Madame Cuapa was out of my league. She's a *lot* out of my league. We don't even play the same game. She's out of your league, too. You say that you

69

want me to help you bring Cuapa in? That's a lot of hooey, and you know it. The YCPD can't handle Cuapa. She could eat the whole department for breakfast. It would be like a school of guppies trying to take down a shark. Do you know that Cuapa has a pet manticore? It's as tall as you are, with teeth like spikes, wings like sails, and a scorpion's stinger as long as a bullwhip. It's a four-hundred pound killing machine. You know what she calls it? Mr. Whiskers. She lets it wander around her house without so much as a leash. It rubs up against her leg and purrs like a kitten. It does whatever she tells it to do. And you think you're going to haul her downtown? And do what? Sweat a confession out of her? You don't drop the arm on someone like Cuapa. The most you can do is keep her happy and hope that she's on your side when the shit hits the fan."

I took a sip of my coffee. It burned my lips, so I set it back down on my desk to let it cool.

Kalama had let me speak my piece without trying to stop me. Now that I was done, she reached for her coffee and took a small sip. Finding it acceptable, she took a longer drink. Then she set it down and pointed at me with her chin. "And what about you? Do you do whatever she tells you to do, too?"

I shrugged and let my lips curl into a smile to let her know that she wasn't going to get under my skin that easily. "I do my job. Same as you."

The detective sat back and frowned. I could see that she was thinking. She looked across the desk at me. "They talk about you at the department. You were out on the pier with Stonehammer and Captain Graham the night they bought it. I've seen your statement. I've never been happy with it."

I shrugged. "It wasn't a happy occasion."

She ignored me. "According to you, Stonehammer and Graham got caught up in some gang violence. Stonehammer got plugged and fell through the railing into the ocean. You weren't clear on how Graham got killed."

"It was all kind of a blur."

"I've seen the autopsy reports, too," the detective continued. "Graham got his neck broken. Did some gangster do that?"

I shrugged. "It was stormy. The wind was whipping the waves up over the wharf. Maybe he slipped and fell."

The detective let that go. "Funny thing about Stonehammer. His body washed up a few days later. The coroner did an autopsy. According to his report, the only bullet wound he found came from a small-caliber slug that barely dented the troll's thick hide. He probably never even felt it. No way it pushed him over a railing and out to sea."

"I might have got some of the details wrong in my statement," I admitted. "A lot of things were going on at once. It was hard to keep it all straight in my mind."

Kalama's eyes narrowed. "Sure. I could see how that might happen."

"Hey, Stonehammer and Graham got buried with honors in a big police ceremony, right? I read all about it in the papers. They died in the line of duty while protecting the city against the bad guys."

The detective nodded. "Except that Internal Affairs found enough dirt on them after their deaths to shake up the whole department. The corruption went pretty deep. Some administrative big-shots were yanked out by the roots, and a lot of dirty cops were pulled out with them. The YCPD is a lot cleaner place now that Graham and his pet troll are gone. I guess you played some small part in that."

"Shucks, ma'am. I was just being a good citizen."

Kalama didn't look amused, but she nodded and seemed to come to a decision. She leaned toward me and narrowed her eyes. "You're right about one thing. Cuapa is too big for the department. As soon as the top brass found out that she was involved in Shipper's death, they gave us the full stop. Cease all investigation. Send the witnesses home. Case closed."

I blew on my coffee to cool it and then drank some down before setting it back on my desk. "I take it you're not here on official business."

She picked up her cup and held it out. "You got something you can spice this up with?"

I reached into a drawer and pulled out a half-empty quart bottle of bargain-priced joy juice and topped off Kalama's cup. She stirred it in with her pinkie finger and took a drink. I put a slug of the hooch in my own cup and joined her.

Chapter Seven

"Let's level with each other, Southerland. Cards on the table."

I sipped my loaded coffee. "All right."

"Shipper didn't just spontaneously combust. He was killed by a curse, a curse put on him by Madame Cuapa. And I know that Cuapa is your client, so you can stop being all coy about that. It's insulting."

I nodded. "Fair enough."

The detective went on. "The department shut down the investigation into Shipper's death as soon as Cuapa's name made its way up the channels. My lieutenant—that's Lieutenant Sanjaya—called me into his office right after you left with your lawyer and gave me the news: 'We're letting this one go.'"

Kalama polished off the rest of her coffee and made a sour face. "Fuck that! Let me tell you something, Southerland. My shield says that I'm a fuckin' homicide detective. Not a lot of females make detective, especially not in homicide. I worked for eleven years to get that shield, climbing my way up through the ranks and leaving a lot of the boys in my dust. I've kept that shield for four years because I'm good at what I do. Yeah, we both have jobs to do. When someone gets murdered, I find out who did it and I bring them in. I don't know what your job is, but that's mine."

"Even when the department orders you to lay off?"

She glared across the desk at me. "I don't let murders slide just because some political animal who has never spent a day in the streets gets all limp-dicked at the thought of taking on a witch." The detective paused. "Even if the witch has a pet manticore."

I looked at her. "Lubank told me that you were a smart cop. He didn't tell me that you were batty."

The detective smiled. "Lubank told me that you were crazy as a bedbug!"

"Yeah. But did he tell you I was smart?"

Kalama shrugged. "It never came up."

Figures.

Kalama leaned forward. "Your turn. Convince me that I shouldn't be going after Cuapa for murder one."

I finished off the last of my coffee and set the mug down on my desk. "Madame Cuapa came here yesterday morning. She told me that Shipper was going to die because of a curse that she had put on him. But she said that she had been under what she called a 'compulsion.' She hadn't intended to drop the hammer on Shipper, and it wasn't until the spell was cast that she woke up to what she'd done."

"Wait a minute." Kalama frowned. "You're saying that she did it in her sleep?"

"Not exactly. It sounds more like hypnosis, only stronger. Or maybe like possession. According to her, someone got inside her head, switched off that part of her brain that allows her to tell right from wrong and to make choices, and turned her into a willing tool."

"And you believe her?" asked the detective.

I hesitated. "I'm not ruling anything out, but, yes, I think she's giving it to me straight."

"Why?"

"Because she's scared. Cuapa knows that she is a weapon of mass destruction, and she knows what could happen if someone else is in charge of the launch codes. And, powerful as she is, she knows that she needs help."

"She wants you to find out who forced her to kill Shipper?"

"Yes, but it's more than that. I don't know if Shipper was a primary target or just a test case, but, if what Cuapa is saying is true, then someone out there is in a position to do damage on a level we can't even imagine."

Kalama rested her elbow on the arm of her chair and reached up to wipe perspiration off the top of her lip. "I don't know." The detective thought for a moment. "She admits that she put the killer curse on Shipper. That sounds like premeditated murder to me. The rest sounds like a setup to cop an insanity plea. A way to say, 'I did it, but I wasn't in control of my own actions.' I hear this kind of hooey from perps all the time."

"Why would she bother? Face it, she could sign her name to this murder in blood, put up a billboard next to City Hall saying, 'I did it,' and no one would bat an eye. You said it yourself—even the department is afraid to touch her."

The detective considered this. She pushed her empty coffee cup toward me. I poured her a generous slug from the bottle of booze and poured one for myself. She took two sips before saying, "No one should have that kind of power. She's too dangerous to exist, especially if she's not in control of her own actions."

I shrugged. "Maybe so. But that kind of thinking is a cable car to nowhere. You start worrying about all the things you can't do anything about and you really *will* go batty. She's not even the *most* powerful thing out there."

"Maybe not. But I've yet to meet anything smaller than a troll that couldn't be stopped by a well-placed bullet."

I smiled and took a drink. "It would have to be bigger than a nine millimeter," I told her.

The eyebrows arched again, and this time the surprise was the real deal. "No way!"

I pointed my index finger at her and let my thumb fall like a hammer. "Bang. Point blank. Right in the center of her chest." I held my finger up to my lips and made as if blowing away the smoke. "Barely left a bruise."

She sat silent for a while after that. Then, remembering her drink, she picked up her cup and downed the remaining booze with one gulp.

She took a second to get control of her breath and asked, "When was this?"

"Last night."

"Why did you shoot her?"

"She poisoned me." I smiled at her. "I wasn't in control of my senses. Another drink?"

She looked at her empty cup. "Not before lunch. I have standards."

I told her that she'd caught me before I'd even had breakfast, and she offered to drive me to a nearby diner.

"Separate checks," she told me, and I accepted.

***

75

An hour later I was finishing up a side of bacon and a slice of buttered sourdough toast in a downtown eatery. After the previous night's ordeal, I didn't have an appetite for much else. Kalama was sliding her half-eaten tuna salad around on her plate with a fork. A portable floor fan set up on one side of the dining area to cool the room had only managed to push the aroma of cigarettes, maple syrup, and coffee from booth to booth. The fan had no chance against the heat of the mid-morning sun peeking through the half-shut horizontal window blinds. I had caught the detective up on the events of the previous evening, and, although she was still shaking her head, I think that she believed I was telling the truth as I knew it.

"What I don't understand is how you survived the poison. Cuapa told you that it was supposed to do you in. You'd think she'd know a thing or two about the effectiveness of poisons, what with her being a witch and all. I find it hard to believe that she miscalculated the dosage."

"She thinks that maybe I was protected somehow."

"What do *you* say?" she asked me.

I shrugged. "I'm just happy to be breathing."

Things were jakeloo between the detective and me, and we were supposed to be laying our cards on the table, but I wasn't ready to tell her about the elf. I wanted to keep that ace up my sleeve, at least for now. Besides, bringing up the elf would take us to a whole new conversation, and I wanted to stay focused on the Madame Cuapa case.

I could see that Kalama wasn't satisfied, but she decided to let it ride. She looked over the table at me. "I need to get statements from Shipper's family."

"Okay."

"But I have a problem."

"The department has dropped the case."

"Uh-huh."

"Which means that you can't legally conduct interviews."

"Uh-huh."

"Which is the reason you came to see me this morning."

Kalama gave me a wry smile. "I figured that you were going to talk to them anyway. I just want you to fill me in if you dig up anything useful."

"Standard rates?" I asked.

The detective's smile disappeared. "I'm not *paying* you. I'm a cop, remember?"

"I'm supposed to work for nothing just because you've got a badge?"

"You're not working for nothing. Cuapa is paying you."

"Then I'll give any dope I uncover to Cuapa."

"Fine. But if that's the way you want to play it, I'm going to have to arrest you."

"For what?"

"Trespassing, for starters. You were escorted out of Emerald Bay Mortgage, but you came back. And then there's property damage for blowing up that door. Oh, and you assaulted their head of legal services."

"Silverblade? I doubt that I hurt him as bad as he hurt my feelings."

"Tell it to the judge."

"You're not serious."

"Shipper's executive assistant, what's her name—Turlock? She doesn't like you at all. She wants to press charges."

"I'll bet. By the way, she should be a person of interest in Shipper's murder. She did everything she could to keep me from warning her boss that he was in danger."

"Now, see? That's useful information. And you gave it to me for nothing. That wasn't too hard, was it?"

Our waitress laid our checks on the table. I slid mine across the table to Kalama. "Buy my breakfast and I'll see what I can do for you."

The detective took the check. "You drive a hard bargain, gumshoe."

***

Kalama dropped me off at my place so that I could clean up. I'd been wearing the same clothes since the previous morning, and

77

I needed to scrape my face and camp out under a shower, preferably for a couple of hours. Unfortunately, I ran out of hot water in ten minutes. Kalama had agreed to meet me at the Shipper house at one o'clock. The idea was that she would use her cop clout to get me in the door, and then I would make with the third degree while she took a powder. She had two other active cases that she was working on, and they needed her attention. We would meet up again at my office later in the afternoon.

When I hit the road in the beastmobile, the temperature was in the high eighties. The heat wave had peaked, although it looked like it might still hit the low nineties by mid-afternoon. I drove by Shipper's house at five to one and spotted Kalama parked nearby. I found a space of my own about a block up the road and pulled in.

The detective met me as I was approaching the house. "What's that thing you're driving?" she asked. "Is it military? Looks like you could roll through a village in that tank!"

"It's a long story."

"I thought that you private dicks liked to be inconspicuous."

"It's an inconspicuous color."

She shook her head. "Good thing we're not doing covert today."

Shipper's house was in a high-end residential district near the financial center. It was a two-story modern cookie-cutter suburban-style home, about five thousand square feet plus a three-car garage. The street was lined with homes built in the same basic design, distinguishable from one another mostly by color and by which side of the house was connected to the garage. The houses were pushed within arm's distance of each other, and rectangular patches of lawn separated the homes from the street. After double-checking to verify we had the right house—the yellow one with the light green trim, not the dark green one with the yellow trim next door—we made our way to the front porch. Kalama pushed the doorbell, and we could hear a chime inside the house play a short friendly tune.

The door was answered by the woman I'd seen in the photo on Shipper's desk. She was a tall breezy brown-eyed doll about my age. Her strawberry-blond hair had been styled by expert hands, and her lightly made-up face was highlighted by a faint row of freckles that crossed over her nose to both cheeks. She was wearing a knee-length pale blue spaghetti-strapped dress that did an admirable job of highlighting the soft curves in her slim figure and showing off the kind of tan more typical of Angel City than Yerba City. It was obvious that she had been taking advantage of our recent heat wave. The doll greeted us with a cool smile.

"Mrs. Shipper?" asked the detective.

"Yes?"

"I'm Detective Kalama, YCPD." She took out her buzzer and let Mrs. Shipper examine it. "This is Mr. Southerland. He's a private detective. May we come in?"

Mrs. Shipper gave me the look of curiosity that I often get from people when they discover that they are on the same planet as a real-life private eye, and then she stepped back and allowed us to enter her home.

"Ma'am, we're very sorry for your loss," Kalama offered when we were inside.

Mrs. Shipper lowered her eyes. "Thank you." Her voice was low and breathy. It was convincing. I suspected that she'd been practicing.

"I know that you've already been interviewed at length, and we appreciate your cooperation in this difficult time." The detective indicated me with her chin. "Mr. Southerland is going to ask you a few routine follow-up questions. We've brought him in to help us find out what happened to your husband. Think of him as an outside consultant, unaffiliated with the police department. Unfortunately, I can't stay. My duty requires me to be elsewhere. So, unless you have any objections to talking to a P.I., I'll leave you in his capable hands."

Mrs. Shipper glanced at me and then turned back to Kalama. "How long will this take?" she asked the detective.

"Not long," I cut in, trying to seize Mrs. Shipper's attention away from the detective. "I just need a few minutes of your time." I smiled at her, turning on the old Southerland charm, and, after a brief hesitation, she returned my smile with one of her own. Good sign. At this rate, we'd be pals by suppertime.

"Are your children home?" I asked.

"Yes. Kaylee and Dwayne are upstairs. We don't need to bother them, do we?" Mrs. Shipper's expression turned sour. "They're processing their grief," she explained, and I caught more than a little note of sarcasm in her tone.

"Probably not," I assured her. Actually, I intended to have a chat with both of them before I left, but for the moment I needed Mrs. Shipper's undivided attention. In the meantime, the kids could continue "processing," whatever that meant. They were probably texting with their friends.

Kalama excused herself, and I followed Mrs. Shipper into a living room the size of a volleyball court. It appeared to be little used. The furnishings were immaculate, the hardwood floors smooth and unmarked by the scuffing of shoes. The walls were painted in a shade of green so pale that it was almost white. The only decoration in the room was a painting, about two feet high and six feet wide, of a black bird, seen from behind, perched on a mesa and looking out over a desert landscape. I took an instant liking to the painting. I don't know why. It's not like I have any expertise or interest in art, but something about the way the bird regarded the emptiness of the orange and purple sands appealed to me. The painting hung over a sofa large enough to sit six full-grown adults. Mrs. Shipper sat down on one end of it. I sat on a chair that appeared to be more decorative than functional, but at least it was within conversational distance of the only other person in the room.

"Mrs. Shipper," I began, "let me tell you how sorry I am about your husband. I know how hard all this is on you and your children."

"Mister...Southerland is it? For starters, please call me Cindy."

"Okay, Cindy." I smiled. "I'm Alex."

Mrs. Shipper smiled back, making sure that it was a sad smile. "Nice to meet you, Alex. Next, please stop treating me like a grieving widow. I mean, it's not like I was *hoping* that Donald would die, but it's not like I won't get along just fine without him. Marrying him was not one of my better ideas."

"How long were you married?" I asked.

She sighed. "It would have been five years in June."

80

"The children are from a previous marriage?" I asked.

"Kaylee is from wife number one, and Dwayne from wife number two. I was wife number three."

"What happened to one and two?"

Mrs. Shipper shrugged. "He paid them off and divorced them after they got too old. I figured that I had another five years before he sent me packing." She looked at her nails, turning them to get different angles. "I guess I'll be out of here a few years before I thought I would."

"You'll be leaving? You won't continue to live here?"

Mrs. Shipper looked up at me. "Most of his money goes to his children. Oh, I'll get a share. But Kaylee gets the house.

"How old is she?"

"Old enough to kick me to the curb. She turned eighteen earlier this month."

"She won't let you stay?"

Mrs. Shipper snorted. "Only long enough for Donald's estate attorney to hand her the deed. The funeral is next Saturday, and we meet with the attorney on Sunday. Let's see, that's in five days. She'll be finished packing my bags by then. I'll have to make sure that she doesn't steal any of my jewelry."

"I take it that the two of you don't get along?"

Her lips curled in a wry smile. "My! You really *are* a private eye, aren't you." She thought for a moment before answering my question. "I'm only ten years older than she is. As far as that little bitch is concerned, I was nothing but a rival for her father's affections. Donald spoiled her rotten. Spoiled them both. I never had a chance with either of them. Believe me, I won't be missed, and I sure won't miss them."

"How old is Dwayne?" I asked.

Mrs. Shipper sighed. "He thinks he's thirty and he acts like he's ten, but he's sixteen."

I decided to re-focus on her late husband. "Did your husband have any enemies?" I asked.

"My husband had nothing *but* enemies," Mrs. Shipper replied. "He ran a mortgage company, and he thought everyone he did business with was trying to cheat him. If a borrower was behind on payments, he skipped negotiation and jumped right to

81

foreclosure. As far as he was concerned, driving people out of their homes was one of the perks of the job. It made him feel strong. He would always want a good screw afterwards. Sometimes with me."

"What about Mrs. Turlock?" I asked.

"Patricia? Are you asking if he was screwing her? Maybe. I wouldn't be surprised. But she might have been above his age range. She's almost forty, you know. For Donald, that was ancient." Mrs. Shipper's eyes met mine, and I knew that she was inviting me to pursue this line of questioning. The not-so-grieving widow wanted to dish some dirt.

"Do you know about anyone else that he might have been...sleeping with?" I asked.

Mrs. Shipper sighed. "Donald cared about nothing more than money. He liked younger women, but he didn't waste a lot of time and energy chasing them down. He was fine with renting them whenever the urge struck. If you check his phone, I'm sure you'll find a few professional agencies among his favorite contacts."

"When you say that he liked younger women...." I let the question hang.

Mrs. Shipper brushed an imaginary strand of hair off her forehead. "I can only imagine. I hope that they were all above the age of legal consent, but...." She shrugged and looked away.

I put a sympathetic expression on my face and nodded, but I felt like our conversation was heading off the rails. I tapped at the arm of my chair. "Getting back to Mrs. Turlock. Do you know if she had any ill feelings toward your husband?"

Mrs. Shipper sighed and shifted her position on the sofa. "I don't know. Maybe. Donald couldn't have been easy to work with. But I don't know about anything specific."

"And Mr. Silverblade?" I asked.

Mrs. Shipper's face lit up. "Claudius? He's a sweetheart! He's the one who introduced me to Donald, you know." Her smile grew wider. It was a pretty smile, especially for someone who had just been widowed. "But I forgive him. He meant well."

"What were the circumstances?"

"I was a legal secretary for an attorney who worked with Claudius on a number of occasions. Claudius impressed me. He's good at his job. We got to know each other a little. Not socially, but as colleagues. One night my boss and I were at a banking conference, and Claudius was there. He bought me a drink and asked me if I wanted to meet his boss. That's how I met Donald. He seemed charming, and he let me talk about myself. A few months later, we were married. I found out later that Claudius had engineered the whole thing. Donald had just paid off wife number two, and Claudius decided to play matchmaker. It would have been cute if Donald hadn't turned out to be such a shitheel. After we were married, he stopped being charming, and he stopped listening to me talk about myself or anything else. My job was to keep his kids out of his hair, to look pretty and hang on his arm at public events, and to keep him satisfied in bed whenever he needed it. I don't blame Claudius, though. I went into my marriage with eyes wide open." She looked down and brushed a speck of something that I couldn't see off the hem of her dress. Then she looked back up at me and met my eyes with her soft brown ones. "Just bad judgment on my part."

"If you were unhappy, why didn't you leave him?" I asked.

She shook her head. "I was so full of myself. I was young and pretty and utterly convinced that Donald would never want to live without me. When he asked me to sign a pre-nup, you know, just for legal purposes, I didn't give it a second thought. In the event of divorce, I get nothing." She closed her eyes. "When things went sour, I just rode it out." Her eyes opened. "He'd buy me things. I guess I got a little too accustomed to having nice things."

"But you'll get something now, though, right?"

She looked straight at me, and her eyes narrowed a bit. "Yes, I will. It won't be a fortune, but it will be enough for me to start over while I've still got some good years in me. Dying was the best thing that Donald has done for me since I married him. I owe a debt of gratitude to whoever killed him."

Heavy footfalls hurrying down an unseen staircase caused us both to turn our heads in that direction. The sound of the footfalls changed, and soon a pudgy teenaged boy came padding around the corner of the room. His unkempt light brown hair needed a trim, and his faint attempt at a mustache and chin whiskers needed another couple of years. His body was doughy and his face was the shape of a balloon that was leaking air. I recognized him as the boy I'd seen in Shipper's photo.

"Cindy—!" The boy began, but he pulled up short when he saw me. "Who the hell is this?" He demanded.

"Dwayne! Mind your manners! This is Detective Southerland. He's come here to ask a few questions about your father."

The kid leveled a glare at me through half-lidded eyes.

"Hello, Dwayne. I'm sorry about your father."

"Why?" Dwayne did his best to let me know how much I disgusted him. "Did you even know him?"

"No, but I know how tough it is when a boy loses his father."

"You don't know shit, motherfucker!"

"Dwayne!" Mrs. Shipper shouted. "Stop that! You're embarrassing me!"

Dwayne shifted his glare to his stepmother. "Shut up, you whore!"

Mrs. Shipper looked like she was about to explode, but before she could say anything I jumped out of my chair, closed on the boy with two rapid steps, and wrapped my hand around his throat. The boy looked up at me in shock and tried to pry my grip off his neck with both hands. The harder he tried, the more I squeezed.

I kept my voice low and steady while putting as much menace in it as I could manage. "Where I come from, a boy who is old enough to call a woman a whore is old enough to lose some teeth for it."

"Alex, please!" Despite her protests, Mrs. Shipper didn't sound all that distressed. "Don't hurt him. I'll deal with him later."

I held my grip for a second or two longer, then pushed the boy away from me. Dwayne stared at me openmouthed, and then turned on his heel and ran out of the room. Once out of my sight, he screamed, "I'll kill you, you son of a bitch!" Then I heard the front door open and slam shut.

"I'm sorry about Dwayne." Mrs. Shipper let out a sigh of resignation. "I know he's upset, but there's no excuse for that kind of behavior toward a guest."

"I guess he doesn't like cops." I sat back down in my chair.

"He probably thinks you're after him for trying to catch glimpses of me when I'm naked." Mrs. Shipper showed me a sly smile. "I had to change the locks on my bathroom door to keep him from walking in on me when I'm taking a shower."

"Want me to have Detective Kalama take him downtown?" I asked.

"That won't be necessary." She let her eyes fall to her lap while maintaining her smile. "I'm not going to be living here that much longer anyway."

My attention was diverted once again by the sound of someone coming down the stairs. This time, however, the footfalls were slow and so faint that I doubted I would have heard them at all if it hadn't been for my elf-enhanced awareness.

I kept my voice low. "I think that your daughter is trying to sneak past us. Do you think you could tell her to come in here for a minute?"

Mrs. Shipper raised her eyebrows in surprise. "Kaylee? Are you out there? Could you come here a second please?" A few silent moments passed. "I know you're there, Kaylee. There's someone here who wants to meet you."

I heard footsteps make their way down the rest of the stairs without stealth, and then a young woman rounded the corner into the living room. Kaylee might not have been Cynthia Shipper's biological daughter, but the two looked enough alike to be related. Like her stepmother, Kaylee had strawberry-blond hair and a trim figure. Unlike Mrs. Shipper, though, Kaylee's eyes were the color of the sky on a sunny day. She would have been a swell young looker in the company of people she cared about, but with her stepmother and me she opted for an attitude of surliness that caused her posture to slump and her face to sag into a mask of sullen dullness.

"Yeah?" she asked, challenging the two of us to give her a good reason for wasting her valuable time.

I put a pleasant tone into my voice. "Hello, Kaylee. My name is Alex. I'm a private investigator. I'd like to ask you a few questions about your father."

"He's dead," she informed me, as if that would end the matter.

"How do you feel about that?" I asked.

She straightened herself up to her full height. "How do I feel? Seriously? That's what you want to ask me?"

"Yes. How do you feel about your father's death?"

"How do you think I feel? I hate it! He was supposed to teach me to sail this summer. He promised! And now he's dead! It's not fair!"

"Do you know anyone who would have wanted to hurt your father?"

She half-closed her eyes and glared at me. "You mean besides Cynthia?"

"Oh Kaylee." Mrs. Shipper sounded tired. "Just stop."

"You despised him!" Kaylee insisted. "You're happy as a lark that he's dead!"

Mrs. Shipper smiled. "And you're not?"

Kaylee's fists dropped to her side as she looked somewhere above our heads and generated an incoherent noise that started somewhere deep in her chest and forced itself past her clenched throat, "*Oooouuuhhhhhhhnng!*"

Mrs. Shipper was unfazed. "By the way.... I'm going to need you to get up early on Saturday morning to help me get things ready for the funeral."

Kaylee turned her half-lidded glare at her stepmother. "I'm. *Not*. Going. To the *funeral!*" She spoke in a tone that suggested her stepmother was too dimwitted to understand complex thought. "I'm going out on Glenn's *yacht* on Saturday. I already *told* you that."

Mrs. Shipper flipped back her hair and smiled up at the girl. "But you'll be here to officially receive the deed to this house on Sunday, won't you. You wouldn't want to miss out on your inheritance."

Kaylee glared at her stepmother in silence, trying to slice her throat with her eyes.

Mrs. Shipper, unperturbed by the glare, continued speaking in a voice as smooth and hard as marble. "Come help bury what's left of your father on Saturday, Kaylee. Otherwise I'll have his remains put in your room and let you deal with them yourself."

In an instant, Kaylee's face turned red as a lobster. She glared at her stepmother, who leaned back on the couch and held her eyes in a relaxed manner that suggested she'd be happy to play this game all day. After a few moments, Kaylee broke her gaze, turned, and stomped away. Again I heard the front door open and slam shut.

Mrs. Shipper gave me a rueful smile. "Such little darlings. Now you know what I've been putting up with for the past five years."

"Mrs. Shipper," I began.

"Cindy."

"Cindy. Is there anyone you could call to stay with you for a few days?"

She smiled and waved off the suggestion. "Oh, don't worry about me. I'll be fine. When the kids come back they'll lock themselves away in their rooms and sulk. They won't be any problem. And I've got a lot of things to do. I've got to pack my things and start looking for a new place to live." She looked around the room. "Funny. I don't think I'm going to miss this place very much at all." She grew thoughtful for a second. "Oh, and I guess I need to go shopping for a black dress. And a veil, too, I suppose. Yes, definitely a veil. They'll all be expecting that from me at the funeral."

"Mrs. Shipper—"

"Cindy!"

"Cindy, you're right. You'll be fine. I don't think I need to worry about you at all."

Mrs. Shipper's face reddened. "That's one hell of a way to talk to someone who just lost her husband *and* her house!"

"Don't be in such a hurry to pack those bags, Cindy. You're protected under the law. You can't be evicted from a home you've been living in for five years without a court order, and not without a thirty-day notice. With a good attorney, you could tie the case up in the courts for months, maybe years. And I'm guessing that you know that already. So you can drop the victim act. I'm not buying it."

I expected Mrs. Shipper to fly into a rage, but she surprised me. Her face softened, and she smiled. "Was it too much? I

87

suppose so." She shook her head, and her smile vanished. "I've never had a husband murdered before, Alex. I have no idea how to act. You don't know how close I am to just losing it and screaming." She looked at me and her eyes were sad. "I might have been trying too hard for sympathy, but, in my defense, I might just go ahead and move out on Monday. I don't have any real reason to stay here anymore. I hope that you'll accept my apology. I'm truly sorry."

It was time to go, and I stood up. "Mrs. Shipper—Cindy—I want to thank you for answering my questions. I know that this is a tough time for you." I took a business card out of my pocket and offered it to her. "If you can think of anything else that you think might help me find out who did this to your husband, don't hesitate to call me."

Mrs. Shipper took my card. "I'll do that, thank you." She stood. "Let me walk you out."

We reached the door, and I opened it. But before I could step through the doorway, Mrs. Shipper reached out and put a hand on my elbow. "Can you do me a favor, Alex?" She asked in a low voice. Her eyes, which had been dry the whole time that I'd been questioning her, began to moisten. "I know it sounds silly, but could you just hold me for a minute before you go? Please? It would make me feel better."

I hesitated for half a second, but gave in. I told myself that it was the polite thing to do, and not unprofessional of me at all. "Sure."

The newly widowed Mrs. Shipper stepped into me and I embraced her, ignoring the way her breasts pressed against my chest and her thigh lightly grazed mine. We stayed that way for several seconds until she let her arms slide off my body. She backed away a half step and grabbed both of my hands with hers. "Thank you," she breathed.

"You'll be okay?" I asked.

She nodded, and, after squeezing my hands, released them and allowed me to step outside. I closed the door behind me without slamming it.

Chapter Eight

While I was walking to my car, the squawking of crows reached me from high overhead. I looked up and watched the murder streaking toward me, their screeching growing louder as they advanced. I prepared to summon Badass, but hesitated as seventy or eighty crows pulled up and began flying wildly in a loose circle in front of me, cawing and shrieking. Then all at once the racket ceased, and the birds swooped and landed, about a third of them on the roof of the Shipper house, and the rest on the Shipper's front lawn, where they nestled in the grass and stared at me in eerie silence.

I stood without moving under the blazing early afternoon sun and stared back. The birds, black as coal, turned their heads from side to side as they regarded me with one gold-colored eye at a time. Their inch-long gray beaks looked hard as granite. I kept the summoning sigil for Badass in the front of my mind and waited for the crows to make the first move.

After about a minute, the crows nearest me began to stir. They parted, forming a corridor, and a crow in the center of the group walked through the opening in my direction. He was larger than the others, about the size of a small chicken. When he was a few feet in front of the rest of the birds, the crow stopped, cocked his head, and stared up at me with one eye. Then he spread his wings, stretched out his neck, and emitted three piercing shrieks at me in rapid succession: "*cawww, cawww, cawww!*" Having delivered his warning, the crow refolded his wings, pulled back his head, and stood motionless.

I got the message. One cautious step at a time, I began walking away from the crows toward my car, keeping an eye on the birds until I had put some distance between us. The birds didn't react as I opened the door to the beastmobile and climbed in.

My favorite elemental is a pint-sized air spirit that I named Smokey. Once inside my car, I let the summoning sigils for Badass melt away and replaced them with the ones I used to call the smaller spirit. Thirty seconds later, a two-inch swirling funnel of light gray haze zipped through one of the car's air vents and hovered over my steering wheel. I detected the faint odor of cigarette smoke and alcohol fumes from the rafters of my favorite neighborhood watering hole, the Black Minotaur Lounge, which is where Smokey liked to hang out. A trembling whisper of a voice rose from the tiny whirlwind, "Hi, Aleksss--how's tricksss?"

Nice! It had taken me days to teach it to say that. "Hello, Smokey. Are you ready for some action?"

The funnel of swirling haze hopped onto the top of my steering wheel and began bouncing up and down in a manner that my teachers would have insisted was definitely *not* eager anticipation, because, they told me, elementals were incapable of such emotions. The elemental leaped to my shoulder and whispered, "Smokey is ready to rumm-ble."

***

It was a little after two-thirty when I got back to my office. I found Kalama waiting for me on my front porch eating a cheeseburger. She pulled another one out of a paper bag and handed it to me.

"Got your appetite back yet?" she asked.

My mouth was watering. "Affirmative."

"Want some fries with that?"

"Absolutely!" I was surprised by how hungry I was. I guess the poison had worn off.

She pulled a cardboard carton of fries out of the bag, and I let her into my office. When we were seated she asked, "So what's the lowdown on Shipper's family? Anything interesting?"

"Mrs. Shipper wants me to call her Cindy," I told her.

Kalama waited. I waited, too. The detective broke first. "That's it? After buying you breakfast *and* lunch, this is all I get?"

I took a healthy bite of the burger. After I finished chewing and swallowing, I said, "She hugged me at the door as I was leaving."

Kalama's features hardened. "I'm so happy to hear that you managed to accomplish something after I left."

"There's more." I took another bite of my burger and let Kalama wait for me to finish while she bored a hole in my skull with her stare. I endured it for a few extra moments and then relented. "Cindy's a gold-digger who wants me to feel sorry for her because her husband didn't pay enough attention to her after they were married. She says that he was into the joy girls, especially young ones. Possibly *really* young. She let slip that he might have some interesting sex-trafficking agencies on his contacts list. She would have divorced him, she says, but a pre-nup would have left her with bupkis. Now that he's dead, she'll get enough to satisfy the average jane, but she'll have to uproot herself and start over. The daughter is getting the house, and she can't wait to give her stepmother the boot. The widow could be out on the streets by Monday."

The detective swallowed. "That's rough."

"She doesn't seem to mind much. She made it clear that she can't get away from the Shipper children fast enough."

The detective swallowed a bite of her burger. "So how are the kids handling things?"

"Young Dwayne is going to miss his stepmother. He likes to watch her take showers." I wiped mustard off my face with a paper napkin.

Kalama grimaced and shook her head.

"Also, he called his stepmother a whore. I had to get a little physical with him."

"You're a regular knight in shining armor. How did the distressed damsel take it?"

"Remarkably well! She wasn't bothered at all, not even when he threatened to kill me as he was running out the front door."

"Cute kid. What about the daughter?"

"The charming Kaylee is going to skip her daddy's funeral. She's going yachting with some rich young worthy named Glenn. Her stepmother thinks that he's too good for her. On the other hand, daddy promised to teach her to sail this summer, and now he can't 'cause he's dead. She thinks that's unfair."

"Sounds like a lovely family. Maybe Shipper committed suicide."

91

"It's an option we should consider."

The detective chewed thoughtfully on some fries. "They all have motives."

I nodded. "Yeah."

"Mrs. Shipper wanted out of the marriage, but she can't just walk out, at least not if she wants an adequate return on her investment. Now that he's dead, though, she gets a slice of the pie."

"Not a big slice," I pointed out, "but a lot more than she would've gotten otherwise. And she's free from a husband who didn't love her while she's still young and pretty enough to do something about it." I bit off half a fry and added, "I don't think that she'll be alone for long."

The detective nodded. "And then there's the daughter. She gets the house."

"Is that enough to kill for?" I grabbed for more fries.

"It's a big house."

"Bigger than mine, but smaller than the mayor's."

The detective shrugged. "People have killed for less."

"But now daddy can't teach her to sail."

"She'll be able to afford private lessons once she gets her inheritance. Plus, she gets to go yachting whenever she feels like it."

"Hmmm." I swallowed some fries. "How about the son?"

"Kills the father in order to possess the mother," Kalama offered. "The headshrinkers love that shit. It's a time-honored classic."

"I don't know." I shook my head. "Those are all tough sells."

The detective looked thoughtful. "As motives go, they might be weak, but that doesn't mean they won't fly. And there could be more to it. Where there's smoke, there's more smoke. And eventually there's a fire. We should keep digging."

"Yes, we should," I agreed. "I'm not ready to clear the grieving family just yet. They all had some kind of justification for wanting Shipper dead, and what seems like a piffle to us may have been reason enough for one or more of them. But what bothers me is the means."

Kalama finished off the last of her fries and leaned back in her chair. "And that brings us back to the witch."

"Yeah," I nodded. "Let's say that someone in the Shipper household wants to bump off the old man. I could see them spiking his martini with rat poison. Or knifing him in his sleep. Or shooting him in the head as he walks in the door after a hard day's work. But gaining control of a witch and using her to rig up a fatal curse? And not just any witch, but the Barbary Coast Bruja herself? That's a little rich for me."

"I don't like it much either," Kalama admitted. "But if that was their play, it worked."

"How could any of them pull it off?" I asked. "They don't strike me as talented."

"One of us should ask them," the detective said.

"And why would they go to all the bother?" I added. "If you're going to kill someone, just kill him. Why get all cute about it?"

"To beat the rap by framing the witch?"

"I don't figure any of them for that much imagination."

"It's early days." Kalama crossed her arms. "You just met them. And it doesn't sound like you spent much time with the kids."

"It was more than I liked. I can still smell them."

"You need to do more digging. You're an investigator, right? The department isn't going to let *me* go after them, so like it or not the Shippers are your meat. Go peep through some keyholes or whatever it is you private dicks do, and try not to make a hash out of it."

I finished off the last bite of my cheeseburger. My office smelled like a greasy burger joint. It usually smelled like burnt coffee and old sweat, so things were looking up. "And while I'm groping around in the dark pretending to be a real copper, what are you going to be doing in your official capacity as an honest-to-goodness professional detective?"

"I figured I'd do some honest-to-goodness professional police work. You know, detecting and shit. For starters, I'm going to call on your friends Turlock and Silverblade."

"Your handlers at the clubhouse will be jake with that?"

93

"Sure. The book on the trespassing case against you is still open. I need to assure that poor secretary that us cops are ready and able to protect her against menaces like you."

"Executive assistant."

"Right. She's been traumatized. She needs to be able to sleep at night."

"Sending a homicide dick out to look into a trespassing beef doesn't sound like efficient management of department resources," I noted.

"Trespassing and property damage. And assault! Don't forget about the assault! That will give me a chance to talk to Silverblade, too. And the matter of Shipper's death might happen to come up." She locked my eyes with her own. "There are cops, and there are cops, Southerland. And maybe your experience with the department hasn't been aces. Some of my fellow coppers should be in other lines of work, like dealing, pimping, or leg-breaking. It's hard to tell some of the so-called good guys from the animals we're trying to clear off the streets. And that's even more true the higher you climb up the food chain. But most of us coppers put in an honest day's work, day-in and day-out, against impossible odds. And my lieutenant is one of the good ones. He wouldn't mind hearing a little more about Shipper's murder, no matter how much the brass might want to sweep it under the rug."

"Fair enough." I sat back in my desk chair. "I'll nose around a little in the Shipper family's closets. Who knows, if I look through the right keyhole maybe I'll catch Cindy in the shower."

***

After Kalama left for Emerald Bay Mortgage, I popped open a bottle of suds to wash down the burger and fries. I'd offered one to the detective, but she took a glass of water, instead. She said that she didn't want beer on her breath when she interviewed Turlock and Silverblade. I had wanted to talk to the two of them myself, but, after the impression I had made on them the day before, I was forced to admit that the detective was the right person to handle that pair. Before she left, Kalama agreed to keep me in the know if she found anything interesting, such as whether Shipper had been enjoying some private time with his executive assistant, or whether he was involved in some sort of financial beef with Silverblade. Like I had told Madame Cuapa, motive for murder usually comes down to love or money in one form or another.

Kalama was right. I needed to be digging into the Shipper family closets, looking for skeletons. I had no doubt that I'd stumble into a few with almost no effort. A family like that would be lousy with guilty secrets, and one of them might have pushed someone into turning out Shipper's lights. But I had something else to do first. I put out a call for Smokey, and it only took a few seconds for the tiny funnel of gray haze to whisk its way into my office and swoop down on my desk, where its whirling winds rustled the cheeseburger wrappers and pushed fried potato crumbs to the carpeted floor.

"Greetings, Aleksss," hissed Smokey. "This one did as you asked."

"Tell me."

"Aleks went away in beast."

I'd been trying to teach him to identify my car as the "beastmobile," but, for now, "beast" was the best he could do.

Smokey continued. "Birds fly from ground and sit on roof of house. Smokey watch birds. Some birds fly around house, but come back to roof. Then all birds rise into wind current and fly away from house fast. Smokey follow. Birds not as fast as Smokey. Birds fly with current to place where Smokey never before be. Birds fly to ground."

Smokey hesitated, and the speed of its whirring increased. I recognized this as a sign of frustration. I'd been increasing Smokey's vocabulary, but there were many things in the world that it could not communicate. In this case, though, I thought that I knew what it had seen. "Did the birds come together and become a human?"

"Yesss," Smokey hissed. "Birds are there then not there. No birdsss. Just human."

A were-crow. I had suspected as much. I had never encountered one before, but a friend of mine named Crawford was a were-rat, and he had told me about many types of were-creatures. He'd also told me that were-creatures tended to have a

95

few screws loose, and that if I met one I should consider it to be at least borderline deranged until it proved otherwise.

"Did you follow the human?" I asked Smokey.

"Human walk into moving building. Car. Big like beast. Smokey means that human walks into car. Car goes away. Smokey does not follow car. Aleks asked Smokey to follow birdsss."

True. Elementals are great at following instructions, but they tend to interpret those instructions literally. Smokey had done what I'd asked it to do.

"Would you be able to return to the place where you saw the human?" I asked.

"Yesss."

"Could you lead me there?"

Smokey spun in silence, searching for a way to explain to an earthbound creature how to locate the last known location of the crows it had followed as they flew through the sky. I often used Smokey for tailing duties, because nobody notices a tiny funnel of haze darting about in the wind. But air elementals live in a world of interconnected wind currents, whereas I find my way around by means of paved streets and intersections. Communicating locations and directions elemental-to-elementalist was a tricky business, but it was something that we'd worked on, and we'd developed a few tricks.

"Smokey will try," it whispered at last.

"Good!" I got up from my chair. "Follow me."

***

In the beastmobile, Smokey perched on my dash and leaned in the general direction of our destination, like a compass needle pointing north. While I drove, Smokey popped in and out of the car in order to fly into familiar wind currents and orient itself. After a complicated series of turns, including one u-turn and four consecutive rights that took me in a complete circle, I found myself driving steadily westward. A half-hour or so later, it became clear to me that I was headed straight to the home of Madame Cuapa.

96

On the way, I pulled out my phone and called Lubank. My attorney was without doubt a morally bankrupt asshole, but he was a good lawyer with a shrewd mind, and, for reasons I didn't completely understand, I could count on him to have my back. Maybe it was because we had a mutually beneficial business arrangement. I did investigative work for him, and he represented me in legal matters, which all too often included rescuing me from the clutches of the YCPD. The diminutive bucktoothed gnome with the shitty fashion sense and horrible hairpiece had enough dirt on police department brass and local politicians to bury them, so they had to be careful how they handled his clients. I'd been busted up by the bulls, but I'd never been lost for good, and I owed some of that to Lubank's legendary blackmail files. It wasn't that our relationship was equal—somehow or another I always seemed to be owing him more for his services than he did for mine—but maybe that's why I could trust him. To him, I was a source of steady income. And besides, Gracie would have killed him if he ever let me come to any harm, and Gracie was the only person, besides himself, that Lubank really cared about.

"Mrs. Shipper sounds like a piece of work!" Lubank exclaimed when I told him about my interview with the passive-aggressive widow and her self-entitled stepchildren.

"Everyone handles grief in their own way."

"Too bad she's not making more off the will. In her vulnerable state, you might have had a chance to scoop her up on the rebound and marry some money. Maybe you should anyway. Even a portion of her late husband's fortune is probably more than you'll ever make peeping through keyholes."

"That's what I love about you, Lubank. You're so sentimental."

"Sentiment doesn't pay for the groceries, pal!"

I rolled up to a stop sign. "Whatever. Anyway, that's not the real reason I called. I'm headed back up to Madame Cuapa's, and she tried to kill me last night."

"Th'fuck you say?"

I gave Lubank the highlights of the previous evening's events, and he responded with his characteristic concern.

"You're a fucking idiot, peeper! She slips poison into your drink and you're going back to give her another shot at you? Fuck you! You deserve whatever you've got coming!"

"Thanks, buddy. I'll check in with you tonight when I'm done. I wouldn't want you to lose sleep worrying about me."

"Who is this again? I've already forgotten your name!"

***

I hadn't quite made it to the witch's house when Smokey told me to stop. I pulled over and parked the car. Fortunately, there was a spot available next to a fire hydrant. According to the elemental, the were-crow had reverted to human in a grove of trees a few yards off the road where no one was likely to see the transformation happen. I couldn't see Madame Cuapa's house from where I was, but I knew that it was just around the next corner, less than a quarter of a mile away on foot.

I dismissed Smokey and watched the elemental zip away, probably on a direct route to the Black Minotaur. With any luck, I'd be there myself later that night. Still sitting in my parked car, I pulled my cellphone out of my shirt pocket and called Madame Cuapa's work number.

A female voice answered the phone. "Madame Cuapa's office. May I help you?"

"Is Madame Cuapa available?" I asked.

"Madame Cuapa is not in the office today. May I take a message?"

"Is she at home?"

"I wouldn't know, sir. I can take your number and have her call you."

"Never mind," I told her, and I disconnected the call.

I tried Madame Cuapa's home number, and Cody answered after the second ring. He informed me that the Madame was home and went to tell her that I was on the line. Two minutes later, just as I was ready to disconnect the call and try again later, she picked up the phone.

"Mr. Southerland? Have you found anything?"

"I'm working some leads. I'm nearby. Can I come on over?"

"Unfortunately, this is not a good time," Madame Cuapa told me. "A couple of guests have arrived, and we've got some important matters to discuss."

"Cody told me that you were bringing in members of your coven."

"Yes. I'm in need of some reliable friends to keep an eye on me. I called two members of my inner circle last night, and they've agreed to stay with me until this mess is sorted. They arrived today, and they're here now. They will endeavor to keep me out of mischief." The witch's tone was light, but I thought I could detect some underlying tension in her voice.

"I have something on the crows that I told you about this morning," I told her.

"The crows? Oh yes, I remember. What about them?"

"They found me again today after I spoke to the Shipper family. They seemed to be warning me away from them, or maybe they were warning me away from the whole case. I summoned an elemental to follow and observe them. The elemental saw the crows transform into a human just down the road from your house about two or three hours ago."

"A were-crow? How interesting!"

"When did your friends arrive?" I asked.

"About two hours ago," she replied.

I let it hang in the air for a moment. Then Madame Cuapa said, "Neither of them are were-crows, Mr. Southerland. I can assure you of that."

"One hell of a coincidence, though."

"True," Madame Cuapa conceded. "I'll bring the matter up with them and see what they say. In the meantime, I've taken some other precautions."

"What sort of precautions?"

"Magical ones. Nothing you would understand."

I hesitated before asking my next question. "Madame Cuapa," I began. "I need to ask.... Were you alone when you whipped up these magicks?"

I could hear the witch sigh. "I suppose I should be indignant, but given the circumstances I understand why you feel the need to ask. But rest easy. Cody was with me through the whole process."

"He's not actually a practitioner, though, is he?"

"He knows enough to tell if I am doing anything I shouldn't be doing. No, I think that the world is safe from me for now."

"If you say so." Despite Madame Cuapa's reluctance, I still wanted to see her, especially since I happened to be in the neighborhood. "I'd like to meet your guests. I promise that I won't be long."

The Madame wasn't having it. "Tomorrow would be better," she insisted. "They came here in a hurry on very short notice to help me, and I would rather not subject them to questioning from an investigator until they settle in a bit. It would be inhospitable."

"Maybe so. But—"

Madame Cuapa interrupted me before I could finish my objection. "No, Mr. Southerland. Today isn't good. Trust me, I'll be in no danger from were-crows, if that's what you're worried about. Now if you'll excuse me, I have to tend to my guests. They are important people who are sacrificing their valuable time to do me a service, and I feel that it's important that I treat them with the courtesy that their sacrifice requires. I've known them for longer than you've been alive, and I trust them with my life."

"You're sure about that?"

Madame Cuapa didn't respond right away. Just when I thought that she must have disconnected the call, her voice broke the silence. "You have to understand how spells work, Mr. Southerland. No two spells are exactly the same. Every spell contains a bit of the...personality...of the spell-caster. When you've been at it long enough, as I have, you can detect the spell-caster in the spell, especially if the spell-casters are people who are close to you. If one of my friends had cast a compulsion spell on me, I'd have known that it was them. But whoever it was that cast that spell is someone unknown to me. And besides, Tloto and Itzel may be greatly skilled practitioners, but neither of them is the Barbary Coast Bruja." She paused for effect, and then dismissed me. "Please continue your investigation, Mr. Southerland. I'll have Cody get in touch with you tomorrow."

She disconnected the call without saying goodbye.

I put my phone down and drummed my fingers on the steering wheel. I didn't know what to think about these "important people." They were witches, and, if they were old members of Madame Cuapa's coven, then they were powerful witches. They had dropped everything to come to Madame Cuapa's aid, and they had traveled from who knows where in less than a day. Madame Cuapa had asked them to stay with her and keep her from dropping any bad juju on unsuspecting victims. As a target of some of this juju, I should have been feeling a little safer now. She trusted them, but should she? I wanted to ask them a few questions, but Madame Cuapa had nixed that idea. Should that bother me? Maybe not. But it did.

I started the beastmobile, and then switched it off. My head was telling me to drive away, but my gut was telling me that it was time to do some snooping. As usual, my gut won the argument, and I climbed out of the car.

I crossed the road, hopped a fence, and trespassed across a rich man's spacious yard, hoping that no attack dogs patrolled the property. My luck held out, and I hopped another fence into another rich man's yard. This one contained a chicken coop, and, while I was marveling at the unexpected presence of farm animals in the city, I noticed a rooster, about two feet tall and angry, heading in my direction with clear and hostile intent. His three-inch talons were no joke, and, in deference to the king of the coop's authority over his territory, I hustled away and over the fence before he could teach me the error of my ways.

I dropped onto an undeveloped plot of wilderness area consisting of sand and scrub brush. A lizard eyed me with suspicion, and then scurried away under a gap in the fence. I wished him luck with the rooster. I had taken no more than four steps before my shoes, meant for cement sidewalks and carpeted floors, were filled with sand. I hiked my way up the side of what amounted to a large sand dune that had somehow survived the surrounding urban development. When I reached the crest of the dune, I found myself looking down at the property behind Madame Cuapa's house, which stood about thirty yards away from me. Lowering myself into a prone position in the sand, I scanned the back yard, which contained a large caged area for Mr. Whiskers and a utility shed, probably filled with yard equipment. I wondered if Cody's many duties included gardening. I noted that the manticore was not in his pen. He was probably cuddling up to the houseguests.

Nothing was happening in the yard, so I lifted my gaze to the back of the house itself. Spotting a sliding glass door, I focused my attention on what was going on inside. I spotted Madame Cuapa, and the two guests—one male, one female—seated at a dining room table, smiling and talking like old friends.

Technically speaking, I couldn't really "see" the three witches as if watching them through binoculars, nor could I "hear" them as if tuning in to a listening device, but after the elf had amped up my awareness the effect was almost the same. When I concentrated on the three witches, I could sense the way their body movements disturbed the environment around them, read the vibration of their voices, and feel the way that they interacted with each other. I gathered that this was the way that elves perceived the world around them. It was all too alien for my human brain to deal with, so my brain interpreted my enhanced awareness as improvements in those things it was more familiar with, namely, my five senses: sight, hearing, touch, taste, and smell. But, practically speaking, let's just say that I could "see" the witches clearly, and I could "hear" most of what they were saying to each other. Truth is, I didn't much care how it worked. It was a handy thing to have around, and I was grateful that the elf had decided to grant me this bit of "elf magic." I also knew that I owed a big debt to the elf, and that someday he would want to collect.

I studied the female guest first. She had an impressive display of silver-colored hair that framed her face like a lion's mane. Her face was wrinkled and dominated by a large hooked nose. She appeared to be ancient. She had a round, plump figure, and I saw that her chair had been augmented with cushions. I realized then that she was a gnome, her gnomish ears hidden by her hair. She was wrapped in a multi-colored striped shawl that covered most of her upper body. She wore a pair of brown slacks that looked like they had been woven from thick fibers of hemp. I'd seen many older women dressed like that in the Borderland. A ball of yarn sat on the table in front of her, and her hands moved non-stop as she knitted the yarn into something that I couldn't identify.

I focused my concentration on the male guest. He had thick jet-black hair and a face built around a trim mustache that he probably thought made him look dashing. He looked to be about forty, which didn't mean anything. In contrast to the casual attire worn by the woman, the man was dressed in a sharp business suit, complete with jacket and tie. He was tall and rakish, but appeared to be fit, like a good light-heavyweight. Even from a distance, I was drawn to his dark, hypnotic eyes. He looked like he could have been a movie star, but whether as a leading man or a featured villain I couldn't say.

They were engaged in a casual conversation. Near as I could make out, the male guest was describing the beauty of some twist he had met at a party. Madame Cuapa's mind was elsewhere, and he was mostly talking to the ancient gnome, who responded with an off-color quip that I couldn't quite catch. As I watched, Cody walked into the dining room carrying a bottle of wine and three glasses on a tray. He was wearing a flamboyant open-collared blue suede suit with a wide collar outlined in bright red trim. He wore no shirt under the coat, which was clasped with a single button just above his navel. His belt and shoes were the same red color as the collar trim. I figured that he had broken out his formal wear in honor of the Madame's guests. He placed the tray on the table and filled the glasses. I noticed that the others had stopped talking when Cody entered, and the conversation didn't resume until he had finished serving them and left the room.

As soon as Cody was gone, the male guest leaned toward Madame Cuapa and began speaking in an agitated fashion. The gnome leaned in as well. I couldn't "hear" the exact words, but by reading the body language and facial expressions of the three witches, I could pick up the gist of the conversation. The man didn't trust Cody. As far as he was concerned, Cody was the mastermind behind Madame Cuapa's current predicament. Madame Cuapa dismissed the accusations out of hand. She trusted Cody completely. He had a sweet disposition and had proven himself to be completely loyal. The gnome looked from one to the other as they spoke, remaining neutral and waiting to be convinced one way or the other. The man was becoming more and more animated. He pointed a stiff finger at Madame Cuapa, and insisted that Cody should be dismissed from the premises until things were back to normal. He went on in that vein for a bit, and Madame Cuapa kept shaking her head until she pounded the table and shouted, "Enough!" The man and the gnome both pulled back. Madame Cuapa glared at the man, and, though he towered over the bruja, the way he lowered his eyes and slumped his shoulders made him seem to be the smaller of the two. Madame Cuapa began to speak, and I sensed the words as if I was in the room with her. "I know why you mistrust Cody, and I'm telling you right now that he's off limits. He belongs to me, and you'll treat him with the appropriate respect. If you need a toy, I'll have one delivered to you. You understand me?" The other witch nodded, again, again, and again.

Suddenly, the gnome spoke up. "Someone is here!" Then all three witches turned and peered in my direction.

I lowered my head and slid down the dune a few feet until I was out of the line of sight. It was time to go. As I started to rise from the sand, I turned my head and stopped short, suppressing a yelp of surprise. Crouched in the sand no more than ten feet from me, tail whipping back and forth through the air, watching me in complete silence with his feral unblinking yellow eyes, was Mr. Whiskers.

The manticore lowered its head and began to growl.

Chapter Nine

"Nice kitty. *Niiiiice* kitty." This close to me, the unrestrained monster appeared to have tripled in size. He seemed larger to me than the beastmobile, with meat hooks for claws and a mouthful of gleaming ivory spikes.

The growl that Mr. Whiskers emitted was so low in pitch that it was almost beyond a human's capacity to hear. I felt its vibration deep in my gut, and it threatened to shake my internal organs from their foundations. His folded bat-like wings inched away from his body, and his tail began to uncoil and rise into the air. His hind end twitched back and forth like a housecat about to spring on an unsuspecting bird.

"Let's talk about this." I tried to sound calm and confident. I didn't even convince myself.

I had two thoughts. The first was outrage. Who lets a dangerous animal like a manticore roam free in a residential neighborhood? My second thought was the realization that it didn't matter. I was fucked. It was all I could do to control my bowels. If I was going to die, I wanted to preserve some dignity.

But then I had a third thought, and it gave me a hint of hope. Madame Cuapa had told me that this creature was psychically linked to Cody. Perhaps it wasn't as wild and uncontrolled as it appeared. I stared into the beast's eyes. "Cody? Are you in there somewhere?"

The manticore stared back at me. Its hindquarters had stopped twitching, but it was still growling, and its body remained tensed and ready to spring. I considered my options. Running wasn't one of them. I didn't have many others. Finally, inch by agonizing inch, I rose from the sand into a seated position, never looking away from the manticore's eyes. Then, just as deliberately, I raised my arms and folded my hands behind my head. I waited.

One minute passed. Then another. Then several more. I didn't know how many. It seemed like hours, but the sun was still hanging above the thickening marine layer, so probably not. Neither of us moved. I concentrated on controlling my breathing and thinking non-threatening thoughts. Beads of sweat rolled down my forehead and into my eyes, but I ignored the itching and stinging. Finally, I heard a door open and close, followed by the sound of footsteps heading in my direction. When the steps drew near, I risked a glance back over my shoulder and saw Cody making his way over the top of the dune. He didn't look happy to see me.

When he was within spitting distance, I greeted him. "Hi, Cody. How's tricks?"

"What the fuck are you doing here, sir?"

"Birdwatching."

Cody glared at me. "Are you spying on the Madame?"

"I wasn't spying on Madame Cuapa. I was spying on her guests."

To my surprise, that brought Cody up short. "So what did you find out about them?" he asked.

"Not much. Hey, your pussycat is making me a little nervous. Shouldn't he be on a leash? Or in a cage? With iron bars?"

Cody smirked at me. "Unlike you, sir, he belongs here. Madame Cuapa owns this whole plot all the way down to the next street, and Mr. Whiskers has the run of it."

"The neighbors don't object?" Mr. Whiskers had settled down into the sand and was now scratching behind his ear with his back leg.

Cody shrugged. "He doesn't bother them as long as they stay off the Madame's property. Besides, that guy back over there has chickens. If he can have animals in his yard, then so can we."

"Sounds fair. Hey, do you mind if I stand? My legs are cramping up down here."

Cody stared down at me without speaking for another moment or two, and then he seemed to come to a decision. "Follow me, sir." He began walking past me down the dune away from the house. Mr. Whiskers sprang to his feet and trotted off beside him. I got up with a lot less grace, knees popping, and took a moment to stretch out my legs before scrambling to catch up.

We reached the bottom of the dune and walked about a hundred yards through scrub brush and long grass until we came to the back of a wooden structure about the size of a large two-story house. The wall was covered with unfamiliar symbols that for some reason made me think of desert landscapes under the light of a full moon. The building seemed to be a warehouse of some sort, or perhaps a hunting lodge, though why someone would build a hunting lodge in the Upper Peninsula was beyond me. There were two doors in the back wall, but Cody led me around the side of the building to the front. When we got to the front of the building, I saw that it was separated from a residential street by a good-sized yard covered with decorative rocks and cactus plants. No symbols had been painted on the side of the building facing the street, and from this vantage point the structure wasn't likely to draw a second look from anyone passing by. A driveway from the street curved its way past the cactus and a couple of scrub oaks to a circular parking area in front of the building. Cody led the way to a wide double-door, which he unlocked with a key on his keyring. The door let out a loud creak when he opened it. Mr. Whiskers bounded into the building, and, with an "After you, sir," Cody waved me on through. Cody followed me in and closed the creaking door behind him. Then he flicked a switch next to the door and the room was lit by dim floodlights built into the walls. I noted that a few of the bulbs were burned out.

The building was one large windowless room with wooden walls, a cement floor, and a ceiling about twenty feet overhead. The air in the room was hot and earthy, and it carried a faint fetid odor of long ago death. A cement table, about three feet off the floor, was embedded in the center of the room. A dozen wooden foldout chairs were set up in front of the table. The walls of the room were adorned with tapestries, each ten or twenty feet wide and nearly as tall. The artwork on the tapestries was beautiful and primitive. They showed scenes of ceremonies involving witches, spirits, animals, and, on one of the tapestries, human sacrifice.

I walked up to the nearest tapestry and studied it. Six witches, three men and three women, danced around a bonfire in the middle of a jungle clearing. The images had been woven into the tapestry by an expert hand. One of the dancers, a man who appeared to be in his fifties, wore the pelt of a wolf like a hooded cloak on his head, over his shoulders, and down his back. A necklace of claws hung around his neck. He was otherwise naked

107

except for a pair of moccasins. I decided that the creator of the tapestry had taken some measure of artistic license with the size of the man's erection. The other dancers all seemed to be in their late teens or early twenties. They wore moccasins, but nothing else. Above the bonfire, the outlines of a demonic dog-like face could just be seen in the plume of smoke. A tongue of red flame hung down from its snout, but where the eyes should have been I could only see darkness. The image seemed familiar, but I couldn't think of a reason why it should. Various animals peered out of the surrounding jungle at the ceremony, their eyes gleaming in the reflected light of the fire.

I started to look away from the tapestry, but my eyes were drawn back to one of the female dancers. One of the girl's arms stretched to the sky, the fingers on her hand splayed wide. Her other arm, bent slightly at the elbow, swung out to one side, the hand closed in a loose fist. Her torso was contorted, breasts pointed in one direction and her midsection in the other. She was in mid leap, the tips of her toes at the end of one outstretched leg just leaving the ground, while the knee of her other leg was raised above her waist and pulled to the side, exposing a small patch of dark red hair between her upper thighs. Her head tilted to one side, long auburn hair flying about in all directions, mouth open in ecstasy, and dark eyes flashing as she abandoned herself to the chaos of the dance. I examined the face until I had no doubt. The dancer, who looked to be in her late teens, was the young Citlali Cuapa.

"Yes, that's the Madame." Cody's voice came from over my shoulder, sounding muffled in the cavernous room. "That was the day of her initiation into the coven she now leads." He paused, and then added, "The tats came later."

"Who's the cluck with the wolf-skin poncho?"

"That 'cluck' is her father, Master Cuetlachtli."

From my days in the Borderland, I knew that "cuetlachtli" was the Nahuatl word for "wolf."

"That explains the fur coat."

"They say that Master Cuetlachtli was the high priest of the coven for a hundred years." Cody studied the tapestry "He died fifty or sixty years ago, and the Madame became the high priestess after that."

I stepped away from the tapestry and looked around the room. "What is this place?" I asked.

"It's a meeting room for the coven. They don't use it very often anymore. The brothers and sisters of the coven are scattered all over the place, but groups of them still come together for special occasions."

I stepped over to the tapestry depicting a human sacrifice. The victim was tied to an altar with ropes. His chest had been cut open, and blood spilled from his body down the sides of the altar to the floor, where it disappeared into a gutter surrounding the altar. A dozen or so men and women in colorful robes stood in the foreground, watching. Master Cuetlachtli, half dressed in his signature wolf skin, stood over the victim with a knife in one hand and a blood-soaked human heart in the other. He held the heart aloft, as if offering it to the gods. Or maybe he was just entertaining the spectators. Probably both.

The altar in the tapestry scratched at something in my head, and I walked over to get a closer look at the cement table in the center of the room. I could see now that the surface of the table was stained a brownish color that could only have been from old blood. Funny how hard it is to clean that stuff off a porous surface, especially after repeated spills. Looking down, I saw that a narrow gutter had been carved out of the floor around the table. It was stained, too.

"It's just animal blood," Cody explained. "Chickens mostly. We get them cheap from the guy next door. Madame Cuapa doesn't do human sacrifices."

"But her father did?" I asked.

Cody shrugged. "That's what they say."

"How do they say he died?"

"He was taken by a god."

"Uh-huh."

"Well," Cody hedged. "He was very old, so maybe it was just his time."

I turned away from the table.

"Shall we take a load off, sir?" Cody led me to the chairs. Mr. Whiskers was already napping in a corner of the room.

After we were seated, Cody caught my eyes and held them. "Tell me why you're here, sir."

"What do you know about were-crows?" I asked.

"Were-crows?" Cody looked skeptical. "You mean like a were-wolf, except that he turns into a crow?"

"Into a lot of crows, actually."

"Those really exist? Huh! I've heard of them, but never seen one. At least as far as I know."

"Well, one's been bugging me the last couple of days. A flock of crows has bumped up to me twice since Madame Cuapa came to my office yesterday morning. The crows were spotted transforming into a human earlier this afternoon in another part of this neighborhood. I came to investigate."

"Does Madame Cuapa know about this?" Cody asked.

"I called her. The were-crow seems to have arrived at roughly the same time as your new guests." I looked at Cody, but his face betrayed no reaction to this news. "I asked her if I could talk to the two witches, but she put me off. So I decided to climb up there behind the house and get a gander at them without her knowing about it. It seemed like a good idea at the time, until your patrol mutt showed up." I looked back at the sleeping manticore. "I'll give him this—he's a silent little devil! I'm a hard man to sneak up on, but I never saw him coming."

Cody's eyes lit up with pride. "He's a born hunter. Good thing for you that he's well trained."

"So you're the reason I'm still alive? Nice work! I appreciate it!"

Cody smiled, then grew serious. "So what did you see?"

"Like I told you before, not much. The tall guy piqued my interest."

Cody's expression tightened ever-so-slightly. I'd have to play poker with him sometime before he learned how to control his tells. "Why's that?" he asked.

"I saw you enter the room with the wine. Did you notice that they all clammed up when you came in?"

"They don't discuss business within earshot of the domestic help." Cody gave me a self-deprecating grin.

"Maybe they were stunned by your outfit."

"Oh, this old thing?" Cody ran a hand over the red-trimmed collar. "It was on sale and I couldn't pass it up."

I shook my head. "Say, what all do you do for Madame Cuapa anyway? You keep the animal trained and fed." I nodded toward Mr. Whiskers. "You drive the Madame around. You're her butler and bodyguard. You wait tables. You do some doctoring. You assist in the lab. What else? Cooking? Gardening? Tax returns? I bet you fix the leaks and change the lightbulbs, too."

Cody shrugged. "Whatever needs doing. Like I told you before, I'm the Madame's personal assistant. And her only servant at the moment."

"That must keep you plenty busy." I nodded in the direction of the house. "She's probably wondering where you are."

"She'll let me know if she needs me."

"And you'll come running?"

"Of course, sir! Serving the Madame is a privilege. And it comes with plenty of perks."

"Such as?"

He smiled. "I'll leave that to your imagination. Sir."

"Right." I looked around the room, taking it all in. "Just one more question. Is Madame Cuapa teaching you to be a witch?"

Cody looked at his hands, and I noted that the thin scars I'd seen before on the palm of one of his hands were present on both. "No, not really. She's taught me enough so that I can help her out a little in the lab, but I'm too busy with my other duties to become a full-fledged apprentice. Besides, that's not my calling. Assisting the Madame is enough for me, and I hope to be doing it for a long, long time."

I nodded at Cody. Despite his ridiculous glam-rock garb and his arrogant swagger, I found myself beginning to admire the jasper. Not that I'd ever want to switch places with him, or that I could be happy waiting on someone hand and foot. Not even someone as powerful as Madame Cuapa, no matter what kinds of perks she could offer me in return. "He belongs to me," she had said about her "personal assistant." But Cody struck me as a man who knew what he wanted, and as someone who took pride in his work. When it comes down to brass tacks, maybe it doesn't get any better than that.

"Right. Well when you left the room, the dark-haired joker got in Madame Cuapa's face. He said that he wants you out of the house until things get back to normal. He was adamant about it. The other one, the gnome, she was watching it all go down, but she wasn't taking sides. It got heated."

Cody nodded. "The man's name is Mr. Falconwing. Tloto Falconwing. He was the Madame's first apprentice. He lives in Angel City, and he's a prominent player in those parts." Cody locked eyes with me, and his expression was serious. "Don't cross him if you know what's good for you."

"Madame Cuapa put him in his place," I told him. "One word and he practically fell on his back and showed his belly."

Cody smiled. "Yeah, she can do that to people."

"Anything else you want to tell me about Falconwing?"

"Yeah. He's a motherfucking prick."

It didn't take a detective to see that there was something personal between Cody and Falconwing, but my gut told me not to press it. At the moment, the young man was cooperating with me, and I wanted to keep it that way.

"What about the broad?" I asked.

"That's Old Itzel. She may not look like much, but she's as dangerous as Mr. Falconwing in her own way. She's from Tenochtitlan, and they treat her like a goddess down there. She's older than Madame Cuapa. She might have been older than Madame Cuapa's father, I don't know. You're in the ring with heavyweights, Mr. Southerland. Don't doubt it for a second."

"Is anyone else there?"

Cody shook his head. "No, the Madame just called for the two of them."

"Did they bring anyone like you along?"

"You mean servants? No. They came alone. Well, they brought familiars. Old Itzel has this little hairless dog." Cody shivered. "Creepy little bastard! Looks more like a rat than a dog."

"And Falconwing? Let me guess."

Cody smiled. "Yup. He's got a falcon. Go figure."

112

"Are they loose on the property?"

"No, and don't worry, sir," Cody assured me. "Mr. Whiskers doesn't like either one of those animals. If they get within sniffing distance, he'll know it. And when he knows it, I'll know it."

"How far is sniffing distance?"

In response, Cody raised his eyes and peered off at nothing. In the corner of the room, Mr. Whiskers raised himself to his front feet, sniffed at the air, and then plopped down again, never bothering to open his eyes. Cody looked back down at me. "The familiars are still in the house. Caged, I hope."

I looked at the sleeping manticore, who was giving off harmless-as-a-housecat vibes that I didn't buy for an instant. "Neat trick."

Cody's lip lifted in an "oh, that?" half-smile that crinkled his eye into a wink.

I looked in the direction of the house, as if I could see it through the wooden walls and past the sand dune. "Look, Cody. Keep an eye on those two witches. Madame Cuapa says that she trusts them, but I don't. Someone put a compulsion on the Madame, and you know as well as I do how hard that's gotta be. But a witch with some heavy mojo might be able to do it."

"You're thinking that Mr. Falconwing or Old Itzel might have turned against the Madame?" Cody was making a show of being skeptical, but I could see that his heart wasn't in it.

I nodded at him with my chin. "You've been thinking the same thing. Especially about Falconwing, right?"

Cody looked uneasy. "I trust Madame Cuapa's judgment."

"That's fine. But keep your eyes open. One of them might be using something on the Madame on the sly. Maybe she was compelled by one of them to bring him up here. Or to bring *her* up here. I don't trust the broad any more than the joker."

Cody looked down. "And they're the ones who are supposed to be watching out for her. And keeping her from casting anymore harmful spells."

"You got it, kid." I clapped a hand on his shoulder. "And if one of those witches is the puppet master pulling Madame Cuapa's strings, your boss just invited the enemy right into her stronghold."

***

Cody let me go then, and I walked along the winding residential streets to my car. To my surprise, I hadn't been ticketed for parking in front of the fire hydrant. Maybe the traffic cops left this neighborhood alone unless they received a complaint from the residents. It was getting to be early evening, and I had a few things I wanted to do before putting a wrap on the day. First, I wanted to call Coyot. I hadn't talked to him since the cops dragged him downtown for questioning, and I wanted to touch base. Among other things, I wanted to pump him for the skinny on Madame Cuapa's houseguests. As a full-fledged member of the brujería fraternity, I figured he might have something enlightening on Falconwing and Old Itzel. Second, I had promised Lubank that I'd check in with him. And third, I was hoping for some quiet time at the Black Minotaur before I hit the hay. Sounded like a plan. I felt like I had a handle on things. I felt organized.

I hit my first snag when I called Coyot. Turned out that he was dead.

Chapter Ten

"Alkwat's balls!" Lubank shouted at Detective Kalama. "Why did you drag my client here at this hour? He has nothing to do with this shit show!"

"No one dragged anyone anywhere," Kalama replied in a calmer voice. "Southerland came here of his own free will. You're the only one here without an invitation."

Lubank thrust a finger toward the detective's chest. "Somebody's gotta stop him from implicating himself. He's too much of a nitwit to protect himself from your dirty cop tricks."

"Hey!" I protested.

"Button it, peeper! They're trying to entrap you!"

We were crowded cheek to jowl in Coyot's office. The place was a wreck, with broken bottles, vases, herbs and powders, and other debris scattered over the floor, and Coyot's shredded corpse lying in the midst of it all. Various uniformed cops were picking up items and putting them in evidence bags, while someone in plain clothes was taking snapshots of the stiff. When I called Coyot earlier that evening, Kalama had answered. She'd informed me that Coyot was not available to come to the phone on account of the fact that his recently mangled body was stretched out at her feet. I'd told her that I was going to drive over and have a look, and she hadn't objected. I'd called Lubank to give him an update, giving him a shorthand account of everything that had happened to me since I last saw him, and he'd insisted on meeting me at the scene. It was well past ten when we arrived.

"We're guessing some sort of animal attack?" I asked Kalama.

"Coyot's receptionist says that he had a big dog. Its prints are in the blood on the floor, but it's gone missing."

"I've seen that mutt. He might have been a terror in his day, but at this point that old boy couldn't hurt a fly. Whatever did this to Coyot probably scared the dog away."

"Maybe. But the dog was Coyot's familiar. And familiars don't run off when their master is in danger, and they don't slink away from their master's dead body, either."

Lubank had been leaning over Coyot's corpse. He straightened up and turned toward the detective and me. "Well, something with teeth and claws did a number on that stiff. That's why I don't own a fuckin' dog. You never know when they'll turn on you."

"Lubank, I'm stunned that you don't have a dog," I told him. "They're experts at digging up dirt—just like you!"

"Always with the wisecracks! You're lucky I'm here. They'd be grilling you in a sweatbox downtown right now if it weren't for me."

"Why? I didn't have nothin' against Coyot."

"Didn't the two of you bust into that mortgage company yesterday? Don't answer that!"

"Some lip you are. Are you trying to protect my interests or get me arrested!"

Lubank poked at my chest with a stubby finger. "I can rack up more billable hours if they arrest you. You're no good to me if you're clean."

Kalama interrupted us. "You two comedians wanna take your act outside?" She looked down at Lubank. "I want to ask your client some questions, but we need to give these boys some room to work."

"Whatever you say, detective." Lubank gave Kalama a disarming smile. "I'm always ready to cooperate with the law."

Lubank and I followed Kalama out of the office and into the waiting room, which, at this late hour, was dark and deserted. The detective turned on a table lamp, and we all took seats.

Kalama dove right in. "Why did you call Coyot tonight?" she asked me.

"You don't have to answer that question," Lubank interjected, lighting up a cigarette.

"It's okay," I told him. I turned back to Kalama. "Madame Cuapa invited two of her fellow witches to stay with her for a while. I thought that Coyot might have some information about them.

Besides, I hadn't talked to him since he was let out of the station yesterday. I wanted to see if he was all right."

"Did you have any reason to think he might be in danger?" asked the detective.

"Not really. Guess I was wrong."

Kalama nodded. I watched the smoke from Lubank's cigarette rolling through a streak of lamplight. It reminded me of the tapestry I'd seen earlier that evening. I searched the cigarette smoke for empty-eyed dog-faced demons but saw only indistinct swirls.

Kalama asked, "What do you know about those two witches?"

Lubank again interjected himself into the questioning. "Is that pertinent?"

"It is if they had some connection to Coyot."

I nodded at Kalama. "They're all brujería. There are a lot of different branches of witchcraft, and they can be as different as apples and oranges, but Cuapa, Coyot, and the two others—they're called Falconwing and Itzel—all of them practice the Nahuatl arts. But compared to the other three, Coyot was strictly bush league. Cuapa and the other two, they're the big cheese."

Kalama thought about that. "Coyot witnessed Shipper's death. Maybe somebody thought that he had seen too much."

I shrugged. "A lot of us saw Shipper get it," I pointed out. "Including me."

Kalama held my eyes, letting it sink in.

"You think I might be next?" I asked.

Kalama shrugged. "I don't know what to think. Run into any big dogs lately?"

I didn't say anything to that. I hadn't run into any big dogs, other than old Chichi, but I'd run into a flock of crows, not to mention a manticore. I'd told Lubank all about both the were-crow and Mr. Whiskers when I called him before coming out to Coyot's office. I looked his way, but he'd developed a sudden interest in a speck of lint on his tie, which he was removing with the careful patience of a surgeon.

"Can you do me a favor?" I asked Kalama. "When they find out what killed Coyot, can you let me know?"

"Sure thing, gumshoe" Kalama deadpanned. "My bosses love it when I leak out confidential police reports to private citizens for no good reason."

We stared at each other without blinking. Lubank stopped picking at his tie and leaned toward me. "You're going to have to give her something."

I stopped trying to stare Kalama down and glanced over at Lubank. "Like what?"

Lubank lifted an eyebrow and shrugged.

I let out a breath. "Okay, copper. On advice from counsel, maybe I can offer you some quid pro quo."

"Spill it and we'll see."

I told her about the were-crow, beginning with my first encounter with the flock of crows on my way to see Shipper at Emerald Bay Mortgage. I told her how the crows had faced me off outside Shipper's house, and how Smokey had seen the crows transform into a human near Madame Cuapa's house.

When I was finished with my story, Kalama asked, "You think that Coyot might have been killed by this were-crow?"

"I don't know. But crows have claws and sharp beaks. It's a possibility."

Kalama frowned. "If this were-crow killed Coyot, and if it's connected to Cuapa or her two witch friends, then Coyot's murder and Shipper's murder are tied together in some way."

Lubank snorted. "Either that or the dog did it, in which case there's no connection between Coyot and Cuapa at all. Which means that Southerland isn't involved in Coyot's murder in any way, shape, or form. It's getting late, boys and girls. What say we all blow this pop stand and go home. Poppa needs some shut-eye."

Kalama nodded. "I've got to wrap things up here, but the two of you might as well scram. Don't leave town, Southerland. You got yourself involved with the murder vic yesterday, and I'm going to need a statement from you." She looked at Lubank. "You'll probably want to sit in for that, just to keep things on the up-and-up. You know how tricky us cops can be."

Lubank reached up and gave his hairpiece a slight adjustment. "Fuckin' right!"

***

I was exhausted when I hit the sack that night, but after sleeping for less than an hour, my eyes sprang open, as if with a sudden realization. Although my body was still overcome with fatigue, my mind was stuck on full speed ahead. The memory of an important dream danced through my head, but when I tried to pin down the details they dissolved like wet tissue paper into vague images of crows and dogs. I knew that my instincts were trying to tell me something, but I'd missed the message. I told my subconscious to keep trying and attempted to find my way back into dreamland.

I dozed on and off for the next few hours, but by five-thirty I decided to give it up. I took a hot shower with a cold rinse, which cleared away any further need of sleep, and put a couple of frozen waffles in my toaster for breakfast. By six-thirty, with the sun nothing more than a glow beneath the horizon, I was already in my office pumping the internet for dope on the Shipper family.

I didn't find much that I didn't already know. Donald Shipper hadn't left much of an electronic footprint while he'd been alive. I read a brief article from a scanned Emerald Bay Mortgage Company newsletter written to announce Shipper's promotion to General Manager, but all it told me was that he'd earned a master's degree in finance, joined Emerald Bay as a loan officer trainee, and worked his way up through the ranks of the company. I found his name listed as an attendee at various conferences and expos through the years. At the Tolanica Bankers Associations marketing conference held six years earlier, Shipper had been part of a four-member panel called "Overcoming the Failed Promise of the Deposit Competition Revolution." Further digging showed that two years ago he had given the keynote address at the annual meeting of the Yerba City chapter of the Entrepreneurs in Real Estate Association. His speech had been titled, "Innovations in Document Custody: Buy Your Ticket and Climb Aboard!" I tried to imagine being the kind of person who would be excited enough about deposit competitions and document custody to speak about them in front of an audience. The effort threatened to undo the effects of my shower and breakfast and send me back to bed.

119

Two hours after sunrise I concluded that Shipper had led a prosperous, somewhat accomplished, and altogether ordinary life, completely at odds with the spectacular nature of his departure from this world. He had spent his adult life in his chosen field of expertise and risen as far as his skills, capability, and ambitions were likely to take him. If he hadn't come to an untimely end, he would no doubt have continued to hold board meetings and browbeat middle managers until receiving his gold watch and lucrative retirement package. After that, it would have been ocean cruises and visits with the grandchildren until one day he ceased waking up in the morning. Ten years later, people would be straining to recall something memorable about old Mr. Shipper. Would they be saying, "Wasn't he the whiz who gave that brilliant appraisal of the Deposit Competition Revolution? He sure had them standing in the aisles with his masterful comparison of the innovations in document custody to boarding a train!" Not likely. Remembering my own brief encounter with the man, I had the feeling that without his money few people would have given that self-important son of a bitch the time of day. I could understand why someone, acting impulsively, might want to plant a fist into his kisser and smack some of the arrogance out of his ugly mug. But someone had gone to the trouble of finding a way to compel a witch to dig into her bag of tricks for a piece of heavy artillery in order to punch his ticket. That was more than an impulsive act; that was a boatload of cold calculation. To me, Shipper didn't seem worth the bother. Somebody disagreed with me, which meant that I was missing something important.

Changing tactics, I decided to see what the internet had on Cynthia Shipper. Turned out that the internet knew her quite well. Cynthia Shipper, née Packwood, had been an honor student at a private prep school on the Peninsula, where she had also been a cheerleader, the female lead in two different school plays, and homecoming queen. In her high school yearbook, she had been described both as "Prettiest face," and "Most likely to marry into money." She had attended community college and received an associate's degree in liberal arts. From there she had embarked upon her short career as a legal secretary before becoming the third wife of the late Donald Shipper. After her marriage, she had become involved in a number of charity organizations, all well-known and non-controversial. They indicated a desire to keep busy without becoming enmeshed in any particular cause.

I thought about Mrs. Shipper. She had been a big deal in high school but seemed to have lacked the ambition or drive to reach for more than a well-heeled husband. Her secondary school credentials could have put her in a prestigious university, but she had opted for community college. Maybe that was all she'd been able to afford. After college, she'd used her skills to get a high-level clerical position, which she'd abandoned as soon as she fulfilled her yearbook prediction of marrying money. Since then, she'd taken to the good life, taking care of her meal-ticket while playing enough of a public role to maintain a sense of self-realization. Like her husband, she'd been living an ordinary life. Unlike her husband, she had not come close to tapping her potential. After meeting her, I had the feeling that she had felt trapped in her marriage. Was murder her way of freeing herself? The nature of the murder was dramatic, and she *had* been an actress. But it seemed a bit much, and my gut told me that I was reaching. I needed to take a break.

I rose from my desk and stretched. I considered all of the facets of the Shipper case. I thought about tattooed witches, spoiled rich families, and executive offices in the top floors of downtown skyscrapers. I thought about executive assistants and personal assistants, and manticores, murders of crows, and tired old dogs. I thought about exploding bodies and blood-soaked stiffs stretched out on floors. Somehow, all of these pieces fit into the same tapestry, like the ones in Madame Cuapa's meeting hall, but the picture was too big and the pieces too scattered and too few. I was missing important links, and they weren't going to walk into my office and lay themselves at my feet. I'd have to find them.

I couldn't think anymore. My brain was misfiring like an engine with two bad plugs. I needed a workout. I went upstairs and changed into some sweats. Then I went down to my laundry room, taped my fists, and began hammering on my heavy bag with measured blows, making each one count. The bag hung from my ceiling and took it without complaining. After beating the shit out of the bag for a half hour, I guzzled down some water, followed it

121

up with a slug of whiskey straight from the bottle, and went outside for a run. The morning was cooler than it had been for a week, and, as I pounded the pavement I lifted my face to the breeze, thankful for the layer of familiar Yerba City fog that had rolled over the city during the night. I ran through neighborhood streets, dodging pedestrians and traffic, focusing on my footfalls, my breathing, and on the motion of my legs and arms. I ran up and down hills, because no neighborhood in Yerba City sits on level ground. I ran at a comfortable steady pace, running but not racing. I ran on the sidewalk from intersection to intersection. If the light was green, I crossed the street running. If the light was red, I made a running right turn. I zigged and zagged through the neighborhood, circling blocks, doubling back, and never getting too far away from where I'd started. After running for an hour, I stopped and took a few long, slow breaths. Every part of my body was tired, but my mind felt more alive than it had since Madame Cuapa had slipped me a mickey. The walk home took fifteen minutes.

As I walked, I thought about Madame Cuapa's houseguests, Falconwing and Itzel. Madame Cuapa didn't believe that either of them had anything to do with Shipper's death or her own predicament. She had told me that she trusted them with her life. But I didn't know anything about them, and I told myself that before the day was over, that would have to change.

The first thing I did when I got back to my office was check my phone for voicemails. I had two calls, one from Detective Kalama, and one from Cody. Kalama wanted me to call her back as soon as I had a minute. Cody informed me that I could come by that afternoon and meet her guests. I called Cody back to confirm. Then I went upstairs to take my second shower of the morning and change into clean clothes. When I was ready, I picked up my phone and called the detective.

***

When Detective Kalama entered Lubank's reception room, Gracie's face lit up. "Laurel! Who are you here to arrest, my husband or my boyfriend? Either one is okay, but make sure you just take one of them. It's no fun around here by myself."

"Hi Gracie. No arrests today. You get to keep them both."

"Whoopie!" Gracie twirled her index finger in the air in a sign of celebration. Then she took a strong draw on her cigarette and added more smoke to the thick gray cloud that was as much a part of the Lubank office as the furniture.

Gracie was a carton-a-day girl with a voice to match. Her blond hair came from a bottle, and the way she squeezed her generous curves into her vast collection of skin-tight dresses may have been considered less than respectable by most, but Gracie somehow made it all work. She was the most outrageous flirt I'd ever met, and I never knew how much of it was just for show. Her love for her husband was obvious, if hard to comprehend. It wasn't so much that enduring human/gnome unions were rare, it was more that Gracie was as vivacious and spirited as a bottle of sparkling wine, and Rob Lubank was, well, Lubank.

Kalama turned to Lubank and me and asked, "Shall we get started?"

Lubank started crossing the room. "Let's go back into my office. You too, Gracie. I want you to take everything down. If this sly cop pulls a fast one, I want it on record."

"Stop it, Rob." Gracie's blond hair, stiff with hair spray, swept over her shoulders as she shook her head. "You know that Laurel is one of the honest ones." She turned to Kalama. "Robby says that if you ever do put the arm on him he'll know that he's done for. He says that no one builds a case like you do."

"Pass that on to my lieutenant, would you? And don't worry. Your husband is too slick to get himself caught. Not that I don't have a file on him a yard thick."

"Well, if anyone puts my Robby away, I hope it'll be you."

"Alkwat's balls, woman!" Lubank yelled. "Are you trying to send me up the river?"

"Of course, Honey!" Gracie wrapped her arm in mine and pulled me tight against a luscious breast that was threatening to pop out of its wrappings. "How else am I going to be able to make time for *this* handsome lug?"

We spent the next half hour in Lubank's office where I answered Kalama's questions about Coyot. Lubank listened intently, making sure that I didn't give the cops any more material than necessary, and Gracie recorded it all both in shorthand and on a recorder. I noticed that Kalama was careful to steer me away from any mention of Madame Cuapa. She would save those questions for a less formal venue.

When we were done, I grabbed my hat and coat and started to leave with Kalama. Gracie kissed me on the cheek and looked from me to Kalama with a wink and a smirk. She took my hand and whispered to me, "Careful with this one, Sweetie. Remember, now that Robby has a copy of your official statement, he'll make sure that anything you tell her in a—shall we say more intimate setting?—will never see the light of day in court."

I rolled my eyes at her. "You know you're the only girl for me, Gracie. And, despite what Rob may think, Detective Kalama isn't trying to pin anything on me. She's just doing her job."

Gracie drew her lips within an inch of my ear. "Just remember, Honey. It's a copper's job to close the book on criminal investigations. Any way she can."

I nodded, squeezed her hand, and followed the detective out the door.

Chapter Eleven

I met up with Kalama at a bar and grill down the street from Lubank's office. The lunch rush was just beginning, and the joint wasn't yet half full. We slid into a vacant corner booth, and a waiter came by as soon as we were settled in. I ordered a steak sandwich and a beer, and Kalama ordered a tuna melt and a club soda. As soon as the waiter was gone, the detective got right to business.

"I think that we can eliminate Mrs. Turlock and Silverblade as suspects in Shipper's murder," she told me.

"Why's that?"

"Turlock's the kind of secretary who takes pride in her work, and part of that is being loyal to her boss. But apart from that she didn't have any strong feelings about him one way or the other. She didn't have any reason to want Shipper dead."

"She's quite a looker. No funny business between them?"

"She says that Shipper made a pass at her once when he was drunk. The crew was at a bar to blow off some steam after some successful big deal, and he got a little excited. She says that he pinned her to a wall when she was coming out of the ladies room and tried to stick his tongue down her throat, but she managed to fend him off. She says that the next day he was so embarrassed and apologetic that she couldn't help but forgive him. And it never happened again. He wouldn't even tell off-color jokes if she was in the room after that night."

"How long ago did it happen?" I asked.

"Three or four years ago."

"Turlock's married, right?"

"Divorced. But she was married when Shipper tried to get himself some."

"Hmmm. Maybe the ex-husband is still sore about it."

Kalama looked doubtful. "Long time to hold a grudge. Besides, that little incident had nothing to do with their divorce. Turns out that the ex is a divorce lawyer, and he ran off with one of his clients."

"What a sweetheart. She still calls herself Mrs. Turlock, though."

"I asked her about that. She says that it's for convenience. She's been with the company for a long time, and that's the name they know her by."

"Hmm. Apart from that one indiscretion, what did she think about Shipper as a boss?"

"Turlock says that he was a hard son of a bitch with no empathy for his customers, but the company turned a nice steady profit under his direction. She works hard, but she's well paid." Kalama smiled. "She got a nice little raise after Shipper's swing-and-a-miss."

"Sounds like she's doing okay. And she's single?"

Kalama's smile widened. "Think you might have a chance with her, hotshot? I wouldn't get too excited if I were you. Apparently, you didn't make much of a first impression. She thinks you belong in a booby-hatch. Also, she still wants me to charge you with trespassing and property damage."

"Terrific. What about Silverblade?"

Kalama frowned. "He's harder to read. I couldn't find a single reason why he might have wanted Shipper dead. He's well respected in the office, and he seems like a straight arrow. He heads up the company's legal department, which mostly involves handling litigation and keeping the company in compliance with changing regulatory and tax laws. I gather that he enjoys his job and that he's good at it. If anything, he seems over-qualified."

"Is he ambitious? Maybe he wanted Shipper's job."

Kalama shrugged. "I didn't get that impression. He makes a lot of dough as it is. This might be interesting, though. He and your client are pretty tight, professionally speaking. According to Mrs. Turlock, Cuapa got Silverblade his current position at Emerald Bay, and he's on a track to get promoted into her corporate headquarters. So I doubt that Shipper's job would be of much interest to him."

"Any way that Shipper's death benefits Silverblade?" I asked.

"Not that I can see." The detective thought for a few moments. "I guess we shouldn't rule him and Turlock out completely, but I think we're barking up the wrong tree with those two."

I agreed with Kalama, but I made a mental note to ask Madame Cuapa about Silverblade. When I'd asked Cuapa about him earlier, she'd said that she knew him, but hadn't elaborated. Maybe the connection between the two was closer than she'd let on. Probably nothing there, but it was worth making sure. It wasn't like I was buried in leads.

***

That afternoon, I drove out to Madame Cuapa's house. On the way, my phone rang, and I saw that Cindy Shipper was calling me. Traffic was crawling, so I connected the call.

"Hello? Mrs. Shipper?"

"Hello, Alex." Mrs. Shipper's voice had a breathy quality over the phone that wasn't as apparent in person. Maybe it was the effect of having the phone's speaker right up to my ear. "Is this a bad time?"

"No. I'm in traffic, but it isn't going anywhere."

"I'd like to see you. There's something I wanted to tell you."

I thought for a second. "I'm going to be tied up for the afternoon. Is later tonight okay?"

"That would be perfect!"

I made some mental calculations. "I can swing by at about nine or so. That too late?"

"No, but not here." She paused. "Can we meet somewhere? It's just that I need to be away from the two little monsters."

I wondered what the grieving widow had in mind. "Do you know a place called the Black Minotaur Lounge? We can meet there if you like."

"I can find it. You'll buy me a drink?"

"Mrs. Shipper...." I began.

"Cindy, please. And don't worry. I'm not asking you to go on a date. But I really need to get out of this house. It's, well...."

She faltered, and I jumped in. "I understand. Must be rough for you right now."

127

"Yes," she agreed, and I thought that she might be fighting back a tear. "A little. I think it's just starting to...sink in. You know what I mean?"

"I do. And I'll buy you a drink, but just one."

She laughed a little. "Believe me, it will help. Thank you."

"I'll see you tonight, then, Cindy."

"Bye, Alex."

I put the phone down and slapped my hand against my forehead. I hoped that Mrs. Shipper was calling me because she had thought of something that might help me find her husband's killer. I hoped that's all it was.

At least most of me did.

***

I called Madame Cuapa's home number, and Cody answered. I told him that I was running late. He told me that it was okay, and that Madame Cuapa would receive me whenever I got there. Traffic picked up as I made my way out of the downtown area, but it was already after six when I parked the beastmobile in front of Madame Cuapa's house. The sun was hidden behind a thick gray layer of low-hanging clouds, and a stiff wind whipped through the branches of the oak trees growing in the Madame's front yard. The house was lit up on the inside, both downstairs and upstairs. I hoped that I wasn't interrupting dinner. I hoped even more that Madame Cuapa wouldn't try to offer me any.

Cody opened the front door before I had a chance to ring the doorbell. Today he was wearing a black tuxedo coat with tails. A cummerbund circled his waist, and black skin-tight stretch pants hugged his legs. He held a white cane in one hand and wore no shirt. He greeted me and let me in.

"Madame Cuapa is in the dining room, sir," Cody told me. "Please follow me. Have you eaten?"

"Yes," I lied. "Are you doing a song and dance number tonight?"

Cody smiled and twirled his cane. "Got any requests?"

"No."

"Too bad." Cody brought himself to attention, lifted the cane to left shoulder arms, executed a snappy about face, and led me through the house at a march.

Madame Cuapa and her two guests were seated at the table in the same seats where I had seen them from my vantage point the day before. They were sipping red wine from crystal goblets. None of them rose when I entered.

"Mr. Southerland, thanks for coming." Madame Cuapa indicated a chair at the opposite end of the table from her. "Please, have a seat. Would you like some wine?" When I hesitated to answer, she turned to her assistant. "Cody? Please bring another glass and a fresh bottle." Looking directly at me, she continued instructing Cody. "Pick a bottle at random and make sure that the cork has been undisturbed."

I nodded at Madame Cuapa. "Thanks." I lowered myself into the offered dining room chair and glanced around the room. It had a lived-in vibe, with plants on shelves and paintings of birds, flowers, and landscapes on the walls. I got the feeling that Madame Cuapa did much of her entertaining in this room.

"Mr. Southerland, these are my friends." She turned first to the woman on her left. "This is Miss Itzel. She's been a member of the coven since before I was born, and that's saying something."

The gnome looked up from her knitting and smiled. "Charmed," she said. Her voice was firm, but with a faint rasp on the edges that reminded me of rustling paper. Up close, she looked like an ancient corpse. Her eyes were slits in her wrinkled face. A huge hooked nose curled over her upper lip. Her teeth were so crooked, I wondered how she could chew. A bird's nest of curly gray hair exploded out of her head and hid her oversized rounded gnome ears. She was propped up in her chair on a mound of cushions, and I wondered how her stubby legs could support her enormous round torso if she had to climb off and walk.

I listened to the rhythmic clacking of Old Itzel's knitting needles as the gnome worked the yarn with the unerring ease of someone who had been at it for decades. Her hands were a blur, and she paused only long enough to take small sips from her wine goblet. Whatever she was making trailed down from the knitting needles to a crease between her inflated belly and her sagging breasts. Poking out from beneath the woven thread was the tiny hairless head of a gray dog, so small and still that I mistook it at first for a doll. Then I noticed the rapid widening and narrowing of its nostrils as it panted through its nose. Bulbous worried-looking brown eyes dominated its face and stared at me without blinking.

Itzel looked me up and down. "My, you're a big one, aren't you! Almost as big as Cody. Citlali certainly likes to surround herself with tall men. I wonder what that says about her. Some sort of fantasy wish fulfillment, I suppose."

"Don't be rude, Itzel," Madame Cuapa scolded. "Old age is no excuse."

Itzel's face twisted into a pout. "Pish posh! When one gets to be as old as Old Itzel, one may say anything that's on one's mind. It's one of the rights earned by the aged." She scratched the back of her dog's neck and cooed at the tiny creature in a baby-talk voice, "Isn't that right, Nessie? She's a good little girl, yes she is." The dog blinked once, licked its lips with a small pointed pink tongue, and continued to stare at me.

Madame Cuapa, indicating the gentleman on her right. "And this suave gentleman is Tloto Falconwing."

"Pleasure to meet you." Falconwing's solemn expression seemed to contradict his words. Up close, his deeply tanned face, dark eyes, and trim mustache made him look even more like an old-time movie star than he had when I'd seen him from up on the sand dune. He had a sad aloofness about him, and I had no doubt that women of all ages dashed themselves on the rocky shores of his indifference in an attempt to bring a hint of happiness to his brooding face. He held out a limp hand, and I wrapped my fingers around it without squeezing.

"Mr. Southerland would like some details on how the two of you are helping to keep me from laying waste to the neighborhood," Madame Cuapa explained to her guests. "He has personal knowledge of how much of a threat I've become. Two nights ago I nearly killed him."

Falconwing looked over at me, but spoke to Madame Cuapa. "Yes, Citlali, we're both aware of the danger." He was about to say more, but he stopped himself when Cody arrived with four crystal goblets, a smaller glass, and a bottle of unopened wine on a tray. His eyes lingered on Cody as the big man set the tray on a marble counter and brought the wine and glassware to the table. I noticed that Cody never looked Falconwing's way.

The big servant held a bottle out for Madame Cuapa to examine. "I brought this up from the cellar, Madame." Madame Cuapa glanced at it and nodded. Cody held the bottle out for me to see, "This is a good vintage, Mr. Southerland. The only thing you have to fear from this bottle is that it will all-too-soon be empty." He produced a corkscrew from somewhere and removed the cork with practiced precision. With an understated flair, he poured a splash of the wine into the smaller glass and handed it to Madame Cuapa.

The Madame swirled the wine around the bottom of the glass and examined the deep red color with a critical eye. She brought the glass to her nose and breathed in the fragrance. She nodded once, poured the wine into her mouth, and swished it around a few times before swallowing it.

"Excellent!" she proclaimed with a smile. She nodded at Cody, and he filled the four fresh goblets from the new bottle. "Mr. Southerland, please choose a glass for yourself."

"Thank you, Madame Cuapa." The truth was that I was starting to feel a little silly about all these precautions. I took the nearest goblet, and the other three each took one for themselves. I waved away my misgivings and took a healthy slug of the red juice. It tasted like wine. I'd have to take Cody's word that it was a good vintage. Judging by the expressions of the three witches as they sipped from their goblets, they all seemed pleased enough with it.

"What do you think, Southerland?" asked Falconwing, holding up his goblet and gazing into my eyes with focused intensity.

"I'm more of a beer and whiskey man, myself, but I'm always willing to expand my horizons."

Falconwing's quick smile told me that I had failed some sort of test. That was fine with me. I wasn't there to make new pals. This was a business call.

It was time to get everyone's attention. "If you don't mind, I have a few questions. Cody, I'd like you to stay." Cody had been about to depart the room, but he stopped and looked at Madame Cuapa, who gave him a slight nod.

Before I could continue, Madame Cuapa, accustomed to being in charge, seized the floor away from me. "You'll want to know what arrangements we've made. Starting tonight, Itzel, Cody, and Tloto will be sleeping in eight-hour shifts. Itzel will retire early tonight."

"I need my beauty sleep," Itzel cooed, bouncing the curls on one side of her head with her hand while placing the other on her hip like a pin-up girl.

Madame Cuapa favored Itzel with a bemused smile, and the old gnome went back to her knitting. Turning back to me, she outlined the rest of the sleep schedule. "Itzel will awaken at about four in the morning, and Cody will take his turn. Tloto took a nap earlier today and will remain awake until noon tomorrow. And I will sleep whenever I feel like it, knowing that two sets of watchful eyes will be upon me at all times. We'll repeat that schedule until you find out who is tampering with me." Madame Cuapa met my eyes with a penetrating stare. These witches and their hypnotic eyes! It was as if they could see parts of me that weren't visible to anyone else. I wondered how much of that was intentional, how much was habit, and how much was just for show. After peering into my soul for a few moments, the Madame continued, "Please make haste, Mr. Southerland. We'd all like to get back to our everyday lives as quickly as possible."

"I'll do what I can," I assured her. "What else have you done to protect yourself?"

"I've bolstered the wards around this house." She waved her hand around the room without pointing anywhere in particular. "It should be more difficult for anyone to 'get to me' without my knowledge. I've also enhanced the protections on my own body. I won't go into detail. Some of these procedures are quite intimate, and some are secret."

"Even from your friends and companions?" I asked.

The Madame's lips curled to form a coy smile. "Some things are strictly between me and certain unearthly spirits."

Old Itzel's expression twisted into an exaggerated leer. "From the way she was moaning, I think that some of those unearthly spirits are pretty damned good in the sack!"

"Itzel!"

"Hey!" Itzel half-turned toward Cuapa with a look of pure innocence. "Your relationship with your gods is nobody's business but your own!"

Madame Cuapa shook her head. "You're incorrigible."

"You have no idea. By the way, I'm almost done with this tea cozy. I hope you like it."

"It's darling! I can't wait to use it."

Cody was looking off into space, and Falconwing heaved a dramatic sigh to signal his boredom. I decided to reclaim the conversation. "As I understand it, the three of you are members of the same coven."

Madame Cuapa answered. "Yes. Itzel was a sister in the coven when my father was the high priest. When my father died, I became the high priestess, and Itzel became my chief advisor. Tloto joined the coven soon after that. In fact, he was the first member that I personally recruited."

I turned to Falconwing. "What were you doing before you met Madame Cuapa?"

Falconwing shrugged. "Making a nuisance of myself. And using my raw powers to make money."

Madame Cuapa *hmmphed*. "He was a little shit. When I found him, he was seducing rich ladies and living off their fortunes."

Falconwing smiled, as if his past life was a matter of no consequence. "Guilty as charged. And rich old queers, too." I glanced at Cody and caught a slight hardening of his otherwise impassive face. Falconwing continued, "I was young, arrogant, and on a course that was taking me nowhere except over the edge of a cliff. Fortunately, Madame Cuapa came along and showed me a more fulfilling life."

Itzel looked up from her knitting. "That doesn't stop him from seducing the young maidens, though, does it Tloto. And the young boys, too. With an emphasis on the young!"

Falconwing shrugged. "I don't seduce anybody. But if someone wants to come to me willingly, well, far be it for me to discourage her. Or him."

"At least he's not after their money anymore," said Madame Cuapa.

"No ma'am. Thanks to you I've learned that there are far more important things than money in this world."

I tried to meet Falconwing's eyes, but found myself looking at the center of his forehead, instead. Something about those dark eyes made me uneasy in a way that I couldn't explain. I forced myself to speak. "But you still have plenty of dough, I'll bet."

He shrugged. "So my accountants tell me."

Throughout this exchange, I kept shooting glances at Cody. He was struggling to keep his face from betraying his thoughts, but it was clear that the young man had a beef of some kind with Falconwing. I was forming some ideas about that, and I made a mental note to ask him about it the next time I had the chance.

I took a sip of wine and asked Falconwing, "Did you know Donald Shipper?"

"He's the man who died, right?" Falconwing looked at Madame Cuapa, who nodded. He turned back to me. "I'd never heard of him until Citlali called me."

I nodded and turned my attention to Old Itzel. "How about you? Did you know Donald Shipper?"

She shook her head. "Never had the pleasure."

I stayed with Itzel, but changed the subject. "You were in the coven before Madame Cuapa was born. Why didn't you become the coven leader after her father died?"

Itzel barked out a laugh. "You're not subtle, are you! I like that. Subtlety is for pussies."

"Itzel!"

"What!" Itzel put on her expression of innocence. She could turn it on at will. "He suspects that I might be doing something nasty in order to take the coven away from you. Me or Tloto. Or maybe we're working together. That's why this nice young man is here today, right?" Her lips split into a broad smile as she looked up at me, and her eyes nearly vanished into the wrinkles in her face. "Don't worry, my boy. I'm not offended in the least. You're just doing your job, and, anyway, I've got nothing to hide. Do I, Nessie? Such a sweet little girl she is...."

I waited for the old witch to finish nuzzling her little rat-dog, whose eyes never left me. After a few scratches and pets, along with some baby noises, Itzel sat up and told me her story over the clacking of her knitting needles. "I was a coven sister when Old Cuetlachtli—that was Citlali's father—was high priest. He was a great, great man! Citlali was his only child and heir. When Cuetlachtli died, the position of high priestess was Citlali's by right. And besides," she looked at the Madame and smiled, "she's much more qualified to lead a coven than Old Itzel. You might be surprised to hear this, but I lack people skills." Her eyes disappeared in another broad smile. "It's true! I don't have a diplomatic bone in my body, and, apparently, complete and total honesty is a bad trait in a leader. Anyway, after her father died, Citlali modernized the coven in ways that wouldn't have occurred to an old stick-in-the-mud like me, and the coven became stronger than ever as a result." Looking away with an I-don't-give-a-shit expression, Itzel waved a languid hand. "I'm more than happy just being along for the ride."

"You're much more than that," said Madame Cuapa. "We wouldn't be where we are without you, and you know it."

"Well, that's true enough I guess," Itzel agreed. "The voice of experience still means something in this world, and Citlali has always been smart enough to know it."

I pressed forward. "If Madame Cuapa were...out of the picture, who would lead the coven?"

It was Falconwing who answered. "It would fall apart!" A scowl twisted Itzel's face, but she quickly suppressed it.

Madame Cuapa put her wine glass on the table. "Nonsense. Tloto will become high priest, and the coven will flourish. Not that I'm going anywhere!" she hastened to add.

"So Mr. Falconwing will become high priest? Not you, Miss Itzel?"

She kept her eyes on her knitting and put on a sour face. "I want nothing to do with leading a coven. Oh, I want to be in the inner chamber to make sure that no one fucks it up, but I'm too old and tired to take on that much responsibility. Isn't that right, Citlali?"

Madame Cuapa smiled. "No, that is not right, you old bitch. You're as capable as anyone in the world to run the coven. But you don't want it. You've never wanted it. You've made that very clear to me."

Itzel didn't look up. "Eh. Such a bother. I'd rather be free to operate without a lot of prying eyes and overeager young novices questioning my every move."

Something occurred to me then. "How many members does this coven have?

Madame Cuapa answered. "The three of us are the inner circle. Total membership? Cody? What's our official membership count now?"

Cody had the answer at the top of his head. "One hundred twelve practicing witches, plus support staff, scattered over western Tolanica. As of the beginning of the week."

I whistled.

Itzel beamed at Madame Cuapa like a proud grandmother. "Far cry from the old days. Your father would be proud."

"How many members did you have when you took over leadership?" I asked Madame Cuapa.

"Sixteen."

"You've been busy."

"Yes, I have."

Chapter Twelve

One hundred twelve witches in a single coven. That was a lot of firepower!

"Are you all right, dear?" asked Madame Cuapa. "You look a little stunned."

"I had the impression that covens tended to be...well, smaller than that."

"It's true that we're one of the larger ones, but the number is a little misleading. It's really a lot of loosely confederated smaller cells. The individual group leaders submit weekly progress reports to me through our website. Cody reads through them all and lets me know if anything needs my attention."

"Could you mobilize them if you wanted to?"

Madame Cuapa swirled the wine in her goblet. "I suppose so. I can't imagine ever needing to, though."

Falcolnwing nodded at me. "I keep telling Citlali that we should hold an annual convention." The corners of his mouth twisted into the slightest of smiles.

Itzel's voice rose over the clacking of her knitting needles. "You just want to watch them all dance naked, you dirty boy."

"Just the young ones." Falconwing raised his glass with three fingers and took a delicate sip of wine.

"Bastard," Itzel muttered.

Madame Cuapa let out a weighty sigh. "Honestly, you two. What must Mr. Southerland think about our little group?"

"I think that I'm learning quite a lot."

Itzel cackled. "And none of it good, am I right?"

I brought my wine goblet to my mouth rather than answer her. After a sip, I turned back to Madame Cuapa. "I just have one other thing I wanted to ask about. I heard that you were the one who got Claudius Silverblade his position with Emerald Bay Mortgage."

"You *have* been busy, haven't you! Careful, everybody. This young sleuth will uncover *all* your secrets!" Madame Cuapa's smile was tight and formal. "Yes, it's true. Silverblade is a good lawyer.

He did some work for me when he was at Nymann and Moss. They're the firm that handles a lot of my legal matters. I liked the way he operated, and when a position opened up at Emerald Bay I made sure that he got it."

"I hear that you're grooming him for something bigger."

Madame Cuapa put her goblet to her lips, hesitated, then put the glass on the table. "Nothing is official yet. But, yes, I've been thinking about moving him into the corporate offices at Greater Olmec. He's a bright fellow, and I'm making sure that he's well paid and happy."

"Mrs. Shipper told me that Silverblade is the one who introduced her to Donald Shipper. That he, in fact, engineered the meeting."

Falconwing downed his remaining wine in one gulp. It struck me that he'd only been taking refined little sips up until that moment.

Madame Cuapa frowned. When she spoke, I had the impression that she was choosing her words with care. "Yes.... I think I heard somewhere that he introduced Shipper to his wife. I don't recall the circumstances, though." She shrugged and looked up at me with a quizzical expression. "Is that important for some reason?"

On a hunch, I turned to Falconwing, who was wiping the corners of his mouth with a cloth napkin. "Do you know Silverblade?"

"Huh? Me?" Falconwing glanced at Madame Cuapa. "Any reason why I should?"

A thought popped in my head, and I ran with it. "I wondered if maybe he had ever introduced anyone to you. A young lady, maybe?"

Falconwing flinched. It was ever so slight, and if I hadn't been looking for it, I would have missed it. But it was a definite flinch. Putting an easy-going smile on his matinee-idol face, Falconwing made a quick effort to regain his composure. "You never know. I admit that I do a fair share of socializing, and people introduce people to me from time to time. Men *and* women. I've never seen any reason to discriminate. I don't remember a Silverblade, though." I kept his eyes locked in mine, and it took

him less than a second to look away. "Silverblade, Silverblade...,"
he trailed off, making a show of trying to remember the name. "Did
you say he was a troll?"

"No, I didn't."

"Well.... Silverblade sounds like a troll name. No..., no..., I
don't ever recall a troll introducing a young lady to me. I think I'd
remember that."

"Yes." I stared at his forehead. "I'm sure you would."

I glanced at Cody, who was maintaining a noncommittal
expression on his face and concentrating hard on looking at
nothing in particular.

"Done!" Old Itzel proclaimed, holding up her completed
cozy, her wrinkled face lit up in a smile of triumph.

***

On my way home, I called Detective Kalama. She didn't
answer, and I got her voice mail. "We need to take another look at
Silverblade," I told her. "Call me."

***

The sun had set by the time I pulled the beastmobile into
Gio's lot and started walking home. Clouds covered the sky, but the
air was still dry from the past week's unseasonable heat. I could
just make out the smell of the ocean in the west wind blowing at
me from across the street. I pulled my fedora down over my
forehead with one hand and buried my other hand in my coat
pocket. I wanted a whiskey to wash the wine off my palate and a
cheeseburger to fill my empty stomach. What I didn't want was to
sit in a noisy bar next to a pretty dame with strawberry-blond hair
and freckles across her nose who might have murdered her
husband a couple of days ago. I also didn't want to be late meeting
her, so I hustled home as quick as a jackrabbit so that I could wash
up, comb my hair, and put on a clean shirt.

I reached the Minotaur at nine o'clock on the dot. The
lounge would fill up and get livelier as the evening wore on, but so
far the night's crowd consisted of clusters of middle-aged swells

dressed in business suits and speaking in low troubled tones about the miserable state of the world while knocking back gin and tonics, martinis, and whiskey and sodas. I was inside in a side booth nursing a brew and munching on some deep-fried calamari when Mrs. Shipper came through the door. She was wearing three-inch heels that lengthened the calves of her legs. Her sleek navy blue dress stopped just short of her knees, and a light blue lacy shawl threatened to slide off her shoulders. Her matching navy blue cloth hat included a decorative veil that covered three-quarters of her face, because, after all, she was in mourning. The heads of the swells pivoted toward the door and the low buzz of conversations around me paused as Mrs. Shipper stood in the entryway and searched the room. When her eyes fell on me she smiled and walked my way. I stood and waited for her arrival. The disappointed swells all turned their eyes away from the two of us as they resumed their discussions.

Mrs. Shipper held out a gloved hand when she reached me, and I gave it a light squeeze. After we were seated, I asked her what she would like to drink.

"A white wine, please." I signaled to a cocktail waitress.

"How's your day been?" I asked her.

"About as good as could be expected," she answered. "Dwayne pestered me with questions about you. He's convinced that you're going to be his new stepfather. I let it slip that I was going to see you tonight, just to drive the little shit crazy. Kaylee and I have been screaming at each other all day. She still thinks she's going out on her boyfriend's yacht instead of coming to her father's funeral. Oh, and she threatened to call a moving company to pack all my belongings and put them in storage if I'm not out of the house by next week. Other than that, it's been peaches and cream."

"Are you really going to move out of the house?" I asked. "You don't have to, you know."

She shrugged. "To tell you the truth, I'm not sure I want to stay. The idea of moving away from those two brats is about the only thing keeping me sane!"

The cocktail waitress came then, and I ordered a glass of the house white for Mrs. Shipper, another beer for me, and some more calamari appetizers for the two of us.

When the waitress was gone, Mrs. Shipper opened her purse and took out a packet of cigarettes. She removed one for herself and then offered me the pack. I held up the palm of my hand. "No thank you. I never picked up the habit." She raised her eyebrows at me and then pulled out a lighter.

After she had taken her first slow puff and blown smoke at the ceiling, I got to business. "On the phone you told me that you had something you wanted to talk to me about."

"Yes." She took a second puff. "I don't know if it means anything, but it's very strange, and I thought I should tell you about it." She hesitated and took another drag on her cigarette before resuming. "Now that it comes down to it, I feel a little embarrassed. You're going to think that I'm off my rocker, but here goes." She took a deep breath to steady herself. "My house has become infested with crows."

I picked up my beer mug and held it just off the table. "Crows?"

"I know it sounds silly, Alex, but, please, hear me out. For the last several weeks, this flock of crows has been flying to my house. They come and go, but they come at least once or twice a day. They've been perching on my roof, sitting in my front yard or in my back yard."

"Crows do that."

"Yes, I know. But they never go to any of the neighbor's houses. Just mine. And, here's the crazy part." She tapped her cigarette on the side of the ashtray. "They peek through my bedroom window."

"Really."

"You think I'm nuts, don't you."

"No. Actually, I don't."

"They watch me!" Mrs. Shipper adjusted her veil with nervous fingers. "And they've been doing it for weeks!"

"What did your husband have to say about them?"

"Well, that's the other crazy part of all this. They never seemed to come around when he was home. Not that he was home

141

that much. He was *always* working. Or so he said." She puffed furiously on her cigarette.

The waitress came with our drinks and calamari. I thanked her and waited for her to leave before turning back to Mrs. Shipper.

"You think he was...."

"I'm not stupid, Alex. Donald started getting bored with me a week after we were married. In the past year, it got worse and worse."

"But these crows were never there when he was home?"

"Hardly ever! Weird, isn't it? And now that he's...gone...the crows don't seem to want to leave me alone. They came late last night and scratched and pecked at my bedroom window until I closed the curtains on them. Crows aren't dangerous, are they? I mean, they aren't that big, but they've got claws, and there's a lot of them. I was afraid to leave the house this morning. I don't want them to swoop down and start scratching at my face!"

Mrs. Shipper's eyes were wide and her lower lip quivered a little. She seemed to be aware of it and stuck her cigarette in her lips to keep them steady.

"It's weird, all right," I agreed. "But why are you coming to me? Shouldn't you call animal control if you're worried?"

Mrs. Shipper took her cigarette out of her mouth and stuck it in the ashtray. She leaned across the table. "I talked to Claudius Silverblade today. He called me to see how I was doing. He's always been very sweet to me. Anyway, he told me that you are working for a witch who might be involved in my husband's murder. Is that true? Be honest with me."

I took a sip of beer. "The identities of my clients are confidential," I explained. "But I can tell you what I've already told Silverblade and Mrs. Turlock: your husband was cursed by a witch."

Mrs. Shipper nodded. "These crows. They don't behave like normal crows. Do you think that a witch might be involved? I guess what I'm asking is, am I safe?"

I didn't know how I wanted to respond to that. I studied Mrs. Shipper's face. It was the face of someone who was holding back real fear. The were-crow, whoever it was, seemed to have a thing for Mrs. Shipper. That was interesting. Had the were-crow been behind Donald Shipper's death? It was certainly possible. Was it a danger to Mrs. Shipper? That was just as possible.

"Would you like me to follow you home tonight?" I asked. "If the crows are there, I may have some ways of dealing with them."

"No!" Mrs. Shipper objected. "I don't want to face them tonight. I'll be moving out of that house pretty soon, and, until I do, I'm thinking of checking myself into a hotel. It will be inconvenient, since I still have to deal with Donald's funeral, but, to be honest, those crows are giving me the heebie-jeebies. I can face them in the daylight, but at night.... At night, it's a different story."

Mrs. Shipper picked up her wine glass and downed it in a few gulps. "I could use something stronger...." She looked up at me, pleading with her soft brown eyes.

So I bought her a glass of whiskey and water. I ordered some whiskey, straight, for myself. When those drinks were gone, I ordered another round. Things got a little fuzzy after that. Sometime around midnight, I offered to let her stay at my place, where she'd be safe, and we left the Minotaur together, arm in arm.

***

I woke up to the sound of heavy, persistent pounding on my front door. It had to be cops. Everyone else used the doorbell. But cops love the sound of their knuckles beating on door panels. They think that the rapping makes them sound more authoritative than chiming bells. The last thing I wanted to do was open my eyes and roll out of bed, but the boys in blue seemed ready to kick in the door if I didn't. Well, let 'em, I thought. I could afford a new door. I let myself sink deeper into my sheets.

"Shouldn't you answer that?"

My eyes shot open. Mrs. Shipper lay next to me, huddled under the blankets, her alarmed face a foot away from my own. The memory of the previous evening came back to me in a flash, along with a searing pain in my temples.

"Morning, sunshine." Mrs. Shipper pulled herself closer to me until her head was touching my shoulder. "I don't know who's

143

doing all that knocking, but, on the bright side, at least we know it isn't my husband."

"Let's hope not," I muttered. "Sorry about my breath."

Mrs. Shipper's smile broadened. "If that's *all* you're sorry about I'll call it a win." She raised herself up on her elbow. "Who *is* that?" she asked. "They're making enough noise to wake the dead!" The she covered her mouth and giggled. "Oops! Maybe my husband will be showing up after all!"

I reminded myself that everyone handles grief in their own way.

I was relieved to discover that, except for my shoes, I was still fully clothed. I wasn't sure about the woman in my bed, who was still under the covers. I found her eyes with my own. "I need to ask you a question."

Mrs. Shipper kissed my forehead. "No." She smiled. "We didn't. Can't say I didn't try, but you're a tough nut to crack." She threw off the covers then, and I saw that she was still in her dress. "I'll never get the wrinkles out of this thing. Guess I'll have to buy me a new one."

I got out of bed and opened my window. Looking down, I saw three uniformed cops at my front door. "You mugs want to keep the noise down?" I yelled. "Some of us are trying to sleep off hangovers!"

"Police!" one of the blues shouted up at me, as if I couldn't tell. "Open up!"

"Yeah, yeah. Hold your horses, I'll be there in a minute." I closed the window.

I turned to Mrs. Shipper. "Stay here. I'll see what this is about."

"Don't worry about me." She sank back under the covers. "I could use more sleep. I may have had a little too much to drink last night."

I went into the bathroom, took care of business, and changed out of my clothes into a robe. I left the bedroom, closing the door behind me. I passed through my living room to the stairs and took my time climbing down. By the time I got to my office, the cops were once again pounding on the door. I unlocked the door and yanked it open. "You bulls need to learn some manners."

"Can the wise-lip." One of the officers, apparently the leader, sneered at me. "We're taking you downtown. Captain wants to see you."

"Captain! In that case, I'll shower up and put on a tie. You boys can wait in my office. I'll put on some coffee."

The lead officer tried to get tough. "No time for that. Get going!"

"Don't be silly." I stepped into my office, leaving the door wide open. "I've got all day."

"The captain says now!"

"Your captain can conduct an unnatural act on himself."

"Huh?" The lead officer looked confused.

"He says that the captain can fuck himself," explained one of the other officers, being helpful.

"What?" The lead officer's face reddened. "Why I oughta...."

"Yes," I agreed. "You should. But first I'm going to wash up and get dressed. I don't think that your captain wants you dragging me into his office in my robe. Think about what that would look like."

While the lead officer thought this over, I walked to the stairs and began to climb. "Be right down," I called back. "You boys make yourselves at home."

Once in my living room, I took out my phone and hit the speed-dial for Lubank's office. Gracie picked up after one ring. "Lubank's Law Office. How may I help you?"

"Hi Gracie, it's me. The boss in?"

"How many times I gotta tell you—I'm the boss around here. You just get outta bed? Whatcha wearin'?"

"White boxers with little pink hearts."

"Ooooo," Gracie moaned. "You're making me all quivery. Robby's not here. Why don't you pop on over before he gets back?"

"Sorry, Doll-Face. Some coppers want to take me to their clubhouse to meet their captain. They seem to be in a hurry."

"Oh, Sugar. What've you done now?"

"Who knows? Maybe they need a fourth for bridge."

"I'll let Robby know the minute I see him, Sweetie. You know the drill. Nothing but name, rank, and serial number until he gets there. And be polite!"

A shout came from downstairs: "Come on, pally. We ain't got all day!"

"I've gotta go, Baby," I told Gracie. "The buttons are getting restless."

"Don't let them break your pretty little nose again," advised Gracie.

After I disconnected, I went back into the bedroom. "Everything okay?" Mrs. Shipper asked, keeping her voice low.

"They're taking me downtown. You can stay as long as you like. I've got eggs in the fridge."

"Thanks. You're sweet, but I should be getting home. I'll call myself a cab. And thanks again for letting me stay the night. It helped." She met my eyes and grinned. "Maybe next time you'll be less of a gentleman."

"We'll see."

I went into the bathroom, splashed some cold water on my face, gargled, and got dressed. When I came out of the bathroom, Mrs. Shipper pulled a delicate hand out from under the covers and gave me a small wave. "Good luck," she breathed.

I returned her wave. "Likewise."

After closing the bedroom door behind me, I paused and took a long deep breath. My head was filled with the image of Mrs. Shipper's freckled nose and her strawberry-blond hair spread over my pillow. Then I shook myself awake and prepared to go meet the law, hoping with every fiber of my being that the gorgeous doll curled up under the bed covers in the room I'd just left had not been involved in the death of her husband.

Chapter Thirteen

When I got downstairs, the officers surrounded me and hustled me out the door to the back seat of a prowl car. Two of the officers sat in front, and the lead officer drove away solo in his own black-and-white. He took the point so that the rest of us wouldn't get lost on the way. He even used his siren to get us through the red lights. I wondered whether there was any real urgency or if he was just showing off. Probably the latter.

When we got to the station, the officers whisked me through the waiting area and straight into an interrogation room. I've probably been questioned in all of the Yerba City Police Department sweatboxes at one time or another. The building contains several such rooms. I don't know how many, because they all look the same: small, boxy, a camera in one of the upper corners, a one-way glass on one of the walls, and one metal table attached to the floor in the center of the room. The officers told me to sit down in a chair on the far side of the table, so I did. They disappeared without cuffing me, which I took to be a good sign.

After a thirty-minute wait that made me wonder why the cops had been in such a dither to get me there, the door to the room opened and a troll walked in. He was well dressed in expensive casual clothing: dark brown linen slacks and a short-sleeved light green silk shirt with no tie. Two long, thick cigars stuck out the top of his shirt pocket. Like all trolls, this one was massive, close to eight feet tall and more than five hundred pounds, with biceps like medicine balls and a chest like a full-grown bull's. This troll also had a gut the size of a hot-air balloon, but I wasn't going to criticize him for it. The pointed tip of his right ear was a mass of scar tissue, as if someone had once tried to burn it off. More scar tissue streaked down the right side of his face from his hairless skull to just past the corner of his glowing red eye. He held a cigar stub the size of a small tree stump at the corner of his thick, ruddy lips.

The troll raised the palm of his hand. "Don't get up, Southerland. I'm Captain Coldgrave."

147

Troll names. I guess you can't expect something that big and menacing to be named Fuzzypuppers.

The last captain of the Yerba City Police Department that I had met was a politically ambitious human slimeball named Graham. He had used his office to peddle influence, conduct dirty jobs of behalf of the mayor's office, direct a street gang, and run all kinds of rackets that I'll probably never know about. Ostensibly a family man, he had also kept a mistress—an adaro water nymph named Leena—in a downtown luxury townhouse. Graham had been involved in the murder of Leena's sister, a basically decent, if borderline homicidal young fireball named Mila, and I had been instrumental in making sure that he paid for that crime. I'd been told that Graham had been replaced by a troll who had formerly been in charge of the vice department in the Angel City Police Department, and I deduced that I was looking at him now. I didn't doubt that he had already formed a strong opinion about the private dick who had been partly responsible for the shakeup of the YCPD, and, by extension, his own promotion. I hoped that he was grateful.

Coldgrave clamped down on his cigar stub with his teeth. "I hear you're a piece of shit."

So much for hope.

Coldgrave pulled the cigar out of his mouth. "Well?"

"Well what?"

"Are you a piece of shit?"

"Is that a trick question?" I asked.

Coldgrave's thick lips widened into a smug smile as he replaced the cigar stub back between his lips. He lowered himself into a chair opposite the table from me, his back to the door, and looked me up and down with his flaming troll eyes. I flashed back to the last time I'd sat opposite a troll in a YCPD sweatbox. For all I knew, this was the same room. I slipped my tongue into the empty socket where my tooth had been. At least my face had healed. Mostly. I braced myself for the worst.

Coldgrave's smile widened. "Relax, Southerland." The troll appeared to be following his own advice. "You're not in any trouble. I just wanted to meet the son of a bitch who killed my predecessor."

"You've been fed some bogus dope, partner. I didn't kill Graham."

"You got him squibbed," Coldgrave countered. "Amounts to the same thing."

"Graham got himself whacked. That asshole was his own worst enemy."

Coldgrave rubbed the scar tissue near his eye. "Maybe so," he admitted. "Internal Affairs says that Graham was up to his neck in graft, and he paid the price. But he was a cop, and you had a hand in his death. That makes you a piece of shit." The troll leaned back in his chair and moved his cigar stub to the other side of his mouth without using his hands. "But that's not why you're here today."

"Well, that's dandy. If I agree that I'm a piece of shit, you think that I could get a cup of coffee? I had to run out of my house this morning without any."

Coldgrave sat up straight and once again removed his cigar stub from his mouth. "What? You want coffee?"

"That's right. Black, please."

"This look like a fuckin' café to you?" Coldgrave crushed his cigar stub out on the top of the table.

I glanced at the crushed stub. "It's lacking a little something in ambience, and the service is lousy, but if the coffee's hot I'll give it a good review."

Coldgrave stared at me, and then he began to laugh. "You're a card," he forced out between chuckles. "A real card. They didn't tell me you was a funny man. Lacking in ambience—that's a good one!" He laughed a little more and wiped a non-existent tear out of one red eye.

I got impatient, which is maybe what the troll wanted. "Look, Coldgrave. You seem like a real swell guy, and I could trade gags with you all day, but your boys said you were all in a buzz to see me. So why don't we cut the crap and get on with it. I got some supermarket flyers in the mail yesterday, and those coupons aren't going to clip themselves."

"Huh? What's that you say? Oh, I get it. You've got better things to do than hang around here wagging chins with the likes of me. Okee, dokie." He sighed, long and slow, and shook his head. It was all theater, but I wasn't getting the point. Why was I here? Coldgrave looked into the one-way glass at some unseen figure on the other side, pantomimed drinking from a cup, and pointed at himself and me. "Black," he called out at the glass. He turned back to me, smiling. "We'll get you that coffee."

Then, with no warning, he pasted me right in the kisser with a lightning jab from out of left field. Stunned by the suddenness of the punch, I tumbled ass backwards over my chair, crashed into the wall, and slid to the floor in a heap. I wiped my lip and examined the smear of scarlet on my hand. I pulled a handkerchief from my pocket and pressed it on my lip. At least my remaining teeth were all in place. With an effort, I staggered to my feet and pulled my chair up from where it had fallen. I slid it back to the table and lowered myself back down into it with as much grace as I could muster.

"You're a funny man, Southerland." Coldgrave wasn't laughing now. "A regular comedian. But one thing you should know about me: I'm not a big fan of comedy. Got that, funny man?"

"Yes sir. Loud and clear." Hard as he had hit me, I knew that the troll had pulled his punch. Otherwise, my head would be dangling off my neck. Coldgrave had been a longtime veteran of the Angel City police force before coming up north, which meant that he'd had a lot of time to hone his interrogation skills. I figured that he knew just how much juice he could put into a punch without doing any meaningful damage.

"Hnff," Coldgrave grunted once I was reseated. "Well, you're probably wondering why I called you in here today."

I bit back on a clever retort and pressed my handkerchief down harder on my lip.

Coldgrave leaned forward and used his hand to swipe his crushed cigar stub off the table and onto the floor. He pulled a fresh cigar, about a foot long and nearly two inches thick, out of his shirt pocket. He bit off the end and spit it to the floor. He shoved the head of the unlit cigar into his mouth. "Tell me everything you know about Dwayne Shipper."

"Dwayne Shipper?" I hadn't been expecting that. "You mean Donald Shipper's kid?"

"That's the one." Coldgrave pulled a lighter the size of a hand grenade out of his pants pocket. "He was killed last night."

"What?"

"Slashed to ribbons." Coldgrave flicked a three-inch flame out of his lighter and held it up to the end of his cigar. "And his heart and eyes are missing."

***

Coldgrave kept me in the sweatbox for an hour, and I never could figure out what he wanted from me. At least he hadn't slugged me again. Once was enough to convince me to put a lid on the funny business and be straight with him. It's not like I had much to tell him anyway. What I knew about Dwayne Shipper could fit into the bottom of a shot glass. He showed me some photos of the crime scene, and I could see that someone had really done a number on the kid. Like Coyot, Dwayne had been sliced to ribbons. He had bloody holes where his eyes used to be, and he had a big hole in his chest. Coyot's corpse still had its eyes when I had seen it on his office floor two nights earlier. Had the heart still been in his chest? I didn't know. I remembered a lot of blood, but I hadn't examined the body all that closely. Either way, the killings had to be related. Two people with a connection to the Donald Shipper murder being reduced to bloody messes on consecutive nights? Some people claim that they don't believe in coincidences. I wouldn't go that far. In a world of infinite possibilities, some amount of coincidence is inevitable. But I was convinced that this was not one of those times.

When Coldgrave decided he'd had enough of me, he sent me packing. Detective Kalama was waiting for me near the front door.

"Had any breakfast?" she asked me.

"I don't know if I can eat. My teeth are a little loose."

"I hear you're a tough guy." She held the door open for me. "You can suck down some soft-boiled eggs. Let's go."

I followed her out of the station, and neither of us spoke until we reached the street. The wind whistled as it passed between buildings, and the sun was lost behind a thick layer of clouds. It

151

was hard to believe that we were just a couple of days removed from a record-breaking heat wave, but that's Yerba City for you. Each year will bring a few days of unseasonable heat and a few days of unseasonable frost, but it's always quick to revert to the norm: foggy, windy, and damp. It was my kind of weather. I jammed my hat down on my head with one hand and pulled my coat tight across my chest with the other.

"What was that all about?" I asked Kalama as we took a right up the sidewalk.

"To be honest, I think that the captain just wanted to get to know you."

"Hell of a way to introduce himself," I dabbed at my lip with my bloody handkerchief.

"What, that? That was just his way of saying he likes you."

"He needs to work on his small talk."

"Listen, Southerland. Coldgrave only lays his hands on two kinds of people. Those he likes, and those he doesn't like. You can tell which is which by how hard he hits them. You're still conscious, so he must like you."

"What if he doesn't know whether he likes you or not?" I asked.

"It doesn't take him long to form an opinion one way or the other."

"And I'm on his good side?"

"For now. But be careful. He's been known to change his mind."

Kalama turned into a corner diner called The Acorn Grill across the street from the police station, and I followed her inside. She led me to an empty booth as far from the front door as she could get and sat with her back to the wall. I sat down across the table from her. It was mid-morning, an hour past the breakfast rush, so the place was nearly empty. A waitress who looked like she should be sitting at a desk in Antonio's algebra class hustled over and set a couple of glasses of water on the table in front of us. She had a cute fresh face and a black braid that hung down her back past her waist.

The waitress arched an eyebrow at me, then turned to Kalama and smiled without saying anything.

"Coffee for both of us," Kalama told her. "He wants his black."

"Could you bring me two eggs and a slice of ham with that coffee?" I asked the waitress.

"How do you want the eggs?" she asked.

"Lookin' at me. And a couple of slices of sourdough toast."

The waitress turned back at Kalama. "You eating?"

"No, just coffee."

The waitress glanced at me with an odd expression that looked like a mixture of curiosity and hostility and left without writing anything down.

"You must come here a lot." I used a spoon to fish a cube of ice out of my water and pressed it on my lip.

Kalama glanced at the ice on my lip and smiled. "Why do you say that?"

"She didn't ask you how you wanted your coffee. And she seems to know you."

"She's wondering who you are."

"Me? Why?"

"She wants to know why her mother is having coffee with a strange man with a fat lip."

"She's your daughter?"

"Yup."

"Shouldn't she be in school?" I asked.

"Graduated last year. She's older than she looks.

I stared at Kalama. "She's not the only one."

"Well aren't you the charmer!" Kalama smiled at me. It was a nice smile. "But Nalani's as old now as I was when I brought her into this world."

"So you're, what, about thirty-eight? Thirty-nine?"

Kalama's smile twisted, but her eyes looked amused. "Don't you know that it's impolite to ask a woman her age?"

"You kind of brought it up," I pointed out.

"Next you'll be asking me if I'm married." She chuckled. "Look at you. You're getting embarrassed."

"So?"

"So what?"

"So are you married?"

153

"Yes, very much so. Not to Nalani's father, though. I relieved him of the responsibility of fatherhood as soon as he found out I was pregnant, and he was so grateful that we never saw or heard from each other again, which is the way I want it. I met Kai a couple of years after Nalani was born, and we've been happily married for fourteen years. He's a history professor at YCU. He also heads up an archeological dig in Azteca outside Teotihuacan, which is where he's been for the last month. That's why your waitress is so curious about you. I'm sure she's thinking the worst about both of us."

"Terrific. I hope she doesn't take it out on my eggs."

"She won't. She thinks that her dad neglects me. She's probably hoping that I'm having a spicy affair with a tall dark younger man. Oh dear, you're blushing again. Don't worry. Despite my daughter's suspicions, Kai and I couldn't be happier with each other."

At that point, Nalani came by with our coffees. Kalama looked up at her and waved a hand toward me. "Nalani, meet Southerland. He's a private investigator helping me on a case. Southerland, meet my daughter, Nalani."

Nalani smiled at me then. "Nice to meet you." She offered me her hand.

I gave it a shake. "Likewise. Your mother's a good cop."

"I hope so. Most of them are incompetent assholes."

"Nalani!"

"Well it's true, Mom. You tell me so all the time."

"Well, yeah," Kalama admitted. "But that's not something you want to be tossing around to anyone you meet."

Nalani looked at me with a smile as sweet as strawberries and announced, "Your eggs will be ready in a minute, sir." She turned and walked away, her braid whipping past my head as it swung after her.

"She seems like a nice girl."

"Careful, hotshot. I think she likes you now. She's not nearly as innocent as those dimples make her look, and she's reached a phase where she thinks that older men are cool and mysterious. Especially ones with scars and interesting faces."

"I'll watch my back."

154

"You won't be the only one," Kalama warned me.

I held up my hands in mock surrender and gave her my best look of innocence.

Kalama smiled and took a sip of coffee. "I had another late night last night."

"Your captain told me that the Shipper kid was killed."

Kalama nodded. "That's two suspicious deaths in two nights. Both vics look like they were mauled by an animal, although I haven't seen any lab reports yet. Both of them people of interest in our case." She looked up at me. "Thoughts?"

"Gotta be connected. But we need more info. If the killer was an animal, was it the same one? Coldgrave said that Dwayne Shipper's heart and eyes were ripped out." The detective nodded. "Coyot still had his eyes," I noted, "but I don't know about the heart."

"It was cut out, too. We didn't catch that at first because of all the blood, but when we heard about the Shipper kid, we checked, and sure enough."

"Definitely related, then," I said, and Kalama nodded. "And I'm right in the middle of it," I added. "Coyot wouldn't be involved in any of this if I hadn't brought him into it."

Kalama frowned. "What I want to know is where Cuapa fits into the picture."

"Wish I knew." I took a sip of my coffee. "These two killings are connected to the original one, and Cuapa's in that one up to her eyeballs. But these other two deaths are different. Donald Shipper's body exploded a week after he was cursed. Nothing left of him but red slime. Coyot and Shipper's son were torn apart by something with claws, or at least something *like* claws. And someone removed their hearts and took them away. That sounds more like a man than an animal."

"Or maybe an animal did the killing and a man took the heart."

"A were-crow could have done both," I pointed out.

"And the kid lost his eyes, although maybe they were just slashed out in the fight."

I considered this. "Or pecked out."

Kalama nodded. "Could have been the were-crow. Could have been a big dog."

I didn't respond. Kalama gave me a hard look, full of meaning. "Or maybe it was someone with a vicious pet."

I shook my head. "No."

"Sure about that? I hear that a certain witch keeps a manticore in her parlor. And that she has a mysterious manservant who tends to it."

I shook my head. "Look. Mr. Whiskers is a monster. Big as a big lion. Bigger. Claws bigger than this knife and a lot more lethal. But a manticore didn't kill Coyot or the kid."

"What makes you say that?"

"Because a manticore can swallow a full-grown man in three bites. Those stiffs were a mess, but they would have been beyond recognition if Mr. Whiskers had got to them, and that's if we found any pieces of them at all."

Kalama nodded. "True. But I'd still like to talk to that servant."

"Like it or not, we'll have to see what Cuapa says about that." I took another sip of coffee. "Better leave Cody to me. If I get suspicious of him, I'll tell you, but I don't think that he or the manticore had anything to do with this. My money's on the were-crow, but we'll have to see what the lab reports say."

The detective frowned, but nodded. "All right. We'll do it your way for now. Lieutenant Sanjaya still doesn't want me to get too close to Cuapa. But that doesn't mean you get to stand between her and me, gumshoe. If I want to put the screws on the witch or the servant, I don't need your permission to do it."

"I'm telling you everything I know."

"No you're not. You're protecting your client. I get it, that's your job. But we've got three in the morgue now, and it needs to stop. You hearing me?" Kalama met my eyes and held them steady.

"I'm hearing you," I assured her.

Kalama nodded, but continued to hold my eyes. "What about these two witches staying with Cuapa? You talk to them yet?"

"Yeah, I saw them at Cuapa's house yesterday afternoon. Both of them need to be on our radar. Falconwing looks like a movie star and lives like one, too, from what I gather. He's next in

156

line to lead Cuapa's coven if she gets shoved out of the picture. And it's a big coven, too. More than a hundred members."

"No shit? Hell, that's a fucking army!"

"Yeah," I agreed. "Cuapa doesn't seem inclined to use them like one, but Falconwing could be a different story. He strikes me as, I don't know, less inhibited than Madame Cuapa."

"What about the other witch?" asked Kalama.

"They call her Old Itzel. She's a gnome, and she looks like she's a million years old. She's gotta be two hundred, at least. Hellspawn live longer than humans, but she's old even for a gnome. She was a member of the coven before Cuapa was born, back when Cuapa's father was in charge. Crusty old bitch! She claims that she wants no part of leading a coven, but I think she'd be more dangerous than Falconwing if she did. There's something about her. She tries to come across as a toothless old crone, like a once-feared queen in her declining years, but I'm not buying it. I think she's still got a lot in the tank."

"Do you think that either of them are powerful enough to force Cuapa to curse someone against her will?" Kalama asked.

I sipped my coffee and thought about the detective's question. It had been on my mind, too. "Cuapa doesn't think so. She says that spells contain the personality of the spell-caster, and that she would have recognized Falconwing or Itzel in the compulsion spell if either one of them had cast it. Also, she seems confident that neither of them are good enough to take her one-on-one."

"Do you believe her?"

"I have to assume that she knows what she's talking about."

"Hmmm."

"But that doesn't mean that one of them couldn't have found a way past her defenses," I added. "Truth is, I'm not sure what to think. I don't know enough."

Kalama nodded and mulled it over. After gulping down some coffee, she looked across her cup at me. "What about the pretty widow? The Shippers are dropping like flies. It would be a shame to lose more of them."

This was the question I'd been dreading, but I was spared for the moment by the arrival of my ham and eggs. Nalani put my plate in front of me and topped off our coffee cups. She gave me a pleasant smile. "Enjoy your meal." Her eyes lingered knowingly on her mother as she turned away from the table and headed back down the diner toward the kitchen.

Kalama shook her head. "I'm definitely going to be talking to her tonight," she muttered.

We took a break from discussing business while I grabbed a bottle of red pepper sauce from the condiments tray, poured a liberal amount over the eggs, and attacked my breakfast like a starving hyena.

Kalama watched me with a look of awe. "When's the last time you ate?" she asked me.

"Can't remember," I mumbled around a mouthful of ham soaked in egg yolk. In less than a minute, the ham and egg whites were history. I began using a slice of toast to scrape up leftover pepper-sauced egg yolk and tried not to think about slashed bodies leaking puddles of blood.

When my plate was scraped clean, I leaned back, satisfied, and sipped some coffee.

"The widow?" Kalama prompted.

"Hmm? Oh yeah." I cleared my throat. "I talked to her again last night. She met me at the Black Minotaur Lounge."

"Oh? Do tell?"

"She wanted to get away from her stepchildren."

"I'll bet!" Kalama's lip twisted into a half-smile as she folded her arms across the table and leaned forward, eager to listen to my story.

I had a sudden desire for more coffee.

"Out with it. Spare no details."

"It's not as bad as all that."

"Uh-huh."

"We had some drinks," I began. "She told me that she's been bothered by crows for the past several weeks. She said they'd been coming to her house every day and watching her. Nobody else's house, just hers. She says that they came to her window a couple of nights ago and acted like they wanted to get inside. She was afraid to go home last night."

"You think it was the were-crow?"

158

"Without a doubt."

"And the stepson was slashed up by an animal last night."

"Yup."

Kalama nodded. "Okay. So then what?"

"We drank too much and I took her home with me."

Kalama leveled her eyes at me. "That wasn't very professional of you."

"No," I admitted. "It wasn't. But I kept my hands to myself."

"That must have taken some of the fun out of it."

"She just slept there, that's all. In her dress." I held up two fingers pressed together. "Scout's honor."

Kalama studied my face. "Uh-huh. Was she still there when the boys rousted you this morning?"

"Yeah, but she kept out of sight."

Kalama's eyes narrowed while she examined my story for plausibility. After a few seconds, she nodded and folded her hands in front of her on the tabletop. "Continue."

"She got a little drunk last night. And at one point she told me something interesting. The first time I talked to her, back at her house the other day, she told me that Silverblade had introduced her to her husband. She said that he had played matchmaker for the two of them after Shipper's second divorce, and she made it sound like he had done it to help out his boss. I made note of it, but didn't pay it much mind at the time. But last night she told me that Shipper wasn't the only man that Silverblade had set her up with. He'd previously hooked her up with two other gents. Both of them well-heeled. And both of them married."

"You think Silverblade has some kind of racket going?"

"It's possible," I nodded. "Mrs. Shipper also told me that Silverblade didn't stop introducing her husband to other ladies after she married him. Young ladies." I paused.

"How young?" Kalama asked.

"Young. Teens. Early teens."

"Alkwat's flaming balls!" hissed the detective through clenched teeth.

"She kept calling them 'his little toys.' She said that Silverblade kept him supplied with 'cute little play toys.'"

"Lord Alkwat's balls!" Kalama's expression was hard as steel. "Those fucking assholes!"

"There's more. I asked the witches about Silverblade yesterday. Cuapa confirmed that she got him his job at Emerald Bay, and that she was grooming him for something bigger. But she wasn't comfortable talking about it. I thought I detected a tell from Falconwing when Silverblade's name was mentioned, and I caught him off guard by asking him if Silverblade had ever introduced any young ladies to him. He said no, but he was lying, and not doing a good job of it. Oh, and Falconwing also likes them young. And he isn't particular about gender, either. It's possible that Silverblade's racket might include a variety of delights."

"Shit," Kalama muttered, looking down at the table. Then she looked up and met my eyes. "Wait a minute! What was that you said about Cuapa? That she was grooming Silverblade for something? And that she didn't want to talk about it?"

I didn't move.

"Are you trying to tell me that Cuapa's involved in Silverblade's racket?"

I still didn't move.

"Wait! Are you trying to say that Cuapa is *in charge* of Silverblade's racket?"

I reached for my coffee cup and took a long slow sip.

***

When Nalani brought the check, I picked it up, and Kalama didn't object. As we walked out of the diner together, I looked back over my shoulder and watched Nalani bring water to two graying squires who stared at her backside as she walked back to the kitchen. When she was out of sight, they turned to each other with lascivious grins and giggled like twelve-year-old boys who had just discovered how to disconnect the parental controls on their internet server. I decided that if I ever had a daughter I wouldn't let her out of my house until she was thirty, which was a good reason for me to never have a daughter.

"I want to talk to Mrs. Shipper," I told Kalama when we were outside.

"I'll drive you."

I started to object, but one look at the detective's determined expression told me that it would be a bad idea. "All right," I conceded. "But I need to call Madame Cuapa first."

"Go ahead. Wait here while I get my car."

After the detective left I punched in Madame Cuapa's home number on my phone, but received no answer. You'd think that the Madame would invest in voice mail, but I guessed that she was too old-fashioned for that. She was probably downtown holding a board meeting, or buying up stocks, or otherwise taking care of her CEO business. I decided not to bother her at work but resolved to call her again at her house later in the day. I had business with Madame Cuapa, and she was going to see me before the day was done whether she wanted to or not.

I wondered how Mrs. Shipper was coping with her stepson's death, especially coming so soon after the murder of her husband. She had never in my presence referred to the kid as anything but a shit and a monster, and little love seemed to be lost between them, but the two of them had lived together as mother and son for five years, and it seemed to me that over that time they must have a had a least a few bonding moments. Then again, maybe not. Sometimes familiarity breeds nothing but contempt. Maybe the initial resentments resulting from two strangers vying for the attention of the same central figure had blossomed into a mutual hatred that festered over the years like a wasting disease. Had the stepmother had a hand in her stepson's death? She had an alibi, and it occurred to me then how convenient that alibi was. All the more reason to see her as soon as possible. Even more disturbing was my sudden desire to go home and give myself the shave and shower that I'd missed that morning, to make myself more presentable before seeing Mrs. Shipper again. Well, screw that! This wasn't going to be a social call. I shoved my hands into my coat pockets and waited for the detective.

161

"You think that Silverblade is running an unlicensed sex-trafficking ring out of this city?" Kalama braked behind a line of cars stopped at the red light.

"Right now, it's just a theory," I admitted. "But it's got a few things going for it."

"Your theory's got some holes in it," Kalama pointed out.

"Yes, it does," I agreed. "But that just means we need more info."

"You think that Silverblade is procuring young girls for people like Shipper."

"And Falconwing. Girls *and* boys, in his case."

"Which means that his operation extends into Angel City."

"Maybe further."

The light changed, and traffic began to worm its way forward. Kalama looked thoughtful for a few moments, then frowned. "How does he have the time to run a racket like that? You'd think that heading up legal services at Emerald Bay would keep him plenty busy."

"I don't know. Maybe it's not that much extra work. What does it take to arrange a meet between one person and another? Maybe a couple of phone calls?"

"What about lining up the talent? Where do they come from? Is he running a smuggling operation?" Kalama made a quick lane change to get around a double-parked delivery truck. "And then there's transportation, and I'm sure there's some health issues."

"Silverblade is most likely a facilitator. He might not have that much personal contact with the merchandise, or even with the clients."

"And he might not even be in charge of the racket," Kalama noted. "He might be a cut-out insulating someone higher up."

"Yeah, maybe." I didn't like the idea that Madame Cuapa might be operating a network that hooked underaged girls and boys up with wealthy clients. I didn't want the pieces to fit. But for now, it was a good working model. I thought about how the YCPD had reacted when Madame Cuapa's name came up in the Shipper investigation. The department had dropped the case like a hot potato. The police brass wanted no part of her, which meant that she was free to do whatever she pleased.

Well, who was I to squawk? I was taking her money, wasn't I? I needed some answers from Madame Cuapa. I still wanted to get to the bottom of Shipper's murder, not to mention the deaths of Coyot and Dwayne, but at this point I didn't know if I was working *for* Madame Cuapa or *against* her.

Something must have shown on my face. Kalama, who had been watching me, brushed a loose strand of hair from her face and turned back to scan the traffic. "Hey, don't beat yourself up, kid. We're making some big assumptions. First, we're assuming that Mrs. Shipper was telling the truth when she told you that Silverblade was supplying her husband with young girls. Second, even if she was telling the truth, it doesn't mean that Silverblade is involved in some kind of organized crime. Maybe he just knows a lot of people and is good at matchmaking. Third, even if Silverblade is crooked, maybe Cuapa has nothing to do with his sex-trafficking racket. What have you really got on her besides the fact that she's taken an interest in Silverblade's career?"

I picked at the stubble on my chin. "She didn't want to talk about Silverblade. Why not? There's something fishy going on there."

"Maybe. But it could be anything."

"I hope so." I sat back and watched as Kalama raced through a yellow light just in time to pull up behind the line of cars waiting for the next light to change.

"Okay. Let's try this on for size. Say that Cuapa is at the top, overseeing the operation. She leads a coven with members scattered all over western Tolanica, maybe further. She has ready access to a pool of loyal personnel. They're witches, but they could be other things, too. Like drivers, talent scouts, accountants, muscle, whatever she needs for the operation to work. Silverblade is her lieutenant. According to the pretty widow, he's a sociable guy. He attends conventions and other functions. He brings people

164

together. Cuapa rakes in the dough, and Silverblade gets a big slice of the pie."

I picked it up from there. "And then Silverblade and Shipper have a falling out. Shipper threatens to expose the racket and blow it out of the water. So Silverblade complains to Cuapa, and she knocks Shipper off."

"But why a curse?" Kalama asked. "Why not a bullet to the back of the head?"

"Cuapa's curse is showy. It sends a message to the other clients: don't fuck with me!"

Kalama frowned. "Hnnph! But then why does she go and hire a private dick and tell him that someone else made her do it, and please go find him for me before I kill again? Especially when the gumshoe might be lucky enough to stumble into her trafficking racket?"

"Don't you mean *smart* enough?"

Kalama glanced at me. "You don't *look* that smart. Maybe she took one gander at you and figured you for a patsy."

"Hmmm. But what's the angle? What am I supposed to be the fall guy for?"

The detective shrugged. "Who knows? Maybe that's still to come."

That wasn't reassuring. "Okay, so how about this. What if Silverblade was behind Shipper's murder. Maybe he's ambitious and wants to edge Cuapa out of the racket. He finds a way to make her bump off Shipper in a way that implicates her and then uses the murder to push her aside."

"That's a lot of guesswork," Kalama noted.

"Guesswork is about all we've got at the moment."

"And how do Coyot and Dwayne Shipper fit into the picture?" asked Kalama. "Or do they?"

I shrugged and gave up, at least for the time being. It was too much speculation leaking out of too few facts. I couldn't hold it all in place. The pieces started to whirl around in my head, which was starting to ache even worse than it had when I woke up that morning.

I turned to Kalama. "Are we there yet?"

She smiled. "Anxious to see the pretty widow again?"

165

I sniffed. "Well, I wish the coppers hadn't run me out of the house without giving me time to brush my teeth."

Kalama took advantage of an opening in the traffic and changed into a faster-moving lane. "Listen, loverboy. If you were fresh enough to take me to breakfast and meet my daughter this morning, you'll be fine and dandy for a chat with a murder suspect."

***

The Shipper home was a beehive of activity when we arrived there. Since it was a crime scene, we had to sign in with the sergeant at the front door. Scanning the names on the list, I was surprised to see a familiar one.

Kalama saw it, too, and looked up at me. "What's Lubank doing here?"

I shrugged. "Beats the hell out of me. Let's go find out."

We walked past a cop carrying a loaded cardboard box, presumably filled with evidence from the late Dwayne Shipper's room, out the front door.

Kalama scowled. "That's probably the kid's porno collection. The boys always find some justification to collect that kind of shit, but in this case it might be legitimate evidence. You'll never guess what was on the little pervert's computer last night when the killer caught him."

"Do I get three tries?"

"I'll spare you the effort. The vic was watching video of his stepmother sunbathing nude in the back yard. From the angle it looks like he took it himself through his bedroom window with his phone. We found a bottle of baby lotion and a box of tissues on the floor. And the kid wasn't wearing pants."

I shook my head. "Figures."

We walked through the house to the dining room, where we found Mrs. Shipper sitting at the table with her stepdaughter, Kaylee. Standing next to Kaylee, head barely clearing the tabletop, was Rob Lubank. A stack of three or four stapled sheets of paper lay in front of Mrs. Shipper, and Lubank was holding out a pen.

"Sign the agreement, Mrs. Shipper," the lawyer was saying. "It's in the best interests of all parties."

"What's going on?" I asked.

"Southerland! Th'fuck you doing here? This is a business matter that doesn't concern you, so butt out." The lawyer turned back to Mrs. Shipper and put a smile on his face. "The sooner we get this done, the less you'll have to put up with bums like this guy padding through your lovely home."

Mrs. Shipper turned and favored me with a sunny smile. "Hi, Alex. It's good to see you again."

"What's going on?" I repeated.

"Kaylee has made me an offer through her attorney, Mr. Lubank. I may get to continue living in this house after all."

"Oh?"

"Yes. Isn't that generous of my stepdaughter? All I have to do is sign this agreement waiving my rights to Dwayne's share of my late husband's inheritance."

"Is it a good deal?" Given Lubank's presence, all I knew for sure is that the little bloodsucking leech would be walking away with a big pot of dough if Mrs. Shipper put her signature on that agreement.

"Mr. Lubank assures me that it is." Mrs. Shipper put a schoolgirl smile on her face. "But I don't know if he's aware of the fact that I spent several years as a legal secretary, and that I've typed up hundreds of documents like this one. So if the learned counsellor will keep his pen in his pocket for a few more minutes, I'll glance through this and find out just what kind of offer my darling stepdaughter is making me."

"Mrs. Shipper," Lubank pleaded. "There's no need for that. I've summarized the basics for you already, and I can promise you that signing this agreement will keep you in this house and ensure that you live in luxury for the rest of your life."

"Oh, I'm sure it will, Mr. Lubank. Tell you what. Just leave this with me and I'll let Kaylee know what I think of her offer before the end of the day." She picked up the papers and started leafing through them. "Thanks so much for coming by. Kaylee will see you out."

"Very well, Mrs. Shipper. I'm just happy to be able to help you out in your time of need."

Lubank put his pen in his shirt pocket and picked up his briefcase. "Kaylee? It was nice seeing you today. I'll let myself out, thank you. Call me later." Kaylee didn't look pleased, and she opened her mouth to make an objection, but the lawyer was already making his way out of the room.

I waited, and when Lubank passed by me, I turned and followed him.

"What are you up to?" I asked him in a low voice.

"Lawyer business. You wouldn't understand."

"Oh, I think I get it. You're trying to take advantage of a distraught widow mourning the recent loss of her husband and son."

"Who, Mrs. Shipper? She's a fuckin' barracuda! Nobody is going to take advantage of *that* dame. The stepdaughter hired me to screw her over, but there's no way she's going to fall for it. It's a horrible deal for her, and she had that figured out before I even stepped into the house. What you saw was me going through the motions, but the outcome was never in any doubt. That's okay, though. I'm still raking in a nice chunk of change from the stepdaughter for taking her case."

"So it wasn't the grieving widow you were trying to take advantage of. It was the grieving child."

"Legally she's an adult. It ain't my fault that she's self-entitled, greedy, and not what you would call overly bright. She's the one who wants to take advantage of her father's grieving wife, so I figure I'll give her an opportunity. I work out a deal and we present it."

"And you win either way."

"Of course! Who do you think you're talking to? Hey, catch me up on your investigation when you get a chance. I hear that you got your ass dragged downtown again this morning, and that you were grilled by a captain! You must be some kind of VIP! You get that lip from him? I bet that hurt!"

"I've had worse."

We reached the front door. "Gotta go, kid."

"Give my love to Gracie."

"She'd rather you bring her some Huaxian! I promised her that you would, and now you're breaking her heart!"

I returned to the dining room and found Kalama chatting with Mrs. Shipper. The agreement that Lubank had left for Mrs. Shipper to sign was laying on the table, torn in two. Kaylee was nowhere to be seen.

"Bad deal?" I asked.

Mrs. Shipper smiled. "Poor Kaylee. She really must think I'm an idiot." She sighed.

"How are you holding up?"

"I'm okay, all things considered," she told me in a weary voice. She looked at me with dry eyes that didn't contain a trace of red. Her face was lightly made up, and her hair was washed and brushed. The only indication that she had suffered any recent hardship was some puffiness under her eyes, and that might have been from the hangover she'd woken up with that morning.

She indicated the detective with a nod of her head. "Detective Kalama was just offering me her condolences. Again." She lowered her eyes and sighed. "I think she's about to ask me some questions. Would you like to sit in?" She turned to Kalama. "Would that be okay?"

Kalama shrugged. "Sure, why not. I love it when civilians sit in when I question material witnesses. The more the merrier." I took that as permission and sat down in a chair at the end of the table, as far from Kalama as I could get. She pulled a small notepad out of her pocket.

Mrs. Shipper tossed back her hair and folded her hands on the tabletop. "I'm ready."

Kalama looked over at me. "Comfortable?" she asked. I nodded, and she turned her attention to Mrs. Shipper. "I know that you've already made a statement to an officer, so please forgive me if I ask you to answer some questions that you've already answered."

"That's okay, detective. Unfortunately, I've spent some time this week learning how this works."

Kalama nodded, but her expression was unreadable. "I understand that you were away when your stepson was attacked."

Mrs. Shipper's lips twisted into a slight smile and she glanced quickly in my direction. "That's right. I was out all night. If you want, I can provide you with the name of someone who will verify my whereabouts at the time of poor Dwayne's death."

Kalama's expression remained blank. "That won't be necessary. When did you learn that Dwayne had been killed?"

"I checked my phone for messages this morning. I had several from an Officer Teofilo. I called him back, and he told me what happened. I came home right away."

"And that was the first you'd heard that something had happened?"

"Yes."

Kalama paused to read from her notepad. When she looked up, she asked, "You're aware of the terms of your husband's will?"

"Yes. It's very simple. Taking the house out of the equation, he left me one-eighth of his estate."

"And you know what he left to his children?"

"Yes. Kaylee got the house and a three-eighths of his remaining estate. Dwayne was to receive everything else."

"So if my math is correct, Dwayne was to receive half of your husband's estate?"

"Yes, minus the house."

Kalama nodded. "Comparatively speaking, you're not getting much."

"No. But comparatively speaking I hadn't been with him as long as they had."

Kalama consulted her notepad again. She wasn't reading anything from it. It was just her way of controlling the pace of the questioning. She paused for a long space before asking, "Are you aware of any provisions in the will that account for the death of any of his heirs?"

Mrs. Shipper met Kalama's cop's eyes with her soft brown ones. "My late husband's will states quite clearly that if either of his children die within two years of his own death, the full amount of their inheritance is transferred to me."

Kalama wrote something in her notebook. "That seems like an odd provision. What happens if *you* die within the next two years?"

Mrs. Shipper shrugged. "My share of the inheritance will be split between the two of them. I guess that Donald wanted to make sure that his money stayed in the immediate family. He was always paranoid about his hard-earned wealth winding up in the hands of the state."

"I see." Kalama wrote something else into her notepad. "So with Dwayne's death, his share of the estate.... Half of it, right? Minus the house, of course. Half of the estate is now added to the portion that you were already set to receive."

"Which means that my share of the inheritance will now be five times what it would have been originally. And, yes, before you ask, I knew all of this before my stepson's death."

Kalama paused, staring at Mrs. Shipper, who stared back. Kalama broke the silence. "That's a lot of dough."

"Yes, it is," Mrs. Shipper confirmed. "Enough for me to live quite comfortably, wherever I find myself."

I jumped in. "What kind of deal was Kaylee offering you?"

Mrs. Shipper turned to me and smiled. "It was complicated. Mr. Lubank is clever, and he tried to disguise the basics of a bad deal with a lot of fancy jargon, but fortunately I speak fluent legalese. The gist of the deal was that if I waived my right to Dwayne's inheritance, my loving stepdaughter would give me the house outright and vacate the premises within thirty days. But Dwayne's share of the inheritance was more than this house is worth. More than twice as much according to an appraiser that I happened to run into recently. Which is why, of course, that Kaylee made the offer." Looking like a cat that had finished off a bowl of cream, she added. "She's a little disappointed that I decided to turn her kind offer down."

Kalama resumed her questioning. "Where was Kaylee last night?"

"You'll have to ask her, but I think that she was with her boyfriend, Glenn. Charming boy. Much too good for her. I can't imagine the lengths she must go through in order to keep his attention."

Kalama turned the page of her notepad. "She returned at about twelve-thirty this morning and found her stepbrother?"

"That's what she says."

"And called the police?"

Mrs. Shipper smiled and shrugged.

"What time did Lubank get here with the agreement that he wanted you to sign?"

"I guess that it was about eleven or so."

Kalama closed her notepad. "Had you and your stepdaughter discussed an agreement like this before today?"

"No, of course not. How could either of us have predicted that Dwayne would...meet with an accident?"

Kalama frowned. "So Kaylee discovers Dwayne's body at just after midnight, and less than twelve hours later, her lawyer is in here making you an offer for Dwayne's share of his father's inheritance? An inheritance that he hadn't even collected yet?"

Mrs. Shipper shrugged. "That about sums it up."

"Is Kaylee upstairs in her room?"

"That's the direction she ran off to."

"Mrs. Shipper, would you do me a favor and go up and tell Kaylee to come down? Tell her that I'd like to ask her a few questions."

After Mrs. Shipper had left the room, I leaned in toward Kalama and asked, "What do you think?"

Kalama let out a weary breath and slouched in her chair. "I think that when I'm done here I'm going to go home and give my daughter a big hug."

Kaylee came into the dining room a minute later looking sullen. "What do you want?" she demanded.

Kalama, straightened herself up in her chair. "Sit down, Kaylee."

"What for?

"I have a couple of questions. It won't take long."

Kaylee made an exasperated noise that rose out of the back of her throat and sounded like, "*Uuuaaawwg*." Then she stomped to the table and plopped down on a chair opposite Kalama, where she slouched and glared at Kalama from beneath her brow.

Kalama met Kaylee's glare with an impassive expression. "How long has Lubank represented you as your attorney?"

"Couple of days," Kaylee muttered.

"After your father's death?"

172

"He called me the day after. Told me to call him if I needed any help with my inheritance."

Typical Lubank. The minute I'd told him about Mrs. Shipper's stormy relationship with her two bratty stepkids, the slimy weasel had wasted no time in calling Kaylee, and maybe Dwayne, too, to stir up a battle over the inheritance. Much as I sometimes wanted to wring his scrawny neck, I had to admire Lubank's uncanny nose for sensing opportunity where others might only see tragedy.

"And when did you first talk to him about trying to trade the house for your brother's share of the inheritance?" Kalama asked.

Kaylee's face fell into a pout. "That was Mr. Lubank's idea."

"You called him after you discovered Dwayne's body?"

"I wanted to know how his death affected my inheritance. He had all the details."

I wondered who she had called first, her attorney or the police. "And Lubank suggested the idea to you?" I asked.

Kaylee turned her half-lidded glare in my direction. "He said it would work. He promised!"

I nodded. "And what are you paying him for his work on your behalf?"

She shrugged. "I don't know. He told me not to worry about it. But she tore up the agreement. That means I don't have to pay him, right?"

I turned away so that she couldn't see me stifling a laugh.

Chapter Fifteen

Kalama had no further questions for Kaylee, who flew up the stairs to her bedroom where she could sulk in private. The cops had finished tossing Dwayne's room for evidence and were on their way back to the station, where they would no doubt spend some time going over his video collection. Kalama offered to drive me home, but I told her that I would call a cab and get in touch with her later. She headed off to the station.

I needed to check in with Madame Cuapa, but first I wanted a quiet word with Mrs. Shipper. I found her in the living room sitting by herself on the sofa with a glass of wine.

"You okay?" I asked.

She shrugged. "Everything is happening so fast. I woke up Monday morning, and it was just another day. Now it's Thursday, and I've lost my husband and my stepson. By the time Monday rolls around again, I may be waking up somewhere else. I know that I don't *have* to move right away, but I don't know if I want to live alone in the house with that... that..." She searched for an appropriate word and finally settled on "That *child*! Especially with an eviction case winding its way through the courts for weeks or months. We'd be at each other's throat every day."

"Any ideas on where you'd go?"

Mrs. Shipper looked up at me with a slight smile. "I enjoyed waking up in *your* bed this morning. But, don't worry. I'm not trying to worm my way into your life. Maybe I'll check into a hotel until I figure out something more permanent. I might like living in a hotel. I'll be able to afford a nice one now."

"Not a bad plan."

"Or maybe I'll stay here a while longer. Kaylee may find it harder to live here than she thinks. She's not very strong. Donald never forced her to do anything for herself, or to take any responsibility. I wonder how long she'll want to live in a house where someone died such a horrible and violent death. Especially after I tell her a few ghost stories. By the time I'm done with her, I wouldn't be surprised if she offered to pay me to take the house off her hands." She chuckled at the thought. "You must think I'm an evil bitch."

"I think you know how to survive."

"Let's hope so." She smiled and picked up her wine glass. "Everyone else around here seems to be dropping like flies." Her eyes never left mine as she put her glass to her lips and downed the wine with one long, slow sip.

***

I didn't stay much longer. When it was clear that the death of her stepson was less of an inconvenience to Mrs. Shipper than the death of her husband had been, I took out my phone and booked a cab. When it arrived, Mrs. Shipper saw me to the door, and before I could do anything about it she wrapped her arms around my chest and pulled up close for an embrace. She pulled back after a moment and pressed her lips against mine. But the kiss was quick and light. I recognize a goodbye kiss when I get one, and this one was sweeter than some but no less definitive. I put my hat on my head, tipped it in her direction, and walked out to the waiting cab.

When I got back home, I treated myself to the shave and shower that I'd missed out on that morning. I even brushed my teeth. I put on fresh underclothes and a clean shirt. I went into the kitchen, spread some chunky peanut butter on a slice of sourdough bread, and placed it on a plate. I cut a banana into chips and piled them on top. Then I took a plastic bottle of chocolate syrup out of the refrigerator and squirted a liberal amount over the bananas and peanut butter. I slid the plate into the microwave, set the timer for thirty seconds, and hit the start button. When it was done, I ate the heated open-faced sandwich with a fork and washed it down with a shot of whiskey and a bottle of beer. You can't find a meal like that in a restaurant, no matter how many stars it gets on the travel sites. When I was finished, I felt like a new man.

It was time to drop in on Madame Cuapa. I wanted to see how the arrangement was coming along. If I remembered right, Cuapa, Cody, and Old Itzel would be awake, and Falconwing would be sleeping. That suited me fine. I put on a tie, grabbed my coat and hat, and headed out the door.

When I got to Gio's shop, I found the mechanic leaning over the open hood of a snazzy silver ragtop and working at something with a ratchet wrench. The convertible was a real eye-catcher. I guessed that it belonged either to an upscale teenybopper who cruised the city streets on Friday nights, or to a forty-year old swifty in serious denial concerning his inevitable slide into old age.

Gio saw me and waved. I walked over to him, "How's Antonio?"

"How should I know? I'm only his father."

I waved at the ragtop. "Nice car."

"I don't know why anyone would drive a convertible in *this* town." Gio wiped at his face with a dirty red rag. "Too damned cold!"

"Weren't you complaining about the heat a couple of days ago?"

"A couple of days ago, it was too hot!"

"When is it just right?"

"Never! That's what I love about this fuckin' city."

I laughed. "Gio, you might be the wisest man I've ever met."

"If only I could be the richest."

"You'd just want more," I pointed out.

"Prob'ly". He studied me for a second. "You keeping out of trouble?"

"Yeah. Why do you ask?"

He pointed at my face with the ratchet wrench. "Looks like someone punched you in the teeth and your lip got in the way."

"Occupational hazard."

"Ever think about reconsidering your choice of careers?"

"It's crossed my mind. But my job gets me out in the world and I meet a lot of interesting people."

"Hmmph! I'd rather work with cars than people. Cars are more interesting than their idiot owners. Take this baby here." Gio pointed at the ragtop with his wrench. "It's got the body of a race car. Looks fast! Costs a pretty penny, too, let me tell ya! But you look under the hood, and it's got the same cheap four-banger engine that the manufacturer puts in its low-priced economy

177

model. Same exact engine, different body." Gio shook his head. "And it's a crappy engine, too. This one's got thirty thousand miles on it. The timing belt is already stretched, and when it breaks, which it will, the pistons will drive themselves through the valves and the engine will more or less self-destruct. I told the owner that he needs to replace the belt with a chain, but he thinks that the engine won't fall apart because it's only two years old. All he wants me to do is fix the air conditioner! In a freakin' convertible! In Yerba freakin' City! Fuckin' moron! He'll wash and wax the body, because it's shiny and pretty. But he doesn't give two craps about what's going on under the hood. Crazy, isn't it?"

"How old's the owner?" I asked.

"Huh? I don't know. Around your age, I'd say."

***

An hour later I was sitting in the beastmobile across the street from Madame Cuapa's house, wondering what I was going to say when I saw her. I hadn't called ahead because I wanted to pop in on them when they weren't expecting me. During my last visit the three witches had acted like a happy little family, and Madame Cuapa seemed to trust her friends without reserve, but I still had questions about their relationship, both personal and professional. My plan was to stir the pot a little to see if anything that might be bubbling under would rise to the surface.

I should have known better. Cody greeted me at the door, "Come in, sir. Madame Cuapa is waiting for you."

"How did she know I was coming?" I asked.

Cody's lip curled into a half-smile. "She's a witch, sir. A real one. Not one of those fake fortune tellers you see at the piers charging tourists to read their palms."

I nodded. "Point taken."

Madame Cuapa and Old Itzel were sitting on the sofa in the living room, drinking tea and chatting like a pair of old gossips. Old Itzel was at work on another knitting project. Another tea cozy, perhaps. I wondered how many tea cozies any one person needed. Maybe she sold them online.

"Mr. Southerland!" Madame Cuapa smiled up at me when I entered. "Just in time!"

"For what?" I asked.

"For a ritual! Itzel and I are going to see if we can identify your were-crow." Madame Cuapa stood, and Itzel hopped from the sofa to her feet, leaving her knitting behind and revealing herself to be far more agile than I would have thought. Sometimes it's the engine that's sound and the chassis that gets neglected.

Madame Cuapa put a hand on my elbow and began guiding me toward the staircase. "Come up to the lab, Mr. Southerland. I've been thinking about your were-crow. What if he's the one behind the compulsion spell? You haven't found out who he is yet, have you?"

"No," I admitted. "I've only seen it as a flock of crows. I haven't seen him in his human form."

"That's what I thought. But you say that your elemental saw him, right?"

"That's right. Smokey saw him transform."

Old Itzel looked up at me. "Smokey? The elemental has a name?"

"I assigned it a name. It makes things easier."

"How cute!" Itzel beamed. "I may have to start naming my favorite powders. Instead of taking a pinch of muscle relaxant, I'll go fetch me a little Betsy!" I had no doubt that I was being mocked, and I found myself grinding my teeth at the old witch's condescending laughter.

Madame Cuapa sensed my unease. "Itzel, you're annoying our guest! Mr. Southerland, how long would it take for your elemental to get here if you summoned it? I need the one who saw the were-crow transform."

I hesitated. "What are you intending to do with it?"

Madame Cuapa smiled. "Oh, don't be so suspicious. Just because I tried to kill you once doesn't mean that you can't trust me."

How about the possibility that she was hiding her involvement in a sex-trafficking ring? Would that be a reason? But I didn't want to confront her with that just yet. "What are you going to do?" I asked again.

"We just need the elemental's memory of the were-crow," Madame Cuapa assured me. "With the proper questioning, we should be able to get an image of the fellow. It will be a little like hypnosis, nothing more. The elemental will not be damaged, I promise."

I did some calculation. "I can probably get Smokey here in about twenty minutes or so."

"Perfect! It will take us about that long to set up the ritual. Let's go upstairs."

When we got to the lab, I asked, "Is Mr. Falconwing sleeping?"

"Yes, he's downstairs in the guestroom. We won't need to disturb him for this ritual. It's a relatively simple one. You can help. Cody, get Mr. Southerland some candles and show him where they go. Itzel and I will take care of everything else."

Old Itzel let out a mocking laugh that sounded like it was coming from a leaky bellows. Yes! I'll go fetch my pouch of Matilda!" I bit back a smirk when her wheezing laugh degenerated into a hacking cough.

***

Smokey was edgy, and I had to reassure the tiny spirit before it would agree to cooperate. Itzel's wrinkled face screwed in disgust. The old crone couldn't understand why I wouldn't simply command the elemental into obedience.

"Such a waste of energy," she grumbled.

The elemental drew close to my ear and hissed, "Smokey is afraid."

"I'll protect you," I promised, knowing how empty my promise would be in the face of these two powerful brujas. "But if you feel yourself to be in immediate danger, fly away fast."

Old Itzel gave me a look of disapproval and shook her head.

"Okay, we're ready," Madame Cuapa announced. "Cody, switch off the light. Mr. Southerland, direct your elemental to place itself inside the ring of candles."

Six white candles in brass candle holders formed a circle in the center of Madame Cuapa's worktable, and I sent Smokey to hover in their midst. The elemental floated over the ring of candle flames with reluctance and hovered a foot above the table, its whirling drawing the candle flames slightly inwards. Cody and I stood just inside the door to the room, keeping out of the way. The two witches, who were standing at either end of the long table, began to chant. As they did so, smoke from the ring of candles began to gather in the air over the elemental. As the smoke grew thicker, some of it poured into Smokey, and the elemental began to grow. After a minute, Smokey grew in height from two to four inches and increased in width from an almost insubstantial sliver of rotating air to a solid funnel of wind about two inches thick. In another minute, Smokey had stretched to eight inches in length, and in five minutes the elemental had become a fiercely spinning dark gray whirlwind that stretched a full three feet from top to bottom and a full two feet wide. The elemental created a draft so powerful, that the flames from the candles now stretched from the wicks into the elemental itself, where the fire spun with the smoke and caused Smokey to shine with a piercing yellow light.

I kept a close eye on Smokey through the whole process. At first, Smokey had seemed edgy bordering on agitation, or even fear. As the spirit filled with smoke and grew, however, the apprehension seemed to give way to curiosity, and maybe even something like wonder. As it spun, glowing with flame, I began to sense something like exultation. For my part, I was as nervous as a parent watching his kid swinging on a trapeze with no net.

Old Itzel continued to chant, but Madame Cuapa now began to speak directly to Smokey in a low, soothing voice. "Remember the black birds. See them flying in the wind. Show me the birds, Smokey. Show me the birds flying."

At first all I could see was smoke and flame spinning in a tight funnel. But then the smoke in the center of the funnel seemed to stop spinning and to start meandering across the surface of the funnel with its own independent motion. The smoke circled in on itself and then began to resolve into the outlines of flying black birds. They looked like shadow figures tinged with bright red streaks that stretched and flickered.

"Good, Smokey!" Madame Cuapa's hypnotic voice rose above Old Itzel's rhythmic chanting. "Now remember the birds coming out of the air to the ground. See the birds landing."

On the surface of the funnel, I could see the birds swooping to the earth. The colors of the swirling candle flames began to change, sorting themselves into the green of the trees and bushes that grew where the crows had landed.

"That's very good, Smokey." Madame Cuapa's soothing voice was a smooth counterpoint to Old Itzel's rhythmic intonations. The effect was calming, and I struggled to keep my concentration on the images forming in the midst of the whirling elemental. "Now remember the birds coming close to each other. Remember the birds coming together and changing. Remember the birds changing into a human. Remember the human. Show us the human."

I was aware of Madame Cuapa, Cody, and I staring intently at the images on the surface of the roiling twister that Smokey had become, watching the shadow figures of birds come together into a shapeless mass, and watching as that mass began to resolve itself into a more cylindrical form. We all stared at the shape, trying to will it into a more identifiable image.

Madame Cuapa's hypnotic voice filled my head. "You're doing great, Smokey. Remember the human. Remember the color of the human's hair, the curves of its face, the form of its body. See the human, Smokey. Remember the human."

Smoke and tendrils of flame eddied and churned through the mass, and the cylinder began to grow legs and arms. A head began to make its appearance. At this point, we couldn't even tell if the human was male or female, but in seconds we would be able to see something more defined.

The shape was still amorphous and featureless when Falconwing stepped into the lab. "What's going on?" he whispered to Cody and me.

All of Cody's attention had been on the images on the surface of the elemental, and when he heard Falconwing's voice, he gave out a high-pitched yelp. That caused me to whip my head around and break my connection with Smokey. Before I knew what was happening, Smokey shot up to the ceiling, swooped down

182

toward the open doorway, whisked past my ear like a rifle shot, and vanished down the hall.

From over the table, smoke was dissipating throughout the room. Where the candles used to be, a ring of six unlit wicks rose from blobs of melted wax. Looked like the show was over.

"Tloto, you fucking oaf!" Itzel shouted from one end of the table. "You ruined everything!"

"What happened?" asked Falconwing. "What'd I do?"

Madame Cuapa and Old Itzel glared bloody murder at Falconwing, who looked from one to the other with an expression of such pure confused innocence that the other two witches couldn't maintain their irritation with him. First Itzel snorted through her nose, then Madame Cuapa hissed between clenched teeth, and then the two of them were bent over laughing. It went on for a full minute.

When they had expended their laughter, the two women crossed the room toward Falconwing, gasping for breath and wiping tears from their eyes.

Old Itzel started in on him, but her tone was light. "Ah, Tloto. You fucking oaf. You sure know how to spoil a party."

"I'm afraid you made a mess of things, Tloto." Madame Cuapa was still gasping for breath.

"What happened?" Falconwing was blinking in confusion. "Last thing I remember clearly was going to bed. Then I think I dreamed that someone was calling to me. Next thing I know I'm standing outside the door, wondering where the bloody hell I am. And then you two old crones are guffawing like maniacs."

"You don't remember walking upstairs?" asked Madame Cuapa, eyeing Falconwing with curiosity.

Old Itzel's eyes gleamed from deep within her wrinkled face. "The ritual must have attracted him. Like a moth to flame."

Madame Cuapa nodded. "That must have been it. You never could stand being left out, could you. Just had to be part of the action."

I was growing more and more irritated. "Excuse me," I interrupted. "Is Smokey okay?"

Falconwing looked at me. "Smokey?"

"His air elemental," explained Old Itzel.

"His elemental has a name?" Falconwing looked bewildered.

Old Itzel snorted. "Says the man who names his cars."

"My cars have personalities!"

"So does my elemental." I probably sounded a little testy. Hell, I *was* a little testy! "I need to find out how it's doing."

"Your elemental is fine," Old Itzel assured me. "You'll find that it's still fully functional." She laughed through her nose. "I've never seen one scram out of a room so fast!"

I wanted to bounce the old gnome down the stairs.

Madame Cuapa put a hand on my arm. "You go find your elemental," she told me. "It's okay. Nothing we did today caused it any damage. I can see that you are concerned about it, though. I may be the Barbary Coast Bruja, but I'll concede that when it comes to elementalism, your knowledge exceeds my own. Much as I hate to admit it. We'll have to have a long discussion about it someday."

Cody walked me to the front door and followed me to my car. Looking around to make sure that no one could hear him, he held out a torn piece of paper with a number written on it in ink and whispered, "This is the number to my private cellphone. When you get a chance, call me."

"Why? What's up?"

"Falconwing!" Cody hissed the name at me. "That was no accident up there! He stopped that ritual on purpose!"

I considered this. "I don't know. He seemed confused to me."

"I don't believe him for a second, and you shouldn't either."

I studied Cody. His face was twisted in anger. "What's the thing between the two of you?"

Cody's eyes flared, but the anger in his expression gave way to a look of uneasiness. He glanced around him. "Not here," he whispered out of the side of his mouth. "Call me later. Soon as you can. We'll meet somewhere safe."

"Okay, we'll do that." I pocketed the paper with his number on it.

Cody nodded. He started to walk away and stopped. "Watch out for falcons," he warned me. "If you see one, it's probably his familiar." He turned and jogged back to the house.

***

I drove down the block a bit, stopped, and sent out a call for Smokey. The little elemental appeared right away, blowing in through my heating vent. It hovered over the dashboard, spinning like a maniac and sending smoke shooting through the inside of the car. At least it had reverted to its normal size.

"Greetings, Aleksss!" Smokey hissed. "Smokey wantsss more!"

"You're okay then?" I asked.

"Smokey is...." The elementals vocabulary reached its limit.

"Jacked to the gills?" I offered. "Hopped to the edges?"

"Smokey doesn't know what those thingsss mean."

"Never mind." I couldn't help smiling "You'll come crashing down soon enough. I don't suppose you've ever been hungover."

The elemental didn't respond. It was spinning to beat the band and looked ready to fly apart at the seams.

"Relax, buddy," I said in what I hoped was a soothing voice. "If you were human, I'd advise you to take a few deep breaths. Come to think of it, that might be just the ticket. Take in some fresh air and blow out the rest of that smoke."

Smokey shortened and broadened as it whirled. Hot smoke flew away from it, and it became more transparent. The spinning began to slow by increments.

"Smokey is better now." It's hiss seemed almost normal.

"Wish it was that easy for me. Hey, that was quite an experience."

"Smokey...likes it."

"Don't get addicted! Can't have my favorite elemental becoming a juice head."

"Smokey doesn't know what that means."

"And yet you live in a bar. Oh well. Hey, you were pretty good in there. We almost saw the were-crow."

"Smokey can show you."

185

"Smokey can what? You mean you can still show me what the were-crow looks like?"

"Smokey can show you. Smokey needs smoke and fire, but Smokey knows how to show you were-crow." The elemental began whirling out of control again, stretching and thinning itself until it looked like a spinning straw.

Chapter Sixteen

I had to send Smokey away to sleep it off, or whatever elementals do after absorbing more stimulation than they can handle. In its present condition, the little elemental was too wired up to focus. But I planned to get back in touch with it as soon as I had a chance to see if it really could display an image of the were-crow without help from the witches. Finding the were-crow could break this case wide open. I wondered if later that night would be too soon for Smokey.

When I got the beastmobile back to Gio's lot, I took out my cellphone and discovered that I had missed a call from Kalama. She left a voicemail. "Call me," was all she said.

I punched up her number after I'd reached my office. She picked up after two rings.

"I reported our suspicions concerning Silverblade and the sex-trafficking ring to Lieutenant Sanjaya," Kalama told me.

"And?"

"An hour later I was put on indefinite administrative leave."

We were both silent for a few seconds.

"Wow! They suspended you?"

"More or less. I still get to collect my salary."

I stared at my front window, where the late afternoon sun was shining through the vertical slats of my half-drawn blinds and casting long shadows on my office floor. Outside the window I could see the cypress trees that lined the street swaying in the stiff breeze. The cypress directly in front of my office had been reduced to a ragged stump, the result of an encounter the year before between Badass and Detective Stonehammer. I smiled at the memory of the troll running away in defeat. I also remembered that my victory had come with a heavy price. But that's the way it works. Life rarely gives something away for nothing, and it comes collecting when payment is due.

"So what now?" I asked.

"There's more. As I was headed for the door, I got word that Coldgrave wanted to see me in his office. So I went in and Sanjaya was in there with him. They told me that as soon as the brass heard I had run across an unlicensed trafficking ring, word came down the line faster than a bullet train to send me home indefinitely. Coldgrave was furious! He says that when Internal Affairs cleaned up the department last year, they only scratched the surface, and that he was sent to us with a mandate—finish the job! And here I was thinking that the captain was going to be business as usual. Turns out that Coldgrave might be one of the good guys. More or less, anyway. He has his eyes on the prize, and he's not too picky about how he gets there. He says that I've got someone up top running scared, and he wants me to keep digging. Off the books, of course. I'm supposed to report to Sanjaya on the q.t. And get this— Coldgrave told me specifically to convince you to help me! He told me to recruit you any way I could. I think he expects me to seduce you. Do you think that will be necessary?"

"Start small. Buy me a beer and we'll take it from there."

"You got it."

"Make it a beer and a shot."

"Don't push it, hotshot."

"Actually, I don't think that I can take your case. Madame Cuapa is paying me for exclusivity."

"Oh, come on, gumshoe. She can't object to you giving a hand to the police. It's your civic duty."

"Maybe so, but if I'm going to do this, then I'm going to have to charge the department for my services. In fact, I'm going to have to add a liability surcharge to my usual rates, and we'll have to make sure that Madame Cuapa never finds out that I'm working for you."

"You can't charge the department. The department isn't hiring you."

"Then I'll charge Coldgrave directly."

"Why can't you just bill your time to Madame Cuapa?"

"Because this is a different case. Madame Cuapa wants me to find out who nailed her with a compulsion spell. Coldgrave wants me to look into a trafficking ring. I'm not going to charge Madame Cuapa for work that I'm doing for Coldgrave."

"It's all part of the same big picture," Kalama argued. "The trafficking ring has something to do with Cuapa's problem."

"Maybe." I admitted. "But maybe not. They might be totally unrelated."

I heard Kalama sigh. "Fine! I'll bring it up with the captain."

"I'll need his signature on a legal contract."

Kalama paused before responding. "Remember what I said about working off the books?"

"I don't work without a contract," I insisted. "I'll email one to your private account."

"You sure I can't just seduce you?"

"Sorry. I'm flattered, but...."

"You're an asshole, you know that?" Kalama laughed. "Okay, email me a contract and I'll get the captain to sign it. He'll probably find a way to bill the department. But he'll expect something for the money."

"He'll get it," I assured her. "How long did it take for them to bounce you off the case?"

"I filed my report and was sent packing a little over an hour later."

"That's fast. Did you mention Madame Cuapa?"

"In fact, I did not. The connection seemed too tenuous, so I held it back. You know what that means, right?"

I did. The department had dropped the Shipper investigation because of its connection to Madame Cuapa. The YCPD brass wanted no part of her. I understood why. The witch was too powerful in too many ways for the department to mess with. Investigating her would be suicide. But if Kalama hadn't included Madame Cuapa's name in her report on the trafficking ring, it meant that someone high up in the department didn't want the ring itself to be investigated. That could only mean that an investigation into the ring risked exposing some very important people as participants or clients. Maybe people in the police administration itself, or maybe some important politicians. Who knows, maybe the mayor was implicated. If he was, I doubted that anyone, including his own family, would be surprised.

Kalama interrupted my thoughts. "We're in over our heads, aren't we."

"Probably."

"Want to get out of the pool?"

"Of course I do. But I can't. That trafficking ring could be the reason someone compelled my client to kill Shipper. And my client might be running that ring. That means investigating it is my job. And I've already deposited the retainer. What about you?"

"Can't. My bosses have given me an assignment, and it's up to me to fulfill it. Even if it's off the books."

"I guess we're stuck."

"Does this mean I still have to buy you a beer?"

"At least you don't have to seduce me."

"My daughter will be disappointed."

The light shining through my blinds disappeared as the sun descended into the thick marine layer blowing in from the ocean. Time was passing, and I felt a restless need to be outside the four walls of my office, hitting the streets in pursuit of the vital lead that would be the key to the case. That's how they did it in the movies. Well, why not? Sometimes the best way to go forward is to stick your chin out and see who takes a poke at it.

Neither Kalama nor I had said anything for about a minute or so, but neither of us had disconnected the call. I broke the silence, "Do you have Shipper's cellphone in evidence?"

"What's left of it. You remember that Shipper's body exploded, right?"

"I'm not likely to forget! Were you able to access his contacts file? Mrs. Shipper told me that her husband might have some escort agencies listed in it."

"Well, the department dropped the case, so we didn't subpoena any records from the phone provider, but Coldgrave convinced a couple of the lab guys to see what they could get from the phone itself, off the record. If there was anything left of the memory, they might have been able to find something. Hang on, I may have a report from them. The lieutenant slipped me a folder on my way out of the station, but I haven't had a chance to look at it yet. Let me see.... Yeah, here we go. This is what they had as of this morning.... Hmmm, the memory was severely damaged.... Looks like most of the contact data was lost.... They managed to retrieve some loose information.... Hmmm, nothing interesting so far.... Wait a second.... Yeah, they managed to find a couple of contact pages. Not many, though. Nothing useful yet.... Hey, here's something. A Tony Atwater from Classic Escorts. Got a pencil?"

"Not necessary. I've already got that number."

"Oh, really?" I could hear the leer in Kalama's voice.

"Can the wise-lip, copper. Atwater was involved in the Graham case. Remember Leena, his adaro mistress? She used to work for him."

"I remember her. Some of the guys downtown think that she was the one who bumped Graham off."

"Stonehammer killed Graham. But Leena was there. Anyway, Atwater is the mug who sold me my car."

"Figures. It *looks* like a pimp's ride."

"You should have seen it before I had it painted."

"You think that Atwater was working with Silverblade?" the detective asked.

I thought about it for a second. "No. Atwater is no boy scout, and he's connected with the mob, but he doesn't deal in underaged girls, at least as far as I know. He's in the business, though, and he might know something. I'll give him a call."

"You hang out with some interesting people. Makes me wonder which side of the law you're on."

"Yeah, I know all kinds of shady characters. I even know someone who got suspended from her job by our city's police department today."

"Point taken. Okay, let me know what you find out."

After we disconnected I punched in the number for Classic Escorts. My call was answered by a seductive female voice. "Classic Escorts. How may I help you?"

"I can't begin to imagine how many corny responses you've had to that question."

"You have no idea."

"Is Tony Atwater in?" I asked. "Tell him it's Alex Southerland."

"Thank you Mr. Southerland." The voice sounded less dreamy and more businesslike. "I'll see if Mr. Atwater is available."

I only had to wait a few moments. "Alex!" Atwater's voice boomed into my ear. "It's been a while! How're you doing?"

"Can't complain. How's business?"

"Never a dull moment! I can always use more security. Why don't you come work for me? Trade in that contract work for a nice steady income. Lots of benefits, too."

"Thanks, but I'm muddling through."

"Still impressing the dolls with that car of mine?"

"I'm thinking of moving into the thing. It's bigger than my apartment."

"Classier, too, I'll bet. So what's the occasion? You looking for a companion? I've got a couple of lovely new adaros that will make you look like a superstar and then make you feel like a champion."

"I'm sure they would. But you know me, I'm just a working stiff with simple dreams."

"Don't tell me. You're working on a case and you want to ask me a few questions."

"Afraid so."

"Whatever it is, I didn't do it. You know me, flatfoot. I'm so clean I squeak!"

"I doubt that." I chuckled a little. "But you're not in my sights for this one. Did you know a mortgage company exec named Donald Shipper?"

"I heard he died a couple of days ago."

"That's the one. Was he a client of yours?"

"Alex, please. You know I can't answer that."

"Your name and number were found in his contacts file on his phone."

"So?"

"According to his widow, Mr. Shipper made use of agencies. She says that he liked young girls."

Atwater didn't say anything for a few seconds. Then he asked, "How young?"

"Teens. Maybe early teens."

"I hope you don't think—"

"No, I don't think he got them from your agency. I know that you run a tight ship, and that you're on the up-and-up. But someone was supplying him, and I was hoping that you might be able to steer me in the right direction."

"Because I'm in the business? Is that it?" Atwater's voice was clipped. He sounded a little sore.

"Don't take it that way, Tony. As far as I'm concerned, you're a respectable businessman. You're licensed and legal, and you treat your employees right. But someone out there is running an unlicensed sex-trafficking ring, and they're supplying rich fat cats, like Donald Shipper, with underaged girls and boys. I figure that's gotta be a slap in the face to honest operators like you. You don't have to tell me whether I'm right or wrong, but I'm gonna make a guess. I'm guessing that Shipper used to be a client of yours, but you haven't heard from him in some time. I'm guessing that someone else started booking him dates with thirteen-year-olds, and he stopped coming to respectable agencies like yours. Whoever these unlicensed lowlifes are, they are taking clients away from you. And what are the chances that they are protecting these girls? You think they're giving them dental insurance and doctor appointments? I'm betting that you want these guys stopped as much as I do. Maybe more. Tell me I'm wrong."

I could hear a sigh on the other end of the line. "No, you're not wrong. But I'm sure that you can appreciate the position I'm in. Yeah, scum like that are bad for business. But telling you who they are might be bad for my reputation, not to mention my life expectancy. With all due respect, and I like you Alex, I really do, but you're an outsider. This is the kind of thing that has to be taken care of internally. Speaking as one professional to another, I know you understand."

"Yeah, I get it. I don't want to make your life difficult. Let me throw out a name. Claudius Silverblade. Anything you can tell me about him?"

"Like what?"

"Is he someone I want to talk to?"

Atwater didn't say anything, but I could almost hear the wheels turning in his head. When he spoke, he sounded distant. "Mr. Southerland, I'm sorry that you aren't interested in any of the fine escorts my agency provides. But if you're looking for something a little more exotic, then you might consider the Daucina Club."

"The Daucina Club?"

193

"Excuse me?"

"Did you say the Daucina Club?"

"I'm sorry, Mr. Southerland, but I've never heard of the Daucina Club. Best of luck to you, brother! I hope to hear from you later. And take care of that car of yours!"

He disconnected, leaving me to stare at my phone. I had a name: the Daucina Club. I'd never heard of it and didn't know what it was. Atwater was telling me that he had never heard of it either, should he find himself dragged further into this case. I'd gotten all I could from him, and it was up to me to do something with it, if I could.

A search of the internet revealed next to nothing. Daucina was a legendary trickster god who roamed the seas off in the southern Nihhonese Ocean, lighting the way for ships at night and seducing young women in his spare time. I found no references for a Daucina Club in Yerba City or anywhere else. I needed a deeper search.

I was acquainted with a shady character named Tom Kintay who designed exotic recreational drugs for the Hatfield Syndicate. For some reason, he had taken a liking to me, even though I had run him in for stealing pharmaceuticals from an army hospital when he was a corporal and I was an M.P. It was Kintay who first told me about a hidden part of the internet, where, if you had the right passwords, you could find all of the unlicensed items that the government didn't want you to know about. Even accessing this shadow space was enough to get you a free trip up the river if you got caught, but Kintay taught me how to stay ahead of the government spooks.

In a locked drawer in one of my filing cabinets, I kept a half dozen cellphones with unused numbers. I had paid cash for the phones to a street vendor who didn't require any contracts and received a limited amount of user time. The phones weren't any more secure than any other phone, but by accessing a network somewhere away from my home I'd be able to conduct a search in the shadow space without alerting anyone to my identity. I'd never be able to use that number again—the number would henceforth be "burned"—but that's why I had six of them.

I didn't know how much time I would need to find the Daucina Club, so I took three of the burners and walked to Gio's lot to get my car.

A half hour later, I pulled into a grocery store parking lot and turned on one of the burners. I accessed the internet and downloaded a special browser, one that would allow me to search for websites that legitimate search engines were not equipped to find. Once I had the browser, I used it to access a web address that Kintay had told me about. I got a sign-in page and entered a password, hoping that it would still work. Kintay had warned me that these shadow sites often moved or disappeared, and that passwords were changed frequently. But this was my lucky day. The password gave me access to an unlabeled search engine window. I typed in "Daucina Club," and waited.

**

Two hours and two burner phones later, I drove the beastmobile to Placid Point, grabbing a cheeseburger, some fries, and a coked up cola at a drive-through on the way. I caught the tail-end of the evening commute, and the streets were still jammed as the last of the nine-to-fivers made their slow way home for dinner and television before hitting the hay and pulling in their eight hours of dreamtime before jamming the streets with their morning commute.

Night had fallen by the time I pulled into a public garage that would cost me more than a dinner at a passable steak house. I parked the car and hit the sidewalk, securing my hat and lowering my head so that the brim would channel the Yerba City breeze. Most of the shops around me were closed or closing, and the sidewalk was lit with neon signs and streetlights. Sidewalk traffic was light. In this part of town, it would pick up again when the neighborhood bars began to fill.

I passed tattoo studios, hock shops, and second-hand clothing stores, their interior lights out and their doors chained shut. Every window was protected by iron bars. My mouth watered as I walked past the open door of a passable barbeque joint. I passed by a decent hash-house that was packed with working stiffs

195

and an empty greasy spoon that would fill up later with the night-owl crowd. After walking for a block and a half, I came to a closed glass double-door with a painting of a fierce-looking adaro wearing a jeweled crown and holding a large spiral shell. Lettering over the painting identified the store as the Nautilus Jewelry and Novelty Shop. A red neon sign on the door read "closed." I walked over to the window next to the door, peered through the bars, and saw a small man with thinning brown hair locking up the orderly rows of jewelry displays. I knew that he kept all of his best stuff out of sight in a secure vault. I rapped at the window to get the man's attention. He turned at the noise, and I waved.

Crawford waved back, mouthed a hello, and signaled for me to meet him behind the store. I gave him a two-finger salute and walked around the corner to the alley that ran down the back of the stores on that block. I leaned against the garage opposite Crawford's back entrance where I knew that he kept his car and waited for him to finish closing up. About ten minutes later, Crawford emerged through the back door, his face lit up in a broad smile.

"Uh-oh!" he shouted. "Here's trouble!" He crossed the alley and we shook hands.

In many ways, Crawford was the reason why I had become a private investigator. After my discharge from the service, I had made a point of visiting Mrs. Colby, the grandmother of one of my army pals who'd been shipped home in a box. Mrs. Colby owned rental property all over Tolanica, and she offered me a place in Yerba City for a reasonable rent if I would do a background investigation on a mysterious gentleman named Crawford, who had submitted a rental application for another of her Yerba City properties. With nothing else to do, I took her up on her offer. It took some effort, but I discovered that Crawford was a were-rat, a shape-changer who could transform himself into a swarm of more than a hundred rats. Most people tend to harbor an instinctive aversion to were-rats, and Crawford himself later warned me that most were-rats were at least borderline psychotic. But when I revealed Crawford's secret to Mrs. Colby, the old dame didn't bat an eye. She granted him his application and told me afterwards that Crawford was one of her quietest and most reliable tenants.

196

I found that I had enjoyed my introduction to investigative work, and with Mrs. Colby's encouragement I got a license and became a full-time P.I., living and working out of the place I rented from the grand old lady. Eventually, I sought Crawford out and the two of us started meeting for drinks. I even began asking him to assist with some of my cases, because, as he put it, rats can go just about everywhere and see just about everything. For reasons of his own, he was always more than willing to help me out.

I followed Crawford up the stairs that led above his shop to his apartment. When we got inside, Crawford produced two bottles of suds from his refrigerator and we sat down at his dining room table.

"Want some pretzels?" asked Crawford. "I've also got peanuts, potato chips, and cheese balls."

I accepted the pretzels, and Crawford poured some cheese balls into a bowl for himself. He sat in an overstuffed easy chair and drained half his bottle of beer in one gulp. "Tell me you need some help. I need some action!"

"I need some help."

"Yes! Tell me it's dangerous!"

"Probably not. But you never know."

Crawford's eyes widened. "I'm about to explode!"

"Been quiet?"

"Too quiet for too long." Crawford popped a cheese ball into his mouth. "I'm getting twitchy."

I knew what that meant. Once, when he'd tipped a few and was plastered all the way to his receding hairline, Crawford told me what life was like for a shape-shifter. He'd said that keeping the human and animal integrated was a lifelong challenge, a challenge that not every shape-shifter could meet.

"And it's harder when the animal is a rat," Crawford had told me, "because everyone hates rats. Most of us lose our minds when we reach puberty." He had grown quiet then, lost in bad memories. After another shot of whiskey, he had simply added, "If we're lucky, we live to regret the things we do and move on."

Crawford had eventually come out of his dark period and learned that he could achieve mental stability by surrounding himself with structure and routine. He'd established his jewelry business and lived an ordinary, run-of-the-mill life. But it wasn't a lifestyle that he could stick to for more than a few months at a time.

I sipped some of my beer. "Sounds like I came over just in time."

"You know how it is. Every now and again, I need to let the animals loose! Otherwise, I'll go a different kind of mad."

We drank our beers and I filled him in on the events of the past few days. It had seemed like weeks, but Madame Cuapa had stepped into my office on Monday morning, and it was only Thursday night. By the time I had brought him up to speed, Crawford was on his third beer and second bowl of cheese balls.

"So what's the plan?" he asked. "Are we going to find this club? What's it called again?"

"The Daucina Club. It's a gentleman's club for the well-heeled. There's a branch in just about every major city in the world, including Yerba City, but hardly anyone knows about them. They are protected at the highest levels, and, from what I've read, just about anything goes. I thought we'd go to the local establishment and have a look around. Problem is, it's invitation only, and there is no chance of a workingclass nobody like me getting through the front door."

"And that's where I come in!" Crawford rubbed his hands together like he was washing them under a faucet. It reminded me of, well, of a rodent. "If you start licking that hand and rubbing it behind your ear, I'm leaving," I told him.

He licked one of his hands and began to rub it behind his ear. "Bigot." I shook my head and grabbed another pretzel.

"You ready to go?" I asked.

"Just need to grab my coat. Want me to drive?"

"Yeah. I'm paying the parking garage for an all-night pass, so I may as well get my money's worth."

Crawford scooted back into his bedroom and emerged in a black leather jacket and a pink and white checked fedora. He'd put on black driving gloves and was carrying a worn leather briefcase.

"Where'd you get that hat?" I asked him.

"Pretty snazzy, isn't it? Can you believe I found it in a thrift store? It's amazing what some people will let go of!"

I shook my head and we walked out to get his car.

Chapter Seventeen

Thanks to my search through the shadow pages, I knew that the Daucina Club was located in an unmarked basement below the five-star Huntinghouse Hotel in the heart of the financial district. A Yerba City native could walk right by the landmark hotel a thousand times and never know that below street level the world's elite were leaning back in plush leather easy chairs, smoking fat cigars and deciding the fate of the world. They were also enjoying the privileges of wealth, which often included secret rendezvous with practitioners in the ways of all pleasures in the luxury suites upstairs. Most of these professional companions were well trained and had been at it long enough to attain the necessary skills to control their encounters. But some of the workers were much too young and way too new at the game to be more than playthings, and playthings all too often are disposable once the novelty wears off.

Crawford parked the car in a spot he'd found down the block from the Huntinghouse and switched the engine off. "Do you have a plan?" He gulped down a mouthful of whiskey from a bottle that he'd brought along to "fight off the night air."

"Yeah, I have a plan." I grabbed the bottle away from him and took a slug for myself. "The plan is, we're going to wing it."

Crawford reached for the bottle. "That sounds like a swell plan."

"The best!" I agreed.

We left the bottle in the car and walked to the front door of the luxurious Huntinghouse Hotel. The crisp air did us both a world of good, and we were barely staggering at all as we entered the spacious lobby and found an unoccupied sofa as far from the front desk as possible. Crawford sat on the far side of the sofa. On the wall next to him was an electrical outlet.

I sat next to him. "Think you can find your way into the basement?"

Crawford grunted at me and pulled a screwdriver out of his briefcase. "Go distract the concierge while I remove the cover off this outlet. I'll let a couple of rats gnaw at the wall a little to widen the opening. Then I'll send ten rats through into the inner wall. They'll follow the electrical wiring down to the club in the basement and shuttle back and forth to let me know what they find."

I got up from the sofa and walked over to the concierge, who had been watching the two of us since we walked in the door.

I met the concierge's stare with a friendly smile. "Hello." The concierge somehow managed to look down his nose at me even though I was a good three inches taller than he was, evidently not liking the cut of my jib. I had the feeling that he disapproved of the smell of cheap liquor on my breath. The alcohol scent on most of the hotel's clientele undoubtedly came from more expensive brands of spirits. "My friend and I are waiting for our partner to arrive. The reservation is in his name, but he phoned and said that he's been held up. We don't know when he'll get here, but it might be a couple of hours. If it's okay, we'll wait for him here in the lobby. We've been traveling, and I know that we look like a couple of bums, but don't worry, we'll be out of the way."

The concierge looked doubtful, but he nodded. "As you say, sir."

I started away, but then stopped. "You don't happen to have a copy of today's paper, do you? I haven't had a chance to look at it yet."

After a brief hesitation, the concierge reached under his stand and produced a folded newspaper. "Here you are, sir."

"Thank you. Say, where do you suppose I could purchase a cigar?"

"Cigars are available at the bar, sir. That's just past the desk and around the corner to the left."

"Thank you. You've been very helpful."

I walked back to where Crawford was sitting. "I don't think the concierge likes us. You ready?"

"Just finished with the hole." Crawford let his arm down his side of the sofa, and as I watched him shrink in size I knew that a line of rats was emerging from his unseen hand and scurrying through the hole in the wall. I handed him the newspaper.

"I'm going to the bar to get us a couple of drinks. It's likely that we are going to be here for a while. Want a cigar?"

"Sounds good." He sat back, laid his fedora next to him on the sofa, and opened the newspaper.

***

"How much longer we going to sit here?" Crawford asked. "I'm about to nod off!"

We'd been at it for an hour and a half, and I was beginning to think that we were wasting our time. Crawford's rats had been relaying messages from the basement, but not much was happening in the Daucina Club. A couple of well-dressed gents had been drinking expensive brandy and muttering to each other in a corner table, probably plotting the takeover of some small province halfway around the globe, but, other than that, it had been a quiet Thursday night in the elite social club, at least so far. The rats had found their way into an office down the hall from the main room, but there was no incriminating information lying around waiting to be discovered. There was a computer on the desk, but it was powered down, and it would be protected by a password that I didn't know.

I took a puff on my cigar, leaned my head back, and blew the smoke upwards into the air. I don't smoke cigarettes, but I sometimes get a craving for a quality cigar, and this one was worthy of the hotel's five-star rating. It cost a ridiculous amount of scratch, but I was planning to pass the cost to my client. She wouldn't mind. She probably had enough cash stuffed in her mattress to buy the factory if she wanted to. "Let's hang around until midnight," I told Crawford. That was just ten minutes away. "Then we'll call it a night. Sorry to have wasted your time."

Crawford smiled. "The glamorous life of a private snoop." He relit his own cigar, which had gone out. "If I ever get the notion to open my own agency, I'll remember the fun we had tonight." The tip of his cigar flared as he puffed it to life.

"Hey, it isn't every day you get to drink in a classy joint like this." I blew more smoke at the ceiling.

"Yeah, I.... Hang on a sec." Crawford's face went blank for a second. "Someone just came into the club. And he's definitely weird."

"What do you mean?"

"I don't know. There's something about him.... The rats are spooked. They don't want to go near him."

"Ever seen him before?"

"I don't think so."

"What's he look like?"

"Tall. Thin, but not too thin. Jet black hair. Bronze skin. Chocolate-colored eyes. They're kind of, I don't know, hypnotic, I guess you'd say. They look right through you. Expensive suit, tailor-made. Handsome, like a film star. He's got this thin mustache."

"That's gotta be Falconwing! Keep watching him, but be careful. No fast moves, or he'll notice."

"Bad news?"

"He's one of the witches I was telling you about."

Crawford's eyes widened. "Lord's balls!"

"What's he doing here? He's supposed to be watching over Madame Cuapa."

"Is he the one that you think is getting supplied with joy girls?"

"And boys. That must be why he's here. But I can't imagine that Madame Cuapa knows about this. He must have snuck out while she was sleeping."

I thought to myself. Who was supposed to be awake with him? Cody! Itzel would be halfway through her sleep shift, and at this hour Madame Cuapa was likely to be sleeping, too. Maybe Falconwing had talked Cody into letting him leave the house for a while. Maybe. I had the sensation of something slithering up the back of my neck.

"What's Falconwing doing?" I asked Crawford.

"Sitting at a table by himself. Drinking."

"Let me know if anyone joins him." Crawford nodded.

At two minutes past midnight, I saw a familiar figure enter the hotel and head straight for the front desk. I picked up the newspaper and held it up so that he wouldn't see my face.

Crawford looked up at me. "What is it?"

"That troll at the front desk. That's Silverblade."

"Holy shit!" hissed Crawford. "What do we do?"

I thought for a second. "Here's what I think is happening. Falconwing slipped away from Madame Cuapa somehow. He's tired of being cooped up in the house babysitting the old dame. He lives the high life. He's not used to sitting around all night long doing nothing, and he's bored. He wants...a diversion. So he calls Silverblade, who has set him up before, and they arrange a meet at the Daucina Club. Look! Silverblade is headed to the elevators. He got a room key from the desk clerk. I'm guessing he's got a nice little bit of entertainment stashed in the room. If I'm right, he'll take the key down to Falconwing, and Falconwing will go up to the room and have himself some feel-good time."

Crawford's eyes turned inward for a second, and then lit up. "Silverblade came into the club and joined Falconwing. He gave him the key, just like you said. Looks like they're going to have a drink first, though."

"Okay, bring the rats back. Wait! How many elevators go to the club level?"

"Just one, as far as I can tell."

"Go ahead and bring the rats back, but stay here. I'll be right back."

I crossed the lobby, trying not to move so fast that I would attract unwanted attention. I turned down a hall to the elevators, where I found three doors. I punched the call button, and the door on my right opened right away. When I stepped through, however, I saw that there was no button leading to a basement. I punched the button for the highest floor of the hotel—the twenty-fifth—and stepped back out of the elevator before the doors closed.

After the elevator car started its journey to the top of the building, I punched the call button again. This time I had to wait.

"Come on!" I muttered to myself.

After what seemed like ten minutes, but was probably only about thirty seconds, I heard the elevator on the left slide to a stop. The door opened and I stepped in. This one had a keyhole where a basement button would be, so that only someone with the right key would be able to take the elevator into the club. I punched all twenty-five buttons and stepped out.

I walked back to the lobby and waved Crawford over to join me. When he reached me I took him to the elevators and pointed to the floor indicator above the elevator on the left. The indicator was lit with the number eight. Stopping at every floor, it was going to need a few minutes to get to the top. "That's the one that goes to the basement. Let me know when it starts heading down," I told Crawford.

I closed my eyes, formed the sigil for summoning Smokey, and waited. The elemental hadn't arrived yet when Crawford grabbed my arm. "It's coming down!"

We watched the indicator light make its way to twenty, fifteen, ten, five, and then "L" for lobby, but the elevator door did not open, and I could hear the car slide past our level to the basement. A few seconds later, I heard the elevator car rise upward.

I couldn't think of any reason why Falconwing would stop off at the lobby level, but, just in case, I nudged Crawford. "Get ready to scram out of here if that door opens."

Fortunately, the elevator car continued upwards without slowing down. We watched the indicator reach fifteen, and then stop.

A couple more minutes passed, and then Smokey zipped into view and hovered over my shoulder. "Hi, Aleksss. How's tricksss?"

Smokey was thick with the gray haze from the Black Minotaur, and the frantic spinning that I'd observed earlier that evening had slowed to a more relaxed whirling.

"Feeling better?" I asked.

"Smokey is ready to serve." The elemental sounded eager.

Crawford was smiling. "You've been training it," he noted.

"Smokey, do you remember Crawford?"

"Smokey remembers. Greetings Crawford. How's tricksss?"

Crawford glanced at me. "I guess we're about to find out."

I punched the call button. The elevator in the center opened, and we got in. "We're headed for the fifteenth floor."

When the elevator arrived at the fifteenth floor we stepped out into a small waiting area situated between two hallways. A sign indicated that the even-numbered rooms ran down one hallway, and the odd-numbered rooms ran down the other. I sent Smokey to check both hallways, and the elemental reported that both were empty.

"Okay, Smokey. Now for the tricky part. Do you remember earlier tonight when you were growing big with smoke and fire?"

The elemental stretched itself upwards and its spinning speed began to increase. "Smokey remembers!"

"Do you remember the man who walked into the room?"

"Smokey remembers. Smokey is afraid."

"You're afraid of the man who walked into the room?"

"Yes. Smokey is afraid of the scary human."

I hesitated. "Why?"

"Smokey doesn't know. Smokey knows that scary human is scary."

Crawford muttered, "I know what you mean."

"Smokey! That man is in one of the rooms in one of those two hallways. I need you to find him without letting him see you, and then I want you to show me which room he's in. Can you do that?"

Smokey's spinning slowed, and the elemental shrunk in on itself. When it spoke, it seemed unsure, but willing. "Smokey is...ready to rumm-ble."

"Okay. Be careful. Make sure that no one hears or sees you. Ready? Go!"

***

Ten minutes passed before Smokey returned, but the elemental had found our target.

"Is the man with someone?" I asked.

"Yes. Two other humans are with the scary man."

Crawford grimaced. "Two! Lord's balls! He's a greedy bastard." He looked up at Smokey. "Male or female?"

Smokey didn't respond.

"Elementals can't tell," I explained. "They don't really understand the concept of gender, maybe because they don't have one."

"Huh!" Crawford grunted. "What about age?"

I glanced at Smokey, and then turned back to Crawford. "Can't tell that, either. We're going to need you for that."

Crawford nodded. "Okay."

"Smokey. Lead us to the room with the scary man in it."

The elemental led us into the hallway with the even-numbered rooms, and it stopped in front of a door at the very end of the hallway: Room 1580. Then we crept back to the elevators. I was trying to be as light-footed as I could, but I couldn't help but notice that I was the only one making any noise at all. Smokey was as silent as a puff of air, and Crawford had a real knack for creeping. Even with my enhanced awareness I couldn't hear him at all, although I was walking right beside him. If I hadn't been able to see him, I'd have never known he was there.

I had no idea what I'd do if Falconwing suddenly decided to leave his room to get a bucket of ice, but we made it to the elevators without incident. "Smokey, were any of the rooms in this hallway empty?"

"Yesss," hissed the elemental.

"Show us."

It turned out that several of the rooms were empty, and I decided on Room 1510 near the other end of the hallway from Falconwing, mostly because it was right next to the stairwell, which offered us a quick retreat if we needed it. I thanked Smokey for a job well done and released it from its service. It whooshed away, probably to the rafters in the ceiling of the Minotaur where, its work complete, it would bask in the combination of tobacco, marijuana, and hashish smoke drifting through the air above the lively weeknight crowd. Lucky fellow. It was well past midnight, but my work was far from done. Crouching on one knee in front of the door, I pulled out my set of picks and turned myself loose on the lock.

Picking locks is harder than it looks in the movies, and after a couple of minutes of patient fumbling, I could feel Crawford getting antsy.

"Hang in there," I muttered "Almost got it."

"What if someone comes?"

"Stay calm and let me know."

"Okay, man, but I've seriously got to pee!"

I was just about there a minute later when I heard Crawford draw in his breath. "Someone's coming," he whispered.

I stood and leaned against the wall next to the door, screening the keyhole, with my pick still in the lock, from sight. A middle-aged couple came out of the elevator area. They were followed by a uniformed bellboy carrying two heavy-looking suitcases. They turned in our direction and stopped three doors short of us on the other side of the corridor. Crawford and I waited while the bellboy unlocked the door and followed the couple into the room, bringing the suitcases. We waited a little longer until the bellboy left the room, pocketing his tip. The bellboy hesitated, and then walked in our direction.

"Need any help?" he asked.

"No, we're fine." I offered him my most innocent smile. "Thanks, though."

The bellboy eyed us for a couple of seconds longer, then shrugged and started back to the elevators. When he was gone, I crouched down and started back on the lock.

"Think he'll be a problem?" Crawford asked.

"I doubt it," I lied, fighting the urge to move faster. Picking a lock is like cracking a safe: haste most assuredly makes waste. It took me another minute, and, to his credit, Crawford held it together.

When the door opened, he let out a breath that he'd been holding and stage-whispered, "About fuckin' time—where's the toilet!"

While Crawford was taking care of business, I opened his briefcase, took out his screwdriver, and removed the cover from a wall outlet next to a sliding glass door that led out to a balcony. I used the screwdriver to chip away at the plaster and enlarge the opening. By the time I was done, Crawford was standing over my shoulder, watching me.

"Think you can find your way to Falconwing's room?" I asked him.

"No problem. You just want me to peek around?"

"Yeah. I want to know if the two pros with him are underaged. But be careful!"

"He'll never know I'm there," Crawford assured me. "I'll be quiet as a mouse."

Crawford crouched down and extended his hand, palm upward, to the opening in the wall. As I watched, a tiny brown rat emerged from the palm of his hand and leaped into the opening. Then a white rat popped out of Crawford's palm and ran after the first one. "Two should be enough." He muttered under his breath. "One to watch, and the other to come back and report." He turned and sat back against the wall to wait. I headed for the bathroom.

A few minutes went by, and then Crawford extended his hand to the outlet. The white rat leaped into the palm of his hand and vanished inside, like it was diving into a swimming pool. Crawford's eyes arched. "A girl *and* a boy! And both are kids. Couldn't be more than fifteen, at most. Younger, I'd bet, especially the girl."

I nodded. This was what I needed. I took out my phone to call Kalama.

Crawford sat back so suddenly that the back of his head slammed into the wall. His arms straightened at his sides, and his legs flattened themselves to the floor. His eyes shot open and his lower jaw dropped. He turned his head and stabbed me with a malevolent glare. Then his eyes rolled back into his head and I found myself staring at two white balls streaked with thin red veins. His mouth worked, and he began to speak in a voice that was not Crawford's. "Southerland! Is that you? And you've hired a were-rat to spy on me! Well, this is inconvenient. No, this won't do at all."

Crawford's mouth opened wide, and the hairs on the back of my neck snapped to attention as a cloud of oily black smoke began to pour out of the little man's mouth.

208

The cloud of smoke grew larger as it spilled out of Crawford's open mouth and rolled into the room. Falconwing's face appeared in its midst, his dark eyes boring into mine. My instincts switched into high gear, and I called the summoning sigils for Badass to my mind's eye. The elemental had assured me that it was always nearby, but I wondered how quickly it could get into the hotel room. The window was closed, and, although the room wasn't air-tight, I was afraid that the oversized bag of wind might not find its way inside fast enough to be of any help.

My cellphone was in my hand, and I tried to punch the speed dial link to Kalama, but Falconwing was ready for that. When I glanced down at my screen the phone flew out of my hand and slid across the carpet. I looked up to see the silhouette of Falconwing, barely visible inside the black cloud that now filled half the room. He appeared to be naked, but it was hard to tell through the thick roiling smoke. When the smoke thinned for a split second, I thought I could detect a large glittering tattoo on Falconwing's chest, but I couldn't make out the details.

"I'm disappointed in you, Southerland." Falconwing's voice sounded odd, like it was being amplified through a speaker. The cloud was still billowing from Crawford's mouth, and Falconwing was making no move to step away from it. "You seem like a man of the world. Sitting all night in that drab little house—I needed a break, that's all!" The figure shrugged. "I don't expect the others to approve, but I thought you might be a little more understanding. And yet, here you are, peeping at me through windows, as if I were some vile philandering husband. I guess you're just a little man after all."

"Madame Cuapa needs you to watch her. She's depending on you. She trusts you." I needed to keep him talking for a few moments longer.

Falconwing had other ideas. His face twisted into a look of scorn as he slowly raised a finger and pointed it at me. "Oh, please. Do shut up." I tried to respond, but when I looked into the dark brown pools of his eyes, I found that I could no longer form words. So much for negotiation. "Well, enough of this." Falconwing let out a theatrical sigh. "You stuck your nose where it didn't belong, you and your rat friend. What a shame."

I couldn't tear my gaze from Falconwing's eyes, which seemed to be filled with black flames. The witch raised his arms and I felt my body rise from the floor. I could hear Falconwing muttering in a low guttural voice, but I couldn't understand the words. With my arms and legs hanging limp, I flopped over backwards, but I didn't fall. Helpless to prevent it, I felt myself floating back toward the center of the room until I was levitating a foot above the king-sized hotel bed, staring up at the ceiling. As I watched, a section of the ceiling began to dissolve, forming a circular opening several feet wide. Suddenly, a light poured through the opening, and, although I knew that I was in a room on the fifteenth floor of a twenty-five story building in the middle of a dark night, I was somehow staring at a brightly lit green-tinged sky through a hole in the room's ceiling.

Falconwing continued to mutter, and I felt a gathering tension in the air, as if a breeze in the room had suddenly gone still. I was having trouble drawing air into my lungs, and my whole body had gone numb. I tried to turn my head, but it wouldn't move, and my eyes remained fixed on the opening in the ceiling.

Like the sun rising over the horizon, a glowing green-feathered head pushed its way over the edge of the hole. It was the head of a giant hummingbird, shining with its own glistening green light, its dark crimson eyes staring at me without blinking, and its three-foot beak sticking out from its head like a spike. I knew that it would be able to pin me to the bed with that beak like a bug in a display case. As it crept over the edge of the hole, I saw that the creature had a winged human body beneath its hummingbird head. It began to lower itself head first from the hole, its eyes fixed on my chest. I became intensely aware of the beating of my heart.

My head filled with images of priests in ceremonial dress sacrificing victims on altars with stone knives and tearing out their hearts. I had a brief vision of a priest raising a still beating heart into the air, where it was plucked from the priest's hand by the same winged monster that was now slithering like a snake over the edge of the opening in the ceiling and flowing toward my floating body. My own heart began to pound, and it felt as if it would leap out of my chest.

My senses began to fade, and my elf-enhanced awareness took over. I realized that although Falconwing *appeared* to be standing inside the cloud of black smoke, in reality it was only an image of the witch, rather than Falconwing in the flesh. I could also sense Badass speeding toward the closed glass door, just seconds away. And I could tell without looking that the base of the antique table lamp at the side of the bed was made of a thick, solid ceramic. The lamp was too well constructed and way too expensive for a more family-friendly hotel. Hell, I didn't have anything close to this kind of quality in my own home. But it was just the sort of room furnishing one would expect to find in a luxurious joint like the Huntinghouse. My instincts told me what I needed to do. The problem was that I was unable to command my body to do it.

Then I heard a sudden rapping noise. Someone was knocking at the front door of the room with a firm fist. I heard an authoritative voice shout, "Hotel detective! I know you're in there! Open up!"

The glowing creature above me and the hole in the ceiling vanished as if they were never there, and I plopped onto the bed. Without pausing to think about it, and without a second to spare, I reached out and grabbed the antique lamp. I ripped it from the wall socket and threw it directly at the image of the openmouthed Falconwing with everything I had. The lamp passed right through the apparition and into the sliding door, which shattered into pieces as the heavy lamp crashed through the glass and onto the balcony. A split second later, Badass sped through the broken glass and swept into the room.

"Badass!" I shouted through my restored voice. "Get that fucking smoke out of this room!"

The elemental whirled through the room like a small tornado, absorbed the oily black smoke, and whooshed out the sliding glass door into the night. With the smoke gone, the image of Falconwing disappeared from the room.

Badass left the room in a shambles. Chairs were toppled, pillows scattered, and lamps lay broken on the floor. A wall-mounted painting had been torn to pieces, and only a portion of its wooden frame still hung from the wall. Crawford was slumped to the floor next to an uncovered electrical outlet surrounded by broken plaster. He let out a painful moan, but at least he was alive and conscious. Every muscle in my body ached. I sat on the edge of the bed, leaning over my knees with my head in my hands. As I sat there groaning, a large pane of glass that had been hanging from the top of the door frame crashed to the floor and broke into pieces.

That was the scene that the hotel detective found when he unlocked and opened the door to Room 1510.

..*

"What in the hell are you doing here, Southerland!" Captain Coldgrave's teeth were clamped so tightly on his cigar that I thought he would break it in two.

"Getting some shuteye until *you* showed up." I yawned. "I had a rough night."

Coldgrave turned to a uniformed officer standing just behind him. "Get him out of there!"

The officer unlocked the door to my cell and waited for me to crawl out from under the threadbare blanket and roll off the thin mattress. I stood on the concrete in my stocking feet and looked around for my shoes.

"Where the hell are his shoes?" Coldgrave turned his burning red troll eyes on the officer. "Go find his damned shoes!"

Another officer came hurrying up the corridor with my shoes dangling from one hand and my trench coat tucked under his arm. "They're right here, sir!"

"What the hell did you think he was going to do, hang himself by his shoelaces?" Coldgrave grabbed my shoes away from the officer and tossed them through the bars to the floor near my feet. "Put them on and get out of there. We're not running a flophouse here."

I refrained from pointing out that I hadn't spent the early morning hours in one of his cells by my own choice. I had, in fact, been dragged there by some of Yerba City's finest after the house

212

dick at the Huntinghouse had called for them and had me arrested for breaking into Room 1510 and trashing it. The johns were supposedly searching for a second man who had somehow vanished without a trace, but I don't think that their hearts were in it. They had better things to do in the wee hours of the morning. They went through the motions, though. They asked me where the second man had gone, and I told them that he had escaped through the hole in the wall. It was true: Crawford had indeed melted down into more than a hundred rats who had taken it on the lam down the electrical wiring inside the hotel walls. I'd been standing in the house dick's way, so he didn't see it happen, but the bellboy had told him that two men were acting suspiciously outside the room, so he'd insisted to the johns that there was a second vagrant on the premises. While they were searching the closets and shower stall for him, I grabbed up Crawford's clothes and stuffed them into his briefcase. The cops assumed that the briefcase was mine, and I didn't correct them. I hoped that Crawford's hat hadn't suffered any damage. It would be hard to find another like it.

Coldgrave handed me my coat and took me right to his office, which was a definite upgrade from the station's sweatboxes. After we were both seated, he lit up a fresh cigar, turned his glowing eyes on me, and arched his eyebrows. "Well?"

I cleared my throat. "It's safe to talk in here? I assume that you've checked your office for bugs."

Coldgrave puffed on his cigar without speaking, so I continued. "There's a local branch of the Daucina Club in the basement of the Huntinghouse."

Coldgrave blew smoke into the air above my head. "Go on."

"Claudius Silverblade runs a sex-trafficking racket there. Last night he provided two underaged pros to a witch named Falconwing. Tloto Falconwing. They were playing their games in room fifteen eighty last night starting a little after midnight."

Coldgrave removed his cigar from his mouth. "Falconwing is in town?"

I nodded. "I had a little run-in with him last night. You've probably got pictures of the results."

"You had a run-in with Falconwing? And you're still alive?"

"I got lucky."

Coldgrave seemed impressed. He jammed his cigar back into his lips and spoke around it. "This is the Silverblade from Emerald Bay Mortgage?"

"Yes sir. I saw him pick up a room key, and an operative of mine saw him give it to Falconwing, who subsequently rode the elevator up to the fifteenth floor to join his rented companions for the night. My operative witnessed some of their activity."

I expected Coldgrave to ask me about my "operative," and he may have been thinking about it as he chewed his cigar, but in the end he gave a sharp nod and let it go.

"My officers reported that you told them to look in on room fifteen eighty."

I nodded. "Before your boys got there I tried to get the house dick to check it out, but he insisted in no uncertain terms that the room was unoccupied and that I should mind my own business."

Coldgrave smiled. "My boys checked the room, but no one was there. No surprise there. But the bed was unmade, and we found some other items of interest. The house dick is currently waiting for me in Interrogation Room D. The night clerk is in Interrogation Room C. The hotel manager is in Interrogation Room A. I've got some questions for all of them. One of them might remember giving someone a key to room fifteen eighty. You never know."

Coldgrave stood, so I did, too. "You talk to Detective Kalama recently?"

"Not since yesterday."

"Get in touch with her and give her the details from last night. With any luck, we'll have Silverblade in custody by the end of the day." He reached out a giant four-fingered hand. "Thanks, Southerland. And, by the way, you were not at the Huntinghouse last night, and you weren't here enjoying one of our free beds this morning. Got it?"

"Got it."

I turned to leave, but Coldgrave stopped me. "Hang on a sec." He picked up a file folder from his desk and handed it to me. "Now get outta here."

214

After I left Coldgrave's office, I opened the file folder. Inside was a copy of my standard contract, signed by Coldgrave. I closed the folder and tapped it against the side of my leg. All I'd have to do now was write up a report and send a bill. I don't know if it made up for spending a cold night in the can, but it sure beat a punch to the kisser!

***

When I left the station, I called Crawford, but got his voice mail. I left a message asking if he was okay and letting him know that I had his briefcase and his clothes. I asked him to call me when he could. Then I crossed the street and walked into The Acorn Grill. My head was aching from a night of whiskey and cigars, not to mention nearly being sacrificed to a giant hummingbird. I needed coffee like a politician needs donations. Nalani wasn't working, and an obese blond-haired waitress took my order. She wore a nametag that identified her as Irene. I asked Irene for a slice of ham, two eggs sunny side up, two slices of sourdough toast, and coffee, and she shuffled off to the kitchen without writing anything down. When the order arrived, it was perfect, and, whenever my coffee cup was less than half full, Irene hustled by and refilled it to the brim from a pot that she held a foot above my cup without ever spilling a drop. I admire professionalism in any field, and Irene was a champion in hers.

I sat alone in a side booth, sipping my coffee, and thinking about where I was with my case. I kept coming up with the same two answers: "nowhere," and "nowhere fast." I had Silverblade on the sex-trafficking rap, but I hadn't tied his racket to Shipper's murder. I had little doubt that Silverblade had supplied Shipper with underaged girls, but I had nothing to indicate that the two of them had fallen out with each other. I suspected that Madame Cuapa was involved in Silverblade's trafficking ring, and that she maybe even ran it, but I had to admit that my reasons for thinking so were weak. I knew that the Madame had been grooming Silverblade for a high position in her company, and it was inconceivable to me that she could have been unaware of his criminal activities, but that didn't have to mean that she was a part of them. And even if she was, where was the link to Shipper's death? I'd been sure that the sex-trafficking ring and Shipper's murder must be related, and that all I needed to do was find the strings that tied them together, but maybe I'd been all wet. Now I was thinking that the trafficking ring and the murder were two separate stories that happened to involve some of the same characters. It seemed that I'd taken a wrong turn and run into a dead end.

What else did I have? Well, there was Mrs. Shipper. She'd been shaken up a little by her husband's death, but not that much. In fact, it looked like she was going to come out of it smelling like roses. She was free from a husband who'd neglected her and still young and attractive enough to start over with a better catch. And now, with her stepson's death, she was going to walk away with most of her late husband's dough. On top of that, she was plotting to take the house from her stepdaughter. It all seemed to be falling in place for the less-than-grief-stricken widow.

But the cause of her husband's death still bothered me. How was Mrs. Shipper capable of compelling the bruja to lay a fatal whammy on her husband? Why involve Madame Cuapa at all? Of all the ways to murder a man, why pick one that risks retaliation from the most powerful witch in western Tolanica? It didn't add up. Mrs. Shipper was a shameless opportunist, and she was certainly taking advantage of her husband's death, but that didn't mean that she had planned it. My gut was telling me that she wasn't the culprit in this case, and I liked to believe that I could count on my gut to get it right ten times out of ten. But I also had to account for the fact that Mrs. Shipper was an attractive dame, capable of scrambling my gut and making a monkey out of a pug like me.

I turned my thoughts to the two witches, Itzel and Falconwing, especially Falconwing. After the previous night, I was *hoping* that Falconwing was the mastermind behind everything. I hadn't sensed any lie in him when he told me that he hadn't known Shipper, but he at least had motivation for wanting to discredit Madame Cuapa. If she were out of the way, he would take over a large, powerful coven, giving him an army of witches under his command. Falconwing would be okay with that, the way a rummy would be okay with truckload of Grade-A hooch. But I couldn't discount Old Itzel. She claimed to be happy in a supporting role, but I kept coming back to the fact that she'd been a part of the coven since before Madame Cuapa was born. She was a powerful bruja in her own right; how had the old witch *really* felt when Cuapa's father had passed the coven down to his young, pretty upstart daughter rather than to the one who had been with him longer? Had she been hiding a grudge all these years?

Madame Cuapa claimed that she would have recognized Falconwing or Itzel behind the compulsion spell. I wasn't sure about that, but she was, and she was the expert. Still, she was biased on behalf of her friends, and wasn't it possible that a powerful witch could somehow camouflage a spell? I didn't know, but Madame Cuapa should. I would like to have asked Coyot, but he was conveniently dead.

Falconwing and Itzel made more sense to me than Silverblade or Mrs. Shipper, but what did I actually have on them? Neither of the witches had a motive that I knew of to kill Shipper, and, my speculations aside, I had no solid reason to believe that either of them had it in for the Madame. So there I was. Just a lot of guesses and dead ends. Nowhere and nowhere fast.

Before I knew it, I had finished a breakfast that I could barely remember eating, and I was looking at a bill that Irene had somehow slipped to the table without me noticing. I paid the bill at the register with my credit card, making sure to include a twenty-five percent tip. I could afford to be generous because I fully intended to include the cost of my breakfast in the expense report that I was going to send to the YCPD. After all, I would have eaten at home if I hadn't been arrested for doing surveillance on the department's behalf. I knew that Lubank would have advised me to charge the breakfast to both the police *and* to Madame Cuapa, but I couldn't do that. My standards might be flexible, but I drew the line at double-dipping.

I stepped out of the diner and into a surprisingly warm and still morning. I looked up into a sunny blue sky, not a cloud in sight. It looked like the heat wave, after letting up for a couple of days, might be coming back. I hoped not. I was getting used to breathing foggy sea air again. I unbuttoned my coat and pulled my phone out of my pocket to call for a cab.

As I waited for the hack, I became aware of a sharp ache behind my eyes. I reached up and rubbed my temples, and it occurred to me that my headache had begun somewhere in the middle of my meal. I wanted to chalk it up to too much expensive booze and the aftereffects of smoking cigars, a vice I don't often indulge, but breakfast and black coffee should have alleviated my hangover, and it was getting worse instead of better. Maybe the workload was getting to me. This was the second day in a row in which I'd found myself outside The Acorn Grill after a night of too much drink, too little sleep, too many cops, and needing a shave and a shower. Maybe it was time for a day off.

When my ride arrived, I gave the cabbie my home address and stretched out in the back seat. After ten minutes, I noticed that my head was covered with a layer of sweat, and I wondered if the sudden changes in the weather were taking their toll on me. There was a sour smell in the inside of the hack, and the air was stale and stuffy. The cabbie was running his fan, but the breeze didn't seem to reach me. I tried to shake it off and think about the case, but I couldn't concentrate. After a few more minutes, my whole body was soaked in sweat. I wanted to take off my coat, but it seemed to be too much trouble. I decided that I needed some shuteye, and I closed my eyes. I drifted into an uneasy doze, but after several minutes my stomach began to get queasy. Suddenly I needed to be out of the cab. I started to say something, but my eggs, ham, and coffee threatened to exit my stomach if I opened my mouth. I looked out the window, and everything began to spin.

From somewhere far away I heard the cabbie say, "Hey Jack—you don't look so good!"

I tried to say, "Don't worry about it," but the only thing that came out of my mouth was my breakfast.

"Hey!" the cabbie was yelling. "What the fuck, Jack! That's gonna cost ya!"

"Sorry," I managed. "Just get me home."

"Th'fuck, Jack! You get yourself home." I heard the squeal of tires as the cabbie pulled his hack to the curb. The next thing I knew, strong arms were yanking me out the door and tossing me to the sidewalk. I felt a hand jam into my pocket and I saw the cabbie pull out my wallet. He cleared it of bills and threw the wallet down on the ground next to me. As I tried to crawl to my hands and knees, the cabbie bounced Crawford's briefcase off the back of my head. I collapsed on the pavement. As the cabbie pulled away, I lost the rest of my breakfast.

I don't know how I did it, but somehow I managed to hoof it the rest of the way to my front door while carrying my fedora in one hand and Crawford's briefcase in the other. I don't think that I had far to go, but that's as far as I got. When I tried to put my key in the lock, I dropped it, and it just seemed too hard to bend down to pick it back up. A siren was screaming in my head, and I covered my ears with both hands trying to make it stop. Then the world seemed to dissolve in front of me, and the last thing I remembered was the head of a black dog with no eyes growing larger and larger as it drew closer and closer.

Chapter Nineteen

A screech that sounded like a metal beam being ripped in two lengthwise by something with talons the size of skyscrapers tore me out of the blackness. I wanted to cover my ears, but I didn't have any hands, or ears, either. I was nothing but a collection of thoughts drifting through the noise. Time passed, and the screeching decreased in volume, one decibel at a time, until I could bear it without wanting to scream. I began to hear words in the screeching, until finally the screeching stopped and the words were all that were left.

"That's right," I heard the words say. "Come back. You're not meant for Mictlan yet. Not today."

The words continued. I focused on them, because there was nothing else.

"Come back, Mr. Southerland. Come back."

The sound of the words grew softer and softer until they were a whisper. Another sound threatened to drown them out altogether, a loud pounding noise, like heavy weights crashing to the ground, one after the other: BAM! ... BAM! ... BAM! ... The crashes became softer, thumps instead of bams, and the intervals between them began to decrease: bam...thump...thu-thump...th-thump.... I came to recognize the sound as the beating of a heart. My heart, I realized. I started to feel a tingle, then the jabbing of needles over every inch of my body, and then a burning sensation. I wanted to tell someone that I was on fire, but I couldn't draw a breath. I began to panic. I needed to breathe!

"Easy now. Easy," came the voice. "Stay calm. Just one moment...one moment.... There."

I sucked in a breath and began to cough. I felt something liquid drain from my throat and out my mouth. I sucked in another breath and coughed for several minutes, unable to stop until my lungs had cleared. Eventually, I was able to breathe again without gagging, but I still couldn't see. I tried to open my eyes, but they seemed to be sewn shut.

I felt something moist wiping my face. "Calm, dear boy. Relax. I've got it. Stay calm. I've got it."

I recognized the hypnotic voice. It was Madame Cuapa. When I could, I opened my eyes.

At first I couldn't see anything but soft pulsing lights, purple, red, blue, like the sun shining on an oil slick on the surface of the sea.

"Keep breathing, dear boy. The worst is over now. Long, slow breaths. That's it."

The colors began to resolve themselves into shapes. The shapes were familiar, and I came to realize that I was in my bedroom. The pale light of the city at night shining through my unshaded window provided dim illumination, but everything seemed a bit...off. Not out of focus, not blurry, but somehow not quite real. I could see the shape of my chest of drawers on the other side of the room, right where it should be, but when I tried to focus on the chest, it would slip in and out of my vision. I would see a brown blob, watch it slowly resolve into my chest of drawers, but then the whole side of the room would fade into blackness. After a moment, the brown blob would emerge from the blackness, and the process would begin again.

"Can you wiggle your fingers?" asked Madame Cuapa.

I tried and failed. I opened my mouth, but nothing came out.

"That's okay. Take your time. You've had a long journey, but you're almost back. Breathe, my boy. Breathe. You're safe now."

I closed my eyes, but a sudden fear of slipping out of reality forced me to snap them open again. Looking straight at the ceiling, I focused my attention on my right index finger, searching for it with my mind. When I thought that I could feel its presence, I willed myself to move it.

"Excellent! Can you move the others now?"

One by one, I moved my fingers. Then I moved my hands. I took deep, slow breaths, and lifted my right arm up from the bed. I let it fall, and then I lifted my left arm. I tried to keep it aloft, but after a couple of seconds it plopped back to the bed as if the string holding it up had snapped. I still couldn't move my legs, and, try as I might, I couldn't speak. I closed my eyes and continued to breathe, one long slow breath after another.

"Don't try to do too much too fast." Madame Cuapa's voice was comforting, and I felt stronger listening to it. "You're doing remarkably well. I assure you, you'll be good as new in no time. But there's no need to rush. Your mind is strong, but your body is still very weak. The best thing you can do now is sleep. I've got you. You're safe now. I won't let the darkness take you. You've nothing to fear."

After coming back from wherever I'd been, sleep was the last thing I wanted. I had a feeling that something out there was still waiting for me to slide back to it. Something monstrous. Something that was calling to me to give up and let go. Despite Madame Cuapa's reassurance, I resolved to keep myself awake, no matter what. I forced my eyes back open and turned my head to the side.

Shapes were beginning to crystalize into objects. I turned my head and found myself looking straight at Madame Cuapa. She appeared to be the most real thing in the room. At first I thought that she was dressed in a tight-fitting multi-colored body suit, but then I realized that she was nude, and that I was seeing the full display of her tattooed skin. Her body was like an elaborate canvas, with almost no space untouched by ink. I could see every detail with crystal clarity. I saw every red, yellow, and black scale of the snakes that coiled around her legs. The one on her right leg climbed up her midsection, and its head rested just below her left breast. Its mouth was open just wide enough to expose two gleaming fangs and a forked tongue testing the air. The snake on her left leg curled around her hip and out of my sight. Colorful flowers—not abstract floral designs, but flowers that appeared to be as real as any that I'd seen arranged in vases—covered her torso. Tiny spiders crawled on the petals and down the stems. A hummingbird hovered on her left breast, drinking nectar from a red flower that I didn't recognize. A scorpion crawled beneath a cactus pear on her right breast. But the image that most caught my attention was a black tarantula the size of my hand perched squarely on the bruja's hairless pubic mound. It was facing upwards with one leg extended, as if poised to make a journey up

223

the Madame's abdomen. Every image was photographic in its detail, and all of it was shrouded in night, as if Madame Cuapa's body existed in eternal moonlight.

It was stunning. I was no art expert, but I knew a masterpiece when I saw one. And I'd bet the beastmobile that all of the work had been done by a single artist, a virtuoso with needle and ink. Something about the artwork seemed familiar, but I didn't know why. I tried to think if I'd ever seen anything like these images before, but nothing came to mind, and the sense of familiarity vanished as I lost myself in the jumble of imagery.

I forced air through my throat and whispered, "Wow!"

Madame Cuapa looked down and examined her own skin. "I'd like to think you are referring to my body, but I suspect that you're commenting on the tattoos."

I grunted out a whispered laugh, but then everything started to grow soft and fade.

"Take this." Madame Cuapa poured some liquid between my lips from a spoon. My mouth was bone dry, and I let the liquid sit on my tongue and flow down the back of my throat before swallowing it. It tasted like lukewarm shit, but I didn't care. After a few seconds, the world around me began to grow solid again.

Madame Cuapa's back was turned to me now as she crossed the room and knelt down over a travel bag. As she rummaged through it, I was able to see the skin art on her back. It was so dense and detailed that I had trouble separating the individual images. She was covered in a panoply of flora, birds, arachnids, insects, and four-legged critters. Three of the images, though obviously done by the same hand, stood out from the rest because they seemed a little blotchy and were tinged in an angry red color. I realized that these images, two tiny birds and a spider, must be new. I wondered when she'd had them done. Most of the images on the Madame's skin were small, with the notable exceptions of the two snakes. I could see the head of the second snake now, resting in the middle of the bruja's back between her shoulder blades. Unlike its mate, this one's mouth was closed as it peered intently at a black crow sitting just inches away. The crow stared back without any sign of fear. I wondered at the crow's confidence.

And then Madame Cuapa shifted her position, and the image of the snake's head changed. Maybe it was a trick of the dim light shining through the bedroom window, or maybe my eyes were playing tricks on me again, but where I had seen the head of the snake, I now saw the head of a black dog with tiny bolts of lightning where its eyes should be. Then the bruja turned again, and the snake's head reappeared.

I wanted to rub my eyes and was surprised to discover that I could. Encouraged, I attempted to move my leg and found that I could bend my knee and slide my foot back a few inches. I took a satisfied breath.

"Very good, Mr. Southerland!" Madame Cuapa was back at my side. "You're almost all the way back. The danger is past." She took the clock radio off the table at the side of the bed, and in its place she lined up a small clay bowl, several small cloth bags closed with drawstrings, a glass vial sealed with a cork, and a small pen knife. She opened one of the bags and scooped out a tiny measure of a yellow powder with a small wooden spoon. She frowned at the powder for a moment and then dumped it in the bowl. Then she scooped a pinch more out of the bag and added it to the batch. She reached into the second bag with two fingers and pulled out a tangled clump of dried roots. She studied the clump, put some of it back into the bag, and flicked the remainder into the bowl. From the third bag, the bruja drew out some kind of beetle, about an inch long. Its legs wriggled as she dropped it into the bowl. She used the handle of the wooden spoon to crush the insect and stir it into the mixture. She then took the cork out of the vial and poured half of the syrupy liquid into the bowl. Its color suggested that it was a mixture of blood and oil. Finally, the bruja picked up the pen knife, cut a small slice into the palm of her hand, and squeezed a few drops of her blood into the bowl. She gave the mixture one last stir with the spoon.

"What's all that?" I managed to croak.

"Trust me, you don't want to know." Madame Cuapa closed her eyes and began to mutter something unintelligible. After several minutes she stopped muttering and held the bowl up to my mouth. "Open wide."

I looked up at her and shook my head.

"Don't be a baby, Mr. Southerland."

I squeezed my mouth shut and clenched my teeth.

"Mr. Southerland, there are two ways that I can administer this potion into your system. One is by mouth. You won't like the other option."

I closed my eyes and opened my mouth. The bruja dumped the contents of the clay bowl past my lips and I swallowed without letting the potion linger in my mouth any longer than necessary. It tasted like mud and slid down my throat like a raw oyster. I felt the palms of Madame Cuapa's hands on my temples and heard her chanting in a language that I didn't know. I kept my eyes closed. The alien words were soothing, like the rustling of leaves. My mind began to drift, and, before I knew it, I was asleep.

***

In my dream, I was standing at the end of the wharf at the old Placid Point Pier. The elf was standing next to me in his stained hooded raincoat, his fishing pole propped up against the railing with its line in the water. An empty bucket sat at his feet. The water was calm, and the rippling surface sparkled in the sun.

"What a time you've had!" The elf's melodious voice was as compelling as ever, and, as always, I was transfixed by the sound of it. "Indeed! It was a near thing. The witch needed all the help I was willing to give her."

Willing? I wasn't sure what to make of that.

The elf responded as if I had asked him a question. "To be sure, to be sure. One might argue that much would have been gained by letting the witch suffer the consequences of her actions without interference. That's on the one hand. But on the other hand, I foresaw many intriguing possibilities that could result by lending her my aid, which she greatly needed."

I had no idea what the elf was going on about.

"No, of course not. Please forgive my prattling on like this. It's not often that I get to speak with anyone, and I must confess that I've always been one of those annoying people who takes pleasure in the sound of his own voice. But wheels turn, wheels turn, and no one can truly foresee the results. So many possibilities, so many random factors."

I started to ask the old elf a question, but he was gone. I was now in Mrs. Shipper's living room. She was sitting on her huge sofa and telling me something, but I couldn't make out the words. Then I was in Madame Cuapa's dining room, sitting at the table with the three witches. Old Itzel's hairless dog was staring at me with unblinking eyes. I looked around the room and saw Dr. Coyot's blood-covered corpse face-down on his office floor, his staff still clutched in his hand. "Don't touch that," I heard myself say to Detective Kalama, but I didn't know what I was referring to. Before she could respond, I was back in Mrs. Shipper's living room again. I watched her stand and step out of her dress. But her nude body was not hers; it was the body of Madame Cuapa, covered in tattoos. She turned, stepped up on her sofa, and leaped into the painting that hung over it on the wall. From somewhere far away I could hear the cawing of crows. "No, wait!" I shouted, but I was now floating in the middle of a pure whiteness with no walls, floor, or ceiling.

I woke up then. I was still in my bed, and Madame Cuapa, now clothed in an ankle-length dress, was watching me from a chair that she had pulled in from my living room. Dawn was breaking outside my window. I found my phone on my side table and confirmed that it had been nearly a full day since I had fallen ill and been tossed out of a taxi.

"How are you feeling?" asked Madame Cuapa.

"Like I've been turned inside out and put back together again."

The Madame nodded. "We have a lot to talk about."

***

"First, I find myself having to apologize to you again." Madame Cuapa folded her hands in her lap and looked me directly in the eyes. "I put a curse on you, and it very nearly killed you. I can't tell you how sorry I am. Not just sorry, but ashamed. For someone like me to allow herself to be used like that—it's beyond embarrassing! Once again, I was under a compulsion, which I

227

succeeded in resisting to an extent. And, in my defense, I managed to bring you back from the brink of death, although it was way too close for comfort." She smiled at me. "To be honest, your recovery wasn't *all* my doing. Your ability to resist the curse was unexpected. I sense the old elf's hand in this. His gift to you is very powerful, but I also felt him helping me while I was bringing you back from the gates of Mictlan, the land of the dead."

I nodded, and Madame Cuapa sighed and looked down at her hands.

"I've been betrayed." She sighed. "My old friends, Tloto and Itzel." She looked up at me. "We argued yesterday morning. In light of my recent problems, they wanted me to step away from my leadership position in the coven. Temporarily, they said." Madame Cuapa's face seemed to melt, as if her familiar imperious features had only been a thin wax mask covering a real face that was old and tired. "To be questioned, doubted like that...." She gathered herself, and her regal mask returned as if it had never gone away. "That's never happened to me before. And I won't stand for it, Mr. Southerland!"

"What happened?"

She looked down at her hands again. "They caught me by surprise. It must have been long in the planning." She scowled. "Itzel threw a powder in my face! That she would have the nerve....!" The bruja shook her head, and the scowl disappeared, to be replaced by an expression of disappointment. "At first I didn't realize what she was doing. I never thought that she would ever launch an attack at me. Not Itzel! She's like my old auntie. Very close to a mother. And my best friend, too. We've always had each other's back. She's the last person I ever expected to turn on me. The last! But if it had just been her, I would have been able to handle it, even taken by surprise like that. The powder got through my defenses somehow. Only someone who knows me as well as she does could have developed something capable of doing that. The powder weakened me just enough for Tloto to strike. And even then, if he had just been a second later I could have deflected his spell. But they had planned it. She hit me with the powder and he launched a spell that he had prepared in advance, so that all he needed was a word."

228

The bruja smiled. "It was a devilish spell, I'll give him that. As his mentor, I can't help but be proud of him. It must have taken him months of preparation, hours of ritual, day after day, to invoke the right combination of spirits and convince them to obey his command. When it hit, I was attacked by an army of otherworldly spirits, no one of them strong enough to hurt me, but together, while I was weakened by Itzel's powder, they beat me into a state of immobility. Physically, I was paralyzed. Mentally, I was in a daze. From there, it was an easy matter for the two of them to administer potions that rendered me unconscious and insentient."

Neither of us spoke for a few seconds, and then she let out a long heavy sigh. "Mr. Southerland, the truth is that I wasn't beaten by my friends. I was defeated by my own arrogance. I didn't believe that I could be struck down like that. I took the two of them for granted, never believing that they were a threat. I let my guard down. But live and learn. It won't happen again." Her dark eyes sharpened, and I knew that I wouldn't want to be in Falconwing's or Itzel's shoes right then.

I still felt weak, and speaking seemed to drain my energy, but I took a deep breath and did my best. "Falconwing tried to kill me the night before you cursed me. He slipped away from your house somehow while you were asleep and went to the Daucina Club." Madame Cuapa's eyes flared. It was obvious that she was familiar with the club. "I was watching the club when he got there. Silverblade met him there and gave him the key to a room upstairs in the hotel, where he had a couple of underaged pros waiting for him. A girl and a boy. Falconwing caught me watching. I was lucky to get away."

Madame Cuapa's face fell. She sat there for a minute without speaking, just shaking her head. When she looked up, her features were composed. "We'll talk about this another time. I promise. But not now, and that's final."

I nodded. "How did you get away from them?"

She smiled. "It was the compulsion spell that freed me. Ironic, isn't it? When it hit me, it awakened me."

I thought about that for a second. "That means that Falconwing and Itzel aren't the ones compelling you."

"No, and I never thought they were. I don't feel either of them in that spell. And, as you suggest, it worked against them."

"You said that you were able to resist it."

"Partially." The bruja reached up and pushed a stray strand of red hair off her face. "Remember, it took the curse that killed Shipper a week to take effect. It's a very complex spell, difficult to cast. I was able to block some of the compulsion this time, so that the spell I cast on you was not as strong and air-tight as the curse on Shipper. I was able to skip some of the steps in the ritual, so the curse was missing some of the completeness that makes it so...explosive. But it took effect much more quickly, in just hours rather than days. On the one hand, that made it less dangerous. But on the other, I had to move fast in order to keep you from dying." She smiled. "I made it, but it was a near thing."

"How did you manage to slip past Falconwing and Itzel? Did Cody help you?"

Madame Cuapa frowned. "My first priority was getting to you before it was too late, but I took a minute to look for Cody. You'll have to forgive me for that. I couldn't find him right away, though, and I knew that I'd have to abandon him. I hope...." She shook her head. "Falconwing must have done something to Cody before he left the house to go to the club. He.... He must have done something to me, too, to keep me from waking." The bruja's jaw clenched and her eyes reflected her anger. Then she took a breath, and made an effort to relax the muscles in her face. "I have ways of coming and going from my own home that, well, let's just say that they bypass normal earthly laws. I used one of these paths to find you.

"And Cody?"

Madame Cuapa's face again tightened with anger. "I don't know where Cody is, but I fear the worst. They needed Cody out of the way for their plan to work. Mr. Whiskers, too. If they've hurt that boy...."

The bruja's eyes narrowed. As I watched, her hair began to puff out from her head as if she were charged with electricity. A pale blue nimbus began to emanate from her body, and she began to levitate from the chair. I felt the hairs on my arm start to rise, and I detected a faint odor of ozone in the air.

"Madame Cuapa?"

At the sound of my voice, the bruja turned on me with an expression that would have curdled milk, and I actually felt my temperature rise, but she immediately began to relax. The nimbus faded, her hair resumed its place on her head, and her body lowered itself to the chair. I rubbed my arms, which released tiny sparks of static electricity. I broke into a cold sweat, and my fever abated.

"Sorry." The witch shuddered briefly, and then slumped a bit before straightening back up. "Now is not the time to let my emotions get the better of me."

"What will you do now?" I asked.

She looked up at me, and her lips slowly curled into a smile that never reached her shining black eyes. "Now? Let's just say that my two old friends have a lot of explaining to do."

Chapter Twenty

After checking my peepers, taking my temperature, spoon-feeding me breakfast, and fussing over me like I was an infant for another hour, Madame Cuapa finally left me to finish healing on my own, but not before ordering me to stay in bed for the rest of the day. As soon as she was gone, I got up, brushed my teeth, shaved, showered, and got dressed. I took a good look at myself in the mirror over my sink. My eyes were a little puffy, and it seemed that the number of white hairs on my head had doubled. I also needed a haircut, but I figured that it would be a couple of days before I would have the time to walk into a clip joint. My face looked tired, but, all things considered, I felt okay. Good enough to get the day started, at any rate. I checked my phone and saw that I had three voice messages from Kalama, one from Crawford, two from Lubank, one from another lawyer who occasionally hired me to do investigative work for him, and one from an unknown number. Amazing how the calls pile up when you lose a day.

I listened to Crawford's message first. "Southerland, are you okay? I called the police department, but they claim that they didn't bring you in last night. Said they didn't know what I was talking about. I'm going to call your lawyer, Lubank, just in case they're hiding you away or something. Talk to you later, I hope. Oh, and I'm fine by the way. Last night was, well, I don't know what it was. Wow! Exciting?" This was followed by a short burst of laughter. "Anyway, I'll be happy to just run my store for a few weeks. No more excitement for a while! Okay? And do you have my fedora? I hope so. I'd hate to lose it. Okay, see ya!"

I was relieved to hear that Crawford had made it home okay, and that he was back into his routine. I'd have to stop by as soon as I could to return his briefcase and make sure that he hadn't suffered any permanent damage from his run-in with Falconwing.

I accessed Lubank's first message next. "Hey, asshole! Where the fuck are you? I got a call from a friend of yours who says that you might have been arrested last night. Why the fuck can't you stay out of police custody? Call me!"

Lubank's second message had come a few minutes later. "I called the station. The cops say that they don't have you. Hell, they say that they don't even *know* you! Call me, you dumb fuck! And don't think for one minute that I'm not going to bill you for the time I spent calling the cops on your behalf!"

I smiled in spite of myself. The bastard was worried about me, but that wouldn't stop him from adding another charge to my tab. His call to the station had probably lasted all of two minutes, but he'd round it up to two billable hours.

The other lawyer had called to give me a job offer. I called back and told his secretary to thank her boss for me, but to tell him that I was busy at the moment and would he please consider me the next time he needed someone. I hated to turn good-paying jobs down, but that's the way it goes in this business. Sometimes you can't handle all the offers, and sometimes the phone doesn't ring for weeks.

I listened to Kalama's first call next. "Southerland, it's Kalama. Coldgrave called me at eight thirty and filled me in on your botched surveillance job last night. Popped by a house dick? I thought you were better than that! He told me to expect a call from you. It's ten o'clock already. Just sayin'."

Kalama's second message came three hours later. "Where you at, gumshoe? It's one o'clock. I've got an update on the Silverblade case. We ran down the two underaged pros in Falconwing's room, and they're singing like canaries. The house dick and the desk clerk from last night have also been very cooperative, especially after the captain took over the questioning. Silverblade is through! Problem is, he's flown the coop! We're after him, but I don't know. Just so you know, Cuapa's name never came up. If we ever get Silverblade, maybe he'll take a deal and turn on her, but I don't know what we could do about her even if he does. Truth is, we'll have a better chance of rolling up this racket if Cuapa isn't involved. And, anyway, we have to get Silverblade first. Call me!"

The detective's third message came at a little after six in the evening. "Southerland? Shit! When you're done fuckin' around, call me! I mean it! Any time, day or night."

I nearly hit the reply button, but then I remembered the message from the unknown number. I hesitated, and then decided to check that call first. I heard a female voice that I didn't recognize say, "Mr. Southerland? You don't know me. I'm a friend of Cody's. He needs help. Can you please call this number? Thank you."

I punched the reply button, but disconnected after eleven rings. I punched in Cody's cellphone number, but my call went to voice mail. "Cody, this is Southerland. Madame Cuapa just left me. She's fine. Falconwing and Itzel turned against her, and she's going back to deal with them. You should go on home if you haven't already. She may need your help. Call me back if you need me for anything."

I figured that the kid was okay. He and Madame Cuapa had probably found each other by now, and the two of them would deal with the two witches.

Before calling Kalama, I went to my window and opened the blinds. Billowing white clouds stood out in stark relief against the bright blue sky. I opened the window to let in a breeze that was only just strong enough to rustle the leaves of the cypress trees along the street. It was a morning so pleasant that even Gio would have trouble complaining about it. I left the window open and went back to my desk thinking that this was going to be a swell day, and that maybe nobody would try to kill me with a curse or cut me open and feed my heart to an unearthly spirit.

I called Kalama, and she answered after the first ring. "Southerland?"

"Yup! How's tricks?"

I heard her sigh. "Where you been, gumshoe? You had me worried."

"Near death experience. It's a long story."

"Give me the skinny."

I rocked back in my desk chair and put my feet up on my desk. "Cuapa got hit by the compulsion spell again, and she tried to put me on ice permanently. But she broke free of it and came to my rescue. Just in the nick of time, I guess. I was out of it, but I'm okay now. Sorry about missing your calls."

"Lord's balls! Where's Cuapa now?"

"She just left to go deal with her two buddies, Itzel and Falconwing. They turned on her, but they aren't the ones behind the compulsion spell."

"You sure about that?"

"Yeah. They managed to work together to put a different kind of whammy on her, and then someone launched the compulsion spell and it freed her from their control. It's complicated, and I'm still sorting it out, but it means that I still haven't found my culprit."

"Hmm. Well, we've made some progress on my end. I have preliminary autopsy reports on Coyot and Dwayne Shipper. I don't know if they'll help you, but they might."

"So what got them?"

"Coyot was definitely mauled by a wild animal, probably a big dog, but maybe a wolf. His throat was ripped out, which would have been enough to kill him all by itself. But he would have died anyway from loss of blood from his other wounds. And, of course, his heart was ripped out. But get this, the chest wound wasn't from teeth—it was from a knife! More specifically, a stone knife. And the coroner says that the bleeding from the chest wound indicates that he was still alive when he was sliced open. In fact, he thinks that the vic was still alive when his heart was removed."

I whistled. "So an animal does the damage, and then a man uses a sacrificial knife to cut out the heart?"

"That's what it looks like."

"But the animal was a dog or a wolf? Not a flock of crows?"

"Definitely not crows. These wounds were made by teeth and claws, not by talons and beaks. The coroner is certain about that. Also, we found canine fur in the blood. We'll need further tests, but our coroner has seen were-wolf attacks, and he's leaning toward dog."

I thought for a few seconds. "Couldn't the dog hair have been from Coyot's dog? That hair might have been there before Coyot was attacked."

"Probably," the detective agreed. "It was the only fur we found in the room, so it's a good bet that it belongs to Coyot's dog. And the fur that the coroner dug out of Coyot's wounds matches the other fur."

Something felt wrong to me. "I saw that mutt. What was its name? Chichi! That's it. Friendly old hound, with the emphasis on old. And it was Coyot's familiar! Hard to see it turning on its master like that, and hard to imagine it being capable of killing him even if it did."

"The evidence points to Chichi. We haven't been able to find him anywhere, though."

Something struck me then. I took my feet off my desk and leaned forward in my chair. "Wait! Did you find Coyot's staff at the crime scene?"

"Yeah, Coyot was holding it in his hand."

"Were there any blast marks in the office?" I asked.

"Blast marks?" Kalama paused for a few moments. "No, I don't think so. I don't remember any, and there's nothing about any blast or scorch marks in the forensic reports."

I considered this. "Coyot blew a door down with that staff. If he'd been defending himself, wouldn't he have used it against his attacker?"

There was a pause on the other end of the phone. Kalama broke the silence. "Makes sense. But we didn't find any evidence of that on the scene."

"Then it must have been his dog after all. Coyot couldn't bring himself to fire on it. Maybe he didn't believe that he was in any real danger."

"Wow!" I could almost hear Kalama's shudder over the phone. "Done in by his own pooch. Poor guy. What a way to go. But why would the dog have done it? Wait! Don't tell me. Witchcraft!"

"That'd be my guess. We're dealing with witches here. Maybe the dog was drugged, or cursed, or possessed. I've seen first-hand what witchcraft can make people do even if they don't want to do it. I'm sure it works on dogs, too." I paused. "Poor old dog. If it's still alive, it must be a real mess, knowing what it did to its master."

"Lord's balls!" Kalama breathed. "Let's hope it's dead. It'd be better off."

Something else was bothering me. "Were there any signs of forced entry?"

"No. But the front door was unlocked. The receptionist had gone home, but the doctor was still there, so she didn't lock the door when she left."

"So anyone could have walked in on Coyot and caught him by surprise. And then do something to the dog to turn it on its master."

"Could be."

I tore my mind away from Coyot and his dog. "Okay, what about the Shipper kid?"

"Dwayne Shipper died of heart failure," Kalama announced.

"What?" I hadn't been expecting that.

"Yup!" confirmed the detective. "The kid had a heart attack. Right after being severely sliced up by a flock of birds."

"You're an evil copper." I smiled. "Does your daughter know that you're an evil copper?"

"She suspects. My husband knows."

I paused to get back on track. "So the were-crow did it."

"Probably. All we know from the preliminary report is that the kid suffered numerous cuts from bird talons and beaks. By numerous, I mean hundreds. He was cut up good and proper. And his eyes were pecked out, but probably not until his heart had already exploded. Young Dwayne was not in the best of shape, as it turns out. Too much rich food and no exercise. He probably wouldn't have lived past his forties unless he made some significant changes to his lifestyle."

"Wait! How do you know that it was a heart attack? Didn't you tell me before that his heart had been cut out?"

"Yup! He was sliced open, same as Coyot, and his heart was cut out. But the Shipper kid wasn't cut open with a stone knife. Whoever did it used a kitchen knife that the kid had in his room. I guess he liked to eat his dinner up there. We found all kinds of dirty plates, glasses, and dinnerware in his room. The kid was a real slob. Anyway, whoever cut his heart out tossed it aside afterwards. It slid under his bed, and that's where we found it."

I had a minor moment of enlightenment. "The heart was no good! Coyot's heart was still going when it was removed, but the kid's heart had already given out. These guys weren't just murdered—they were sacrificed!"

"Does that mean we're back to the witches?" Kalama asked.

"Maybe. Probably. Or someone who *wants* to be a witch or *thinks* he's a witch."

"He or she," Kalama reminded me. "We could be dealing with a woman. Maybe the lovely widow?"

"Uhhhh, she has an alibi, remember?"

"Were you awake all night?" Kalama asked. "Maybe you fell asleep and she...flew away?"

"Are you suggesting that Mrs. Shipper is a were-crow?" It didn't seem likely to me.

"Why not? Her story about being bothered by crows could be hooey."

"Hmm.... What was the time of death again?"

"Kaylee says that she found the body at about twelve-thirty."

"Then forget it. Mrs. Shipper and I were still at the Minotaur. Or we were on our way to my place. I'm not sure of the exact times, but I wasn't asleep until at least one."

"Sure about that, hotshot?"

I concentrated on my memory of that night, which seemed ages ago. Yes, we'd left the Minotaur at around midnight. Maybe a little after. I remembered checking the time when we were getting ready to leave. We'd parked the car in Gio's lot and walked the block to my place, where we discussed the sleeping arrangements. I didn't have a clear memory of how the discussion had ended, but it must have been at least one o'clock by the time I fell asleep.

"Positive. We talked a little before we..., before I nodded off. It had to have been at least one o'clock. Probably a little later."

"All right. If you say so. So we can rule out Mrs. Shipper, at least for the death of her stepson. The problem here is motive. If Mrs. Shipper didn't kill her pervy stepson, then who else had a reason to? His sister maybe?"

I thought about that. "Possibly. She's his stepsister, actually. Same father, different mother. If the kid was hinky for the stepmother, maybe he was doing the same sort of things with his stepsister, too. Maybe she'd had enough of it."

Kalama processed this idea for a few seconds. "I don't know. Her boyfriend confirms that she was with him at the time Dwayne was killed. He might be lying, of course, but.... I don't know. I'm not seeing it."

I called up a mental picture of Dwayne Shipper laying on his bedroom floor, leaking blood from a thousand cuts. "Do we know how the were-crow got in the kid's room?"

"Through the window. There was glass all over the floor. Some of the glass had blood on it, and some of that blood was crow blood."

I nodded to myself. "The were-crow is the key to this whole thing. The way I see it, the were-crow killed the Shipper kid while trying to conduct a sacrifice. Coyot was killed the night before, right? And that was also a sacrifice, a more successful one as it turned out. The were-crow did something to cause the dog to kill Coyot, and then he cut out his heart."

Kalama considered the idea. "Maybe. Or maybe the were-crow is part of a group, like a cult. Maybe there's more than one of these creeps out there cutting out hearts."

"Yeah, could be," I admitted.

"It's something to think about, anyway. But I still think that we've got witches behind it all."

"You might be right about that." I thought about my night at the Huntinghouse. "Falconwing attacked me the other night after I caught him with the two pros. He was going to sacrifice me to some kind of spirit." I hesitated, not wanting to tell the rest.

Kalama wouldn't let me stop there. "Go on," she prompted.

"Try to keep an open mind about this." I hesitated. "This story is going to make me sound like I've gone buggy."

"Hey, we're talking about witchcraft, right?" Kalama's voice was encouraging. "I'll believe anything!"

"We'll see. Anyway, I was paralyzed and levitating above the hotel bed. The ceiling opened up, and I could see a daytime sky, all lit up by a green light."

"Not the room above you?"

"I know. But witchcraft, right?"

"All right. Then what happened."

I hesitated, staring out the window. The day didn't seem as bright as it had. A cloud must have passed in front of the sun. "This is the part you're not going to believe," I told Kalama.

"I'll believe you, I promise!" she insisted.

"Some kind of, well, I don't know what it was. A spirit? A god? Anyway, it started to crawl down over the edge of the hole above me. It.... It had a big green feathery head that looked like a giant hummingbird's head. It was glowing like a green sun. And it had a beak like a spear."

"A giant glowing hummingbird? Are you sure that somebody didn't spike your drink?"

"See? I told you that you wouldn't believe me."

"Sorry. Go on."

I gathered my thoughts, remembering. "The head was on a man's body. And it had wings, like a hummingbird's wings, but big."

"Alkwat's balls, man! You *were* drugged!"

I could feel a wave of irritation rising up from my stomach and into my throat, like an attack of acid indigestion. "Are you going to listen, or what? You know, this was only the second-worst thing that's happened to me over the last two days."

"Sorry! Really! I'll be quiet."

"There's not much more to tell. Falconwing was mumbling some kind of chant, and as the monster came down toward me I could feel my heart trying to tear out of my body. But then the hotel dick started pounding on the door, and the noise broke Falconwing's concentration. The monster vanished and I fell onto the bed. After that, I was able to drive Falconwing away with an elemental."

"Wait. An elemental blew Falconwing out of the room?"

"It was a big elemental. And Falconwing wasn't actually there. It was just his image inside a cloud of smoke."

Kalama didn't say anything.

"I know. You think I was hopped up."

"Have you considered the possibility?" Kalama asked.

I ignored her question. "Here's the thing, though. This wasn't like those other deaths."

"No were-crow and no dogs."

"And no knife. You said that someone used knives to cut out those other hearts."

"That's right."

"Well, Falconwing didn't have a knife. He didn't need one. Either that hummingbird spirit was going to cut me open with its beak, or my heart was going to pop out on its own."

Kalama thought for a moment. "Still. We're talking about pulling out hearts. Hearts that were supposed to still be alive and beating. That's a common thread, and an unusual one. Unless you were just hallucinating."

"Trust me, I wasn't. I know the difference."

Kalama *hmphed* at me. "I'm sure you do. Okay, I believe you. We're dealing with witches here, and it all sounds like witchy shit to me. Anyway, I hear that someone else was in the room with you, and I'm sure that he'll corroborate your story."

I had deliberately avoided mentioning Crawford. I didn't want him involved. "Someone else? I don't know what you're talking about."

"Southerland, please. You need to get over the idea that all cops are idiots. We've got hotel footage of you and an unidentified man in the hallway outside the hotel room you broke into. Nice work with the lock picks, by the way. The footage shows both of you entering the room together."

I made my voice firm. "He was never there. It must have been a glitch in the tape."

We both clammed up, trying to stare each other down over the phone. Finally, I heard Kalama let out a sigh. "You'll have to come clean about him sooner or later, Southerland. That hotel footage could show up in court."

"But you don't need him at the moment, do you?" I asked. "I'm asking you to leave him be for now. If he becomes necessary for your case, I'll bring him to you myself. Until then, keep the bulls off him. Deal?"

"Deal," agreed Kalama. "For now. But I need your word that you'll produce him if we need him. Otherwise I'll track him down myself."

I knew that, under the circumstances, that was going to be the best I could do. "Fine. You have my word."

"Thanks." Kalama paused a beat. "Okay, one last item and I'll let you go. You know that we questioned Coyot after Donald Shipper's death on Monday. We were still questioning him when word came down to let all the witnesses go home. I managed to get my hands on an electronic transcript of his interrogation, and there's a section I want you to read. I'm going to email it to you right now. I don't know how much it will help you, but there's some shit in there that looks promising."

"All right."

"Okay, that's it for now," said Kalama. "You're okay? Back from the dead?"

"I said it was a *near* death experience. I'm fine. I'm a fast healer."

"Whatever you say, bub. But stay off the happy juice! They'll be hauling your ass into a clinic for the cure. You don't want the men in white coats strapping you to a slab and poking needles in your butt."

"Right. And be careful going after witches. If you see a winged man with a giant glowing hummingbird head, don't say that I didn't warn you!"

Chapter Twenty-One

The sun was shining through my window, and I got up and pulled the blinds to keep out the glare. I was thirsty, so I popped open a bottle of suds and brought it back with me to my desk. I needed something to wash the witch's brew out of my system. Madame Cuapa's potions had done the job, and I was feeling almost brand new, but the odor of that junk was leaking out every pore of my body, and I smelled like a walking corpse.

I drank down half my beer in three big gulps, filled the room with a belch that I figured did more for my belly than all of Madame Cuapa's concoctions, and called up Kalama's message in my email. I clicked on the attachment and the transcript of Coyot's interrogation popped up on my screen. I took another, smaller sip of beer and began to read.

Q: What do you think killed Shipper?

A: Southerland said that it was a curse. I don't have any reason to doubt it.

Q: You're a practicing witch, right?

A: Correct. I'm a practitioner of brujería.

Q: Are you capable of laying that kind of curse on somebody?

A: Not like that, no. I've never seen a curse that powerful. I've only just heard of them.

Q: How many witches are capable of blowing somebody up like that?

A: In the world? Several.

Q: How about locally.

A: In the Yerba City area? Probably just one. Madame Cuapa.

Q: That's the one they call the Barbary Coast Bruja?

A: That's her.

Q: How does a curse like that work?

A: What do you mean?

Q: I mean how do you do something like that?

245

A: This is not something I can easily explain to a non-practitioner. But in a nutshell, a curse that powerful isn't actually conducted by the witch. The witch calls upon a powerful spirit, and it's the spirit who actually...does the damage, you might say.

Q: A spirit?

A: Yes, and in this case, an especially powerful one. You might even call it a god. A god that only someone like Madame Cuapa could call upon and maintain her sanity. If I had to guess, I would say that the spirit, or god, that actually caused Shipper to explode like that was Xolotl.

Q: Sho.... Who?

A: Xolotl. X-O-L-O-T-L. Pronounced sho-lotj, or sho-lote, if you prefer. It's got that funny T-L sound that most non-Nahuatl speakers can't pronounce.

Q: Right. So—

A: Did you know that Lord Ketz-Alkwat's name was originally spelled Q-U-E-T-Z-A-L-C-O-A-T-L? It got modernized a few centuries ago.

Q: That's terrific. So—

A: In fact, my own name—Coyot—was once spelled with a T-L ending. It means "coyote," with two syllables, properly speaking, but—

Q: But nothing! What the fuck are you talking about?

A: Sorry. The history of the Nahuatl language is something of a passion with me. I forget how boring the subject is for most people.

Q: Never mind, skip it. Tell me about this Sho.... This god character.

A: Xolotl. Oh, he's fascinating. According to Nahuatl tradition, Xolotl brought fire to the Mexica people and was worshipped as a god in Azteca even before the appearance of the Dragon Lords. He's usually portrayed in the form of a dog with no eyes, or with lightning bolts for eyes.

Q: You don't say.

A: When Ketz-Alkwat came to what is now Tolanica, Xolotl led a resistance movement against him, but, as we know, Lord Ketz prevailed.

Q: Yes, well—

A: But, again according to Nahautl tradition, Lord Ketz couldn't kill Xolotl, so he sent him to an otherworldly realm called Mictlan. Xolotl became the ruler of Mictlan, and the Nahuatl people believed that he led their souls to his realm when they died. Some people still believe it.

Q: What do you believe?

A: What I believe is very subtle and would require a great deal of time to explain.

Q: Forget I asked. So you think that Madame Cuapa sent this dog-spirit after Shipper?

A: Southerland thinks that Madame Cuapa was forced to do it by a compulsion spell.

Q: Do you agree with him?

A: I do.

Q: Why?

A: I don't think that Madame Cuapa would willingly invoke Xolotl.

Q: Why do you say that?

A: It's complicated.

Q: Try me.

A: Madame Cuapa's father, a very powerful brujo named Cuetlachtli, the Wolf, used to serve Xolotl. When he died and was taken to Mictlan by Xolotl, Madame Cuapa took over leadership of the coven. She changed its direction in many ways. Among other things, she refused to serve Xolotl and turned the coven away from him. I haven't heard anything that might indicate she's gone back to serving the god that took her father.

Q: And you would know?

A: I think so. I am a member of the Cult of Xolotl. I'm not in the inner circle or anything, but if Madame Cuapa was invoking Xolotl, that would be a big deal. I'm pretty sure that I would have heard about it.

Q: Who else is in this cult?

A: There are a lot of us, actually. Mostly in Azteca, but quite a few up this way, too.

Q: You don't say. Anyone important?

247

Coyot never got a chance to answer. The transcript ended at this point, and a note from the officer doing the questioning told me that the interrogation had been interrupted and the witness sent home. Word that Madame Cuapa's name had come up in the interrogations had rattled some people but good, and they had wasted no time in shutting down the whole investigation. I guess that investigating powerful witches was a bad career move, a worse move than sweeping a murder investigation under the carpet, even when the vic was rich and respectable.

I read the transcript through three more times. When I was satisfied, I picked up my phone. I needed to talk to Madame Cuapa right away. I called and let the phone ring eleven times. I disconnected and tried again. Still no answer. I tried a third time and let the phone ring twenty times before giving up.

I called Cody's cel and nearly fired my phone through the window when the call went to voicemail. I waited for the beep and then started speaking. "Cody! It's Southerland. Call me! I've got something, or at least I think I do. I can't get hold of Madame Cuapa. I'm going out there, now!"

I stood up, and after some hesitation, I put on my shoulder holster and took my heater out of the safe. I ran upstairs and got my hat and coat. I put my phone in my shirt pocket and hustled out the door. I began walking, and then jogging up the block to Gio's lot to get the beastmobile. I made it halfway there when I became aware of something large coming up behind me fast. Before I could turn around, something heavy crashed into my back and sent me somersaulting to the pavement. I looked up to get the license number of the bus that I was sure had hit me, only to have my shoulders pinned to the ground by two massive fur-covered paws. I stared up straight into a pair of feral yellow eyes. The creature's snout wrinkled into a snarl, and a low growl, almost below my range of hearing, filled my skull.

My eyes dropped to the mouth of the creature, anticipating the sight of giant spear-like teeth preparing to tear into my throat. Instead, I saw a piece of paper, rolled up like a scroll, clenched in the creature's mouth. The creature opened its jaws, and the paper dropped to my chest. Then the creature took its paws off my shoulders, sat back on its haunches, and began to lick its front paw.

It was only then that I realized that the monster that had accosted me was Mr. Whiskers.

Without taking my eyes off the manticore, I rose slowly to my elbows. The rolled up paper slid to my midsection, and I grabbed it to keep from losing it in the breeze. That's when I saw that my name, "Mr. Southerland," had been written on the paper. I unrolled the paper and read the words, "Climb on and hold tight. Cody."

I looked up at Mr. Whiskers, who looked back down at me and snarled.

"Not a chance," I told him.

In response, the manticore climbed to his feet and turned so that he was standing perpendicular to my prone body, exposing his flank. He tossed his head in my direction and let out a roar so loud and so vicious that I would have run headlong into traffic if I hadn't been lying on the sidewalk.

"I don't speak manticore," I told him. "But if I did, I'd say that you just told me that you don't like this any more than I do."

Mr. Whiskers turned his head so that he was looking straight out in front of him and snorted in disgust.

I got to my feet, and after making sure that I hadn't broken anything important when the manticore knocked me to the pavement, I walked up to the side of the beast. After tucking my fedora into a pocket on the inside of my coat, I reached out and grabbed the manticore by the mane. Then I pulled myself up onto his back and lay face down between his wings. I extended my arms around the manticore's neck and grabbed some fur.

Before I could say a word, the manticore's wings snapped out from his body, and the beast began to sprint up the sidewalk. His wings began to flap, and the next thing I knew I was airborne.

***

In the past five days, I'd been attacked by a flock of crows, poisoned into a state of delirium, offered up as a sacrifice to a hummingbird god, and snatched from the boundaries of the land of the dead where I'd been sent by a curse, but when it comes to pure terror nothing takes the cake like hanging on by your fingernails to the neck of a winged killing machine while it's weaving its way at close to the speed of sound in a slalom course through Yerba City's maze of skyscrapers. As we banked in a full circle around the Transcontinental Tower, the tallest structure in the city, coming within inches of scraping its walls, I screamed, "You're doing this on purpose, you lousy sack of shit!" In response, Mr. Whiskers let out a roar and went into a sudden power dive that drove the air out of my lungs and threatened to send my stomach flying out my ass. The manticore buzzed the tops of the cars on the street below before launching himself straight up into the air. I tightened my grip on the monster's mane and hung on.

Mr. Whiskers took me high above the streets and streaked away from downtown to the western part of the city. When he swooped to the ground five minutes later in a surprisingly soft landing, I rolled off the manticore's back and fell to one knee in the middle of a paved street. I braced myself with both hands and tried to catch my breath, but Mr. Whiskers had other ideas. With a shove from his giant paw, the manticore sent me face-first into the asphalt, forcing the breath out of my body with a whoosh. Then the big cat grabbed the collar of my coat in its teeth and began to drag me up the street.

"Let go, you mangy fleabag! I can walk!" I managed to scramble to my feet and the manticore released my collar. I remembered that I was packing heat and thought about shooting the creature, but I figured it would just make him mad. Mr. Whiskers roared at me and began walking. I sighed in resignation and followed.

Looking around, I saw that I was in an unfamiliar part of the city. It was a workingclass neighborhood that had seen better days, with small worn houses packed together like sardines in a tin. The houses were at least seventy years old and in varied states of decay. Some were well maintained, but most were run down, and a few looked like they'd been abandoned for decades. Each house had a small yard in front, but most of the yards were overgrown or had been taken over by weeds. The only cars I saw were parked at the side of the street, in driveways, or in the front yards. Many of these were missing tires, and some were missing hood covers and even doors. All around me, people sat on porches

250

or wandered through the neighborhood, using the street, sidewalks, and front yards indiscriminately. They either ignored me or stared at me dead-eyed under hooded brows. Mr. Whiskers walked past them like they weren't there. None of them seemed surprised by the fact that a four-hundred pound bat-winged jungle cat with a scorpion's tail was wandering up their street. Maybe monsters were a common sight here.

Mr. Whiskers led me to an abandoned house in the middle of the block. At least I assumed that it had been abandoned. A portion of the wall at one corner of the house was missing, as was the front door, and there was no glass in the windows, which were covered over on the inside with cardboard. My guess was that a meth lab inside the house had exploded several years before. I followed the manticore through the door-less entry.

The inside of the house was dark, but that was no obstacle to my enhanced awareness. Mr. Whiskers led me past the front room down a short hallway to what had once been a bedroom. Cody was sitting on a blanket on the floor in the corner of the room. Next to him on the blanket was a plate that showed the remains of a meal, black beans and rice by the look of it. A flattened beer can lay beside the plate. Cody, seeming a little groggy, peered up at me. "Hello, sir. Did you have a nice flight?"

Cody didn't look well. The rims of his eyes were red, his face was pale, and his black hair was dank and plastered over his shoulders like strands of wet seaweed. He was wearing an unbuttoned dark purple leather vest with matching leather pants. His feet were bare, and, as usual, he was shirtless. Normally, he wore that look with style, but, bunched into a back corner of that burnt-out house, the big man brought to mind a plastic trash bag waiting to be hauled out to the dumpster.

Mr. Whiskers walked over to the plate and began licking up the remains of the rice and beans. I nodded at the animal with my chin. "That monster gave me an aerial tour of the downtown skyline. He was trying to get me air sick."

Cody's lips turned upwards into a weak smile. "Exhilarating, wasn't it!"

"That's an interesting perspective."

Cody reached up and scratched the manticore between the eyes. "He loves to fly. He's also an outrageous showoff."

"What happened to you?" I asked. "Did you get my phone messages?"

Cody sighed, and his smile disappeared. "I don't have my phone. I left it at the house."

"Are you all right? You don't look too good."

"I'll be okay." As if to prove it, the big man pushed himself to his feet, though he continued to lean against the wall. "Some of the neighbors have been taking care of me. I could use more food, though, and Mr. Whiskers needs to eat."

"What happened?" I asked again.

Cody scowled. "Falconwing! He tried to...hurt me, but I got away, thanks to Mr. Whiskers." He patted the big cat on the head. Mr. Whiskers let out a low growl and bumped Cody's waist with his forehead. "I need to walk a little. Let's get out of here and I'll tell you about it."

***

We walked a block to a grassy area that used to be a park. I guess it still was, but it hadn't been serviced in years. Some kids played on rusty playground equipment, avoiding the jagged metal and broken chains. They laughed and shouted and looked to be having a swell time. They didn't seem to mind Mr. Whiskers, who was nosing through the tall grass searching for snack food. Cody and I strolled through the grass to a sun-bleached wooden bench and sat down.

Cody hadn't said anything on the way to the park, and I let him gather his thoughts without rushing him. He watched the kids running through the remains of the playground for a bit. Then he looked down and took a deep breath. "Two nights ago," he began, "while Itzel was still asleep, Falconwing and the Madame went out to the back yard to talk privately. After a while, I could hear them arguing. I couldn't catch it all, but Falconwing was telling the Madame that recent events had called her competency into question. He told her that she should consider retiring and turn the coven over to him. I couldn't hear what the Madame was saying, but I don't think she was taking him seriously. I think she was just brushing him off and telling him not to worry so much. Anyway, the two of them came back inside, and the Madame said that she needed to go upstairs and get some sleep. Falconwing convinced her to have a glass of wine with him first. They went into the living room and I brought in a bottle and two glasses. I poured the wine and then left, but before I got out of the room I turned and saw Falconwing drop something into the Madame's glass. It was very slick, and the Madame was looking the other way, but I saw him do it. I started to say something, but Falconwing looked right at me, and the next thing I knew I was walking away. It was like I was trying to remember something, but I'd forgotten what it was. It was only later that I recalled what I had seen."

"Falconwing put a spell on you?"

"You have to watch out for his eyes. Never look directly into them."

I nodded. I'd tell Cody about my own experience with Falconwing later, but I wanted to hear his story first. "Okay. Then what happened?"

The Madame went to bed, and a few minutes later my memory cleared up and I remembered what Falconwing had done to the Madame's drink. I went into the Madame's room and tried to wake her, but she wouldn't wake up. Then Falconwing came in and told me not to worry about the Madame, that he'd only slipped her a mild sedative to help her sleep and that she'd be fine in the morning. I went downstairs with Falconwing."

Cody looked down at his hands and clenched his teeth. "That's when he told me to come to his room. I refused. He told me that he could make me. Just like he.... Like he...."

"Like he did before?" I finished for him.

Cody turned his head and glared at me. "You knew?" he breathed.

"It's pretty obvious that something happened between you."

Cody looked down again. "I was twelve years old. Twelve years old." He shook his head. "I was still living in the village down south. The Madame came to visit my family. She brought Falconwing with her. He spent a lot of time talking to me. I thought he was cool. He really seemed interested in me, and, well, even back then I knew that I wasn't like most of my friends. They were starting to notice girls, but girls didn't interest me too much. I was attracted to men. And Falconwing is a good-looking man. Anyway, one night he came to my room and asked me if I wanted to take a walk with him. To me it sounded like an adventure, to be out with this fascinating older guy with no one else around. I was just a kid, but he talked to me like I was a man, and I liked that. We walked into the fields outside the village, and he started talking to me about...ways in which we could become closer friends. Then he kissed me."

Cody paused, not looking at me, and I waited, not wanting to push him.

When he spoke again, the big man's voice was wistful, "I liked it. But he wanted to do more, and I didn't want to. That's when he got mad. I tried to run, but he looked me in the eyes, and I couldn't move. All I could do was lay there and...let him do what he wanted."

He stopped then. "Were there other times?" I asked.

"Yes," Cody admitted in a low voice. Now that he was bringing his secret into the light, his voice began to increase in strength. "Many times over the next few years. Every time he came to visit. But he didn't have to force me after that first time. I was convinced that I was in love with him." He shook his head. "I knew that he didn't love me, but I was just a big stupid kid, and he made me feel grown up. I would have done anything for him, just to have him spend time with me and talk to me man-to-man, like I was an adult. And he told me not to tell anyone, especially the Madame. I used to tell myself that he had put a spell on me so that I couldn't talk about it."

I kept my voice soft. "He didn't, though, did he. You're telling me now." When Cody nodded, I continued, "He didn't need a spell. It's a hard thing to talk about, especially for a kid. Did he tell you that the Madame would get mad if she knew?"

Cody looked at me with downcast eyes. "Yes. He said that the Madame would abandon me for bringing trouble to her doorstep and that she'd never want to see me again. That would have been unbearable for me. So I kept quiet. And I've kept quiet. Up till now."

"Cody. Look at me." Cody hesitated for a moment, and then raised his eyes until they met mine. "You didn't do anything wrong. Madame Cuapa will not blame you. She will not think badly of you. She most certainly will not abandon you. Falconwing didn't put a spell on you, but he still messed with your mind. Madame Cuapa will know this."

Cody nodded. "I know. I know. I know. I guess I've always known, but I just didn't want to stir anything up. She and Falconwing are very close friends."

"Maybe not so much anymore."

Cody's eyes widened. "What do you mean?"

"You've been out of touch," I told him. "The Madame has fallen out with both Falconwing *and* Itzel. They turned on her."

"What!" Cody leaped to his feet.

"She's dealing with it," I put my hand on his arm. "Sit back down. We need to talk about some things before you go running off half-cocked. I have some information that you need to give to Madame Cuapa. But first you have to finish telling me about the other night."

Cody sat down, but I could see that he was impatient to leave. "We hadn't...done anything together for years. I think he'd lost interest in me. But the other night, he told me that he wanted me. I told him to forget it, and he looked at me and I froze up, just like the first time, only worse. I couldn't stop him, but Mr. Whiskers could. He came in and attacked Falconwing. Falconwing did something to confuse him, but Mr. Whiskers was able to drag me out of the room and out of the house. I don't remember too much after that, but Mr. Whiskers flew me out here to this neighborhood. I have some relatives here, an auntie and a couple of cousins, and I know some of the neighbors."

"One of them called me. She told me you needed help, but she didn't leave a name. When I called back, no one answered."

"That was probably my cousin, Tepin. She has a landline phone, but no cel. I was in bad shape when I got here. Whatever Falconwing did to me, it didn't wear off right away. She's been feeding me rice and beans." He looked at me with a smile. "I should introduce you to her. She's a great cook! Maybe the two of you will hit it off."

"Thanks. I'm a little busy these days."

He let out a weak laugh, which turned into a hacking cough. "I'm just now getting my strength back. But if the Madame needs my help, I should go to her right away!" He seemed ready to spring up again.

"Hang on a second." I reached out to restrain him. "The Madame can handle herself. Falconwing and Itzel won't be able to catch her by surprise this time."

Cody looked reluctant, but he didn't bolt. I looked out and saw Mr. Whiskers crouched in the grass, shaking his back end. "Looks like your pussycat has found something. I hope it's not a small child."

Cody smiled. "He won't hurt anybody as long as I'm with him."

As we watched, the manticore pounced and pulled something out of the grass. He shook his head vigorously, and I could see that he had a four-foot snake wriggling in his jaws. "Lord's balls!" I shouted.

Mr. Whiskers slammed the snake to the ground and then lifted it back into the air. His jaws opened and he clamped his teeth back down on the snake. He opened his jaws again, and the snake vanished into the manticore's mouth. Mr. Whiskers swallowed, and started nosing through the grass for a second course.

One of the kids in the playground, a little girl about ten years old, had been watching the manticore hunt. When Mr. Whiskers had finished with the snake, the little girl looked in our direction with wide eyes, grinned, and said, "Cool!" Then she ran to tell her friends what she had seen.

I looked over at Cody, whose eyes were glazed over. He ran his tongue over his lips. Then his eyes sharpened, and he glanced over at me and cleared his throat. "So where were we?" he asked.

Chapter Twenty-Two

When I was sure that I had Cody's attention, I resumed questioning him. "After Falconwing attacked you and chased you and your pet out of the house, he contacted Claudius Silverblade. You know about him, right?"

Cody nodded. "You asked about him the other day. I knew that the Madame has been monitoring his career and that she has plans for him. You asked Falconwing if Silverblade had ever provided sexual partners for him, and he denied it, but I could tell that he was lying." Cody's expression hardened.

I nodded. "Yes, he was. After Falconwing called him, he met him at a place called the Daucina Club. Are you familiar with it?"

"I'm aware of it. I know that it's an exclusive club for rich old fogies."

"They've got branches in every major city in the world, including here in Yerba City." I looked at Cody, but he just shrugged. I went on. "The local branch is located in the basement of the Huntinghouse Hotel. I was there that night and saw Falconwing meet up with Silverblade. Silverblade set him up with two partners. Teenagers. A girl and a boy."

Cody nodded, hanging his head.

I put my hand on Cody's shoulder and then released it. "I've got to ask you something." Cody looked over at me. "The police expect to have Silverblade in custody soon. He's going to be charged with trafficking underaged prostitutes. What I need to know from you right now is whether the Madame is involved in his racket."

Cody's eyes hardened, but then he looked away. When he looked back, he nodded. "She's aware of it."

"Is she running it? Is she Silverblade's boss? Tell the truth!"

"No sir!" Cody shook his head. "Uh-uh! She wouldn't involve herself in anything like that. That's not her kind of game."

"You're positive? She's been thinking about bringing Silverblade into her corporate office."

"You're barking up the wrong tree, mister!" Cody insisted. "It's Silverblade's racket. It starts and stops with him. The Madame has nothing to do with it. I'd know if she did. I have access to all her personal financial records."

I studied Cody until I was convinced that he was telling the truth as he knew it. I wasn't completely convinced that his boss wasn't hiding something from him, but I felt some relief at his vehement denial. I hoped for his sake that he was right.

"Okay." I waved a hand. "Let's move on. Falconwing caught me surveilling him. He whammied me with those eyes of his and tried to feed my heart to some kind of spirit."

Cody's eyes widened. "A spirit? What spirit?"

"It looked with a man with wings and a green hummingbird's head."

"Huitzilopochtli!" Cody exclaimed.

"Wheetso what?"

"Huitzilopochtli. The Hummingbird. He's the central god of the brujería. The Nahuatl people say that it was Huitzilopochtli who led the Azteca people to Tenochtitlan. He's wicked powerful!" Cody stared at me. "You shouldn't have been able to escape him."

"I got lucky. Something caused Falconwing to lose his concentration and the spirit vanished."

Cody nodded. "That makes sense. Holding Huitzilopochtli in this earthly plane is difficult under the best of conditions, even for a master brujo like Falconwing. It would require the shedding of much blood."

"Yeah." I couldn't stop myself from shuddering a little at the memory. "I guess that's why he was after my heart. What is it with your Nahuatl spirits and hearts?"

"The spirits require energy from living beings in order to allow themselves to be used by the practitioners of the brujería. That's why almost all spells require the shedding of blood. The bigger the spell, the more blood that's required. But the major spirits, gods like Huitzilopochtli, need the energy from still-beating hearts. The old Azteca people used to sacrifice their enemies to gods like Huitzilopochtli by the thousands. Nahuatl belief says that Huitzilopochtli holds back the darkness, and that without him life on earth would be impossible. But it's a hard job, and without constant refreshment, the god's own energy would expire in fifty-two years."

"And then what? The sun would go out?"

"The world would be plunged into darkness. Old Azteca belief says that the sun shines with the energy of Huitzilopochtli."

"Sounds like as good an excuse for human sacrifices as any." For a few seconds, I watched the kids play on the broken down playground equipment. "I wonder.... You say that this god—Huitzilopochtli?—you say he needs energy from fresh-plucked human hearts, I guess because they give him the super jolts of living energy that he needs to keep the sun lit, or whatever. What about an exploding body—would that be as effective as a beating heart?"

Cody shrugged. "I was brought up in the culture, but I'm not a priest, or a witch. Maybe. Seems like it would."

"So Donald Shipper's death could have worked as a sacrifice." It was an interesting angle. "But Huitzilopochtli isn't the only spirit that needs sacrifices, is he. What about that spirit in the tapestry on the wall of your Madame's meeting room? The one that looks like a dog with no eyes?"

"That's Xolotl," Cody told me. "He's the ruler of Mictlan, the land of the dead. He's a wicked powerful god, too. The belief is that he brought fire and much knowledge to humanity."

"Madame Cuapa's father used to worship him, didn't he."

"Yes, he did. His whole coven did."

"And he held sacrifices for him. Cut out hearts."

Cody nodded. "Yes, but the Madame put a stop to all that."

"But she participated in sacrificial ceremonies for Xolotl when her father was in charge of the coven, right?"

"Yes," Cody admitted, "But that was a long time ago. She rejected Xolotl and turned the coven away from him. No more worship. No more human sacrifices. She won't have anything to do with him anymore."

"Maybe not willingly. But I'm pretty sure that the compulsion spell forced her to call on Xolotl to kill Shipper."

Cody looked out over the untended grass of the park. "Yes, from what little I know of these things, I can see where that might be the case."

"I'm pretty sure of it," I repeated. "Because whoever is compelling the Madame struck again yesterday."

Cody's head whipped around and he stared at me open-mouthed.

"She was forced to put the same whammy on me that she put on Shipper, although she says that she was able to resist the compulsion to some extent this time. The curse hit me yesterday morning. It's a little fuzzy in my head, but I gather that I was on my way to oblivion, and a big black dog with no eyes was taking me there. But the Madame was able to intervene and pull me back."

Cody reached out with both arms and grabbed my shoulder with his huge mitts. "Lord Alkwat's balls! Fires of Hell!"

"I woke up with Madame Cuapa feeding me potions to heal me from the ordeal." I paused. "She was naked, but the way, and I got a full view of her tattoos."

Cody stared off into the park and said nothing.

"That's some quality artwork. What can you tell me about it?"

Cody blinked. "Her tattoos? What do you mean?"

"That's not ordinary work."

"No, no, it's not," Cody shook his head. "She has this guy named Teca who does them for her. He's an amazing artist! It's a painful process, but the Madame endures it."

"Are the tattoos important?" I asked. "I mean, is it more than just body art?"

"Oh yes!" Cody nodded. "Tattoos are extremely important to the brujas and brujos. I mean, some of the tattoos are just for show, but many of them are enchanted, which means that the witches can cast certain powerful spells on the spot without having to conduct a time-consuming ritual first. Some of the tats actually keep minor spirits trapped in the ink and give the wearers constant protection. That's why you can't kill someone like the Madame by shooting her, for instance."

"So some of Madame Cuapa's tattoos are enchanted?"

Cody nodded. "I think that just about all of them are. That's one of the reasons she's so strong."

"I'm guessing that some tattoo work is more effective than others?" I looked at Cody for confirmation.

"That's right."

"And this guy, Teca?"

"He's the best! He's got a real gift. He must have been blessed. Either that, or he was born with skills similar to a witch's. Madame Cuapa doesn't use anyone else for her skin work."

"How long has she been using him?"

Cody shook his head. "I don't know. As long as I've known her."

I caught Cody's eyes and held them. "Cody. This is important. When I saw Madame Cuapa's tattoos yesterday, some of them looked new. When was the last time she saw this Teca?"

"Let's see. It was Tuesday, the morning after the Madame was compelled to poison you and you shot her. She wanted some extra protection, so she called Teca and convinced him to come over right away. He added some detail to a couple of her tattoos."

"How long was he there?"

Cody shrugged. "Not long. He works fast, and this was just touch-up work. I think he was out by lunchtime."

"Did you see him leave? Did you see him get into a car? Did he call a cab?"

Cody frowned. "He always comes in his van. You can't miss it. He's painted it all up with his work, and it's got Teca's Tattoos written on both sides in big letters."

"So he got into his van? This is important."

"Well.... Now that you mention it, I didn't see the van on Tuesday. He walked away down the street. I assume that he was parked nearby, though. His shop is over in Placid Point, and he lives above the shop. That's way too far to walk."

I leaned back on the bench and closed my eyes. "Got him!"

"Got who? What do you mean?" I opened my eyes to catch Cody staring at me.

"Teca is the were-crow," I told him.

"Wait.... What?"

"After Teca was out of your sight, he transformed into crows and flew to the Shipper house, just in time to catch me walking out after talking to Mrs. Shipper. Then after I left, he flew back into your neighborhood to retrieve his van, which he had parked around the corner from your house. That's where Smokey,

261

my elemental, saw him transform back into his human form. Falconwing kept Smokey from showing us the were-crow, but I don't need that now. Teca's our man. It all adds up. Smokey led me to the spot where Teca reverted to his human form, but, at the time, I suspected that the were-crow was one of Madame Cuapa's guests, who had both showed up that day. I was in the neighborhood, so I took the opportunity to get behind your house to get a look at the two witches."

"And Mr. Whiskers spotted you. And I took you to the meeting room."

"Where I saw the image of Xolotl on the tapestry. And that leads me to my next point." I paused. "Madame Cuapa has two big snake tattoos, one with its head on the front of her torso, and one with its head on her back."

Cody's face was expressionless, but he didn't meet my eyes. I think he was a little uncomfortable with my intimate knowledge of the Madame's skin.

I continued. "The one on her back is looking at a crow, who is staring back at the snake. I think that the crow is Teca's signature."

Cody's eyes widened. "That makes sense! I've always wondered about it. The snakes are representations of the Ometeotl, the dual god of creation and fertility. Omecihuatl, the female creative spirit, is the one in front. The one in back is Ometecuhtli the male principle. They are both one god and two, or one god with two natures, you might say. The Ometeotl is the most powerful spirit in the brujería. The dual god gave birth to some of the other powerful gods, including Huitziliopochtli."

Cody paused and smiled. "Sorry to be so long-winded. Is this important?"

"It might be." I found myself interested despite myself. "Go ahead."

"Anyway, much of the Madame's power rests in the spells embedded in those two tattoos. But the crow is just a crow. As far as I know, it contains no enchantments at all. It might be the Madame's only tattoo that doesn't. So it makes sense that it's the artist's signature." Cody smiled. "Pretty bold of him, to put his signature on the Madame's back. But I guess that the quality of his work justifies a little show of pride."

"His work might be even better than you think." I met his eyes. "When Madame Cuapa was tending to me yesterday, I saw the snake tattoo on her back change. The head of the snake became a black dog with lightning bolts for eyes. It was Xolotl."

Cody looked away and shook his head. "That's impossible. Tattoos don't change. How close a look did you get?"

"It was dark, but that doesn't affect my sight. I'll admit that I was a little woozy, though. It's possible that I was hallucinating."

Cody nodded, but not with much conviction. "That's gotta be it."

"But bear with me here. What if Teca, who you agree is a wizard at his craft, what if he was able to somehow superimpose Xolotl over.... Over.... What was the name of that snake god again?"

"Ometecuhtli." Cody shook his head again. "I've seen that tattoo many times. I would know if there was something weird about it."

"Maybe, but maybe not. Look, I'm going to tell you something that you might not know." I waited for Cody to meet my eyes. "Eight months ago, I met an elf. You know that they aren't really extinct, right?"

Cody gave one slight nod.

I went on. "The elf did something to me that made me abnormally aware of my surroundings. Like I know without looking that Mr. Whiskers is taking a whiz over on that tree behind me, and that a couple of tomato-heads are smoking rock over there behind those bushes. I think that with my enhanced awareness, and maybe because of the state my mind was in after the Madame brought me back from the edge of death, or maybe just because of a trick of the light, I was able to see something that is normally hidden."

Cody thought about this. "Could even an artist like Teca fool the Madame in this way? Introduce a hidden image of Xolotl right on her skin? But it would have to be enchanted for it to work. Teca is special, but he's not a witch. He wouldn't be able to hide that from the Madame."

"Well, I admit that I don't have all the answers, but Madame Cuapa needs to know about this. I'm going to call her now and let her know that I've found you. I'll tell her that you're on your way home."

But when I tried, no one answered the phone. I let it ring ten times, then disconnected.

I let out a frustrated breath. "She's still not answering."

Cody frowned. "It might not mean anything. She has this thing about telephones. She thinks that they are invasive, and she almost always leaves it up to me to answer her calls. She doesn't own a cel, you know. Every time I tell her she should get one, she refuses."

I let out another breath. "I don't like it."

Cody rose to his feet. "I don't either. We need to go."

I stood. "*You* need to go."

"You're not coming?" Mr. Whiskers was trotting in our direction.

"I'll get another ride. Besides, I want to go see Teca and stand him down. If I'm right, he's guilty of at least one murder, and it looks like he could be the one pulling Madame Cuapa's strings. From what you told me about the tattoos, he could be working some kind of magic through the secret tat he put on Madame Cuapa's back. You go to the Madame and tell her everything I told you. She'll be able to untangle things from her end. Meanwhile, I'll brace Teca and see what he's got to say for himself. I'm betting that it will be a story worth hearing."

Cody hopped on the manticore's back with practiced ease, and the beast prepared himself for takeoff.

"Wait!" I shouted.

Mr. Whiskers stopped, and Cody looked at me with raised eyebrows.

"Has either Falconwing or Itzel been inked by Teca?"

Cody blinked. "I don't know about Itzel, but Falconwing has. He's got a big tattoo of the hummingbird god on his chest, and it's in the same style and quality as the tats Teca put on the Madame."

***

As soon as Mr. Whiskers had flown Cody out of the park, I took out my phone and called Detective Kalama. When she answered, I told her. "I know who the were-crow is. Do you want to run him in for the murder of the Shipper kid?"

"I'm suspended, remember?"

"I don't think they'll mind. You can at least call your lieutenant and tell him who to pick up. I'm guessing he'll let you in on it."

"Probably. Who is he?"

"I'll tell you, but I want a run at him first."

Kalama waited a second or two before responding. "I don't think that's a good idea."

"I want to ask him a few questions concerning Madame Cuapa before you guys come in and he lawyers up or gets lost in the system."

More silence from Kalama. Then, "I still don't think it's a good idea."

"But that's not a "no," is it. Just give me a few minutes with him. I think he might be the guy with the compulsion spell on Madame Cuapa. If he is, then Cuapa can deal with him. Either way, you still got him for the Shipper kid's murder."

"Then stand aside and let us take him for that."

"Nuts to that! Once you coppers have him, you'll bury any involvement he might have with Cuapa. The department doesn't want any part of her. And I'll lose my chance to find out if he's the one with the juju on Cuapa."

Kalama sighed. "Okay, how much time will you need?"

"Not much. And maybe I'll be able to tie him to the Coyot murder, too, while I'm at it."

Kalama deliberated for a few seconds before conceding. "All right. What's your plan?"

I suppressed a sigh of relief. I knew that Kalama was sticking her neck out for me, and that she didn't have to. "First, I need you to pick me up."

"Where are you?"

I gave her the intersection nearest to the park.

Kalama whistled. "What are you doing there?"

"Long story. I'm stuck here without a car, and I don't think I can convince a hack to come into this neighborhood, even in daytime."

"Okay, I'm maybe twenty minutes away. Try not to get mugged."

"Don't be slow. A couple of rockheads are giving me the eye even as we speak."

"You got a roscoe?"

"Nine-millimeter."

"Good. You can shoot out your kidneys before they get their hands on you. Those rockheads have been known to sell internal organs to support their habit."

I studied the two ragged figures who had emerged from the bushes, their eyes darting everywhere but at me. "I don't think it will come to that. From the looks of them, I think they'd rather eat my kidneys than sell them. I'd better disconnect, though. It looks like they're about to make me a business proposition."

I disconnected the call and put the phone into my pocket. The two figures crept in my direction, never looking directly at me, and pausing every couple of steps as if reconsidering the wisdom of their actions. I kept my hands in my pockets and my eyes on the pair of them as I waited, but also listened to hear whether anyone else was coming up on me from another direction. So far, I hadn't heard anything, but I stayed attentive.

When the pair were within ten feet of me, I pulled my hands out of my pocket and unbuttoned the top of my coat so that I had access to my heater. Not that I thought I would need to use it. The two junkies were so emaciated that they looked like they'd have trouble holding their own against a strong breeze. Badass could have broken them in half, but I wasn't going to summon the big gun without further provocation.

The junkies advanced just short of spitting distance and stopped to peer in my general direction with hungry eyes. Turning his gaze to my feet, one of them let out a hoarse hissing whisper, "Hey mister—ya got any spare change?"

"Sorry fellas." I spread my arms to my sides, palms up. "Fresh out."

The two of them looked at each other, and one of them nodded. I braced myself for some kind of attack but was caught by surprise when the two scrawny rockheads melted before my eyes, and the grass in front of me was suddenly swarming with snakes.

Chapter Twenty-Three

The snakes had puffed themselves up and were coiled to strike. Some of them were vibrating the tips of their tails. I have to admit that my heart leaped into my throat, and that my instincts were telling me to make tracks. But I didn't. Although the dark brown patterns along their pale brown bodies made them appear to be venomous rattlesnakes, their snub-nosed heads were too narrow, and they lacked the rattler's black and white banding on the end of their tails. Besides, they didn't have rattles. I recognized the reptiles as a non-venomous variety that we used to call gopher snakes when I was a kid. I knew that all snakes bite, and that the bite of even a non-venomous snake can lead to nasty infections. I could see that the grass was seething with close to a hundred of these snakes, each one about a yard or so long, but after my initial second of shock, I relaxed.

I knew a few things about shape-shifters because of my friendship with Crawford. He had revealed to me that were-rats could transform into a finite number of rats. A were-rat could survive the death some of its individual rats, but when too many of the rats died the rest of them could no longer reform and become human. The individual rats would eventually lose the last vestiges of their humanity and become a mere collection of ordinary wild rodents. He told me that it was the same with all of the various types of shape-shifters that transformed into swarms of animals. From the sickly look of those two rockheads, I guessed that they wouldn't be able to lose more than a few more snakes without losing their ability to transform back into humans. I had a feeling that one of them had lost a part of himself just minutes earlier to a hungry manticore

Rather than running, I kept my legs steady and feet planted, put my hands in my pockets, and smiled down at the slithering serpents. "Is this the part where your victim screams and beats feet while you get your kicks?" I stared at the snakes, holding my ground. "Sorry, I'm not playing that game."

The snakes advanced on me, hissing like a leaky gas valve, but stopped before getting too close. "I don't know how many snakes you've got left in you." I reached inside my coat and pulled out my gat. "But I don't think I'd have to blast too many apart before you'd both be kissing your human asses goodbye forever. All things considered, that might be the best thing for you, but far be it for me to make that kind of decision on your behalf."

The closest snakes withdrew a little. I holstered the gat. "Tell you what. Your little gag is going over like a lead balloon, so why don't you pull yourselves together again and we'll talk. I might have a proposition for you. Something you'll like."

The snakes writhed around a little, and then slowly they crawled under the clothes that they had abandoned in the grass and transformed themselves back to human, pulling on their ragged shorts, pants, shirts, and shoes as they did so. When they were finished, they stared down at the ground near their feet, looking sheepish.

"How would you like to earn some dough?" I asked. That perked them up. They didn't lift their heads, but I could see their lips curl up into something that looked like smiles.

***

"Who are your friends?" Kalama had pulled up to the curb where I was waiting with the two disheveled junkies, who were busy staring off to their sides with downcast eyes.

"The one with the runny nose is Yolo."

"They both have runny noses."

"The other one is Zolo. They're coming with us."

"Are they housebroken?"

"I doubt it."

The detective sighed. "Do we need them?"

"They're part of my plan."

"You have a plan?"

"I'm working on one."

"Lord's balls, Southerland!"

"It'll be fine, detective." I turned to the two rockheads. "C'mon fellas. You get the back seat. I'll ride shotgun."

I directed Kalama toward Placid Point. While I'd been waiting for the detective to pick me up, I'd accessed the internet on my phone and found the location for Teca's Tattoos. It turned out that his shop wasn't far from Crawford's place. I filled Kalama in on what I'd learned from Cody as she drove.

Kalama's eyes darted as she maneuvered through traffic and listened to my story. "I get why you think that someone is controlling Cuapa through an enchanted tattoo. Given the level of witchcraft we're talking about, that seems like it could work. That doesn't mean that it's the tattoo artist who's working the spell, though."

"Maybe not, but he's involved."

"You really think he's the were-crow?" Kalama asked.

"No doubt about it. He was in the right place at the right time. And his signature crow tat on Cuapa's back is the kicker."

"But what was his motive for killing the Shipper kid?"

I'd been thinking about this. "The key is Mrs. Shipper. I think that our were-crow is obsessed with her."

Kalama thought this over. "Obsessed? You think that he's some kind of stalker?"

"Something like that. When I was questioning Mrs. Shipper, I noticed a painting in her living room, a desert landscape with a crow in the foreground. I don't know much about art but I think that Cuapa's tattoo artist is the same artist who painted that picture. The style is distinctive enough that even a non-expert like me can see it. The painting could mean that the artist knew the Shippers. He could have been attracted to Cindy Shipper. It wouldn't be hard."

Kalama glanced over at me. "Guess not."

I ignored the glance. "The artist is a were-crow. That's two different kinds of mentally unstable. I mean, most of the artists I've met are at least a little bit nutso, but shape-shifters tend to be downright batty." I glanced back at our two backseat passengers. Both of them were slouched in their seats, their tired eyes uncomprehending and their expressions slack. If they had been listening to me tell Kalama about witches, were-crows, and magic tattoos, their only reaction so far had been utter indifference.

271

I went on. "So the tattoo artist's attraction to Mrs. Shipper gets a little weird. He somehow discovers a way to use Madame Cuapa as an instrument of murder by manipulating her through one of his tattoos. And he uses the witch to murder Mrs. Shipper's husband."

Kalama turned her head and stared at me. "You think he murdered the son *and* the father?"

"Watch the road!" I braced myself against the dashboard with both hands. Kalama slowed the car as an SUV changed out of a slower moving lane and squeezed in front of her. "Yeah. I think that the artist killed them both."

"Okay, I can see why he might want to get the husband out of the way, but why the son?"

"You remember that Dirty Dwayne had videotaped his stepmother sunbathing in the buff out in the back yard. I don't think that he was the only guy in the audience. Mrs. Shipper told me that crows have been hanging out at her house."

"You think that the were-crow was watching Mrs. Shipper sunbathe?"

"I do. I don't know if he's ever actually met Mrs. Shipper, or when he first saw her and starting stalking her, but at some point he discovered that she liked to soak up the afternoon sun in her back yard. This past Tuesday, he did a house call at Madame Cuapa's. Touched up a few of her tats. According to Cody, he worked fast and was done by about noon. He wants to get to the Shipper house to see the show, but he thinks that if he drives, it will take too long and he'll miss it. So he gets out of sight, transforms into crows, and flies. He gets there just in time to see the object of his obsession hugging me in her doorway. So he lands on the lawn and gives me a warning. I suspect that he was telling me to lay off his gal. And then, according to my elemental, the crows hung around on the roof of the house for a while after I drove away. Whether he gets to see Mrs. Shipper or not, I don't know. But eventually he flew back to get his van, which was still parked over by Cuapa's house."

"You still haven't told me why you think the were-crow killed the Shipper kid."

"I'm getting to that. According to Mrs. Shipper, the were-crow came to her bedroom window Tuesday night. I think that he'd reached the point where he wanted to get closer to her, to start a real relationship. The husband was gone, and he was ready to be more than just an observer. It's also possible that seeing me and her together earlier that day might have pushed him to go beyond just watching her from a distance. Anyway, late that night he comes to her bedroom window and starts scratching at it, making a lot of noise and maybe trying to get in. I'm thinking that maybe he came to her window again the next night, but Mrs. Shipper isn't there."

"Because she was getting drunk with you at the Black Minotaur Lounge."

"Yeah. So he goes to look in the other windows, probably hoping to find her."

"And when he looks into young Dwayne's window, he catches him pleasuring himself while watching videos of his naked stepmother."

"And that drives him crazy enough to attack the kid, who drops dead with a coronary. He resumes his human form and finds the knife, which he uses to cut out the heart. But the heart is no good, so he tosses it and gets the hell out."

A hoarse voice came from the back seat. "She was naked?"

I turned. "What?"

Yolo, or maybe it was Zolo, spoke without looking at me. "You said something about a video of a naked lady?"

I stared at him for a long moment. "I think you must have misheard me."

The junkie looked disappointed. "Oh. Okay." His eyes glazed over again.

I turned back to see Kalama staring at me. "You sure about these guys?"

I shrugged. "We'll see."

Kalama honked at a car that didn't move fast enough after the light turned green. "Why does he cut out the kid's heart?"

"I'm still putting the pieces together. Maybe he's part of a cult or something."

Kalama nodded, but she didn't look convinced. "I'm still not seeing how this tattoo joker casts a spell on Cuapa. Is he a were-crow and a witch, too?

"Cody doesn't think he's a witch. But he definitely hangs around them. Cuapa's had him over to work on her skin, and he's worked on Falconwing at some point. Maybe Old Itzel, too, but I don't know about that." I paused, thinking. Something was nagging at me. Suddenly, I had it. "The paintings in Madame Cuapa's dining room! Some of those looked like the tattoo artist's work. Maybe he's closer to Cuapa than I thought."

Kalama shook her head. "You don't learn witchcraft just by putting ink on a witch, or by selling paintings to her."

"No, but a guy who spends that much time around witches might get curious. He's been inking her for years. He sells or gives her paintings. He's worked on Falconwing and maybe other witches, too. Maybe he found something in Cuapa's house, or he learned something from Falconwing, or maybe he did some research on his own. I don't know how, but he could have discovered a way to use his tattoos to work a spell powerful enough to control the bruja."

Kalama frowned. "Seems like a longshot."

"Maybe. That's why I want a chance to talk to him. Make a right at the next intersection. We're almost there."

***

Kalama double-parked the car half a block from Teca's shop. I turned back to face the two burnouts. Judging by their expressions, they were unhappy.

"You guys ready to earn some dough?"

One of them looked up in my direction without quite making eye contact. "Hey, man. You got any rock?"

In response, I pulled my wallet out of my pocket. I reached under a hidden flap and pulled out a bill that I kept folded up in there for emergencies, like when I'd run up my bar tab a little higher than I'd planned. I unfolded the bill and held it up for the junkies to look at. It took about five seconds, but when their eyes widened and their mouths dropped open, I knew that I had their attention.

"This is yours to split if you do what we tell you. It'll buy you a lot of rock, if that's what you want to use it for. But you have to earn it. Are you ready?"

"Yeah, man," came a rasping voice.

"Sure," came another.

"All right, then. Yolo."

"I'm Zolo."

"See that tattoo studio over there? I want you to walk over and take a peek through the windows. See who's inside. Then come back here and tell us. Got it?"

Neither of them moved.

"Zolo?"

"Huh? Me? I thought you were talking to Yolo."

"I'm talking to you, Zolo. You know what I want you to do?"

"Ummm..."

This was going to be harder than I thought. "Walk over to that tattoo studio over there. You see it? Good. Walk over and look through the window. See what's going on in there. Then come back and tell us. Okay?"

"Yeah, man. Okay. And then you give us the dough?"

"You'll have to do a few other things first, but yeah. Do what I say and you'll get the dough. Now go."

"You mean now?"

"Now! Go!"

"Okay, man. You don't have to get sore." Zolo opened the back door and stepped out into the street. He put his head down and, without looking, made his way across, oblivious to the car that screeched to a stop in order to avoid running him down. The car's engine died, and the driver spent a half minute trying to start it up again as a cacophony of horns blared from the vehicles behind him.

Kalama, watched the burnout stumble up the sidewalk. "So much for stealth."

"He'll be okay." I reassured her, trying to sound confident.

We watched Zolo shamble up to the tattoo shop, head down and hands in pockets. When he reached the shop, he took his hands out of his pockets and braced himself against the window, leaning in until his nose was touching the glass.

Kalama glanced my way. "Subtle."

"He's fine."

A minute passed. Kalama glanced my way again. "When he wakes up, I hope he remembers the way back."

I didn't say anything.

Finally, the front door opened, and a hairy-faced heavyset lug wearing a tank top that revealed a colorful array of skin art stepped halfway out. I heard him yell, "Hey! Get lost before I call the cops, you fuckin' juicer! You hearin' me?"

Zolo pushed himself off the window, showed the lug his middle finger, and scurried away back in our direction.

Kalama looked at me and shook her head.

Zolo somehow remembered where we were parked and managed to cross the street to the car in one piece. When he was seated, I asked him, "What did you see in there?"

"Where? In the tattoo shop?"

"Yes, in the tattoo shop. What did you see?"

"Just that guy. He was drawing or something."

"No one else was in there?" I asked.

"Naw. Just him." Zolo's eyes darted to one side and he smiled. "He's got a cool picture of a naked twist on his wall. Awesome tits, man!"

I looked at Kalama. "Go around to the back of the shop. I want to check out the exit points."

"Whatever you say, chief!" She sounded more amused than unhappy, like she couldn't wait to see how this was all going to blow up in my face. But she started up the car and turned into the alley behind Teca's shop.

She stopped the car in the alley, but kept the motor running. I turned to her. "Okay. Me and the two junior g-men will get out here. You go find a place to park and call for your backup. By the time they get here, I'll be done with the were-crow and you can have him."

"You're sure about this?"

"What could go wrong?"

276

I started to get out of the car, but Kalama stopped me. "Wait. Open the glove box. I've got something for you."

Curious, I opened the glove box and pulled out a set of handcuffs. The color was a little unusual, and I realized that they were made of silver. I looked over at Kalama for an explanation.

"The department arrests a fair share of shape-shifters. Those bracelets are enchanted. Get them on your were-crow while he's in human form and he won't be able to transform into a flock of crows."

"That's useful." I turned to face her. "Thanks." I put the cuffs in my inside coat pocket and got out of the car.

The two burned out were-snakes were already out in the alley, slouching with their hands in their pockets and staring off to their sides. Kalama drove off, and, without looking at me, my two new partners followed me to the rear of the tattoo studio. We stopped, and I turned to one of them. "Zolo."

"I'm Yolo."

"Send a couple of snakes up on the roof."

"What for?"

"That guy in the shop is a were-crow." When I saw Yolo's blank expression, I explained, "You know how you can become snakes? That guy in there can change into crows."

"No shit?" Yolo's eyes met mine for a split second before darting away again. "That's fuckin' weird, man."

I stared at him for a few moments, but decided to let it go. "It's pretty likely that he's got a skylight up there so that he can fly out of it when he wants to. I want you to send two snakes up there. See if there's an opening. If there is, send one of the snakes back so that he can tell you."

Yolo looked up to the roof, back to the ground, and then back to the roof again. Then he looked off to the side with an uncomprehending expression. I pointed. "Use that drainpipe."

Yolo shrugged, and then two gopher snakes slithered out from beneath the cuff of his pant leg. They crawled to the drain pipe and climbed it faster than I would have thought they'd be able to. A few seconds later, one of the snakes slithered down the pipe and up Yolo's leg.

I looked at Yolo. He stared at my feet. "Well?" I asked.

"Well what?"

"Is there an opening up there?"

"Yeah, man."

"What's it look like?"

Yolo shrugged. "It's square. It's got bars on it."

"It's not covered? Birds can fly through it?"

"Yeah, man."

"Okay. Here's what I want you to do. Change into snakes and go up onto the roof around that opening. If any crows try to fly out. Grab them. Don't let them get away."

Yolo looked off to his side, and then back at my feet. "You want me to eat them?"

"If you want. Can you eat a crow?"

"Yeah, man."

Zolo swung his gaze toward his fellow junkie. "You can't eat a whole crow, man. They're too big."

"Can too! Most of one, anyway."

"Well save some for me, man. I'm hungry!"

"Fuck you, man!"

"Fuck you!"

I reached out and gripped each of them by a bony shoulder. They looked at the ground near my feet. "Knock it off! I don't care if you eat them or not. Just don't let any crows get through that opening. Got it?"

"I got it, man." Yolo, I think. "And you'll give us that cash?"

"That's the deal. You ready?"

Yolo melted away into a swarm of serpents, leaving his ragged clothes to fall to the alley floor. One after the other, the snakes slithered their way up the drainpipe to the roof.

"C'mon," I told Zolo. "We're going to block off this back exit. Help me push that dumpster over here."

With Zolo's reluctant help, we managed to roll the dumpster about five feet until it was backed into the tattoo shop's rear exit. Then we walked out of the alley and down the street to the front door of the shop.

"When we go inside, you'll come in behind me. If he stays human, your job is to make sure that he doesn't go through the front door. If he turns himself into crows and attacks me, then I want you to turn into snakes and fight him off. Can you do that?"

Zolo continued looking off to one side, but he smiled. "Does that mean I get to eat the crows?"

"Maybe. We'll see how it goes. Are you ready? You know what to do?"

"Yeah, man!"

I wasn't so sure. "If he stays human, you stay human. Got it? Make sure he doesn't leave the shop. If he turns to crows, then it's snake time."

Zolo nodded along without looking at me, and I decided I would have to hope for the best. I made sure that my heater and Kalama's cuffs were where they should be, and we entered the shop.

Chapter Twenty-Four

I had to admit that I was winging it, trying to be ready for anything. What I didn't expect was that as soon as I had taken one step into Teca's studio all hell would break loose. A brass bell rang when I opened the door, and Teca looked up from his work. I had half a second to catch the look of wide-eyed shock in his brown bearded face when he disappeared and was replaced by a chaotic explosion of flapping wings, extended talons, open beaks, and mad screeching so loud that I wanted to cover my ears. Instead, I threw up my arms to protect myself from the frenzied black swarm that attacked me all at once. I swatted a few of the birds out of the air, but I couldn't prevent talons and beaks from ripping at my face. I tried to shake the birds away from my eyes and spotted Zolo—or was it Yolo?—frozen in place, a look of utter confusion on his face.

"Snakes!" I shouted. "Snakes, you fucking wet-brain!"

The message got through, and where the junkie had been standing a moment before, a swarm of snakes now shot their way along the floor and up my legs. I held my arms out in front of me, and snakes wound their way up my torso and shot off my arms to strike at the crows. An ordinary gopher snake imitates a viper, but when it strikes it usually does so with closed jaws, using its blunt nose to fend off its enemies. But ordinary gopher snakes don't collectively share the frazzled mind of a hungry rockhead with a taste for bird flesh. The snakes leaped at the crows, jaws wide open, and clamped down on whatever they could reach. The crows screeched as jaws locked on wings, legs, and necks. They stopped attacking my face and swooped down at the snakes, grabbing at their writhing bodies with their talons and pecking away at their heads with their rock-hard beaks.

Blood flew around the room, and I could see that the birds were gaining the upper hand. "Yolo!" I shouted toward the skylight that I saw in the ceiling, hoping that I got the name right. "Change in plans! We need some help down here! Attack the crows!"

Dozens of snakes began to fall from the skylight. Some fell all the way to the floor. A few landed on my head and shoulders.

But most of them came down on birds and struck at their necks and wings. Free from attacking crows, I jumped on top of a table, kicking aside a stack of canvases and paint brushes.

"Stop!" I shouted. "Stop fighting!"

The frenzy in the room showed no sign of abating. I reached under my coat and drew out my nine-millimeter. "Stop!" I shouted again, and fired a shot into the ceiling.

That got the attention of both snakes and birds. I pointed my rod at the nearest crow. "Teca! If you get anywhere near that skylight, I'll blast you out of the air!"

The crows began to retreat from the snakes, whirling like a dust storm toward the back of the shop. They coalesced and changed into a naked human form, bleeding from several deep cuts and puncture wounds. "Keep those fuckin' snakes away from me!" He yelled.

"Yolo! Zolo! Human, now!" The snakes writhed around in confusion. Most seemed to want to take up the attack again. "Turn back and you'll get the cash. Keep attacking and I'll fill you full of lead."

That did the trick, and soon I was looking at the scrawny naked figures of the two rock addicts. Teca took that moment to run to the back door of his shop. He pulled the door open, but was faced with an unexpected obstacle blocking the doorway. I took advantage of his confusion by leaping off the table, closing the gap between us at a run, and pushing him into the side of the dumpster. I slammed the door into his back, and as he bounced off the dumpster I twisted his arm behind his back and clamped his wrist with one end of the silver cuffs. He screamed in pain or alarm, and I twisted his other arm behind his back and locked his wrist into the other cuff. Then I pulled him by the handcuffs away from the back door and closed it.

I dragged Teca to a chair and forced him into it. I turned to my two assistants. They were banged up, shivering, and bleeding a little, but they didn't look much worse than usual. "You guys okay?" They both nodded. "Get your clothes back on and wait by the door," I told them. Then I turned my attention to the were-crow.

I showed him my heater. "Move and I'll shoot. You'll never make it to the door."

Teca stared at me with sullen eyes, breathing hard. "You're supposed to be dead!"

"Surprise, motherfucker."

The tattoo artist was a big man, fortyish, about my height, and heavier by maybe thirty pounds. It wasn't good weight, though, too much fat in the gut and too little muscle in the legs and chest. His long dark brown hair was streaked with gray and hung past his shoulders. It didn't look like it had been washed in at least a month. Dark bushy brows jutted out over his copper-colored eyes. Dark brown and gray hair also covered the lower part of his face, the ragged edges of his beard hanging down to his chest. Tattoos covered most of his body. The ones on his lower arms, abdomen, and upper thighs were clearly ones that he had done himself. The images were as amazing as the ones I'd seen on Madame Cuapa's skin. His other tats had been put on by professionals who were no doubt experts in their craft, but they seemed ordinary and drab in comparison to his own work. Teca was definitely a master, and without doubt a rare prodigy. He was also very likely a murderer who had killed Dwayne Shipper. I was convinced that he was responsible for the murder of Donald Shipper, as well, and he had pretty much just told me that he believed he had succeeded in killing me. Now that I had him in my power, I wasn't inclined to be gentle with him.

Two of Teca's tats drew my attention. The first was one on his right upper thigh, where, in remarkable near-photographic detail, an image of a nude woman was stretched out on her side and propped up on one elbow. The woman's lips curled into a suggestive smile, one hand rested on her thigh, and her eyes invited the observer to enjoy the seductive display of her body. One look at the woman's face left no doubt that the model for the image was Cindy Shipper, although the oversized breasts were the product of some artistic license on Teca's part.

The second noteworthy tattoo dominated Teca's chest. It was the head of a by-now familiar black dog with lightning bolts where the eyes should be. The black ink in the tattoo gleamed with an almost supernatural shine that made the image seem three-

283

dimensional. In my mind's eye, I had a brief vision of a giant version of that dog leading me into a dark void. I blinked away the vision and lifted my gaze to meet Teca's eyes.

Teca glared at me through the hair on his face. "I ain't talking to you without a mouthpiece."

"I'm a private dick," I told him. "I don't care if you have a lawyer or not."

His eyes narrowed. "I still ain't talkin'."

"I'm not here to question you, featherbrain. I'm here to tell you the score. All you get to do is sit and listen."

"Let me tell *you* the score, asshole!" Teca spat the words at me. "Cindy is mine! Leave her the fuck alone!"

I tried to pin him to the chair with my steely stare. He tried to slice into my brain with his laser-like one. I looked for a way to take control of the conversation. "Is that why you killed her husband?"

He broke eye contact for an instant. "I ain't talkin'."

"You don't have to. I already know everything."

He met my eyes again. "You don't know shit!"

"You *say* that, Teca. But there's nothing behind it. You got to Madame Cuapa through your ink work. I have to admit, that was clever. Overcoming the Barbary Coast Bruja with a compulsion spell! Wow—that took nerve! Not to mention some rare skill!"

Teca smiled, and I could see the pride in his eyes. He couldn't help himself. I knew that I'd found the right button, so I kept pushing. I looked around the shop where, as Zolo had noted, several of Teca's paintings were mounted on the walls, including the one that had captured Zolo's attention. It stretched five feet along the wall and was a match for the tattoo of Mrs. Shipper on Teca's thigh. "I've gotta say, Teca, your work is fuckin' brilliant! I've never seen anything like it. I can see why Madame Cuapa hangs your paintings in her house. And that painting in the Shipper's living room is a masterpiece!"

Teca's face was a mixture of defiance and pride. He didn't know whether to spit in my face or thank me for recognizing his genius. As I waited to see which path he would take, his expression changed and his eyes moved away from me to look over my shoulder.

"Hey, man. Can we get that dough now?"

I cursed under my breath. I'd forgotten about my two soldiers. I glanced back to see that the rockheads had crept up behind me and were shifting from one foot to the other, scratching at their arms and legs, and staring at the floor at their sides. I smiled at them and pulled out my wallet. "You boys earned this," I told them, pulling out the bill that I'd shown them earlier. Their faces lit up like lighthouse beacons when they saw it. I held it out. "Are you sure you want to spend this on rock? Why don't you get some food and some decent clothes and start cleaning up your act?"

One of them, Yolo, I think, snatched the bill from my hand, and the two of them turned and raced out of the shop. As they scurried away, a single bloodied snake slipped from beneath the pants of one of the junkies and plopped to the floor, where it lay motionless. Either Yolo or Zolo was one dead snake closer to forever losing his humanity.

I shook my head and turned back to Teca, whose expression had gone blank. Damn! He'd been close to talking, but the interference from my two erstwhile fellow combatants had cost me my advantage. As I searched for a way to regain the edge, my eyes fell on the image of Xolotl on his chest. Something about the unnatural-looking ink triggered an idea.

"You know," I began. "I've been wondering how you did it. How did you cast that compulsion spell on the bruja. You're not a witch, I know that. So how did you gain control over one of the most powerful masters of witchcraft in the world?" I pointed at the tattoo on his chest. "I've seen that one before. On Madame Cuapa's back. It was hidden, and I don't even know if she's aware that it's there, but I saw it."

Teca's eyes widened, and I knew that I had him.

"Not quite as clever as you thought, right?" I was goading him a little. "But that's how you got to her, isn't it. Through that secret tattoo of Xolotl."

Teca drew in a quick breath at the mention of the dog-faced god's name.

I smiled at the artist. "Oh, I know all about Xolotl. God of lightning. Bringer of fire. Ruler of Mictlan. So on and so forth. But

285

how did you hide that tattoo? That puzzled me for a while. But I think I know the answer now. You're a great artist, no doubt about it. A genius! But you can't enchant a tattoo. And yet, there's magic in the tattoo! So how did it get there?" I snapped my finger. "Through the ink, of course! Ink that was already enchanted when you used it on the bruja!"

Teca tried to bluff. He put a sneer on his lips and looked away. But he was trying too hard. I looked around the shop again until I saw his collection of inks on a long table near the wall. I wandered in that direction, taking my time. "I wonder where you got that ink from," I mused aloud.

Teca stopped sneering and watched me with narrowed eyes.

I reached the table. "These your inks? Nice!" The plastic tubes were neatly arranged, and each displayed the logo from the same commercial supplier. I picked up a tube of red ink, made a show of examining it, and put it down. I glanced at Teca to see if I had his attention. He looked a little nervous, but not much. I picked up a plastic tube of blue ink and set it down. I picked up a tube of black ink and turned toward Teca.

I held up the tube. "This the ink you use to draw the dog?" Then I put the tube down. "No, that's not the stuff. That's just ordinary ink. You've got something special for Xolotl. Let me see...."

I looked through the ink but didn't see what I was looking for. I scanned the room and fixed my eyes on a counter near the front door. A cash register sat on the counter, along with a credit-card machine and stacks of papers. Impulse-buy items, such as prints of artwork, silver rings, chrome action figures, and stylized roach clips were displayed on shelves below the register.

I turned toward Teca again. "I wonder what you've got behind that register." His jaw set just enough to tell me that I was on the right track. Thinking he might do something rash, I held up the nine-millimeter. "Don't move!"

I stepped behind the counter. On a shelf below the register I found a vicious-looking hunting knife, a sawed-off shotgun, and an unlabeled stoppered glass bottle half-filled with black ink. I took the bottle and held it up in one hand for Teca to see. He sprang to his feet but stopped in his tracks when I lifted the shotgun with my other hand and pointed it at his chest. "Sit your ass down," I told him, putting a menacing growl in my voice.

Teca opened his mouth to speak, but I cut him off. "I'm betting that this thing's loaded."

He let whatever he was going to say stay unsaid. Deflated, he plopped back down in the chair and looked down at his feet. He shook his head. "For fuck's sake," he muttered. "Can you at least get that damned snake off my floor? It's giving me the fuckin' creeps!"

I put the shotgun down on the counter and picked up my nine-millimeter from the shelf where I had left it. I put the heater back in my holster. Teca wasn't going anywhere. The fight had gone out of him. I only needed one more important piece of information from him now, and I wasn't sure how I was going to get it.

I stepped out from behind the counter with the glass bottle of ink in my hand. Teca stared at it as if hypnotized. "This is the real stuff, isn't it. The ink that you used on that tattoo on your chest, and the one you used for the secret tattoo on Madame Cuapa. The enchanted ink." I stared hard at Teca. "Five will get you ten that you're planning to use this ink on Cindy Shipper. If you can convince her to let you ink her, you'll use this stuff to form a link between the two of you. Then she'll be yours forever. Is that how it's supposed to work?"

Teca shifted in his chair, looking uncomfortable. I knew that I'd hit the mark, but I wasn't sure what to do next. I held the bottle in the air loosely with two fingers and rocked it back and forth while I considered ways to draw Teca out and get him talking. Beads of sweat started forming on his forehead. I made a show of relaxing. "Teca, Teca, Teca. You've got it all wrong about Mrs. Shipper and me. There's nothing between us. She gave me a hug because she was upset. That's all."

Teca's eyes hardened. "You're lying! I saw her coming out of your house the other morning. She'd been in there all night, you prick!"

"That was the night you killed her stepson, right? Sloppy job, by the way. Mrs. Shipper had some information for me. She

287

told me that she was being stalked by a were-crow. She said that she was afraid to go home. So she slept at my place. But I never touched her. I slept on the couch." The last part was a lie, but I meant well by it.

It didn't matter, though. Teca sat bolt upright in the chair, and I halfway reached for the gat in my holster. "You fucking liar! I wasn't stalking her! She *wanted* me to see her! She told me to come over! It wasn't me she was afraid of! Not me!"

This was going in a different direction than I expected. "What do you mean? Who was she afraid of?"

"Her stepson, you retard! He's a fucking pervert! She wanted me to protect her from him! She told me that he had dirty pictures of her, and that he used them get his fucking rocks off. She was afraid that the kid was going to rape her! She asked me to protect her from him! And I fuckin' *did* protect her! The little dirtbag was watching Cindy on his computer, whacking off, just like she said. But I made him stop!"

Oh fuck. "Mrs. Shipper told you what the kid was doing?"

"Yeah. She told me. And she told me to come back and help her. She told me that she needed me. She told me that.... She told me that she loved me!"

Teca slumped in his chair, exhausted by his confession. "She loved me," he repeated, much quieter now.

I could see Teca withdrawing into himself, but I still didn't have what I needed from him, and I knew that the cops would be arriving soon. I had to regain Teca's attention quick and steer him in the right direction. "You stopped him." I narrowed my eyes at him. "And you cut out his heart as a sacrifice. Who were you sacrificing to? Xolotl? Huitziliopotchli?"

Teca looked up at me, meeting my eyes. His face screwed up into a scowl. "But his heart was no good. It wasn't beating no more. The gods need beating hearts."

"Like when you cut out Dr. Coyot's heart?"

Teca smiled. "I ain't saying no more."

I still needed that last piece of information. Teca hadn't enchanted the ink himself. I needed to know who had supplied it to him. Teca had been pulling Madame Cuapa's strings, but I needed to know who had been pulling Teca's. "Who was it who told you to sacrifice hearts? It was the same person who gave you this ink, wasn't it!" I shook the bottle a little to get his attention, but Teca just smiled. I was running out of time and getting desperate. I decided to play my hunch, hoping that I was right. "It was Falconwing, wasn't it. You did that tattoo on his chest, the hummingbird god. He gave you this ink after he enchanted it. He told you how to use it to hide a Xolotl tat on Madame Cuapa, and he taught you how to call on Xolotl through the tat to cast a compulsion spell on her. He couldn't do it himself, because she would know that it was him. So he got you to do it. You were happy to play along, because you wanted to use the spell to force Cuapa to curse Cindy Shipper's husband. It worked, but Dr. Coyot caught on to Falconwing's scheme. He had to go. So Falconwing gave you something to use on Coyot's dog, something that would drive the mutt crazy and kill Coyot. And Falconwing wanted you to cut out Coyot's heart as a sacrifice to Huitzilopochtli, so you did that, too."

Teca's expression didn't change. His smug grin was plastered to his face.

"Come on, Teca. The police know you killed the Shipper kid. They'll be here any second. Your only chance of saving your skin is to give up Falconwing. Tell the cops that he made you do it. He made you kill Shipper and Shipper's kid. He made you cut out Coyot's heart. You tried to kill me, too, but I won't press charges if you give up Falconwing. Don't be a sap, Teca! Falconwing can't help you now. Madame Cuapa is on to him! Give him up and save yourself! It's what Cindy would want you to do."

I thought that it was a good performance on my part, and that I sounded pretty darned convincing. Teca looked away from me, considering everything that I had told him. His mouth opened and closed as he worked up the courage to give up the man who I was convinced was behind everything. Then Teca looked up at me and smiled. "Kiss my ass, motherfucker!" He spat in my direction. "I ain't tellin' you jack shit!"

Chapter Twenty-Five

"We got enough to pin a murder rap on him for the Shipper kid," Kalama told me. The johns had stuffed Teca into the backseat of a prowl car and were taking him downtown. "But it sounds like the widow was playing him for a sucker."

"Yeah," I agreed. "She was playing me for a sucker, too, I guess. Can't say that I'm surprised."

Kalama nodded. "Her husband's funeral is being held today. It should still be in full swing. We're going to send a couple of officers out there to pick her up for questioning. I'll let you know how that goes."

"Thanks."

She glanced up and down the street. "I don't see your two assistants anywhere."

"They took the money and beat it. I'm guessing that they're holed up in a rock pad somewhere, or will be soon." I shook my head. "It's too bad. In the end, they didn't do a half-bad job for me. I'm not sure that I could have got those bracelets on Teca without their help."

Kalama looked at the cuts on my face. "The were-crow did a number on you. You're lucky you didn't lose an eye or two."

"I'll be all right."

"You realize that those two addicts are beyond help. They might not even make it through the day if they flash that dough around the wrong people."

I nodded. "Yeah, maybe so." I changed the subject. "Hey, I'm worried about Madame Cuapa and Cody. I tried to reach Cuapa again on her house phone, and no one's answering. I tried Cody's cel and got his voicemail. I need to get over there."

"You asking me for another ride?"

"No, I'll get a hack this time."

"Not necessary. I'll drive."

"You sure?"

The detective shrugged. "I'm still suspended, remember? I've got nothing better to do. Let's roll, gumshoe!"

291

Madame Cuapa's house was still as stone when Kalama and I climbed up the porch steps to the doorway. Night had fallen, but the porch light was off, and no lights were shining through the windows, either upstairs or downstairs. I put my ear to the door and strained my senses, but heard nothing. I tried the door handle, and it turned in my hand. I looked at Kalama, who shrugged. I opened the door and we went inside.

Kalama had clipped a flashlight to her belt when we left the car, and she made a move to unfasten it. I put a hand on her arm and shook my head. "I can see in the dark," I told her. She looked at me with a puzzled expression. "Long story. I'll tell you about it later."

Kalama raised her eyebrows at me, but she released the flashlight and followed me through the living room to Cody's bedroom. The door was closed, but unlocked. I listened at the door, and, when I didn't hear anything, I opened it and took a look inside. No one was there, and nothing looked out of place. I led Kalama to the guest bedroom and repeated the process with the same results. We checked the downstairs bathroom. Nothing.

We went up the stairs next, and I gave Madame Cuapa's bedroom and lab a cursory looksee. I checked out the upstairs bathroom. No one was around, and nothing appeared to be disturbed. We went downstairs, through the living room, and into the kitchen. I looked into the dining room. It appeared that no one was home.

I saw a door in the kitchen, and, catching a strong scent of wine, I concluded that it led into the wine cellar. I opened the door and moved to start down the stairs, but Kalama stopped me. "I don't care what you say. If we're going down there, I'm using my flashlight."

"All right. I don't think anyone's there anyway."

A quick search confirmed that the cellar was as empty as the rest of the house. We climbed back up to the kitchen and into the dining room. "Let's go see if there's a car in the garage," Kalama suggested.

We went outside to the garage and opened the door. The garage was empty.

"Looks like they all drove somewhere." Kalama nodded.

"Why don't you try Cody again," she suggested.

I took out my phone and tapped in Cody's number. From a distance, I heard a ringtone. "Do you hear that?" I asked Kalama.

"Hear what?"

"Sh! It's coming from inside the house."

We went back into the house, and I called Cody's number again. This time Kalama heard the ringtone, too. It was coming from Cody's bedroom. We re-entered the room and found Cody's phone on a nightstand next to his bed.

"He told me that when he got chased out of here by Falconwing a couple of days ago, he left without his phone. Looks like he never got it back."

"Any idea where they might be?"

"Yeah, maybe." I frowned at the phone. "But I don't like it. Let's go!"

I led Kalama through the dining room and out into the back yard. "There's a meeting hall a hundred yards or so past the top of that dune. It's got an altar in there where, according to Cody, the Madame sacrifices chickens. But it's a little big for chickens, and that clearly isn't what it was originally built for. The land between here and there all belongs to Madame Cuapa. You can get there by driving down the road in the front of the house and going around the block. I'm guessing that's what they did. It would be a lot quicker if we go overland, but the manticore patrols the property. If Cody is in trouble, though, I'm guessing that the manticore is with him. Besides, I've ridden on that manticore's back. I think he likes me. Want to chance it?"

"Not really."

"If we drive up, they'll see us coming. If we come up on the building from behind, we might be able to catch them by surprise."

Kalama was about to protest further when I stopped her. "Wait!" I pointed off into the distance over the dune. "Do you see that? It's a bird. A falcon, I think."

Kalama peered into the darkness, straining her eyes. "I don't see anything. Are you sure?"

293

"Positive. My eyes are, well, you'll have to trust me. I can see it pretty well. It's definitely a falcon. Five will get you ten it's Falconwing's familiar. If I've got my bearings, it's right above the meeting hall." I looked at Kalama. "Come on."

I started out to the foot of the dune at a jog. Kalama hesitated, and then followed. The night was clear, but the sliver of a moon on the horizon wasn't doing much to light our way. The good news was that the two of us were all but invisible to anyone with natural vision as we made our way over the dune and across the undeveloped land.

We didn't encounter Mr. Whiskers, but the falcon was going to be a problem. I had no doubt that the bird was acting as a lookout. Fortunately, it seemed to be concentrating on the road in front of the meeting hall. But as we drew nearer, I abandoned the idea that Kalama and I would be able to sneak to the building undetected. We crouched down low so that we were screened from the falcon by some brush.

"You want me to shoot it?" Kalama whispered to me with a straight face.

"Sure. You got a shotgun handy?"

"Just this police-issue nine-millimeter. If you could lure it down here within twenty or thirty yards of us, I think I could scare it."

I laughed in spite of myself. "Let's try something else. Sit tight. I've got an idea."

I needed an elemental. I thought about calling Badass, but he was too noisy. As soon as he showed up, Falconwing would know that I was close by. Smokey was too small for what I had in mind. Besides, the little guy was too far away, and I was in a hurry. I needed a local. I closed my eyes and envisioned the appropriate sigils. When I opened my eyes, the sky appeared to be lit by an unnatural light that I knew Kalama would not be able to see. It was like putting on a scuba mask and going under the surface of the ocean. Without the mask the waters would be almost opaque, but with the mask a whole community of ocean life would be visible. I searched the sky for elementals and found several floating about in the wind currents. I chose the closest one of the size that I needed and sent out a call.

A half minute later, a funnel of whirling air about a foot tall floated in front of me above the scrub brush. "Greetings."

A quiet reedy voice that sounded like it was coming from the bell of a clarinet emerged from the funnel. "Greetings, master. This one is ready to serve."

"Do you see that bird circling up there?" I pointed.

"This one sees the bird."

"Attack it. Drive it away if you can. Keep it busy. Do it until I release you from your service."

"This one will obey." And with that, the elemental made a bee-line for the falcon.

"This should be fun," I told Kalama.

Her lips curled ever so slightly into a small smile. "Interesting."

I watched the falcon circling in the sky above the meeting hall. Suddenly, it rolled to the side, feathers flying from its body, as if it had been struck by an invisible boulder. It righted itself but was knocked aside again. The falcon began to plunge downward, and it thrust out its wings to slow its fall. It swooped upwards, flapped its wings and shot straight up into the sky. When it leveled off, it was struck sideways again. It flew away from the meeting hall, darting back and forth, bumped and harassed at every turn, until it was just a darker speck in the night sky.

I nudged Kalama. "All clear—let's go!"

We jogged to one of the doors in the back of the meeting hall. I put my ear on the door and listened. I heard the faint sound of a voice, but couldn't make out the words.

"Someone's in there." I tried the door handle, but it was locked. "Let's go around front."

We moved to the front of the hall and saw a beige luxury SUV parked in the circular lot at the end of the driveway. "That's Madame Cuapa's car," I whispered. "They're here. Give me a second."

I led Kalama away from the front door to the side of the building. I closed my eyes and formed a summoning sigil for the elemental. A few moments later, it shot towards me, but stopped to hover in the air about ten feet away. Its reedy voice emerged from the air funnel: "This one cannot approach any closer. The building pushes this one away."

"No problem," I whispered back. "Attack the bird one last time, and then your service to me will be done. Thank you."

The elemental shot away into the night. I turned to Kalama. "Sounds like the building is warded against elementals. Looks like it's just you and me. Shall we try the front door?"

"Do you have a plan?"

"I don't know what we're going to find inside. Let's be cool and try to talk our way through it. Don't meet their eyes."

"Terrific."

"Do you want to call for backup?"

Kalama thought about it. "I don't think so. There's a good chance no one would come. And if they did, it wouldn't be in time to do us any good."

"Probably not," I agreed. "Well, here goes nothing!"

We walked to the double door and stared at it for a few seconds.

Kalama glanced over at me. "Maybe we should knock."

That seemed like as good an idea as any, so I stepped up to the door and reached up to give it a rap. Before I could, the double doors swung open wide.

Falconwing's voice boomed from the center of the room. "Come in! We've been expecting you."

I made a mental note: never try to sneak up on a witch. I peered through the doorway. The meeting hall was lit by torches in the four corners of the room, and smoke from the torches hung in a cloud at the ceiling. Falconwing stood behind the sacrificial table in the center of the room. He was shirtless, and I got a good view of the hummingbird tattoo on his chest. He held a large stone knife in one hand. Itzel, dressed in what appeared to be a ceremonial robe with elaborate folds in the loose cloth, stood behind Falconwing and a little to his right. Her expression was harsh, her eyes mere slits as she glared in my direction. Cody, dressed in a loose white robe, lay on the table, face up and unconscious. Behind and to the left of Falconwing, surrounded by five lit white candles, each one four feet tall and six inches thick, Mr. Whiskers paced in a circle, his snout curled in a snarl. In front of the table, Madame

Cuapa was slouched unmoving in one of the front-row folding chairs. I couldn't tell if she was alive or dead. She was dressed in a loose white robe, like the one Cody was wearing.

I looked in Falconwing's direction, trying not to meet his eyes, but failing. I found that, try as I might, I couldn't keep myself from seeking his gaze. Once his eyes locked with mine, I couldn't turn away. "Is this a bad time?" I asked. "We can come back later."

"Not at all!" Falconwing boomed. "Please, come in. I insist!"

The witch waved a hand in our direction, and, against my will, I found myself walking toward the chairs that faced the sacrificial table. Kalama fell in behind me, matching me step for step. I guessed that she had been no more successful in avoiding Falconwing's eyes than I had been. We found ourselves sitting down in chairs on either side of Madame Cuapa, Kalama on the bruja's right, and me on her left. I tried to move my arms and legs, but they hung limp and useless from my body. With an effort, though, I was able to move my head. Turning toward Madame Cuapa, I could see the slow rise and fall of her chest. At least she was alive. I looked beyond Madame Cuapa to Kalama. She was turned toward me with a grim expression on her face. I gave her a nod, pleased to see that she hadn't given up hope.

I turned my head back to Falconwing and opened my mouth to speak. I was surprised when I could. "I hope we haven't kept you waiting."

"On the contrary." Falconwing's smile was chilling. "You're just in time. We've been waiting for the new moon to take its proper position, and, by my reckoning, that should happen in another few minutes."

"What happens then?"

Falconwing looked down at Cody. "Isn't it obvious? We begin the sacrifices!"

"Sacrifices? As in more than one?"

"Yes." Falconwing's smile widened. "Four, to be precise."

Chapter Twenty-Six

We apparently still had some time before the sacrifices were to begin, and Falconwing was feeling sociable. "I haven't had the pleasure of meeting your friend," he told me. He turned to Kalama and gave her a slight bow. "Hello, dear. My name is Tloto Falconwing."

"Detective Kalama, Homicide, YCPD. You're under arrest, Mr. Falconwing. I've already called for backup, and they're on their way."

Falconwing smiled at her. "No you haven't, but nice try. As for being under arrest, I'm afraid to say that I'll be resisting. As will Miss Itzel. Isn't that right, dear?"

He nodded over his shoulder at Itzel, but she didn't respond. I glanced at her, and then I looked again. Beads of sweat had formed on her forehead. Her jaw was set and lips pursed. I got the impression that she was focusing her will on something, concentrating hard. A thought tickled my brain, and an idea began to form.

"Falconwing!" I shouted. "I didn't think that your coven did human sacrifices."

"Things change," he told me. "Especially with a change in leadership."

"I take it that you're in charge now?"

"Yes, I am. It's going to be a new age for the coven."

"The Age of Huitzilopochtli?"

Falconwing's usually somber face lit up in a serene smile. "Yes, very good. But you've met the hummingbird god already, haven't you. You nearly had the honor of giving him your heart a little prematurely. It's better this way, though. Now you'll be a part of something very special. When it's over, you're certain to have an honored place in the Realm of Mictlan."

"Well, congratulations. I'll have to hand it to you, I didn't think you'd be able to take Madame Cuapa. She was steaming when she left this morning to throw down with you and Itzel. She didn't think that you two had what it took to stand in her way. I figured that the two of you would be going down for the count."

Falconwing snorted. "I always told her that her pride would be her undoing. But, to be fair, I have to admit that Miss Itzel gets all the credit for bringing the Madame to her knees."

"Through the tattoo that's hidden on her back, right?"

Falconwing's eyes widened in surprise. "How...." He glanced back at Old Itzel "What tattoo?" Then he quickly turned and met my eyes. "A hidden tattoo? How would you know about such things?"

"You didn't know about that? Sir, I owe you an apology. I guess I had you wrong. I thought you were responsible for that tattoo, but it turns out that it was Old Itzel all along." I looked beyond Falconwing to the old gnome. "But I guess she can't talk now. She's busy concentrating on keeping the Madame in check. Tough job, I'll bet, even with the aid of the hidden tat of Xolotl on her back."

"Itzel? What's this about a tattoo? A tattoo of Xolotl?" Falconwing turned back to Itzel, who gave him a brief glare before looking away. The sweat on her brow was thickening.

"Itzel gave Teca some ink that she'd enchanted to use on the Madame's back to touch up her Ometecuhtli tattoo. That artist is pretty clever. I'm guessing that Old Itzel taught him how to overlay an image of Xolotl on the snake's head. I don't think that the Madame even knew it was there. Until now, anyway, if she can hear me. But I caught sight of it."

I couldn't help feeling some satisfaction at the shocked expression on Falconwing's face, but I was still no closer to getting out of this fix. Falconwing didn't say anything, so I kept talking. "Here's what I'm thinking. Old Itzel developed some sort of working relationship with Teca. I don't know when, but Teca is from Itzel's neck of the woods, so it could have been quite a while ago. Maybe she's the one who introduced Teca to the Madame in the first place. But I'm just speculating." I paused to collect my thoughts. It occurred to me that I was convincing myself as much as I was convincing Falconwing.

But I had his attention. "You *do* know who Teca is, right?" I continued. "He's the one who put that big hummingbird tat on your chest. He does nice work, I'll give him that! So, like I said, Itzel got him to put that hidden tattoo on the Madame's back, using ink that she had already enchanted. Then she taught Teca how to use the link to cast a compulsion spell on her. Itzel let him compel the Madame to put a curse on the husband of the dame that he had the hots for. It didn't matter to Itzel who the target was. All that mattered was that it showed the rest of the coven that she was weak. I'll bet she got in touch with you right away, and pushed you to take over leadership of the coven. I'm right about that, aren't I. I can tell by the way your face is getting all dark."

Falconwing, in fact, looked like he was about to have an aneurism. A vein in his neck was swelling, and his eyes were losing their focus as he started putting the pieces into place.

"Yeah," I continued. "Old Itzel played you for a sucker, old boy. You've been thinking that you're the one running this show, but she's been behind everything. Hey! Itzel! How long have you been biding your time, knitting your tea cozies and pretending to be the young upstart's best friend? And all the while, waiting for the chance to push her aside." I filled my voice with scorn. "Her and her 'new direction' for the coven. No more human sacrifices. No more honoring Xolotl. How many years of watching her throw away everything that her father, Cuetlachtli, had built?"

"She dishonored her father!" Itzel shouted. "Without her father, she was nothing. He rewarded her by giving her the coven, and she took advantage of her position to betray his legacy. She's nothing but a filthy traitor!" Sweat was rolling down her face, and she reached up to brush it out of her eyes.

Falconwing turned back to stare at her. I poured it on, knowing that I finally had it right, or at least mostly right, which was good enough. "And then the Madame goes and hires a private dick. And the private dick stumbles onto Dr. Coyot, a minor practitioner, but a member of the cult of Xolotl. You're a member of that cult, too, aren't you Itzel? When Coyot saw the results of Madame Cuapa's curse, he knew that she had invoked Xolotl, something that she would not have done willingly. The poor sap was afraid that some member of the cult was involved. Maybe he guessed it was Old Itzel, maybe he didn't. Did he contact you, Itzel?

301

Or maybe you just found out that he was asking inconvenient questions. Either way, you needed him out of the picture."

I wasn't sure about this next part, but it made sense, so I ran with it. "You got in touch with Teca again, didn't you, Itzel. You weren't in town yet, but you don't need to be a witch to call someone on his cellphone. You convinced him to go see Coyot after his office hours and to keep the call connected so that you could instruct him. You asked him to bring a stone sacrificial knife with him. Did he get one from you during an earlier visit? Was it a present, or a reward for his good work? Well, it doesn't matter where he got it. They're easy enough to find."

I didn't know how much time I had left, so I picked up the pace. "Coyot had one of Teca's special tattoos, a tattoo using your enchanted ink. Thanks to you, I'll bet that a lot of witches do. The tattoos give you the means to keep watch on them and mobilize them if you want to. It's better than the internet!" I was guessing here, but it made sense. "When Teca was in Coyot's office, you used Coyot's tattoo as a link to put a spell on his familiar. The gentle old mutt went crazy and attacked his master. Poor thing. That was cruel, Itzel. That was really cruel. So the dog kills his master and then slinks off, probably to die alone somewhere. And Teca does what you ask him to do. He cuts out Coyot's heart and offers it up as a sacrifice. Not to Huitzilopochtli, though. That's not who you all worshiped when the Madame's father was running the coven. No, you had Teca offer Coyot's heart up to Xolotl. Because that's *your* plan for the coven once Madame Cuapa is out of the picture. To bring back the old ways, right?"

Falconwing swung his head back in my direction and smiled. "That's an interesting story, Mr. Southerland. And I'm sure that a lot of it is true. Maybe all of it. But I see what you're trying to do. You're trying to divide us. You think that you're being clever, but you overplayed your hand. Itzel and I have already discussed the future of the coven, and we've come to an agreement. It's a big coven. There's room for diversity. Under my leadership, the coven will be primarily devoted to honoring Huitzilopochtli, but there will be a special place for Xolotl, too. The two of them easily co-exist in a balance of light and darkness, life and death. If anything, each makes the other greater." He shook his head at me, smiling like a patient father teaching a child an important life lesson. "There's no division here. We're one big united family."

Falconwing gathered himself. "And now, the time is upon us. The new moon is in place. Let us start the ceremony."

Falconwing might have been right. Maybe I'd overplayed my hand. But I wasn't ready to fold just yet. "Hey, Itzel," I shouted. "Detective Kalama's boys arrested Teca this afternoon. He's downtown singing like a nightingale. They've got a captain over there, a troll, and when he gets someone in the sweatbox, he can get him to turn on his own mother. By now, Teca has told the coppers everything he knows. He'll give you up for two murders."

Falconwing laughed. "We're hardly afraid of the police, Mr. Southerland. We work with gods! No more of this bullshit. It's time to begin."

Falconwing was brushing me off, but I knew that I had scored a hit on Old Itzel. She was definitely nervous. But she was also far from losing her nerve. For what it was worth, I had the information that Madame Cuapa had paid me to find. It was Old Itzel, working through Teca, who had been behind the compulsion spell that resulted in Donald Shipper's murder. It was a shame that my only reward for completing my job was going to be an honored place in the land of the dead. Some days you can't win for losing.

***

Falconwing placed the stone knife over the top of Cody's outstretched body and pressed the palms of his hands together in front of his chest. He tilted back his head and turned his eyes to the ceiling, where smoke from the guttering torches was beginning to swirl counter-clockwise in a slow-moving circle. Behind him, Mr. Whiskers paced ever more frantically within the pentagram formed by the five standing candles, grumbling and snorting his frustration. Falconwing closed his eyes and began a muttering chant. Behind him, Old Itzel's lips also began to move, and I guessed that she was fortifying Falconwing's prayer with her own.

I strained to move my arms and legs, and I could see that Kalama was doing the same. Neither of us was having any success. I tried to think of some way to distract Falconwing, but I'd about

303

run out of ideas. "Hey, Falconwing!" I shouted in desperation. "Your fly is open!" This got me a look of exasperation from Kalama, but Falconwing's chanting continued unabated. I managed to shrug at Kalama. "You got anything better?" She sighed and looked away.

I turned my attention to Madame Cuapa, who, except for her slow breathing, still hadn't shown any sign of life. "Madame Cuapa!" I shouted. "Can you hear me? Madame Cuapa! Open your eyes! Madame Cuapa! Madame Cuapa!" Detecting no change in the bruja's breathing, I abandoned my attempts to wake her.

Falconwing's chanting was beginning to crescendo. Looking over his head, I saw the clouds of smoke swirling in a distinct circle. The center of the circle grew darker and darker until I could no longer see the ceiling. And still it darkened, until the darkness deepened into a void. As the volume of Falconwing's chanting increased, the darkness began to spill down from the circle, like an ever-lengthening beam of black light. I watched the blackness extend through the circle, stretching closer and closer to Falconwing. And I smiled.

"Hey, Falconwing!" I shouted. "You might want to open your eyes and check out that light coming down from the ceiling. Were you expecting it to be black? Because I'm thinking that you wanted it to be more of a greenish hue. But I'm not a witch, so what do I know. I'm a little confused, though. I thought you were planning to sacrifice Cody's heart to Huitzilopochtli, not Xolotl."

Falconwing stopped chanting, and his eyes snapped open. He noticed the black beam of light stretching halfway to the floor and frowned in confusion. "What is this?" he asked of no one in particular.

Behind him, Old Itzel's chest heaved as she let out an exasperated sigh. She put her hand into a fold of her robe and drew out a sacrificial stone knife, identical to the one that Falconwing had laid across Cody's chest. The old gnome bounded forward, raised the knife over her head, and plunged it into the center of Falconwing's back. Falconwing's eyes opened wide in astonishment. His back arched, and Itzel withdrew the knife and allowed Falconwing to crumble to the cement floor at her feet like a sack of potatoes. Itzel shoved Cody off the table, and the knife on

304

his chest clattered to the floor, sliding to a stop a few feet in front of me. With a show of strength I never would have dreamed she possessed, Old Itzel grabbed Falconwing's limp body by the neck with one hand, lifted him into the air, and slung him to the top of the table, face up. With no further ritual, chanting, or fuss of any kind, she plunged her knife into Falconwing's chest and sliced this way and that with swift practiced movements. Satisfied, she placed the knife on Falconwing's abdomen, reached into his chest with both hands, and pulled out a bleeding and still-throbbing heart, which she held into the darkening air with a look of triumph.

At that moment, I became aware that I could move again. Kalama discovered the same thing. She reached beneath her coat and pulled out her police issue piece. Without hesitation, the detective fired ten rounds in rapid succession at Old Itzel. I saw Falconwing's bloody heart slip from the old gnome's hands as the flying lead forced her backwards until she fell to the floor in a heap. I knew from experience that a nine-millimeter wasn't going to stop a witch of Itzel's competence, and, sure enough, the old gnome was already climbing to her feet. She glared at Kalama through squinted eyes and cackled. "You fucking bitch—that hurt!"

As Kalama ejected her spent clip and reached beneath her coat for another, I reached into my own coat pocket and pulled out the stoppered bottle of ink that I had taken from Teca's shop. I had no idea of why I had kept it, except that I didn't want to leave such a potent magical substance sitting around unattended. Operating on pure instinct, I reached over and pushed the unconscious Madame Cuapa forward in her chair. Holding her in place, I pulled the cork stopper out of the bottle with my teeth and spit it off to one side. Then I pulled open the back of the bruja's robe and poured the ink down her back, moving the bottle back and forth to make sure that the enchanted ink covered as much skin as possible.

Madame Cuapa's eyes snapped open, and she glared at Itzel with an expression so fierce that the old gnome gasped and fell back a step as if she had been shoved. I knew that Itzel had been using the secret Xolotl tattoo on Madame Cuapa's back to hold her in check, and, without taking the time to reason it all out, I gambled that I could break Itzel's hold on the Madame by blotting

305

out the tattoo with the ink that had been used to make it. It worked. Madame Cuapa, who must have been aware of everything that was happening even though she'd been powerless to interfere, thrust out her arm in the direction of the trapped manticore. Instantly, the flames in the five candles were snuffed out, as if by an invisible burst of wind.

Mr. Whiskers didn't hesitate. With a single bound, he launched himself at Old Itzel, who barely had time to turn before four hundred pounds of wild feline fury sent her crashing to the cement floor and pinned her there by the shoulders. The pointed barb of the manticore's tail slashed down over his head and buried itself into the fallen gnome's sternum. He yanked his tail back out of the witch's chest, and blood shot out of the puncture like a fountain. Then the manticore's jaws opened wide and snapped down on the witch's neck. The monster backed off the witch's body and lifted her off the ground by her throat. He shook his head vigorously back and forth, shaking Old Itzel like a rag doll. A loud crack echoed throughout the hall, and the robe slipped off the witch's body. Mr. Whiskers tossed the wrinkled naked body of the ancient gnome to the floor, threw back his head, and let loose a roar that would have shattered the glass from the hall's window frames if there had actually been any windows in the hall. As it was, I had to hold my hands over my ears.

When the manticore stopped roaring, he walked over to Cody's prone body and began licking him in the face. Kalama looked at me and shook her head. "Wow!"

But Madame Cuapa's expression was still intense. "Wait," she commanded through clenched teeth. "We're not done yet."

She was right. As we watched in horror, the black beam of light that continued to extend through the smoke swirling at the ceiling reached the body of Old Itzel. The beam went out, as if it had been switched off at the source. Old Itzel's fat wrinkled body rose from the floor, righted itself, and regained its feet. A deep open wound gaped high on the body's chest, just below the neck, but it was no longer bleeding. The ancient witch's lips spread into a smile that threatened to split her head, which was bobbing precariously on her shoulders. A soft cackling began to emerge from her lips. It got louder and louder until it was echoing throughout the hall. Then it stopped, and a voice that sounded like Old Itzel's, except a half-octave lower and more resonant, rang out like a trumpet. "You didn't think it was going to be *that* easy, did you?"

***

I let out a slow breath, and I heard Kalama mutter, "What the fucking fuck."

Madame Cuapa kept her gaze on Itzel. "You two stay back. This is *my* fight now." She stood and let her sacrificial robe fall to her feet, exposing her tattooed body, including the black blotch that covered most of her back. She held out a cupped hand, and the black ink rose from the skin on her back and floated into her palm. When she had it all she tilted her hand, and the ink floated away from her and poured itself into the bottle that I was still holding. Then the stopper rose from the floor and sealed the bottle. "Hang onto that for me," Madame Cuapa told me. "It's too valuable to waste." I put the bottle back into my pocket.

Out loud to Itzel, or whoever she was now, Madame Cuapa said, "I've freed myself from the last of your pollutants, including the secret link to Xolotl that you've been using against me. I see that the dog god my father worshiped has filled you with his power. But I rejected him long ago. He has no control over me now that he's stopped skulking in the shadows and has come out into the open."

"Brave words, traitor. They won't help you now. Restore your father's practices and I'll not only allow you to live, but to continue to lead the coven. Refuse, and I'll feed you to Xolotl."

In response, Madame Cuapa reached out with both arms. In the dim light, it appeared that her arms had transformed into red, yellow, and black ringed snakes that now extended well past her normal reach. Falconwing's heart rose from the cement floor where it had fallen and flew into the mouth of one of the snakes. I blinked, and the snakes disappeared, leaving Falconwing's heart clutched in the bruja's fist. She crushed the heart with both hands and let the blood flow down her arms and onto her torso. Then she began to twist her fingers into what looked to me like gang signs

307

and chant in a language that I didn't know. The Madame's body began to glow with an orange-tinged light. The light pushed its way out from the bruja's body and fought against the growing gloom that had been settling over the hall since the black beam had begun to spill out of the swirling smoke. Itzel extended her arm, and darkness began to roll like wisps of smoke from the tips of her fingers. The two witches moved toward one another, taking slow careful steps.

On the floor between them, Cody rose to his knees and shook his head. Mr. Whiskers stopped licking his face and nuzzled him in the shoulder. Cody looked around the room, blinking, and trying to process the scene that was unfolding on either side of him. He looked from Itzel to Madame Cuapa, and back again to Itzel. Then he rose to his feet and charged the old gnome. I admired his spunk, but it was to no avail. Without bothering to turn her head to look at the enraged Cody, the three-and-a-half-foot gnome lashed out with a backhanded swipe that sent the six-and-a-half-foot man crashing to the floor. Mr. Whiskers sprang to Cody's side and stood next to him, ready to protect him from any further assaults.

As the two witches advanced on each other, I assessed their progress. It seemed to me that the Madame had bitten off more than she could chew. She was an extremely skilled witch, one of the most powerful in the world, but she was up against a spirit that even Lord Ketz-Alkwat had been unable to entirely banish from this world. The orange light shining from Madame Cuapa's body was no longer expanding, and, even though the torches in the corners of the hall were still blazing at full strength, the room was growing darker. It occurred to me that Cody might have been on the right track. Taking care to avoid sudden movements, I began to slide to my left in a flanking maneuver. On my way, I reached down and picked up Falconwing's knife from the floor. Kalama saw what I was doing, and she began to make a similar flanking movement to her right, her nine-millimeter in her hand.

Madame Cuapa had ceased moving forward. She stood ten feet from Old Itzel with her feet planted on the floor, body leaning forward as if fighting against a silent gale-force wind. Kalama and I eased past her and advanced on Itzel from opposite sides. When she was five feet away from the old witch, Kalama pointed her piece at Itzel's head and fired off ten slugs. The flying lead disappeared into the darkness that surrounded the gnome, doing no damage, but the shots got Itzel's attention. She turned her head toward Kalama, and I took the opportunity to charge the witch and slash at her neck with the knife. I felt the stone blade slide against something softer than rock, but harder than flesh. The next thing I knew, the knife was ripped from my hand and I was flying through the air. I tumbled hard to the floor, but managed to avoid cracking my skull on the cement by shielding my head with my arms.

Neither Kalama nor I had hurt Old Itzel, but we'd distracted her enough for Madame Cuapa to strike, which she did, literally. Looking up from the floor, I saw the bruja's snake tattoos slither up her body and wind their way swiftly down the length of her arms. The Madame closed the gap between herself and Old Itzel with three running steps and thrust her arms, which were now two striking snakes, deep into the center of the gnome's chest. Itzel screamed and grabbed Madame Cuapa by the throat with both hands. With supernatural strength, the smaller witch forced Madame Cuapa to her knees, but the Madame's hands remained buried inside Itzel's chest.

Black and orange smoke bubbled from Old Itzel and Madame Cuapa like boiling oil, swirling and blending until the two witches were almost hidden from view. But through the smoke, I could see that Itzel's grip on Madame Cuapa's neck was tightening, and the Madame was sinking further toward the floor. Cody scrambled to his feet and picked up the knife that I'd lost. I thought that he was going to use it on Old Itzel, but instead he opened his hand and, with one quick motion, slashed his palm with the stone blade. He ran to Madame Cuapa and grabbed her right shoulder with his bloody hand.

Kalama was a little quicker on the uptake than I was. She rushed over to Cody and, taking the knife from him, she sliced it across the palm of her own hand, which she then used to grip the back of Madame Cuapa's neck. The Madame ceased slumping to the floor and, inch by painful inch, began to rise. I got to my feet and dashed over to take the knife from Kalama. I opened my hand

and slashed the blade across my palm. Then I clapped my palm on Madame Cuapa's left shoulder.

I felt a burst of electricity surge through my body, and I could feel blood pulsing out of the cut in my hand. The blood didn't spill down the Madame's shoulder, though. Instead, her body absorbed the blood and its life-giving energy like a sponge. My knees began to weaken, and I found myself leaning against Madame Cuapa. But the Madame was growing stronger by the second, and she continued to rise until she was off her knees and on her feet. Kalama lost her grip on the Madame's neck and slid to the floor. Cody's hand slipped off the Madame's shoulder and he slumped to one knee. I lost my grip, as well, and fell to my hands and knees. I lifted the hand I had cut and examined it. The slice in my palm was clean, with only a couple of beads of blood trickling out of the cut.

Madame Cuapa now loomed over Old Itzel, and, even though Itzel's hands were still wrapped around the Madame's throat, it was clear that the old gnome was tiring. The Madame shook her head, and Itzel's hands fell free. As Itzel opened her mouth to scream, the muscles in Madame Cuapa's arms swelled and she yanked her hands out of Itzel's chest. Cupped in the Madame's hands was Old Itzel's still-beating heart.

Itzel collapsed to the floor. Black smoke poured from the wound in her chest and hovered above her body. It swirled and coalesced until it came to resemble the outline of a giant dog. Madame Cuapa held the bloody heart toward the dog, which floated in her direction. But before the dog-shaped cloud could reach her, Madame Cuapa drew the heart away from it, and, with a burst of strength, ripped the heart in two. Then her snake tattoos again slithered up her body and down her arms, where the jaws of the two serpents opened wide and clamped down over the two halves of the heart, swallowing them whole.

Pale orange light burst from the Madame's body like rays from the sun, and I had to cover my eyes with my arm. A warm sensation filled me from head to toe. It felt pleasant, like a hot shower on a cold morning. I felt a sudden urge to sleep. Sleep seemed like a good idea. In fact, sleep seemed like the best idea I'd ever had.

"Pass me some of that duck, Baby Doll." I reached for the appropriate cardboard container and placed it in front of Gracie's plate. "This is great Huaxian. Where did you say you got it?"

"Huangdi's Garden on Palace Street," I told her. "It's the authentic stuff. Not the watered-down Tolanican version."

We were sitting at the dining room table in Lubank's house out in the Bayfront District. It had a nice view of the bay, but was otherwise fairly modest given his income bracket. Lubank and Gracie practically lived in their office, usually only coming home to grab a few hours of shuteye in the wee hours of the morning before getting cleaned up and dressed for another day of work. It was rare for them to entertain guests at home.

"I like the Tolanican Huaxian food better," Lubank complained. He slurped some of the sweet-and-sour soup and grimaced. "This so-called authentic shit is too damned spicy! And what are you two doing with those chopsticks? This is Tolanica! Use a fuckin' fork!"

"Oh, Honey," Gracie chided him. "Don't be rude. It was very nice of Alex to stop by and pick us up some dinner on his way over."

"Yeah, and who came up with that idea?" Lubank gave me a meaningful glance.

"Credit where credit is due. Rob's been pestering me to bring you some Huaxian for weeks."

Gracie leveled an evil eye at her husband. "You could have bought me some yourself anytime, you cheapskate."

"Hey! I've been busy!"

Gracie rolled her eyes. "You've been busy all right. Busy spending time with that pretty widow!"

"You mean that pretty *rich* widow! And I'm making sure that a big chunk of her newfound wealth is heading in our direction. You want a new car or not!"

"Oh, Honey! You know I do!" Gracie winked at me. "Go squeeze that bitch for everything she's got!"

311

I coughed and reached for my beer glass. "Sorry. This duck is spicy!"

Lubank pointed at me with his fork. "See? I told you!"

I wiped my mouth with a napkin and looked over at Lubank. "I still don't see how you can represent Cindy Shipper. Aren't you representing her stepdaughter *against* her? Isn't that a conflict of interest?"

Lubank waved his fork at me in a dismissive gesture. "What are you, a fuckin' law professor? Kaylee Shipper withdrew her offer to sell the rights to the house to her stepmother in return for her stepmother's rights to Dwayne Shipper's share of Donald Shipper's estate. That means no conflict of interest. You got that? I represent the whole family now. And Cindy Shipper needs all the help she can get, thanks to you!"

"Me? What did I do?"

"You ratted her out to the cops for manipulating that nutty were-crow into murdering her stepson, you evil bastard! How could you do that to such a sweet young frail?"

"That dame's no frail, and you know it. She manipulated Teca into murdering her stepson. She played him for a sap. She knew that he had the hots for her, and she told him that the boy was threatening her. She convinced him to come back the next night, and then she made sure that she wouldn't be home. She hoped that he would catch the boy, um, engaging in his usual nighttime habits."

I stopped and glanced over at Gracie, who was listening with interest. "Jerking off to videos of his naked stepmother?" she suggested.

"Yeah, that. She wanted Teca to kill Dwayne, because she knew that his share of the inheritance would go to her if he died."

Lubank raised his eyebrows. "Yeah? What's your point?"

"My point is that she's responsible for the murder of her stepson!"

Lubank's face pulled itself into an exaggerated expression of skepticism. "Wha-a-at? Pssshhh! That were-crow isn't some vulnerable junior high kid. He's a full-grown adult, capable of making his own choices. His decision to knock off Dwayne Shipper was entirely his own. Just because some twist sweet-talks him into

312

thinking he's her personal savior doesn't make her complicit in his misdeeds. She never told him to *kill* the boy."

"That 'twist' is your client," I pointed out. "And if she's guilty of causing her stepson's murder, then she isn't eligible to collect his inheritance."

"So? She's innocent! That's what matters. Well, that plus the fact that she'll fork over a nice percentage of that inheritance to me if I can keep her that way." He looked at Gracie. "And the more often I have to go over and consult with her, the more billing hours I rack up." He rubbed his fingers together in the universal sign of money. "Ch-ching!"

"Yeah, well just make sure that money is your *only* motive for seeing her." Gracie shook a chopstick in his direction. "Don't forget that she's spent her whole life making suckers out of men who think with their dicks instead of their brains. She even used poor Alex here, falling all over him in her doorway and coming out of his house in the morning, knowing that the were-crow was watching and that she was driving him crazy with jealousy."

"You have nothing to worry about, Sugar. Unlike Southerland, I'm no dame-dizzy dope." Lubank speared a chunk of duck with his fork.

I couldn't do anything except shake my head. When a guy's right, he's right.

"Poor Alex," Gracie cooed at me. "Don't worry, Honey. Some of us like our men to be a little bit naïve." She put her hand high enough up on my inner thigh to cause me to break into another fit of coughing.

***

The night after Madame Cuapa walked out of her coven's meeting room as the only witch left standing, I called on Crawford so that I could return his belongings.

"Sorry about your hat," I told him.

Crawford's expression showed his disappointment as I handed him his crushed pink-and-white checked fedora. "Could have been worse, I guess. I was lucky to make it out of that hotel with my skin! If I ever see another witch again it will be too soon."

"You and me both."

Crawford examined his precious hat, which was now mashed and misshapen. "Do you think it can be saved?" he asked, looking doubtful.

"Sorry, pal. It's gone. It's my fault. Let me buy you another one."

Crawford shook his head. "They don't make hats like this anymore."

I refrained from telling him that they shouldn't have made any in the first place. "Let me look around. You never know."

Crawford tossed the ruined hat to his couch. "Oh well. Easy come, easy go. What a night that was!"

"I'm glad you made it out in one piece."

"Didn't lose a single rat!"

"Are you sleeping okay?"

"It's getting easier." Crawford picked up an empty shot glass and filled it with whiskey. "This helps."

He filled my own empty shot glass and we clinked them together in a toast. "To quiet nights," I said.

"To quiet nights," he repeated, and we each tossed back our glasses, polishing off the shots with one gulp.

***

But quiet nights proved to be elusive. The next night, sleep wouldn't come my way, so I decided to surround myself with a crowd at the Black Minotaur.

As it happens, it was Monday night and only a handful of people were in the place. I took a seat in a booth and ordered a beer from a cocktail waitress with a lipstick kiss tattooed to her shoulder. It bothered me a little that I would have preferred it to be a snake, or a scorpion, or at least a spider. I tried not to think about what that might mean. When the beer came, I nursed it for a few minutes, and then looked up at the rafters to see if I could find Smokey.

I spotted the tiny elemental looming near the ceiling over the bar, soaking up the alcohol fumes. I called up its summoning sigil and the two-inch funnel of haze drifted to my table.

"Hi, Aleksss. How's tricksss?"

"Hi, Smokey. Can't complain. How're you?"

"Smokey is ready to serve."

"No job today, little fella. Hey, can you really show me the image of the were-crow like the scary women wanted you to?"

The funnel's spinning increased in speed. "Smokey can! Smokey needs smoke and fire."

I picked up a packet of matches from the condiments tray. "There's plenty of cigarette smoke in this place. Gather some up and I'll light a few of these matches."

Smokey jetted off and returned a minute later looking like a miniature gray tornado. "Smokey is ready for fire!" The elemental sounded eager.

I struck a match, and Smokey drew in the flame. The match burned out quickly, and I lit another. Smokey absorbed this flame, too, and I could see that one match at a time probably wasn't going to do the trick. I tore off a match, struck it into flame, and placed the rest of the packet in the ashtray with the cover folded back. I touched the flame to one of the matchheads in the packet, and soon the entire packet was blazing. I tore open some paper sugar packets, poured the sugar out, and placed the wrappers in the flame. Smokey whirled and drew in the fire until the spinning smoke was tinged with orange. The elemental broadened by two inches, enough to be able to produce a small, but visible image.

I concentrated on the image, watching the outlines of a tiny figure form in the center of the whirling gray smoke. At first, it was just a black silhouette of a heavy-set man, but the black smoke within the human outline began to swirl and change color. Soon, I could see a face, but the features remained vague. The colors were odd, tending towards shades of purple, blue, orange, and red, and never shaping themselves into anything distinct.

"Can you sharpen the facial features?" I asked.

"Smokey sees man."

"The colors are wrong," I insisted.

"Smokey sees man. Smokey will know man if Smokey sees him."

Then it came to me in a flash, and I realized what the problem was. "Okay, Smokey. Very good. Excellent! You can stop now."

Smokey stopped whirling, and the smoke and fire dissipated into the air as the elemental returned to its normal size. "Did Alex see man?"

"Alex saw man," I assured the elemental. "But humans and elementals don't see things the same way."

"Smokey doesn't understand."

"I know. It's okay. Don't sweat it, kid, you did good."

"Smokey is happy."

Turns out that Smokey wouldn't have been able to show us a recognizable image of the were-crow in Madame Cuapa's lab after all, even if Old Itzel hadn't secretly induced Falconwing to wake up and interrupt the ritual. At least, that's the way I figure it must have happened. Elementals—air elementals, at least—see different parts of the light spectrum than humans. More specifically, they see heat and cold, or ultraviolet and infrared. These temperature patterns are distinct to them, but invisible to humans. Similarly, certain parts of what we call the visible spectrum are invisible to air elementals. The most that Smokey would have been able to show us was a close approximation of the shape of Teca's body, but the features that humans regard as identifiable would have been rendered as red and purple streaks and blotches representing patterns of cold and heat, making the figure recognizable by another elemental, but not by a human.

Useful information for an elementalist. Maybe I'd write an article about it someday. But probably not.

***

Stopping Old Itzel and driving the spirit of Xolotl back to wherever he'd come from had required Madame Cuapa to absorb a lot of energy-rich blood from Cody, Kalama, and me, and it had taken much of the Madame's power to revive the three of us afterwards. Even Cody, who was used to shedding blood as a part of his service to the Madame, had been shaken by the experience. My elf-enhanced powers of healing helped me in my recovery, but the ordeal had been especially tough on Kalama. She had been the last of us to regain consciousness afterwards, and, as a precaution, Madame Cuapa had insisted that the detective stay the night in her guest room while she and Cody fed her healing potions and looked after her.

I called Kalama on her cel a couple of days later from my office to see how she was doing. Remarkably well, as it turned out.

"I wish the Madame had let me keep a bottle of that tonic," Kalama told me. "It tastes like dirty laundry, but it makes me feel like dancing. Kai flew home yesterday, and let's just say that he's having trouble keeping up with me."

I laughed, not knowing what to say in response. "So you're okay? No bad dreams?"

"No more than usual. You work homicide in this city for a while and you see a lot of weird shit. Watching two old naked ladies throwing down on a Saturday night is no big deal."

I leaned back in my desk chair. "You *did* see one of them rip the other one's heart out of her chest with her bare hands and feed it to a couple of snakes that were crawling up her arms, didn't you?"

"Yeah. That was unusual."

"Uh-huh. Well, glad to hear you're okay. Have they reinstated you yet?"

"The lieutenant called me about an hour ago. He's expecting me back at my desk in the morning."

"Are they going to give you the credit for bringing in Teca for the Dwayne Shipper murder?"

Kalama didn't answer right away. "You didn't hear?"

I sat up in my chair. "Hear what?"

"They found Teca in his cell this morning. He'd been torn to pieces."

"You're kidding!" I knew that she wasn't. "Dead?"

"Oh yeah. Very much so."

"Was he alone?"

"All alone in a locked cell. No way in and no way out."

"How are they explaining it?"

317

"The official word is that he hanged himself with his bedsheet. The department is conducting an internal investigation."

"Right. And what *really* happened?"

"You tell me."

I stared at the chair across from my desk, where a witch with snake tattoos winding up her gams had been sitting just over a week ago. "There are people in this world that you shouldn't fuck with," I told Kalama.

"The department agrees. I don't think that we'll be looking any further into Teca's cause of death."

After we disconnected, I leaned back in my chair and studied the new addition that I'd hung on my office wall. It had been delivered by a private messenger service earlier that morning with no card and no return address, but I knew who had sent it. To be honest, the two-foot tall, six-foot wide painting was too big for my little office, but somehow I'd found room for it above the file cabinets. I let my eyes wander over the desert landscape until they came to rest on the mysterious black bird sitting on the mesa and contemplating the desolate red and gold vista that lay before it. I know next to nothing about art, so I had no idea why I found the painting so compelling. Nor do I know why Mrs. Shipper decided to give the painting to me. Maybe she saw the way I was drawn to it when I was questioning her in her living room. Maybe she was trying to send me a message that I was too dense to decipher. I didn't think about all that too much, though. I just liked staring at the painting.

***

I let my cards fall face down on the table. "I fold."

"Come to papa!" Gio reached out with both hands and pulled the chips from the center of the table to the pile that had been growing in front of him. "Guess it's my lucky night!"

It was my deal, and I gathered up all the loose cards without letting on that I'd just dumped three eights despite knowing that Gio was only holding a pair of aces. I wasn't in it for the dough, but no one had to know that.

318

It had been two weeks since Gio and I had finally gone out for a couple of drinks one night. I spent the evening listening to Gio complain about the weather, educate me on the pros and cons of various types of internal combustion engines, and discuss the joys and tribulations of family life, and he didn't ask much from me in return except for a friendly ear. Turns out that Antonio has two younger sisters. I hadn't known that.

"The oldest just turned twelve," Gio told me. "Twelve! It's not possible! She'll be bringing boys to the house pretty soon. Thinking about it is turning me into a fuckin' nutcase!"

A couple of days after that, Gio told me that Connie was insisting that I come over for fish dinner, and I accepted. Fish dinner turned out to be fresh-baked cod with olives and tomatoes on a bed of pasta noodles, the whole thing covered with a delicious cream sauce. I told Connie that it was the best meal I'd ever had, and I meant it. While we were eating, Antonio asked me where I'd found the beastmobile, and I gave him a heavily watered-down version of the story. The twelve-year-old, Sienna, watched me with large dark eyes for a few minutes before dismissing me as boring. Antonio's youngest sister, a ten-year-old named Gemma, was as fascinated by cars as her father and brother, but she told me that the beastmobile was too big for just one person and wanted to know why I didn't either get a smaller car or get married and have a lot of children. I looked to Gio for help, but he just shrugged and chuckled at my discomfort.

Before I left for the evening, Gio asked me if I played cards. I told him that I knew some games, and he asked me if I'd be up for some poker nights with his buddies. "Nothing serious," he told me. "Low stakes, no more than two raises per hand. We meet once a week, but not everyone comes every time. Just when it's convenient."

So I found myself smoking cigars, drinking whiskey and beer, and playing five-card draw with Gio, a car salesman named Burt, an appliance repairman named Paavo, and Kofi, who managed a hardware store. The first hand wasn't done before I discovered that my elf-enhanced awareness gave me such an unfair advantage over Gio and his pals that I could have cleaned them out of their life savings in a couple of hours. Burt pushed his

319

cards together and looked up whenever he had a winning hand. Paavo's pupils dilated when he drew the cards he was hoping for. Kofi, who was holding most of the chips at the moment, bit down on his cigar whenever he was bluffing. Gio was the worst card player of the bunch. He bluffed way too often, but he only scratched at the corner of his mouth with the tip of his little finger when he thought he had a winner. The four of them surrounded me with talk, rough talk, talk about their jobs, their families, sports, corruption in politics, their health, the health of their family members, the health of their friends, the sorry state of young people today, beautiful women, lousy bosses, lousy cards, and every mundane detail of everyday life, and I immersed myself in every casual carefree profanity-laced minute of it. I won a few hands and tanked enough to break even and lost myself in the smoke, the booze, and the company.

As I dealt the cards, my mind turned to my last conversation with Madame Cuapa. She had invited me to her house to thank me personally for my help and to hand me what turned out to be a generous check. I was appropriately appreciative, but that didn't stop me from asking the Madame about Silverblade's trafficking ring.

I looked the witch in the eye, probably risking my soul. "I have to know. Were you a part of that?"

Madame Cuapa's expression turned blank. She would have been a much tougher opponent at the poker table than Gio and his friends. "I was aware of Silverblade's activities, of course." I waited for more, but she simply smiled and offered me more tea. I told her that I couldn't stay, and stood to go.

"Cody will show you out." She poured herself a cup from a pot wrapped in a knitted tea cozy.

Cody walked me to my car. "You should know something." He paused, distracted for a brief moment by my car. "In the end, the Madame made a choice. She loved Old Itzel, even though it turned out that Itzel was probably planning to betray her all along. Even so, in our culture, Itzel was a worthy adversary. Did you know that she was Cuetlachtli's first disciple? She was completely devoted to him and his ways. In the history of our people, when you defeat your enemies, tradition demands that you honor those

320

warriors by offering up their hearts to the gods. Warriors would walk tall as they were led to the altars, proud and willing to give up the last of their life energy to the gods who had given them a good life. To be freed from captivity was a great disgrace. If they were given an opportunity to escape, they would turn it down."

Cody glanced back at the house, and then continued. "When the Madame took Itzel's heart, tradition says that she should have offered it to Xolotl. The dog god would have then taken the spirit of Itzel to Mictlan, where she would have been given a place of great honor for her services on his behalf. But the Madame chose to forsake her companion. Instead, she used Itzel's life energy to revive me, you, and Detective Kalama. We would all have died otherwise. In the end, the Madame chose the living over the dead, and the spirit of Old Itzel was swept aside to who knows where."

He put a hand on my shoulder. "Don't give up on the Madame. She's been shaken by these recent events in ways you can't understand. She's become aware of her arrogance. She's coming to terms with her pride. She had come to believe that she was above the concerns of the rest of us, maybe even that she was better than us. That's changed. I'm asking you to give her some room, and some time to think about the kind of witch—the kind of person—she wants to be. And I'll be there watching her."

I looked up at the big man. "For your sake, I hope that she chooses the right path. If she doesn't, she might decide that you're in her way."

He shrugged. "It's possible. But it's a chance I'm willing to take. And I think it will turn out okay."

I put out my hand, and he shook it. "Say hi to that pussycat of yours," I told him.

"Let me know if you want him to take you on another flight."

"Let me know when Hell freezes over!"

Cody had a good laugh at that one.

A week after that, Kalama told me that the Daucina Club had quietly abandoned the basement of the Huntinghouse. She didn't know if it had moved to another part of town or if it had left the city altogether. She said that Captain Coldgrave had made it a priority to stamp out child sex-trafficking in Yerba City. I wondered how successful he would be. The sad truth is that where there's a demand, there's likely to be a supply.

For now, I smiled and studied the pair of jacks in my hand. I'd lost four hands in a row and decided it might be time for a win. I sipped some whiskey and clamped my teeth on my cigar. I wasn't going to take up smoking on a regular basis, but when I considered a world filled with witches, manticores, murderous shape-shifters, and deadly supernatural spirits, not to mention underaged escorts entertaining gentlemen clients in fancy hotel rooms, I figured that an occasional puff of a cheap cigar in a dark smoky room with my newfound poker buddies was something I could get used to. That other world would still be there in the morning, and I'd be ready for it. But there's a time and there's a place. Gio, Burt, and Paavo had thrown in their cards, and I'd just seen Kofi bite down on his cigar. It was time for me to start breaking even.

The End

Some Notes from the Author on Aztec Names and Tradition

A Witch Steps into My Office makes use of many aspects of the fascinating pre-Columbian culture of Mexico and Central America. My primary purpose was not to write good history, but rather to write an entertaining story, and, in my attempt to do so, I bent and twisted historical and cultural traditions as I saw fit. Sorry about that. I've included the following notes with the hope that they will provide readers with some insights into some of the names, places, and ideas used in this book.

Tolanica: The stories of Alexander Southerland are set in Tolanica, one of the realms ruled by the seven immortal Dragon Lords. The name comes from Tollan, or Tolan, the mythological place of seven caves in old Mayan folklore where the Ki'ichi' Mayan people learned their language and received their gods.

Lord Ketz-Alkwat: As Dr. Coyot noted, Ketz-Alkwat is the modernized phonetic rendering of **Quetzalcoatl** the ancient feathered serpent god prominently worshiped by a number of peoples in pre-Columbian Mexico and Central America. Quetzalcoatl represented both divinity and humanity, and was seen as a link between the earth and the heavens. He was often associated with the sun and with war, and in many traditions coordinated the efforts of the other gods in the preservation of the world.

Brujería: Brujería refers to a religious practice native to the Caribbean that can be traced back to at least the early sixteenth century. It represents a mixture of Native American, African, and, in the modern day, Catholic traditions. Its leaders (priests and

323

priestesses) are known as brujos (BROO-hōz) and brujas (BROO-hăz). I have taken a number of artistic liberties with the traditional collection of brujería practice and used it to represent a hodgepodge of its own herbalistic and shamanistic customs with a mythical continuation of (and dominance by) Aztec religious traditions. In doing so, I have eliminated almost all of the Catholic influences. The idea is that the mixture of practices that in our history became dominated by Catholic belief became, in my fictional Azteca region of Tolanica, dominated instead by a continued organized Aztec tradition.

Xolotl: The Aztec god of fire and lightning and ruler of the dead. According to one tradition, Xolotl brought fire to humans in defiance of his twin brother, Quetzalcoatl, who banished him to Mictlan, the land of the dead. Afterwards, he served as a guide, leading the souls of the dead safely to Mictlan. Xolotl is commonly portrayed as a giant black dog or dog-headed man, often with no eyes, or with lightning bolts in place of eyes. He is associated with monsters, deformities, and sickness. I used some artistic license in portraying Xolotl, not as Quetzalcoatl's twin brother, but as an ancient Azteca spirit who rebelled against the coming of Lord Ketz-Alkwat.

Huitzilopochtli: Huitzilopochtli, whose name means "hummingbird of the south," or "left-handed hummingbird," was the chief god of the Aztecs. He began as a god of war and the hunt, but eventually became best known as the god of the sun. According to Aztec tradition, Huitzilopochtli guided the Mexica people on a southward migration to an island in the middle of a Lake Texcoco (tĕsh-KŌ-kō) where an eagle perched on a prickly-pear cactus grasped a serpent in its talons (this image is the centerpiece for the modern flag of Mexico). The Mexica built the city of Tenochtitlan on the island, and it became the center of the Aztec Empire. After Tenochtitlan was conquered by Hernán Cortés, it was rebuilt and renamed Mexico City. In my version of history, the Cortés conquest was more of a migration, and Tenochtitlan retained its original name. Huitzilopochtli was believed to be the force that kept darkness and chaos at bay. Tradition says that if

Huitzilopochtli was not nourished with the life energy from human sacrifices, the sun would fall to the darkness after a fifty-two year cycle.

Ometeotl: The dual god who represented the male and female principles. The female principle is named **Omecihuatl**, and the male is **Ometecuhtli**. In some traditions, Ometeotl gave birth to many of the other important gods, including Huitzilopochtli. Some scholars claim that Ometeotl wasn't worshiped by the Aztecs at all, but was a creation of Spanish priests. In *no* tradition that I know of was Ometeotl represented as a pair of coral snakes. That's a shameless bit of artistic license on my part.

Thank You!

Thank you for reading *A Witch Steps into My Office*. If you enjoyed it, I hope that you will consider writing a review—even a short one—on Amazon, Goodreads, BookBub, or your favorite book site. Publishing is still driven by word of mouth, and every single voice helps. I'm working hard to bring Alex Southerland back, and knowing that readers might be interested in hearing more about his adventures in Yerba City will certainly speed up the process!

About the Author

Dr. Douglas Lumsden is a former history professor and private school teacher. He lives in Monterey, California, with his wife, Rita, and his cat, Cinderella.

.

Made in the USA
Monee, IL
03 January 2023

24417783R00187